THE CYANIDE GHOST

A Mina Scarletti Mystery
Book Six

Linda Stratmann

SAPERE
BOOKS

THE CYANIDE GHOST

Published by Sapere Books.

20 Windermere Drive, Leeds, England, LS17 7UZ,
United Kingdom

saperebooks.com

ISBN: 978-1-80055-197-8

PROLOGUE

In the autumn of 1871 Mr Beckler took a photograph which changed his life forever. His one-man business in Twickenham concentrated mainly on family portraits and *cartes de visite*, which he created in his sunlit studio. When he took his camera outdoors, it was to capture artistic images of important buildings or record public events. On that memorable day, however, he had been summoned with great urgency to the home of a recently deceased gentleman. His task was to create a deathbed portrait, a *memento mori*, destined to be both the first and last picture of the loved one, something to be treasured by the bereaved.

The subject, dressed in his best suit, was nicely arranged on quilts and pillows, his body framed in floral tributes, a bible having been carefully pressed into his chilly grasp. The living customer, the deceased's sister, was in a state of abject grief, since the gentleman had been young and his demise sudden and unexpected. Mr Beckler had been obliged to try and calm her as best he could although, as he was painfully aware, comforting ladies was not one of his most notable skills. His thin, oddly elongated body tended to loom over others, so that he resembled a giant predatory and carnivorous insect, and his attempts at smiling only made recipients flinch. He had eventually concluded that the best thing to do was to perform his professional duty as quickly as possible. He was finally able to persuade the lady to sit beside the supine shell of her brother with her hand tentatively resting on a sleeve while gazing upon the dead face in the manner of Her Majesty the Queen contemplating a marble bust of the late Prince Consort.

The bedroom curtains had been thrown fully back to admit the vibrant light of an unclouded sun, and he had brought his largest reflector to make the most of it. The camera was set ready upon its stand, and a glass plate prepared with a light-sensitive coating. Advising the lady to remain as still as possible, Mr Beckler removed the lens cap and, since he lacked the superior illumination of a studio setting, allowed an exposure of several minutes to ensure the best possible image. The gentleman at least could be relied upon not to move.

No other living person was in the room, neither was there a portrait of the dead man hanging on the wall, yet when the picture was later printed onto chemically sensitised paper, a man's face, ethereal and translucent, was seen hovering above the lady's shoulder. Mr Beckler was understandably apprehensive as to how his client might react to this unusual result, but he need not have worried. Although the features of the ghostly image were cloudy and indistinct, she was quite certain from the arrangement of the hair and shape of the beard, that this was the spiritual form of her late brother watching over her, a circumstance which she found at once to be thrilling, only slightly unnerving and deeply comforting.

Mr Beckler, with more professional concerns, was left perplexed as to how he had succeeded in photographing a ghost; however, he supposed that if he had done it once then he should be able to do it again. In this expectation he was doomed to disappointment. Mr Beckler was an energetic young man, eager to explore the latest possibilities in photographic art. During the following weeks he conducted numerous experiments in which he employed the best quality glass, the most modern equipment and the purest chemicals, risking all his small savings in the exercise. He visited graveyards, the bedsides of the deceased and houses widely reputed to be haunted, but he was never able to repeat the feat.

He decided not to mention the occurrence to other photographers. Neither did he write to any of the profession's journals for advice. There was a good reason for this. Only a few years previously an American photographer, William Mumler, had conducted a highly successful business in the creation and sale of spirit pictures only to be arrested and charged with swindling. While Mumler had never been proven to be a cheat, the accusation alone had all but destroyed his career. Mr Beckler knew that he had not cheated, but who would believe him unless he had proof? If, however, he was able to discover and refine the method of photographing spirits, and demonstrate it without any fear of being dubbed a trickster, then and only then would he have sought a means of making his name and fortune, and felt able to advertise this new service to the public with confidence. Fortunately for these private ambitions, the grieving client had retreated into a solitary state and been silent on the subject. For the time being, the spirit photograph was a close kept secret.

That winter, Mr Beckler was interested to discover that Mr Arthur Wallace Hope, the influential spiritualist, renowned explorer, associate of the much admired Dr Livingstone, and author of several popular books, was touring the county of Middlesex with a series of lectures on the spirit world. Mr Beckler attended a lecture hoping to receive some enlightenment and purchased a book, but neither the speaker nor the book referred in any way to photography. Mr Beckler ventured to send a letter to the eminent gentleman hinting that he had something of importance to impart. He was able to secure an interview at which with some trepidation, he revealed the ghostly portrait. To his gratification, Mr Hope became very excited to see what he declared to be clear scientific proof that validated his belief in the ability of persons in spirit to communicate with the living. He urged Mr Beckler to continue his experiments.

Mr Hope was a large fine-looking man with glossy waves of rich, dark hair, a deep voice, and a commanding manner. A scion of the aristocracy, his fame and wealth cast an irresistible glamour over his public. Men felt honoured by his notice, ladies either blushed or paled to gaze on him. Mr Beckler, a humble and unprepossessing person, making his way in the world by his own diligent efforts, acceded at once to all Mr Hope's wishes.

He was told that his work would have a greater chance of success if carried out in Brighton, which Mr Hope informed him was a strong focus of psychic power, and he should therefore move his interests there. Financial considerations were as nothing in Mr Hope's avid pursuit of spiritual truth, and he promised that should Mr Beckler find suitable premises for a Brighton business, he would provide a loan for its purchase. He did, however, have a word of warning for his new acolyte. The one complicating factor about a presence in Brighton was Miss Mina Scarletti. According to Mr Hope, she was both a highly powerful spirit medium who utterly and repeatedly refused to acknowledge her gifts, and a deeply wounding thorn in his side. He had tried every method at his disposal to bring her to a belief in the world of the spirit, and not only had she scorned his advice, but she had actively disrupted his work. She had a small following in Brighton, the ignorant and wilfully unenlightened, who heeded her every word. As a result, her malicious insinuations had brought about the disgrace and even imprisonment of mediums he had championed, wise and pure souls who he knew were destined to change all human understanding.

Miss Scarletti, ordered Mr Hope, was to be shunned at all costs.

Mr Beckler had first encountered the dangerous Miss Mina Scarletti in January 1872. He had accompanied Mr Hope to Hollow House, a haunted Sussex mansion, the home of Mr Honeyacre and his new young wife, Kitty. The household was being terrorised by spirit manifestations of a malevolent nature, so powerful and persistent that Mr Hope felt sure that Mr Beckler would be able to employ his new-found talent to photograph them. On arrival they had unexpectedly found that Mr Hope's enemy, the intransigent Miss Scarletti, was a visitor. She was accompanied by two friends, the enchantingly beautiful Mrs Nellie Jordan and respected man of medicine Dr Hamid. Soon afterwards, they were unexpectedly joined by Mina's younger brother Richard, a handsome idler who spent most of the visit complaining of a toothache, and another gentleman who went everywhere with binocular glasses and claimed that he was visiting the area to write a book on natural history but appeared to know nothing of the subject.

It became rapidly apparent to Mr Beckler that Miss Scarletti's attitude to Mr Hope's blandishments were unaltered. At the first opportunity Mr Hope had taken Mr Beckler aside and advised him that if Miss Scarletti could not admit the truth, then for the good of all mankind she must be made as naught. Mr Beckler had been highly alarmed by the intensity of his patron's manner, and had had to be reassured that he would not stoop to murder, but was obliged to ask, what could be done? The lady, Mr Hope had said, with a sorrowful expression, had already resisted friendly persuasion, reasoned argument, bribery and blackmail. Her medical advisor, Dr Hamid, was a highly regarded Brighton practitioner, and would undoubtedly do everything in his power to prevent any attempt to have her declared insane and put in a place of confinement. Mr Beckler had decided not to ask how Mr Hope knew this last piece of information but received the uncomfortable impression that it was because his patron had already tried this tactic and failed.

There was, apparently, only one more course of action remaining. Mr Hope commanded Mr Beckler to romance his enemy, using every wile in his armoury. Mr Beckler was very much taken aback, and protested that he was no Lothario, but Mr Hope clearly believed that Miss Scarletti, who was extremely small with a twisted spine, and walked with a pronounced limp, would be grateful for the attentions of any man. Mr Beckler reluctantly did his best, but Miss Scarletti was not to be won. A shrewd lady, she easily saw through the young photographer's scheme, and received it with contempt and disgust. The eventual failure of Mr Hope's mission at the haunted mansion was laid firmly at the door of the infuriating Miss Scarletti.

By the spring of 1872, Mr Hope had gone to Africa again in search of his former expedition leader, Dr Livingstone, from whom nothing had been heard for some considerable time, and Mr Beckler had opened his business on the busy thoroughfare of Brighton's Ship Street. Freed from the overbearing influence of his eminent patron, Mr Beckler found himself dreading his return. He had become horribly aware that just as Mr Hope had the power to advance him, he could just as easily abandon or even ruin him if he so chose. It was therefore essential that he carry out the tasks assigned to him, however distasteful they might be.

He dreaded offering Mr Hope still more failures: failure to capture a portrait of the ghost of Mr H G Simpson, the previous owner of the business, which was rumoured to haunt the premises but which he had neither seen nor heard; failure to discover the secret that continued to elude him, how he had created the spirit picture; failure to seduce Miss Scarletti, a lady who had in their brief acquaintance earned his profound respect and who now loathed him. If he could only bring her to the path of the spirit, that would be a fine achievement, but the chances of her ever speaking to him again were remote. In an attempt to mollify her he had even given employment to her brother Richard, who seemed to be blithely unaware that Mr Beckler had insulted his sister. Richard's only skills were a modest talent for drawing, a charming manner with lady customers, and a well-practised ability to waste time in a daydream.

Then quite unexpectedly another spirit picture appeared.

Mr Beckler's second unexpected spirit picture had materialised on one of a set he had taken of the only daughter of Mr Henry Hartop, a gentleman of some means, and a proudly self-made success, who owned and rented superior-quality apartments in Brighton. Miss Hartop, of indeterminate age, but probably nearer thirty-five than thirty, was quite conceivably the only person in Brighton who actually enjoyed hearing the sound of her voice. Her usual conversational volume was a penetrating shout, her preferred register a high-pitched trill with which she greeted even the most mundane event as worthy of loud and excited exclamation.

Despite this, she was not lacking in friends, since she enjoyed a generous allowance from her father, which she spent lavishly on clothes, treats and entertainment. She had gathered about her a small group of less moneyed but respectable single ladies, whom she marshalled and conducted like a personal choir. There was, however, one important accoutrement she lacked. Even the prospect of a substantial dowry had not so far attracted a husband. She often declared herself to be the object of admiring glances from eligible gentlemen, but until recently she had not directed her own gaze in any particular direction. Then she had paid a visit to the new photographer's shop on Ship Street, where her eyes had lighted upon the blond curls and fine features of Richard Scarletti. Miss Hartop liked what she saw.

Mr Beckler had long been in two minds about the wisdom of employing Richard Scarletti. His record-keeping was far from meticulous, his attention to the essentials of cleaning was slapdash at best, his knowledge of basic chemistry was laughable, and he seemed dumbfounded when asked to learn new skills. None of this dented a wholly unrealistic self-confidence in his own abilities. On the other hand, he was useful for carrying equipment, although he often needed to be prodded into action, and he was also able to charm and amuse the customers, skills in which Mr Beckler was aware he was deficient. Ladies admired Mr Scarletti's good looks, whereas Mr Beckler's mirror could only inform him that nature had played a joke on him when allocating his facial features.

Miss Hartop had taken such a strong fancy to Mr Scarletti that she returned to the shop almost daily, on any excuse she could muster, making purchases, studying catalogues, viewing exhibitions and arranging sittings for herself and her friends. Chiefly, however, the purpose of her visits was to flirt with the counter clerk. If he was not at the desk, she would walk about waiting for him to appear, checking her appearance in a mirror. Sometimes she sang to herself, presumably so that if Mr

Scarletti could not see her, he could certainly hear her. If this was meant to be in the nature of a siren's song, Mr Beckler thought it was having quite the opposite effect. Even Richard, who often talked of making his fortune by marrying one, balked at the prospect of Miss Hartop.

Since she was a valuable customer, Mr Beckler was obliged to pander to Miss Hartop's vision of herself, allowing her free choice of whatever gown or pose she felt would display her charms to the greatest advantage. Sometimes her attitudes before the camera lens bordered on the cusp of indecency, and to preserve his reputation he made sure that Miss Hartop's maid was always present and took care that any questionable images, once revealed to his eyes by their development on glass, were never subjected to the fixative solution of potassium cyanide. Instead, they were allowed to fade, the plates returned to the general stock. In his opinion, the performers of the Brighton Music Hall, whom he had recently photographed, showed far more taste and decorum than Miss Hartop.

Business was doing well, but there was one significant worry. Mr Beckler had recently learned that Dr Livingstone had been found alive, which meant that his patron Mr Arthur Wallace Hope might return to England far sooner than anticipated. Before his departure, Mr Hope had tasked his protégé with discovering a reliable and repeatable method of photographing spirits, but all his numerous experiments had ended in failure. The purported ghost of the previous owner Mr Simpson had also refused to appear, either to Mr Beckler's eye or his camera. Areas of unexpected cold on the premises, which suggested the presence of disembodied entities, had disappeared once gaps in the brickwork had been closed up, and nightly muttering noises had provided no useful intelligence, which was understandable, since they had been produced by mice.

Just as Mr Beckler was beginning to lose all hope of satisfying his patron's demands, Miss Hartop made an appointment for a new portrait. She had been eager to immortalise her image wearing her newest summer gown purchased from Brighton's most fashionable emporium for ladies' apparel, Jordan and Conroy. She also carried a bouquet of a size befitting a bride, no doubt an unsubtle hint to potential suitors. Miss Hartop always demanded the best of everything, and the best quality glass plates in the shop were those Mr Beckler had acquired from the estate of Mr Simpson, which only needed a thorough cleaning to be re-used. He took three pictures of the would-be temptress in an elaborate peach silk gown to enable her to select the best one.

Two of the images as they appeared in negative form on glass were as good as any picture of Miss Hartop was ever likely to be, but the third displayed a curiously shaped smudge that seemed to be floating in mid-air. Mr Beckler, who had seen such a smudge only once before, viewed it with excitement and a little frisson of hope. He had fixed it with care, his hands shaking as he bathed the glass in a cyanide solution to preserve the image and make it clearer, sharper, more vigorous. He had hardly dared to print the picture, and trembled when he saw it, trembled even more when he thought of showing it to Miss Hartop.

Miss Hartop had meanwhile arrived with her maid to see the new pictures and he found them in the studio, the maid standing quietly by while her mistress experimented with a variety of seductive poses on a chair. She looked up expectantly as he entered but was instantly and very obviously disappointed not to see Mr Scarletti. It was a reaction that Mr Beckler was finding very familiar from many of his lady clients.

'I have the new prints,' he said, 'but —'

'Oh! Let me see!' Miss Hartop exclaimed, bouncing to her feet. The first two pictures brought nods of approval, and he hesitated before showing her the third one.

The portrait itself was unexceptional. Miss Hartop appeared to be contemplating her future as a bride, and the flowers looked agreeable enough, but there was something else in the picture and when Mr Beckler had first seen it clearly, he had known for certain that the object had not been in the room, or at least not in a form that was visible to his eyes. Floating in the air a little way above Miss Hartop's shoulder was a misty image, half transparent and yet perfectly identifiable as the figure of a woman. The lady was seen in profile, only the upper half of her body appearing. She was clad in a blouse with a high frilled collar and wearing a large, elaborately trimmed hat.

'I am not at all sure where that originated, or whom it could be,' said Mr Beckler.

Miss Hartop, however, was sure. She clutched a hand to her bosom, threw her head back and uttered a scream that was in danger of awakening the corpses in every cemetery in Brighton. 'Mother!' she cried, and fainted dead away into Mr Beckler's arms.

He had managed the situation with as much delicacy as he could muster. When she recovered, which fortunately took only moments, since Miss Hartop could not stay silent for long, Mr Beckler politely but urgently requested that she not mention the picture to anyone until he had had an opportunity to study it. Despite this, within days all Brighton knew that Mr Beckler could photograph ghosts. The news was not, however, taken seriously. To Mr Beckler's severe discomfiture, it was loudly derided at society gatherings and dismissed with heavy sarcasm in the newspapers as ladies' tattle over the teacups; indeed, there were insinuations that the teacups concerned contained something rather stronger than tea.

Mr Beckler knew that he had a great deal of work to do. While the public clamour had been unfortunate, it had thankfully reflected more on Miss Hartop's judgement than his own. The image was of better clarity than his first ghostly portrait, and he had used a magnifying glass to make a careful examination of the plate from which the picture had been printed. As a result, he had at long last gained an insight into how the ghostly images had been achieved, and more importantly, how he might create them again and do better next time. Before he attempted this, however, he made a careful study of both the advocates and critics of the much-maligned American photographer Mr Mumler, to learn what errors he should avoid. Armed with this information, he recommenced his experiments. He needed to refine the images so that they were convincing portrayals of recognisable individuals, discover how to replicate them at will, and then attract influential clients. He could not achieve this last miracle alone, but he had at hand three associates who would not question his actions: the voluble self-centred Miss Hartop, the unwitting and witless Richard Scarletti and the professional legacy of the former owner of the business, the late Mr H G Simpson.

Careful plans were assembling in Mr Beckler's mind as he watched his latest production come to life in the printing frame. After carefully toning and fixing the paper print, he at last hung it up to dry with a smile of satisfaction.

At long last, he had the perfect ghost.

CHAPTER ONE

It was early summer in Brighton. The air sang with salt breezes, the sky was a limpid sheet of uninterrupted blue. There were long sunlit days, blissfully sublime, almost as if they might last forever. When evening drifted in, it brought its own pleasures, painting both sea and sky in red and gold, before finally welcoming in cooler and quieter nights.

The town was in its fresh new holiday colours for the first of the visitors. By day the piers, promenades and pebbled beaches were busy with families determined to make the most of every moment, the sea dotted with boats and bathers, the streets alive with the rattle of pony carts and squealing children in their tiny goat-drawn carriages. On the wide walking promenade of the new West Pier visitors displayed their brightest attire, strolling in the sun, chattering in the shade of ornamental shelters, clustering about the gaslit bandstand in the evenings.

There was entertainment to suit every taste: gardens to visit, theatre varieties, marching bands, the Royal Pavilion to admire, concerts at the Dome, and the usual assembly of fortune tellers and magicians in gaudy booths.

It was four months since Mina Scarletti had been stricken by a lung infection that had nearly taken her life, but with care and determination she had gradually mended. Dr Hamid had been cautious to pronounce his final verdict, but he now felt able to say that he did not believe her illness had left her with any lasting detriment to her already precarious health. He had prescribed fresh air, gentle exercise, warm sunshine, and not getting involved in solving mysteries or undertaking any work that could tax her energy. The first three items on his prescription were easily procured in Brighton. The last was not.

Mina, her mother Louisa, and younger brother Richard lived on Montpelier Road, in one of the tall cream-coloured houses that formed a terrace sloping down to the sea front. Here, all the conversation was about the forthcoming celebration to mark the betrothal of Mina's older brother, Edward. He was the serious, sensible one of the family, a managing partner in the Scarletti family publishing business which had been established by their late father, Henry. Edward resided in London, not far from his office on Regent Street, and last year he had wooed and won pretty heiress Agatha Hooper.

A family gathering had been delayed for several months, first by Mina's long illness and then by the birth of a daughter to Mina's sister Enid, her third child, since she already had twin boys. Throughout the winter of 1871 and the following spring, Enid and her mother had been thrown into paroxysms of distress due to the extended absence on business of Enid's husband, Mr Inskip. His destination had been a remote part of Romania, and although he had promised to write, several months elapsed with no news of him. Louisa had feared tragedy; Enid had dreaded her husband's return and his discovery that her expectant state was incompatible with his being the father. It eventually transpired that he had been languishing under an indisposition that was and remained mysterious. Baby Gwendoline's arrival as a seven-month child had solved Enid's difficulty, and when Mr Inskip finally returned in good health, he had suspected nothing. He, Enid and the betrothed couple were therefore about to descend upon Brighton for a celebratory gathering at the Grand Hotel.

Edward's wedding date had been set for the end of September, to be followed by a tour of Italy. Edward being

18

Edward, he was naturally fretting about how Scarletti Publishing would fare during his long absence from the office but had been reassured by his partner, Mr Greville, who had formerly managed the business with his late father, that all would be safe in his capable and experienced hands.

As family matriarch, Louisa's main contribution to the work of organising the visit and celebration was complaining about the intolerable burden it placed on her, while leaving the actual labour to others. Since Mina usually managed the household, the Brighton arrangements had fallen to her. She in turn consulted Edward, who meekly took his orders on matters domestic from Miss Hooper. The Scarlettis' general maid Rose was frequently dispatched on errands, which she undertook with no audible complaint.

It was a warm afternoon in late June when Mina, her mother and brother Richard gathered at the parlour table for what would probably be the last peaceful family tea before the visitors arrived.

'The fatigue will undoubtedly kill me,' said Mrs Scarletti, with practised confidence, 'but at least I will have the comfort of seeing my family all together. They will gather around my deathbed —' she made a dramatic gesture to indicate the sweeping extent of this expected assembly of grief — 'to say a final farewell, and I will be reunited with my dear departed ones in heaven.' She sighed and piled clotted cream onto a scone. Tall and slender, with an elegant sweep of blonde hair and the complexion of a porcelain doll, Mina's mother could never be convinced that she was far stronger than she looked. She ate heartily and went about in society as much as was appropriate for a three-year widow.

'But there are so many people to crowd into the house!' she continued. 'Enid and the new baby and the twins! Where will they sleep? How can we manage them all? How shall we feed them? Is there bed linen enough? I really can't imagine.' She pressed pale fingers disconsolately to her forehead.

'It is all planned, Mother,' said Mina, patiently. She had advised her mother of the arrangements several times, but Mrs Scarletti had been determined not to absorb the information as it interfered with her protestations. 'I have consulted with cook about the meals, and we have ordered everything that is required. The linens are clean, aired and ready. Enid and Mr Inskip will take the guest bedroom, and one of the upper rooms has been prepared for their nursemaid and children. Edward will share Richard's room, and Miss Hooper will stay at the Grand Hotel with her aunt.'

'I should hope so!' said Mrs Scarletti, with a flash of indignant alarm. 'A betrothed couple cannot sleep under the same roof until they are married. At least, they will not do so under this roof. It would be the talk of Brighton if they both stayed here.'

Richard, looking uncomfortable on a straight-backed chair since it impeded his natural urge to lounge like a dozing cat, inspected a treacle tart and took two pieces. 'Knowing Miss Hooper, she has insisted on the Grand Hotel,' he said wryly. 'She is one of those quietly demanding types and would scorn anything less. Is it just the family lunching there?' he added.

'Yes,' said Mina, 'I have reserved a private room with a special menu and champagne. There will be a string trio to entertain us, and a formal display of Miss Hooper's pressed flowers which have been specially framed for the occasion.'

Mrs Scarletti, who had decided that Miss Hooper's pressed flowers were an abomination, shuddered. 'I trust they will be under glass or I could not endure them. Why anyone would want to look at dead flowers that have been squashed out of their proper shape I cannot imagine. A nice painting or a photograph would be so much better, but the girl can have no talent for art, unlike you, Richard.' She favoured her son with an indulgent smile.

Mina could not repress a little sigh. Richard, who had been granted the fine features and blond locks of his doting mother, liked to wander idly through life with as little trouble to himself as possible. Mina was very fond of him, but his tendency to unintentionally cause confusion and chaos was a constant worry to her. Only last March, Richard had been dismissed from his post as a sketch artist for Scarletti Publishing by his own brother for neglecting his work and general unreliability. This ignominious end to his association with the family business had had to be carefully concealed from their mother to avoid upsetting her further during Mina's illness and Enid's pregnancy. No one wanted to shake her conviction that Richard was the talented one of the family, since boasting of his accomplishments had been her only comfort during a time of severe trial. When Mina discovered the truth from Edward, she had unashamedly used it as a weapon to induce her workshy younger brother to find another honest employment, threatening that if he did not, she would reveal all as soon as family equilibrium had been restored. Since Richard had long ago dissipated his inheritance from their late father, and relied upon gifts from his mother, he had taken the threat very seriously.

This scheme of Mina's had however rebounded upon her with disturbing effect since Richard had found employment at the new business of the detestable photographer Mr Beckler, a man who Mina for her own very good reasons wanted to avoid. Mina had secrets of her own, an unpleasantness she felt unable to reveal to her family. It lay encased in her memory like a hungry viper with sharp little teeth that gnawed at her from within. To her further annoyance, Richard entertained hopes that Mina and his employer might make a match.

'We should have photographs made of the betrothal party,' said Richard. 'I shall ask Beckler to do it; I am sure he will be delighted.'

'That is a good thought, my dear,' said Mrs Scarletti. 'Imagine how we will all look gathered together. We are such a handsome family. Even Miss Hooper has quite regular features, and might look well if carefully lit.' She glanced at Mina as if about to say something else but did not. Mina, her small, frail body twisted by scoliosis, was often placed to one side in family portraits so as to make the least possible impression, and it hardly needed to be said that this would occur again. 'Mr Beckler is a very clever young man,' Mrs Scarletti went on. 'And when I sat for my portrait, I thought his manners were excellent.' She patted her hair. 'Is he still single? I only ask because a young man of promise ought to have a wife. Perhaps I can think of someone for him.'

'He is single and devoted to his business. I doubt he even thinks of marriage,' said Richard, 'although, one never knows…' He gave Mina a sly glance, whose eyes flashed a warning look.

'I passed by the shop the other day and there was an advertisement in the window offering to take portraits of monuments in the Extra Mural Cemetery,' said Mrs Scarletti. 'I thought that very peculiar.'

'Ah, that is his new idea,' said Richard. 'You know he takes *memento mori* portraits, and they are very good ones, but not everyone makes a handsome corpse. There was that fellow who fell off the train, for example. You wouldn't want that sight on your mantelpiece. So Beckler thought that if people have no last portrait they might like one of the monument. He will offer to send them to those family members who cannot travel to Brighton to put flowers on the grave. And of course, if the Brighton customers are pleased with the pictures, they might want to come in and have their photographs taken while they are still alive. He sees opportunities everywhere.'

'You take very fine pictures, my dear,' said Mrs Scarletti, warmly.

Richard had failed to mention to his mother that none of the portraits displayed in the shop were his own work, since Mr Beckler permitted him only the most superficial contact with valuable equipment and none at all with dangerous chemicals. His main position was that of counter clerk. 'It is hard work, Mother,' he sighed. 'He is intending to go out to the cemetery and take some sample pictures to make a display. But the most important task, the one I am to carry out, is to decide which monuments will make the best pictures. I have to go there and find and sketch them first and show Beckler my drawings before we could think of taking the camera out.'

'How do you choose which ones to sketch?' asked Mina. 'The most ornamental, I suppose, or those of the most important families?'

'He gave me a list of names. I have to take it to the cemetery office, and they will give me a plan and tell me where to find the graves. Then —' he paused for thought — 'oh yes, then I put a cross on the map where the monument is and go there and draw it. It's all terribly complicated.'

Mina frowned. Despite the impression Richard had wanted to give, it was obvious that all the decisions were being made by his employer. 'Are these families who still live in Brighton?'

He shrugged. 'Mostly. I suppose so. I didn't ask. One of the graves was that of Mrs Honeyacre. The first one, of course, not the one we know. Oh, and Mrs Peasgood's husband.'

Mina said nothing, but her suspicions had been aroused. She knew from past encounters that spirit mediums made use of graveyards for their research, gathering information about local deceased from inscriptions on tombstones. This information then emerged at séances to convince the clients that they were in touch with the family spirits, since they could not imagine how the medium might otherwise know their history. 'He's not setting himself up as a medium, is he?' she asked anxiously.

Richard looked mystified by the question. 'I don't think so. He hasn't said he would.'

'But why those graves in particular? Unless he plans to cover every monument in the cemetery, which would be a very substantial endeavour.'

Richard searched his memory, which was not a lengthy task. 'I think — I had the impression from something Beckler said that they were families that Mr Hope was acquainted with. Perhaps they were people he met when he was last in Brighton. The spiritualism devotees? Maybe Beckler thinks they would be more likely to do business with him as he is Mr Hope's associate.'

Mina did not reply but thought that if Mr Hope imagined that Mr Honeyacre and her mother's friend Mrs Peasgood might support any protégé of his, he had a far better opinion of himself than he deserved. Mr Honeyacre, who had made a study of spiritualism for many years, had once been a sincere admirer of Mr Hope but this admiration had not outlasted the experience of meeting him. It was one thing reading the gentleman's books, but it was quite another to have him descend upon one's house and take over its domestic arrangements to the discomfort and annoyance of everyone else.

Mrs Peasgood had once taken an interest in spiritualism but had quite given this up after an incident in the Royal Pavilion which had caused her some personal embarrassment. Since she was a constant presence at ladies' tea gatherings and a frequent hostess of elegant soirées held at her own home, she was also well aware that Mr Hope's reputation had been touched by scandal. Mina was obliged to remind herself, however, that Mr Hope was unusually blind to his detractors unless they made some sort of clamour, and he had considerable support amongst those who refused to believe any ill of him. He existed bathed in the sunny glow of an imagined perpetual universal admiration.

'Enterprise and hard work, that is what makes a man a success,' said Mrs Scarletti, softly smoothing the lace collar of her gown with her fingertips. 'If I had a marriageable daughter, I might well consider Mr Beckler as a son-in-law.'

'What about —' Richard began, glancing at Mina. Mina gave him her sharpest look and Richard almost choked on his tea.

'How old is Mr Beckler?' mused Mrs Scarletti. 'I should imagine he is about thirty.'

'I think so,' said Richard, vaguely.

'That is a good age,' said Mrs Scarletti, approvingly. 'He is now past the time of immature foolishness, but still young enough for energy and achievement.' She touched a silver comb in her hair with a smile.

Mina's blood ran cold. Mr Beckler had an obsequiously flattering manner with female customers, which she personally found repellent. Her mother, however, a handsome woman in her fifties who liked to be admired, was unable to tell the difference between self-seeking flattery and a genuine compliment. Mina feared that her mother, in considering that the young photographer might like to be married had not, despite the difference in their ages, placed herself outside the list of potential brides.

CHAPTER TWO

Mr and Mrs Inskip were the first members of the betrothal party to arrive at the Scarletti home. They brought with them their rumbustious two-year-old twins William and Benjamin, baby Gwendoline, who had in only a few months of existence cultivated a determined annoyance with the world, and an extraordinarily patient nursemaid, Mrs Wheedon.

Enid and her husband had always been an ill-assorted couple. Mina was not the only person who had been astonished when her sister had accepted Mr Inskip's proposal, which he had made more in desperate hope than any expectation of success. Enid was a younger version of their mother — slender, even after two pregnancies, with almost white-blonde hair and a perfect complexion. Launched into society at eighteen, she had gloried in the admiration of young gentlemen and thrilled to the excitement of flirtation. There had been no lack of either. She had received many offers for her hand, none of which she had seriously considered, but had married Mr Inskip on a whim, the quicker to escape a household deeply afflicted by melancholy after the death of her father Henry.

Enid was now twenty-three, her husband ten years her senior and the leading light of a law practice in London whose speciality was transactions in land. With neither brothers nor sisters, he had on the demise of his father inherited properties and investments which were a sound foundation for marriage, but he lacked assertiveness and found it hard to engage with other people in a manner which commanded their attention. He had very little conversation, and when he did speak it was of mundane matters that were tedious to the listener. He was, in fact, a bore. Enid might have tolerated this had he been handsome, but Mr Inskip was short and slight, with sallow, sunken cheeks, a sharply pointed nose and sparse brown whiskers. If he had been ugly, he might have been interesting, but the best that could be said of him was that he was plain.

Not long after the wedding, it became apparent that Enid had realised she had made a terrible mistake. Another suitor, a pretty youth who had been her preference but had no fortune, had come into an unexpected inheritance and was now engaged to another. The newly minted Mrs Inskip came to regard her husband with indifference and even distaste.

Enid had been visiting Brighton with the twins the previous year during her husband's long absence abroad. It was inevitable, given the presence of the charismatic explorer Mr Arthur Wallace Hope, who was giving a series of lectures to enraptured audiences, that a passion had been aroused in Enid which had induced her to attend his lectures, and purchase his books. That should have been the limit of her admiration. Further than that she ought not to have gone, but the careless, wilful, unhappy wife had succumbed to the temptation of secret assignations at Mr Hope's hotel, and Mina had by chance learned of it.

Quite what Enid expected to come of this unwise behaviour was unclear, but she had probably not anticipated her paramour's sudden departure from town, leaving her to deal with the unintended consequences. She had discovered too late that he had been conducting similar intrigues with other married ladies, all of whom believed themselves to be his only interest, all of whom he had abandoned without a thought. Fortunately, Enid had escaped any rumours attaching to her name, since the town had been alive with gossip about Mr Hope and the attractive wife of Mr Laidlaw, senior partner in the family solicitors. Phipps, Laidlaw and Phipps. To avoid scandal, Mr Laidlaw had been obliged to retire from practice and remove himself and his contrite wife from Brighton.

Mina had understandably been anxious about the consequences of Mr Inskip's recent return from Romania but to her surprise and relief had learned from Edward's reports that the reunited couple were on far better terms than previously. On their arrival in Brighton, the reasons for this change were apparent.

Mr Inskip's travel and the tribulations he had suffered had made him almost a different man. He had allowed his whiskers to grow mightily during his illness and now sported a full bushy beard of the kind generally considered manly. His skin, which had looked almost corpse-like from his habit of shunning the outdoors now looked weathered, like that of a wanderer in the wilds who had endured harshness of climate and overcome it without complaint. He was full of tales of travel in the far and most dangerous reaches of Europe, which were considerably more entertaining than his previous conversation, which had mainly expounded on the complexities of property deeds, a subject which he alone found fascinating.

In the past, Enid had tended to avoid gazing at her husband. He had been a ghost in her presence, pale and hardly there. Now she looked on him with obvious approval.

'Is your Romanian client very noble and distinguished?' asked Mrs Scarletti as they were seated at the family dining table. 'Does he have handsome features? Is he married?'

'He is quite elderly now,' said Mr Inskip, 'but the portraits in the castle show him to have been very handsome in his youth. The family goes back many hundreds of years. He has no wife, and I believe he is the last of his line.'

'And you, Mr Inskip?' asked Mina. 'Tell me how you fare. Are you now completely well? Please do reassure us.'

He smiled, a bright, toothy beam that made his beard tips quiver. 'Thank you, yes, I am. My illness was cured by the religious ladies who live in a closed order in one wing of the castle.'

'It is a very big castle,' said Enid, with more energy than she usually afforded to a discussion of historic buildings.

'And extremely remote,' added Mr Inskip. 'It is ranged about with high mountains, thus the difficulty of the journey both there and back. The Count has few servants and owns extensive acres of land which are populated by peasants. They live in very poor conditions and raise sheep and fowls. Their constant demands can be a severe trial to him.'

'That is very hard work for an aged gentleman,' said Mina. 'How old is he?'

'I did not like to ask. There was something about him that made him appear both very old indeed and yet in another way — ageless. But he no longer has any taste for land management. That was the reason for my visit. He wishes to appoint an agent to manage the estate, then he will sell the castle and retire to a more comfortable and convenient property in a city. Romanian winters can be extremely harsh. He may even decide to settle in England. If he does, I am to look for a manor house here and make all the arrangements.'

'Then we may see him, I hope,' said Mrs Scarletti, glowing a little with the anticipation of meeting a count. 'You must arrange an introduction. Invite him to dine.'

Mina smiled, seeing that her mother was already preparing for an acquaintanceship with the nobility which would make her the envy of her friends.

'Although —' Mrs Scarletti looked suddenly concerned as Rose brought in the soup tureen, the contents of which were a reminder of the limitations of the Scarletti's cook — 'he must be used to the very best cuisine and cellar.'

'He dines very simply and sparingly, and I believe is a follower of the temperance movement,' said Mr Inskip, reassuringly. 'At least, I have never seen him drink.'

'Perhaps he will find a better appetite in England,' said Mina. 'I am sure he will find the climate more comfortable here.'

'Did you have many adventures?' asked Richard, reaching out to take charge of the wine bottle. 'Edward told us that Romania is a very inhospitable place with all sorts of dangers, like robbers and brigands and hungry wolves.'

Mr Inskip chuckled. 'The main dangers are actually the weather and the terrain. It was a very hard journey and made all the worse by the villagers being nervous of travelling in winter. My return was severely delayed by illness as you know, and when the snows came down, they blocked the mountain pass which was our only route, making any kind of travel impossible. The bad weather also had the effect of reducing the normal food supply of the wolf packs. Wolves don't usually attack travellers but will sometimes do so when starving. Their favourite diet is wild boar, but they will eat anything they can catch when necessary.'

'Starving wolves!' exclaimed Mrs Scarletti. 'How horrible!'

Mina thought that a pack of hungry wild animals and a carriage full of terrified travellers trapped in the mountains by snow would make a very good start for a story. She would have liked to make notes of Mr Inskip's observations but felt that this might be frowned upon at the dinner table. She determined to do so as soon as she could. 'Tell me more about the wolves,' she said.

31

'The wolf,' said Mr Inskip, who clearly needed no encouragement, 'is a large and noble creature, but it is a danger to livestock, which have to be protected. The peasants will sometimes kill a wolf that has been taking their sheep. They use its skin to make belts and suchlike. They believe that wearing a wolfskin belt will protect them from the bite of a wolf; in fact, they presented me with one before I left.'

'Is it effective?' asked Mrs Scarletti. 'Do we have wolves in Brighton?' She looked about her in the hope of information. 'I have never seen one, though Mrs Carmody has a large dog which is almost the same thing.'

'I do not think wolves live in these islands,' said Mina. 'And Mrs Carmody's dog is an Irish retriever.'

Mr Inskip accepted a bread roll. It was somewhat on the dense side, but he tore it in half as easily as if it were made of rice paper. 'I did not encounter any wolves myself,' he said, 'although one does hear them howling from time to time. It was a curious sound, and many people fear it, but the Count seems to like it, he finds it almost tuneful in a way. He does keep guard dogs which are part wolf. They roam in a pack about the estate, which they regard as their territory. The mixed breed creatures are said to be more aggressive than pure wolves, but more territorial than dogs. They do have a handler who they trust. I was warned to stay away from them, but one of the pups gave me a scratch with its claws which turned very unpleasant and may have been the reason for my illness. I was unwell for a long time; I hardly knew myself. But the Count made sure I was looked after and well fed and I feel quite strong again, in fact stronger than I ever was before.'

Enid said nothing but smiled and pressed her fingertips to her cheeks.

'Are you well, Enid?' demanded her mother, staring at her intently. 'You look quite flushed.'

'It is the soup,' said Enid, hastily. 'It is — very hot.'

'I don't regret the hardships of my travels,' Mr Inskip continued. 'In fact, through them I began to understand the spirit of those great men who go to foreign lands and undergo many trials. It awakened in me a curiosity about mankind and other modes of living, and dare I say it, a craving for travel and adventure. I used to spend all my days indoors but now I find myself eager to explore, which I do whenever I can, either on foot or with my new velocipede.'

'Adventure is a very fine thing if only it could be achieved in comfort, while being well housed and fed and not having people shooting arrows at you, or being eaten by lions,' said Richard.

'I don't think I could admire an adventurer who had no spirit,' said Enid. 'A man, a true man, must be prepared to confront danger.'

'How can one tell the difference?' said Richard. 'There was a customer who came to be photographed the other day, and he brought a tiger-skin rug with him so he could pretend he had shot it himself.'

'Perhaps he did,' said his mother.

'It still had the price ticket attached.'

There was a pause as Rose collected the soup plates and brought in the roast and vegetables.

'But we will have a real explorer in Brighton very soon,' said Richard, heaping potatoes onto his plate, 'as Mr Beckler has just heard that Mr Hope is returning to England and intends to come here for a visit, and he wants a new picture done in his best expedition clothes. The studio will be full of potted plants, and he will peer out from between them holding a big gun.'

'That will hardly look convincing,' said Mina. 'Unless they have potted plants in jungles, which I doubt.'

'Jungles,' said her mother, authoritatively, 'are generally composed of a great many trees.'

'It would be very hard to take a camera there,' said Richard.

'One could at least take an artist,' said Mina. 'Mr Hope's lectures on Africa were illustrated by maps, and the pictures in his book were undoubtedly drawn from his descriptions alone. No one poses for a portrait while fighting a giant snake.'

'Just imagine,' said Richard, brightly, 'if one stood before a big portrait of a place and then had one's photograph taken. You could seem to be anywhere in the world without ever having been there.'

'That would be cheating,' said Mina. 'But I am sure Mr Hope has really been to Africa. In fact, he thinks so highly of it I am surprised he does not remain there permanently.'

'I should like to meet him,' said Mr Inskip. 'I noticed you have several of his books on your shelves.'

'He is a shameful creature!' said Mrs Scarletti. 'He has a reputation. I will say no more than that. Read his books of adventure if you wish, but he will not be admitted to this house.'

Enid lowered her eyes to her plate and said nothing.

'Is he writing a new travel book?' asked Mr Inskip.

'I don't know,' said Richard. 'He was hoping to find Dr Livingstone; in fact, that was the whole reason he went back to Africa, but then someone else found him first, some American, who will no doubt be writing his memoirs and making a lot of money.'

Mina smiled. 'I read in the newspapers that when the news came out that Dr Livingstone had been found, Mr Hope lost his financing from the Royal Geographical Society, and half his companions abandoned him at the coast before he had even started his journey to the interior, so I suppose he had no option but to come back. I doubt that he will be writing a new book. I don't think a volume entitled "How I Didn't Find Dr Livingstone" would enjoy much success.'

'Perhaps I shall have a portrait taken,' said Mr Inskip. 'In my travelling clothes, with a feather in my hat and my wolfskin belt.'

'The belt is very rough and coarse, but it is not without charm,' said Enid, taking a sip of water before digging into her roast beef.

'Oh yes, you must have a portrait,' said Mrs Scarletti. 'Richard's business is doing so very well! His partner is a very enterprising gentleman who will be taking photographs for our celebration. Do you know, I read in the *Gazette* today that he can take pictures of ghosts? I never knew such a thing was possible.' She suddenly heaved a great sigh, and Mina knew that her mother was thinking of those family members who would be absent from the gathering.

'Ghosts?' enquired Mr Inskip, looking at Richard.

'Oh, he can't do it to order,' said Richard. 'He took a photograph of a ghost last year, but he didn't know how he had done it, and when he tried to do it again, he couldn't. And then about a week ago another one appeared. Which he might have been very pleased about, except it had to be the mother of that dreadful Miss Hartop.' He pulled a face. 'He pleaded with her not to talk of it, but of course she has gossiped the news all over town, and he can hardly deny it. Ever since then he has spent most of his time in his darkroom hoping to find more ghosts, but mainly I think it is to avoid Miss Hartop, and I can't say I blame him.'

'Is her judgement to be relied upon?' asked Mina.

'She is a silly creature, by all accounts, but I think she can be trusted to recognise her own mother,' said Mrs Scarletti, severely.

No one sought to contradict her.

CHAPTER THREE

Mina feared that one day her curiosity would get the better of her, with unpleasant consequences, nevertheless she was always unwilling and frequently unable to hold it in check. She had agreed, in order to mollify her anxious mother, to pay a visit to the Grand Hotel, to ensure that all the arrangements for the betrothal feast were in order. It was also, she realised, an opportunity to go to nearby Ship Street and see for herself what Mr Beckler was up to. Not that she intended to see or speak to him. Her plan was to gather information by the strategy of studying the contents of the shop window, without actually encountering the man.

Her most reliable source of information concerning the photographer was usually her friend Mr Marcus Merridew, the famous Brighton actor. A theatrical artist of great versatility, he often patronised the shop for *cartes de visite* in which he was portrayed costumed for his most prominent roles. His recent career had been marked by a noted rendition of Hamlet which had thrilled Brighton audiences. He had partly rewritten the play to provide a more palatable ending, as he felt that such a popular hero, however flawed, ought not to end his life so tragically young.

Mr Merridew was constantly in demand for ladies' tea gatherings to give poetry readings; however, his range included entertainments suitable for every taste. Currently, however, he was not in Brighton. He was touring the theatres of coastal towns with a pantomime of his own creation, *The Jolly Milkmaid*, in which he played the role of the milkmaid's mother, Dame Bracket. Mina had never seen this work, which she had been given to understand was much enjoyed by families visiting the seaside, but she had been told that the magical transformation of Dame Bracket to the beautiful Fairy Cherish always brought the house down.

Soon after luncheon, Enid announced that she would like to take a walk on the West Pier, where she was happy to be squired by her attentive husband. Mina's mother was fawning over the new baby while Mrs Wheedon amused the twins, and Rose was kept constantly busy with trivial demands blown into extraordinary proportions. Mina would have to go out alone.

A little expedition of this kind would have been very pleasant in the company of her good friend Nellie Jordan, whose husband was a partner in the fashionable costume emporium of Jordan and Conroy. Nellie had recently returned from Italy, where she had amused herself in the company of acquaintances while her husband visited silk weavers and purchased fabrics and trimmings to astonish and delight his customers.

Nellie kept a smart little carriage and frequented all the best teashops, but it was not possible for her to accompany Mina on this occasion as it meant visiting Richard's place of work. For Nellie, visits to Richard were strictly forbidden, and not without good reason. Richard and Nellie had been affectionate companions before her marriage, and their continuing friendship following that event had not met with her husband's approval. To Mr Jordan, his attractive wife, tricked out in the pinnacle of fashion, was a travelling clothes form, an advertisement for his business; to her, he was the entrée to the life of comfort she had always desired. It was a fragile arrangement. There were watchful eyes on Nellie. One slip and she would be a ruined woman.

Mina took a cab that travelled east along Kings Road. Even after more than three years in Brighton, she still found the views a delightful and invigorating prospect, on one side the cool elegance of Regency Square, on the other, the fashionable West Pier making its dramatic incursion into the glittering endless sea.

On her way to Ship Street the carriage passed the Grand Hotel, its frontage like a high white cliff. Designed to accommodate visiting nobility and gentry, it had first opened its doors in 1864, and had quickly secured its reputation as the premier and certainly the most expensive hotel in Brighton. Next door to the hotel was the important and exclusive photographic business of Mr J E Mayall, the superior fine art portraitist. Mr Mayall's studio occupied an enviable position on an upper floor where large areas of glass could admit the maximum light. He had been a presence in Brighton since the opening of the hotel, leaving his original London business in Regent Street in the capable hands of his eldest son, and was a prominent influence in town.

Photography, Mina knew, was a thriving commercial activity in Brighton. New buildings such as the Grand Hotel and the West Pier held a fascination for the public. They had been portrayed from all angles during the course of their construction, and again when they were opened. Photographers also liked to make wistfully nostalgic images of the old Chain Pier, whose days were most probably numbered, and artistic portrayals of the beaches where rows of pleasure boats were lined up like the bodies of stranded dolphins, ready to take visitors on excursions.

Mr Mayall's greatest claim to fame was having photographed most of the royal family, a fact he never lost the opportunity to advertise. He should have been engaged to take the images of

Enid's wedding, but due to the impetuosity of the arrangement in a household mainly concerned with consoling her recently widowed mother, the photographs had been forgotten until the last moment. Mr Mayall had not been available, and thus the Scarlettis had engaged Mr Simpson of Ship Street. His quiet, respectful and unfussy dedication to his profession had struck the perfect note on such a sombre occasion.

Mina ordered the driver to stop and alighted at the junction of Kings Road and Ship Street. From there it was thankfully only a short walk up to the shop. Mina was obliged to labour a little at the incline but was encouraged to discover that as long as she took suitable care, the walk did not overstrain her cramped lungs.

Mr Beckler's establishment was far humbler than Mr Mayall's, yet there was clearly room for another photographer in Brighton, as long as he knew his business and offered the public something of good quality, and affordable. But the fickle public also clamoured for novelty, and as far as Mina was aware Mr Mayall had never claimed to take pictures of ghosts.

Mina approached the shop cautiously. She had not visited or even passed the place of business since Mr Beckler had purchased it from the estate of the late Mr Simpson. Little had changed. It was a narrow building, with a single entrance door, and there were two floors above the shop. The window was crammed with displays and advertisements. There was every kind of portrait a family might want: stern gentlemen, dignified ladies, betrothed couples, weddings, mothers with babies and large family groups.

A notice announced: 'Memento Mori portraits a speciality. Discretion and good taste assured.' There was the advertisement Richard had mentioned, offering to take pictures of some of the notable monuments in the Extra Mural

Cemetery. These were accompanied by framed portraits of important buildings to show the quality that could be achieved. These pictures, taken in beautiful and intense sunlight, were a marvel of clarity.

Mina, despite her contempt for their creator, could only admire the clear rendition of architectural features, the crisply defined embellishments and sharp contrasts between light and shadow. A printed card suggested that a selection of suitable frames was available inside, or could be made to order, and for a small extra charge the picture could be securely packaged and sent anywhere in the country or abroad.

Overseeing all this photographic plenty was the image of Mr Beckler's distinguished patron, Mr Arthur Wallace Hope, with a notice saying 'By appointment to the nobility' in front of a display of that gentleman's books.

There was, however, one other item which attracted Mina's special attention. Handsomely framed and displayed on a small easel to emphasise its importance, it was a picture of a short, plump lady with a snub nose wearing a gown with so many frills that they threatened to obscure her figure. She was seated on a chair, not sitting upright but leaning a little with her elbow on a circular plant stand, on which there stood a branched candlestick, her head turned to cast a knowing look at the camera. Her eyes were small, dark and shiny, like those of a hungry rodent. Engulfed in her arms was a bouquet the size of a small canoe.

The picture had clearly been taken in Mr Beckler's studio. Mina had seen others and recognised the balloon back chair, the scroll feet and barley twist legs of the plant stand, a draped velvet curtain behind the subject and the edge of a portrait frame carved with acanthus leaves. Hovering above one almost daringly bare shoulder was a cloudy shape which on close study might be taken to be that of a woman seen in profile and wearing a large hat. The lady did not appear to be taking any notice of the subject of the picture, which Mina thought strange, as this was supposed to be the spirit of the lady's late mother watching over her. Instead, the ghostly head was tilted upward, as if gazing to the heavens.

Underneath the picture was a card, which read: 'The famous ghost portrait. As reported in the *Gazette*, the *Chronicle* and the *Illustrated Police News!* Guaranteed genuine. No trickery involved. If you doubt us, come in and see for yourself!'

Mina hesitated, unsure of what to do. For a few moments there was a little tussle going on in her mind. She very much wanted to come in and see for herself. She wanted to learn all about the spirit picture and how it was made. She wanted to see what Richard really did in his daily occupation. She did not, however, want to see the horrible Mr Beckler, but Mr Beckler would undoubtedly be present. The last time they had spoken was in January at Hollow House, when she had told him to his face that she never wanted to see him again, and she had meant it. Richard had informed her that his employer lived in an apartment above the shop, and spent most of his time on the premises, so there was no prospect of his going out for meals, and therefore no opportunity for her to go in when she would be sure not to see him.

Mina decided to take the way of common sense. She comforted herself with the assurance that her curiosity had been partly satisfied, and perhaps a better opportunity for investigation would arise in future. Her best course was to return to Kings Road and stroll gently along to the Grand Hotel where, once her business was complete, she could pause to sit and refresh herself in the peaceful gentility of the tearoom before returning home.

'Oh!' came a little squawk behind her. 'You must be Miss Scarletti!'

Mina turned. She was used to the fact that she was an object of curiosity to those who did not know her, and instantly recognisable to anyone who knew her description. Standing behind her with a broad smile was the plump lady who was the subject of the ghost portrait. She was accompanied by a young woman whose dark serviceable clothing and retiring manner proclaimed her to be a maid.

'It is such a delight to meet you at last; you are so very famous, you know!' enthused Miss Hartop. 'Are you quite well now? Isn't the air just so delicious! And what a pretty little shop this is! I am sure you know that your brother and I are very good friends. He must have mentioned me. I am Hannah Hartop. I feel we practically know one another already!'

'I — er,' said Mina, unsure of how to respond.

'And we will be great friends, too, I am certain of it!' Miss Hartop linked her arm firmly in Mina's. 'Come now, let us go in.'

Miss Hartop's arm was a strong arm and would not be denied, and for a moment Mina had visions of her using that arm to wrestle a hapless Richard to the altar.

'I can see you have been admiring my wonderful picture, and I am sure you want to hear all about how it was taken!'

That was undeniable, and Mina, unwilling to embark on a public quarrel or an unseemly struggle which she would inevitably lose, allowed herself to be guided into the shop. The maid followed unbidden, like a slight shadow of her mistress. She was a plain girl who might have been pretty if her hair had been better styled and her bonnet more flattering, but Mina guessed that this would not have been permitted. She particularly recalled that some months earlier the maid's powers of observation and good memory had provided vital evidence in solving a mystery in which she had been interested, a feat for which Miss Hartop had been happy to accept the credit.

The premises were tidy but cramped, with every inch of available space in use. There was a long counter to the right, with a brass till, record books, leatherbound catalogues, a glass case displaying photograph albums, another with blank *cartes de visite*, and a tiered wooden stand with a selection of frames. On the wall behind the counter were rows of drawers labelled with their contents: printed cards, small frames, folders, picture hanging materials, envelopes and photograph mounts. A large well-dressed lady holding a lorgnette was standing at the counter and poring over a catalogue illustrating picture frames while Richard looked on with an expression of deep melancholy.

The facing wall was given up to displays of pictures featuring notable residents of Brighton, views of the Royal Pavilion, piers, beaches and gardens, and images from a recent exhibition, taken in caves and Egyptian monuments by the light of burning magnesium ribbon.

Mina looked about with some trepidation, but to her relief there was no sign of Mr Beckler. At the far end of the shop was a door which she recalled led to the manager's office and studio. She assumed that he was on the other side of that door and hoped that he would stay there.

'Oh, Mr Scarletti!' exclaimed Miss Hartop. 'You look so pensive today. Like one of those old Roman statues! How refined! How noble! Now here is somebody come to cheer you; see who I met outside looking in the window!'

Richard, who had flinched at the sound of Miss Hartop's voice, stared at Mina in astonishment. 'Mina!'

The customer glanced around with an expression of interest, and after taking a moment to study Mina, went back to contemplation of the catalogue, only giving it rather less attention than before.

'I was going to the Grand Hotel to see if all was in order and I just chanced to be passing, and…' Mina winced. It was not a convincing explanation.

'Well, while you are here, I can make an appointment for you, if you like,' said Richard.

'Thank you, Richard, I don't wish to have my photograph taken.'

'Miss Scarletti is very curious about my portrait,' said Miss Hartop. 'Have you met Mr Beckler? I can introduce you if you like. He is an excellent photographer, although not nearly as handsome to look at as your brother.'

'I have met him,' said Mina. 'He is obviously very busy at the moment.' She glanced enquiringly at Richard.

'Yes, he's in the office with a client. Shall I go and tell him you are here?'

'No, I would not wish to disturb him.'

'But he will tell you all about my picture,' said Miss Hartop. 'Isn't it a marvel?'

'It is remarkable,' said Mina. 'Perhaps one day soon we will talk of it and you can tell me something about how it was taken?' Miss Hartop was about to protest, but Mina quickly interrupted. 'To be honest with you, Miss Hartop, I was not intending entering the shop at all today but was simply on my way to the Grand Hotel where I have important business. I need to make arrangements for my brother's betrothal celebration. I am afraid I shall have to leave almost immediately.' Now that Miss Hartop had released her arm Mina began to move towards the door, eager to take her leave as soon as possible.

Miss Hartop gasped and uttered a cry like that of a wild animal with its leg caught in a trap. 'Oh, Mr Scarletti, oh dear me, oh my word, you have kept such a secret!'

Mina caught a panicked glance from Richard and realised the error. She was obliged to turn back. 'No, no, Miss Hartop, please calm yourself, you are mistaken. I am not referring to Richard but to my older brother Edward, who is engaged to a Miss Hooper.'

The reassurance succeeded only in transforming an emergency into a drama. 'Oh! What excitement! I do declare, you quite took my breath away. I almost think I might faint.' Miss Hartop seemed to be considering fainting, but seeing as there was no means of support within arm's reach other than Mina, who would not have been a good choice, she lurched heavily towards the counter and leaned on it.

In any other person this might have been quite alarming, but Richard merely looked unhappy and the maid, who had been studying the display of photographs, hurried to the side of her mistress and with an expression which suggested that this was a common occurrence, took firm hold of an arm. Miss Hartop clutched a hand to her chest and panted.

Mina, as the cause of the mishap, now felt obliged to remain a few more moments to see the sufferer recovered. The lady customer, who did not appear at all disturbed by the situation, came forward purposefully, dipping into her reticule to retrieve a smelling bottle from which she deftly removed the stopper and waved the pungent restorative under Miss Hartop's nose.

The afflicted maiden gave a loud yelp and straightened up. There was so much attention devoted to her that it was not until then that Mina realised that Mr Beckler and his client, a bald gentleman with a heroic moustache, had emerged from the office and were standing at the far end of the shop, contemplating the scene.

CHAPTER FOUR

A host of conflicting expressions crossed Mr Beckler's face when he saw Mina, and for a moment he appeared unable to move or speak, but confronted by a valued customer being supported by her maid and making a noise like a distressed walrus, he was obliged to recover himself quickly. He swallowed convulsively and stepped forward. 'Miss Hartop, are you well? Is there something you require? A chair? A glass of water?'

'Oh, Mr Beckler!' cried the lady, still convulsively clutching at her bosom with a plump fist. 'I had such a surprise just now, but it was all a misunderstanding.'

Mr Beckler made a curt nod and conducted the moustached gentleman to the counter. 'Mr Scarletti, if you could make an appointment for Mr Winstanley.'

Richard was quick to take up this duty as a welcome alternative to dealing with Miss Hartop.

Mr Beckler regarded Mina and uttered a nervous cough. 'Miss Scarletti —' he began.

'I really ought to be going,' said Mina to no one in particular. She turned towards the door.

'Oh, but you cannot go yet!' said Miss Hartop, reaching out and taking Mina's arm before she could escape. 'I know how interested you are in the spirit picture! I am sure Mr Beckler would be delighted to tell you all about it.'

'Yes, of course,' said Mr Beckler, readily seizing on the opportunity. 'That would be my pleasure. Perhaps you would like to see the studio where the portrait was taken. And I could tell you how the image was created in the camera and printed.'

There was a heavily awkward silence. Mina wanted to see and understand all of those things, but not if it meant being alone with Mr Beckler, however respectful and professional his manners might be in public. Neither did she wish to reveal her reservations to anyone, including her own family. Most especially her own family.

'I would like to know more,' said the lady customer unexpectedly. 'Might I accompany you? Forgive me, Miss Scarletti, we have not been introduced. I am Clara McClelland. My husband is a medical practitioner. We have a mutual friend, I believe, a Mrs Holt.'

Mina had heard much that was commendable of Dr McClelland, although she had never met him. 'I am delighted to make your acquaintance,' she said, realising as she spoke that her voice must sound strained.

'Are you quite well?' asked Mrs McClelland, studying her anxiously. 'You look a little pale.'

'I am not long recovered from a serious indisposition,' said Mina. 'I may have overtaxed myself in coming here. But I would be extremely grateful for your company.'

Mr Beckler flicked an eyebrow at Richard, nodding towards Miss Hartop, then with a polite gesture towards the studio door proceeded to conduct Mina and her new companion to the rear of the premises. He looked to be about to offer his arm to Mina, but Mrs McClelland offered hers and Mina took it. Mr Beckler accepted the refusal with regret and pushed the rear door open. A narrow corridor stretched ahead, leading to an exit from the premises, its walls punctuated by side doors and a rear staircase.

As they reached the end of the corridor, Mina glanced up the narrow unlit stairs which were uncarpeted and made a sharp turn to the upper apartments. There was a faint odour of old wood and chemicals.

'This is the studio,' said Mr Beckler, opening the door opposite the stairs.

'This is where the famous spirit photograph was taken?' asked Mrs McClelland.

'All the indoor pictures are taken here. The conversion to a studio was carried out many years ago by the previous owner, Mr Simpson.'

'Who is rumoured to haunt the premises, I believe?' said Mrs McClelland, but Mina thought from her tone of voice that she was teasing.

'So I have been told,' said Mr Beckler.

Mina had not entered the studio since Mr Simpson had taken the pictures that followed Enid's wedding. There were sets of blinds which were only partially open, and Mr Beckler drew them fully back to reveal a room devoted to the gathering of light. The sun was high and blazed through the glass roof, its heat penetrating the rear wall which was also mostly composed of glass and looked out onto a walled yard. If there had not been some carefully placed ventilation, it would have been unbearably stifling.

Mina now saw, bathed in sunlight, the furnishings depicted in the spirit photograph, the small decorative plant table and balloon back dining chair. There was also, out of range of the camera lens, a garment stand so that sitters could divest themselves of coats and hats if they wished, and a rotating mirror on a wheeled wooden platform to reflect light if needed. The studio also offered a choice of vases, potted plants, ornaments, paintings and seating. The camera, a substantial device with a square bellows arrangement which enabled its length to be adjusted, sat on a robust wooden stand with screws and ratchets and a turning handle. The sight of such apparatus always evoked a slight shudder from Mina. She had once been encased in a steel corset in a futile effort to correct her scoliosis and recalled the rhythmic clicking of the ratchets as the garment was tightened in an attempt to force her spine straight. She breathed carefully to calm herself and pushed the memory away. This was no torture device but simply a means of raising and lowering the camera.

The area of wall that formed a backdrop to the portrait had been newly painted in plain light grey which helped soften the glare, and a set of pale blue curtains hung from a wooden pole enabling them to be drawn across, tied back or tastefully draped as required. Mina regarded the curtains with suspicion. Things or people could hide behind curtains. Was this the secret of the spirit photograph? Did Mr Beckler, unknown to Miss Hartop who would have been facing the camera, conceal an accomplice there? Did the accomplice then surreptitiously draw the covering back to became part of the picture, then adjust it later for concealment?

Mina walked over to the curtains and twitched one edge aside. The fabric hung close to a wall of whitewashed brick, and she estimated that an individual could not hide behind it without revealing his or her presence. A painting, however, or another photograph was very possible, although the surface of the wall had no picture hooks nor any sign that anything had ever been attached there. She glanced around. Mr Beckler was gazing at her, and it was evident that he knew very well what she was doing. She let go of the curtain.

'And is this where Miss Hartop was sitting?' asked Mrs McClelland, pointing to the chair.

'Yes, in this very chair.'

Mrs McClelland moved to stand behind the camera and looked about her. 'I see only the room,' she said. 'And when you took the portrait, there was no other person in the room?'

'Only Miss Hartop's maid, who was seated there —' he gestured towards a chair by the side wall — 'and she did not move from her place during the entire proceedings and saw nothing unusual. I can assure you I did not see the spirit until I saw the image on the glass negative and even then, I hardly believed what it was until the picture was printed.'

'Well, that is a mystery,' observed Mrs McClelland, but offered no further comment.

'It is. I am utterly at a loss to know how the image appeared on the plate and can only conclude that the camera was able to record something that the eye could not see. It may be something that science will one day explain, or it may be forever beyond any human understanding.'

Mina was examining the selection of decorative paintings in the studio, but they were all landscapes.

'Has there been another such image since then?' asked Mrs McClelland.

Mr Beckler risked a shy smile. 'I have been working towards that end, but in view of the public interest I can say nothing more at this juncture.'

'How intriguing,' said Mrs McClelland. She turned to Mina. 'You are very quiet, Miss Scarletti. I had anticipated that you would be full of the most interesting questions.'

Mina was careful to address the lady. 'I am thinking that I know nothing about the way in which a photograph is made. Even my brother who works here has been unable to enlighten me.'

'To give a simple description,' said Mr Beckler, 'I use a process that has been perfected over the last ten years or so. I first coat a clean glass plate in a preparation called collodion, then when that is set, I dip the plate in a solution of silver nitrate which is very sensitive to light. This solution alone will not adhere to glass, but it will form a coat on the collodion. The prepared plate has to be kept in a special slide to protect it from the light until it is put in the camera where in taking the photograph it is exposed to the light coming through the lens. This causes the image to be created on the glass. The image cannot last long and must be fixed by bathing it in a chemical solution. Potassium cyanide is the best thing for that purpose. Then it is varnished to protect it. But this is just the first part. The image that forms on the plate due to the action of the light is a negative. This means that what we see as light is dark on the plate and vice versa. The plate is put in a frame with sensitised paper and exposed to sunlight for the production of the prints.'

'Well, that is a very clear explanation,' said Mrs McClelland. 'So it is not one simple action of the camera?'

'No, there are several stages of preparation before the operation of the camera and then there is further work to be done afterwards.'

She gave him a humorously cynical look. 'Now you must be honest with us, Mr Beckler. Are you sure there was no mischievous person who could have altered the glass plate afterwards?'

Mr Beckler smiled politely. 'No one carried out that operation but myself. Neither are the plates left unattended. When I take portraits in the studio, I use a wet coating on the plate which must be used very quickly. I think it gives the sharpest results. Not long ago, photographers who travelled at any distance from their studio were obliged to take a folding portable darkroom with them. But there is a new kind of coating quite recently invented, where the plate is not wet but allowed to dry, and the glass can be prepared well in advance and processed when it is brought back to the studio. That is the method I use when I take pictures in town. Here, however, the entire operation must be completed in minutes. There is simply no opportunity for any hand other than mine to touch the plates or the chemicals.'

Mrs McClelland studied the camera through the lenses of her lorgnette. 'I suppose the ghost image could not have been an accident?'

'I am unable to say. No lady of that description was present during any of the work done to make the image. In fact, I can truthfully say that I have never photographed or even met the lady whose image appeared. The work is carried out by myself, alone in the darkroom.'

'This darkroom you mention,' said Mrs McClelland, 'it sounds fascinating. Like a dark séance. Spirit mediums claim that darkness is essential for the visitations of the spirits. Light is the enemy. It chases them away. What do you say, Miss Scarletti?'

Mina chose her words carefully. 'It is certainly true that séances conducted in darkness achieve far more convincing results than those where light is allowed.'

'Would you show us your darkroom, Mr Beckler?' asked Mrs McClelland. 'I mean, it makes me wonder — how can you work there when it is dark?'

'It is only white light that has to be excluded but — well, you can see for yourself. I don't usually encourage visitors in view of the dangerous chemicals, but on this occasion … come this way.'

Leaving the studio, Mr Beckler produced a bunch of keys from his pocket and unlocked another door. They entered a room where the light was so dim that it took a little while for their eyes to make out any details. The contrast with the studio could not have been greater. Just as the studio had been designed to admit the maximum light, this room was designed to exclude it. There was a single small window, and this was glazed in yellow glass which allowed in a strange sickly glow.

'Sunlight will affect the silvered plate,' said Mr Beckler, 'as will the light of burning magnesium. Gas and candlelight have very little effect. All the same, it is best to have as little light in the room as possible.'

They moved about the room, Mr Beckler pointing out the tools and materials of his profession. The air was heavily scented with chemicals. There was a pervading deep musty odour, with hints of bitterness and a tang like vinegar. Mina cast her glance over the labelled glass bottles on the shelves. Many were too high for her to reach or read, but she was able to make out *Argentum Nitricum*, *Acetas Natricus*, and more mysteriously *K.Cy*. A paper packet had a faded chemist's label saying simply 'Poison'.

'That is not for photography,' explained Mr Beckler. 'It's white arsenic. I think Mr Simpson used it to destroy vermin.'

'It is as well that the room is kept locked,' observed Mrs McClelland. 'My husband is always so very careful about keeping his medicines secure. Only his most trusted assistants are allowed to touch them.'

Mina said nothing but could only feel relieved that the room was not accessible to Richard. There were other things for the visitors to see: the sink for washing glass plates, racks for drying them, trays for the silver dipping process, a shallow bath for sensitising paper, and printing frames, ready to be taken outside and exposed to sunlight.

Mina, though interested, was relieved to emerge from the darkroom. Mr Beckler locked the door and they returned to the shop to find that Mr Winstanley had departed, and Miss Hartop was engaging Richard in conversation.

'The darkroom is so very fascinating,' Miss Hartop said. 'What a wonder it is that anyone can see to work in there. And the yellow light must make one look quite ill. I am sure my complexion would not look well in there.' She smiled up at Richard, hoping for a compliment. He did not take the bait.

'It is trying on the eyesight, I admit,' said Mr Beckler. 'But one gets accustomed to it.'

'But what of the other gentleman? He is quite elderly; how can he manage?' Miss Hartop asked.

Mr Beckler looked puzzled. 'The other gentleman?'

'Yes, when you showed me the room the other day, there was another gentleman standing in the corner.'

Mr Beckler was silent. He remained surprised, but said, 'Miss Hartop, when I showed you about the room, there was no other gentleman there. The only persons in the room were myself and you and your maid.'

Miss Hartop turned to her maid. 'Tilly, did you not see the gentleman watching us?'

Tilly looked composed, as anyone might who was accustomed to dealing with Miss Hartop's demands daily. 'No, Miss, there was just yourself and Mr Beckler. I suppose it might have been a trick of the light, which was very dim.'

Miss Hartop squeezed her face into an angry frown. 'Really, Tilly, I can think how I might imagine a shadow or a shape, but not an elderly man standing there and gazing at us.'

'Did you hear anything?' asked Mr Beckler. 'Did he speak?'

Miss Hartop thought about it. 'I heard nothing. Now you mention it, it was strange. I didn't speak to him, as the way he stared at me was so unusual. It made me feel quite uncomfortable.'

Mr Beckler made no reply but approached the counter and opened a catalogue which bore the title 'Photograph Frames. Our Premium Selection. Simpson and Co, Ship Street, Brighton'. He turned the pages to locate an insert with a photograph of a gentleman. 'Was this the man you saw?'

Miss Hartop examined the picture. 'Why yes, that was he. You see?' she said with a triumphant squeak. 'I didn't make a mistake.'

The gentleman portrayed was elderly and dignified. He sat beside a table on which was a framed portrait of a lady, and an item which Mina assumed to be apparatus devoted to the art of photography, although she could not identify it. The gentleman, however, was familiar to her, and she hardly needed to read the caption.

Mr H G Simpson.

CHAPTER FIVE

The shock in the little photographer's shop was palpable. Miss Hartop finally appeared to appreciate the implications of what she had seen and began to gasp and pant as if fighting for breath. A chair was hurriedly brought, and Tilly and Mrs McClelland assisted her into it. The smelling bottle was offered again but declined by the patient with a sharp wave of the hand as if swatting away a fly.

Mina looked at Miss Hartop closely. Her mother had threatened to faint many a time, but Mina greeted these remarks with calm acceptance, as there was never any noticeable change in her colour. The prospect of her actually fainting was rarely taken seriously but could never be safely dismissed without examination. Miss Hartop's colour had not changed; rather, there was a calculating look in her eyes and a little smile tilting the corner of her mouth. She was a very long way from fainting.

Richard and Mina exchanged glances. Both understood without a word passing between them that the event would be the subject of later discussion. Mr Beckler was silent, but as he gazed at the photograph of the late Mr Simpson, the tips of his long thin fingers were shaking. Mina could guess his thoughts. The ghostly vision would bring another raft of fame to the shop, another nod of approval from his patron, but he must be regretting that the elusive shade had chosen Miss Hartop as his conduit.

Mr Beckler turned and looked questioningly at Mrs McClelland, then at Mina.

'I am sorry, but I saw nothing,' said Mrs McClelland. 'Miss Scarletti, did you see anything? I would have thought you, with your gifts —' she ventured.

'I have no gifts,' said Mina, patiently. 'I am so sorry to disappoint you, but that is a story put about by the newspapers. I have never seen a ghost. But I have an appointment now, and I must go.' She handed Mrs McClelland her card. 'It has been a pleasure to make your acquaintance.'

'Likewise,' said Mrs McClelland, proffering a card in return. 'We must take tea very soon. I would enjoy conversing with you,' she added, meaningfully.

Mina smiled. She judged that Mrs McClelland was an astute lady who had guessed that her silence during the tour was not because she had nothing to say.

Mina began to move towards the door. As she did so, Mr Beckler darted ahead of her and opened the door with a respectful bow. 'Miss Scarletti —' he began. She continued on her way and left without speaking to or looking at him.

Outside, Mina paused for a moment to inhale the freshness of the clean Brighton air. It was then that the noise started. Miss Hartop had got her breath back and was using it to emit a loud, keening wail. A customer approached the shop, hesitated, cautiously opened the door, peered inside, then quickly closed the door, turned and hurried away.

Mina walked on. It was only a short stroll to the hotel along Kings Road in clement weather, and she did not trouble to take a cab. Her efforts that day existed, she realised, in an awkward place between Dr Hamid's prescription of gentle exercise and his admonition against overstraining herself, and she was unsure as to where this expedition ranked.

Her business at the Grand Hotel was soon done without difficulty, and she was grateful for a rest from her walk, a pot of tea and a little treat. The hotel's scones were a miracle of lightness compared with the redoubtable efforts of the Scarletti cook. The latter had the notable distinction of being able to last several days in a tin box, which was not, thought Mina, the first quality one looked for in a scone.

There was time for reflection. She had now seen for herself that Miss Hartop was, as she had been told, an unmitigated flirt. Like so many ladies she was attracted to Richard's good looks, but since she lacked modesty, was unable to make a secret of it, and would probably propel herself into his lap at the first opportunity which presented itself. There was no doubt in Mina's mind that the lady had only made such strong overtures of friendship to her because she was Richard's sister, a strategy to bring the huntress closer to her quarry.

Miss Hartop's sudden claim to have seen the spirit of Mr Simpson, made in Mina's presence, was almost certainly a ploy to gain her interest and further the friendship. The lady had visited the shop many times and had had ample opportunity to examine the catalogues and see Mr Simpson's portrait. If she had seen his ghost before, Mina would have heard about it from Richard. Mrs McClelland, on the other hand, she thought to be a kind and intelligent person and would be happy to know her better.

Mina had never denied her interest in the activities of spirit mediums. It was clear, however, that her reputation for being a medium herself, initiated by Mr Hope and further spread by the newspapers, persisted. Many practitioners she had found were well-meaning persons. They offered genuine comfort and reassurance to their clients for a modest fee, or even for none. Others, however, were criminals, draining their trusting victims of gold and casting them aside when they offered no further sustenance. Mina's recent exploits in unmasking these leeches were unfortunately seen by some as merely disposing of rivals.

Here, Mina was obliged to pause in her ruminations and consider all the possibilities. Without actual evidence, she could not entirely discount that Miss Hartop really had seen the ghost of Mr Simpson. Perhaps the image on the photograph was genuine, perhaps despite all her vigorous protests she really did have the powers she obstinately refused to acknowledge? Mina sighed and poured herself another cup of tea. Her reflections, she thought, would be so much simpler if she did not spend so much of her private time devising stories with surprise endings.

Rested and refreshed, Mina returned home to find that a telegram had arrived for her mother, advising her of Edward's arrival that evening in time for dinner. Mrs Scarletti, having conveniently forgotten all about Mina's errand, was complaining bitterly about her absence. It was impossible to convince her that she herself had requested it.

As Mina expected, Rose and cook had all the arrangements in hand. Her mother, professing herself to be utterly exhausted due to having done all the work while Mina was out, decided to take a nap, and Mina was therefore able to spend some time at her writing desk. There, supported by the little wedge-shaped cushion which allowed her tilted body to sit upright, she penned her stories, which were published by the Scarletti Library of Romance under the *nom de plume* Robert Neil.

Her family took almost no interest in her writing, which they assumed to be gently moral tales for children. Even Edward was unaware of the real nature of her output since it was his partner Mr Greville who was in charge of storybooks, and only he knew that she wrote bloodcurdling tales of ghosts and demons. Of all her friends, only Dr Hamid had any inkling. His late sister Eliza, an invalid whose scoliosis had been more advanced than Mina's, had been a devotee of the stories. Mina had befriended Eliza in what had proved to be the final months of her life. Her good humour and resilience in the face of her overwhelming affliction was and remained a powerful guide to all who had known her.

It was inevitable that Mina took inspiration for her works of fiction from her own experiences, and the recent events at Hollow House had been a veritable treasure trove leading to a series of tales of mysterious hauntings. She wondered if Mr Hope read her work. She doubted it, and even if he did would he recognise himself as the appalling Mr Hogg, the predatory voluptuary who suffered such a horrible fate? Would Mr Beckler see in the repellent Mr Bickley, whom she had consigned to a ghastly death, a mirror image of himself?

She had begun a new tale, concerning a supposed adventurer who achieved great acclaim from visiting faraway places, but was proved to be a great fraud since the portraits he produced in evidence were all photographs of him standing in front of paintings. He would suffer the consequences of his duplicity when the paintings came to life and swallowed him. She was debating whether he should be strangled by a snake, eaten by a crocodile, or plunge into the seething maw of a volcano, when Richard unexpectedly arrived home early and came to see her.

'The house is very quiet,' he said.

'Mother is resting, Mrs Wheedon has taken the children out for fresh air, and Enid and Mr Inskip are out walking. Let us enjoy the peace while we can.'

Richard stretched out on the bed with a groan of relief, and Mina put her pen down and turned to him. 'Why so early? Have you been dismissed?'

He tried to look offended by the suggestion. 'No, the shop had to be closed because Beckler and Mrs McClelland and the maid had to manage Miss Hartop. There would have been less trouble with an escaped elephant. I was sent off to fetch her father. He didn't look surprised. On the way back he told me what a wonderfully misunderstood girl she is and told me the size of her dowry. In fact, he repeated the figure in case I had not heard it properly the first time. Anyhow, I was pretty grateful when Beckler said I could go home. He was very pleased to see you, by the way.'

Mina ignored the last comment. 'Did Miss Hartop recover from her fright? Or whatever it was that happened?'

'Oh, it is far, far worse than that, my dear. You recall I told you that Mr Hope is on his way back from Africa?'

Mina's heart sank. 'Yes. Has he arrived?'

'Not yet, but he is sure to be regaled with all Beckler's marvellous successes. The new spirit photograph will undoubtedly please him, and now there is Miss Hartop, who once she had calmed down, got all excited again as she has convinced herself that she is a medium. She even thinks that her sighting of Mr Simpson's ghost, which had been rather bashful until now, shows that it is she who is the secret behind both the photograph and his appearance.'

'I don't believe Mr Beckler cares for her very much.'

'And who can blame him? But he must take his success where he finds it. He has more patience with her than I do. She is always babbling on about the society people she mixes with, and I think most of that is true, because her father has so many friends, so Beckler endures it. He is even able to pretend that he finds such conversation interesting.'

'He is a businessman, so he must hope to gain more customers through her connections.'

'I expect so. At any rate, the plan now is that Miss Hartop will develop herself as a medium.'

Even from Miss Hartop this was astonishing. 'Really?' exclaimed Mina. 'Does her father approve? When single ladies take up that profession, they are so often stated to be respectable that the public must see the matter as being in some doubt.'

'He didn't object. After all, it may attract a husband. Some men like a woman with a bit of mystery or notoriety about her. Mr Hartop is a very patient man, but even his patience is stretched to the limit. The plan, which was under discussion when I left, was to place a partition in the ground floor storeroom so a portion of it could be converted into a medium's booth where Miss Hartop will practise her art, with her maid Tilly in attendance. Will you consult her?'

'I shall not. My famous powers of prediction have already revealed what I would learn from it. She can tell me nothing that all the town does not already know or suppose.' Mina gave this strange development further thought. 'What form of mediumship will she practise? She clearly has no experience.'

'That is to be determined. When Mr Hope arrives, he will certainly want to study her.'

'In any other individual, that would excite my sympathy.'

Richard sat up, resting his chin in his hands and gazing up at his sister. 'Mina, my dear...' he began cautiously.

Mina knew that tone of voice and that look. Her brother wanted a favour from her. 'No, Richard,' she said sternly, 'I am not lending you anything. You have wages, and you should learn to use your money wisely.'

He blinked with surprise. 'That wasn't what I meant.'

'Neither will I pass notes to Nellie for you. I know how fond you are of her, but she is a respectable married woman now, and you know what Mr Jordan is like. If he was to find them, she would be ruined.'

'I can't send her notes at all now she has a new maid,' he said disconsolately.

'She does? I am sorry to hear that. Zillah was so sensible and reliable. But perhaps she is getting married?'

'No, I had a letter from Zillah that tells all. She has been sent to Hollow House to look after Mrs Honeyacre, whose baby is due to arrive in about three months. She might stay on for the lying in as well. So I am bereft of my trusted accomplice. And according to Zillah, the new woman is a dragon. Miss Fletcher. Mr Jordan chose her specially. She has eyes that can see through walls. If I came near to Nellie, Miss Fletcher would stare holes in me.'

'And now that you are living here, it is impossible for Nellie to visit and take tea with me without it arousing suspicion. Well, I shall send her a note. Something Mr Jordan can safely open and read himself if he wishes. We can meet at one of her favourite teashops with her dragon in attendance and she can tell me all the news.'

'Mina.'

'Yes, Richard?'

'I know you don't like Mr Beckler, although I am sure it was all a misunderstanding.'

'It was no misunderstanding, and I will not discuss it.'

'No, well, the thing is, with Mr Hope coming back, he told me that he was concerned that Hope is intent on finding ways of discrediting you. He wanted me to warn you about it.'

'Very well,' said Mina curtly, 'consider me warned.'

'Hope is a very powerful man. He has lots of friends and no end of money. Even after the scandal last year there are people in Brighton who will hear no ill of him, no matter what he does. He can say all sorts of nonsense and people will believe him. Ladies especially — they often comment on his picture in the shop window. Some of their compliments are very — well — extravagant. Why do some ladies like bad men? I don't understand. Is it because he is so tall? Or is it something to do with his hair?'

'I really don't know.'

'But I was thinking. Perhaps when he comes back, it would be safer for you if you could pretend to believe in his views.'

'My intention,' said Mina firmly, 'is to avoid him. Both he and his accomplice, if at all possible. I wouldn't have entered the shop today if Miss Hartop hadn't pulled me inside. And I will not subscribe to his views either privately or in public.'

'But you do believe in the hereafter? Please tell me you do,' Richard added plaintively.

Mina could see that he was unhappy and left her desk to sit beside him, linking her arm in his. 'I don't deny the existence of the spirit world, even though I have seen no evidence of it and may never do so until I am of that world myself. The question I doubt is whether the living can see it or hear it or converse with it. But I am not inflexible. If I should find a medium who is genuine, I will gladly become a believer, but so far none of the people I have encountered who have claimed to be in touch with spirits have convinced me. I have no quarrel with those who offer comfort or an evening's entertainment for a shilling or so. But I will not abide heartless, designing individuals who make targets of the bereaved and use conjuring tricks to cheat them out of their fortunes. The proper place for them is prison.'

'Perhaps Miss Hartop is genuine.'

'Is that what you think? Well, one cannot judge the contents by the vessel. We shall see.' Mina heard a carriage approach the house and went to peer out of the window in case it was Edward arriving, but it passed by. She sat down beside Richard again, relishing the moment of peace. 'Richard, you recall our conversation about the sketches you were making of the monuments in the Extra Mural Cemetery?'

'Yes.'

'And you have done this?'

'Yes. They weren't the sort of things I like to draw, but the cemetery is a good place for a quiet smoke.'

'Have they been photographed?'

'Not yet. Beckler wants a time when the light is good, but not during shop hours or when there are too many people about. We may go out early on Sunday.'

'Do you recall which monuments they were? Did Mr Beckler suggest why he had chosen those particular ones?'

'No, he just gave me a list of names.'

'Do you still have the list?' asked Mina, hopefully.

Richard delved through his pockets and came up with a crumpled sheet of paper.

Mina took it to her desk, smoothed it out and studied it. 'And were all these monuments attractive and important ones?'

'No, not all. Some were the usual type of thing. Two were just headstones. Some had statues and one was a large family vault.'

'I don't suppose you still have the drawings?'

'No, Beckler has them.' Richard looked puzzled. 'Why are you so interested? Do you want me to ask him about them?'

'No!' said Mina so sharply it came out as a snap, and Richard jumped.

'I don't understand why —'

'I don't want to give him any excuse to come near me again. Can you respect that?'

He shrugged. 'I suppose so.'

She returned to the list. There were eight names in all, three of which Mina recognised, although she had never met any of the individuals concerned, since they had all passed away before the Scarletti family came to live in Brighton.

Aloysius Phipps had been the senior partner of the prominent Brighton solicitors, which, following the departure of the humiliated Mr Laidlaw and·his wayward wife, was known simply as Phipps and Co. Mina had often used the firm and had seen an oil painting of its founder which was proudly on display at the premises.

Mrs Eleanor Honeyacre was the first wife of the owner of the Sussex mansion Hollow House. Mina had visited him and his second wife Kitty, after they had complained of an outbreak of ghostly occurrences. A portrait of the first Mrs Honeyacre, a gentlewoman with curly grey hair and a mild expression, was hung in a prominent place where the new Mrs Honeyacre tolerated it with perfect grace.

Charles Peasgood was the late husband of a friend of Mina's mother. A surgeon with a substantial practice, and highly regarded in Brighton, he had left his widow comfortably provided for, with an elegant home in Kemptown.

All these individuals belonged to families of the class that Mr Beckler would very much wish to attract to his shop, although Mina thought they would have been more likely to have patronised the fashionable Mr Mayall. Apart from this there was nothing she could see that they had in common.

The other names she did not recognise: Bertram Veale, Hector Samprey, Edith Porterson-White, Frederick Soules, and Robert Mulgrew.

Letters and numbers had been written beside each name, and Mina didn't have to ask what these signified; they were clearly the locations of the burial plots provided by the cemetery office.

There was a noise downstairs. With some prompting from Mina, Richard stirred himself to go and investigate and came back to report that it was the return of the Inskips together with Mrs Wheedon and her charges. There was a certain amount of bustle and conversation before the Inskips went to ready themselves for dinner and the children were taken up to their nursery. Not long afterwards a cab drew up bringing Edward, Miss Hooper and her aunt.

Mina put all her notes aside. From now on, private time would be at a premium.

CHAPTER SIX

Edward Scarletti was thirty, but he had already acquired that quintessential feature of a dedicated middle-aged businessman: two deep parallel lines of worry carved into the bridge of his nose. Even when he was not actively frowning, he appeared to be. His dark hair and stocky build marked him out as his father's son, but the lively imagination and creative joy he might have inherited from that parent either had not found a home in him or been put aside as frivolous. He could not tolerate idleness in himself and abhorred it in others. Every aspect of his life, his business, his obligations as an eldest son, his pursuit of marital happiness was approached with a strong sense of duty and tireless dedication.

Edward's beloved, Miss Hooper, was a demure nineteen. Her grandfather had made a fortune in timber and her recently deceased father, who had never remarried following the early death of his wife, had owned a paper mill. Miss Hooper enjoyed a generous allowance and was due to receive a substantial portion on marriage. Her guardian and mentor, a great aunt, Mrs Gostelow, lived in a charming rural cottage on the banks of the Thames where there was fresh air and a well-tended garden. It was here, rather than her late father's sombre London home, where Miss Hooper spent her happiest times.

The young heiress had received every advantage life could offer. She'd had a sound general education at a genteel school for girls where care was taken not to overheat the fragile female constitution and risk the pupils' prospects of motherhood with too much intensive learning. She did, however, take the valuable extra classes in deportment, music and drawing. Although the demands of fashion had long passed Mrs Gostelow by, she understood that a young girl in hopes of a good marriage should be shown at her best when the time came to enter society, and helped her cultivate a refined taste in dress, and care for her complexion. Miss Hooper's great love, however, was her great-aunt's garden, where she grew a variety of herbs and flowers.

Mina had met Miss Hooper only once before. To hear Edward speak of his affianced lady, she was the very epitome of beauty and grace. She was in fact a tolerably pretty girl with good manners, who knew how to make the most of her appearance. So quiet was she, so daintily reserved, that it was impossible to make any judgement of her true character. Edward was dazzled in admiration, Richard had detected a will of steel beneath the lace, and Mina was curious to know her better.

It so chanced that Miss Hooper's family was connected to that of Brighton's renowned photographic artist, Mr J E Mayall, whose second wife was a distant cousin. Mayall's London business, managed by his eldest son, Edwin, was in Regent Street, close by the offices of Scarletti publishing. Edward Scarletti had become acquainted with the Mayalls when he had initiated a meeting to discuss whether it was possible to publish photographs easily and cheaply in newsprint. To his disappointment he had been advised that this was an innovation whose time was yet to come; however, the two serious young businessmen had discovered strong mutual interests. More social meetings had followed, at one of which Edward had met his future bride.

Miss Hooper, it transpired, had never before visited Brighton, and had long been eager to do so. Mina gathered that this was most probably why Edward had been persuaded to celebrate the betrothal there rather than in London. Mina's mother pounced on this fact at once to outline her plan whereby Edward would move to Brighton as soon as the happy couple were returned from honeymoon. She had obviously given the question a great deal of thought, since she already knew of several houses to recommend, all of them as it so chanced very close to Montpelier Road and of an ideal size to accommodate a large family. She did not actually say so, but the implication was that she anticipated that the new wife would soon have important things to occupy her energies which would leave her no free time for such frivolities as pressed flowers.

The great-aunt, Mrs Gostelow, was a lady of some seventy years, clad in the pearl grey of a long-time widow. In company, she uttered only politenesses. She soon appreciated that no one had any interest in her observations regarding the journey to Brighton, the comfort at the hotel, or the state of the weather, and remained content to watch over her charge, and take stock of the Scarlettis with a shrewd eye.

The dinner bell was rung, and the families assembled, all exhibiting an extreme of civility.

The fare at family dinners for the Scarlettis was variable in nature. Mina always received advance notice of what was to arrive at table, but this did not dispel her uncertainty on the subject. Dining pleasure depended on whether cook had suddenly taken it into her head to strive for an elegance that was not her forte or had bowed to the inevitable and determined on solidity and quantity, at both of which she excelled. The recent influx of visitors had easily decided her on the latter approach, for which Mina was grateful. With eight people at table, the platters and tureens were large, the aromas inviting and the portions generous.

Mina's mother, taking her rightful place at the head of the table, was in her element, dispensing in queenly fashion wisdom, advice and instructions in equal measure. The rest of the company ate silently during her monologues, adding their own observations whenever she was temporarily silenced by food or drink. Any diversion into subjects she had no interest in were doomed to be interrupted. Mina said almost nothing but listened.

Miss Hooper, resplendent in summer yellow and silk daisies, had a pretty figure which she took care to maintain. All her eating and drinking was in small sips and bites. It was a very deliberate and practised restraint. Mina could not help but wonder if, once safely married, the new Mrs Edward Scarletti would be more liberal when dining.

'I assume,' said Edward, during one of his mother's pauses, 'that Mr Mayall will be taking the photographs to record the betrothal?'

'No, no,' said Mrs Scarletti, waving a laden fork and shaking her head in an emphatic manner which admitted of no contradiction. 'I have engaged Mr Beckler of Ship Street. He is a very enterprising young man who has purchased the business of the late Mr Simpson and taken Richard as a partner. Richard is a wonderful photographer; he will rival Mr Mayall one day!'

Miss Hooper allowed a quizzical look to briefly wrinkle her creamy forehead but sensibly made no attempt to protest. She glanced at Edward, who merely grunted.

'Photography is a very exacting business, you know,' said Mrs Scarletti. 'The camera is quite an extraordinary machine. It is all done with sunlight and glass. And then the pictures just appear on paper.'

'I hope you are careful with the chemicals, Richard,' said Edward.

'Chemicals?' queried Mrs Scarletti. 'I never saw any. You must be mistaken, Edward. The pictures are made by sunshine, and that is quite safe in moderation.'

Edward opened his mouth but wisely closed it again.

Once dinner was done, Edward seized the opportunity of taking Mina aside for a private talk. 'Whatever Mother might imagine, I am well aware that photographers carry large stocks of poisonous chemicals. Only last year one of Mayall's employees, a man he had dismissed because of his addiction to intoxicating liquor, took a terrible revenge. He damaged hundreds of pounds worth of equipment with a hammer and then stole a bottle of potassium cyanide, about four or five pounds of it, and consumed some with the result one might expect. I'm not saying Richard would do anything of the sort and I didn't want to discuss it in front of Mother, but he is so very careless.'

'You were right to say nothing to Mother,' said Mina. 'But please don't be concerned. Mr Beckler knows Richard better than you might think and does not entrust him with anything dangerous or fragile. His role in the business is far humbler than Mother likes to imagine.'

'Well, that is a relief. You know that Mr Mayall's son Edwin died just a few months ago? The poor fellow was only a few years older than me. He had been extremely ill for a very long time. Who knows what caused it? But I am confident that Richard's employment will go the way of all the others, as he is likely to get bored before long and look for something else. Either that or Beckler will realise he is not worth the pay and terminate the arrangement.'

Mina said nothing, but she thought the latter eventuality unlikely. She felt sure that Mr Beckler's offer of employment to Richard was nothing to do with his qualities and experience, but everything to do with herself. Either he wished to ingratiate himself with her or he was planning to carry out another horrid scheme at Mr Hope's command. She attached no good intentions to the warning he had sent her, which could simply be another way of earning her trust.

That led her to consider the list of cemetery monuments Richard had sketched for his employer, which lay forgotten in her room. Was this merely a business venture or was it evidence of a more sinister design? Richard's involvement was a concern, and she knew she had to find out more.

Later, when she was alone in her room, Mina made a careful study of the most recent directory of Brighton. She was looking for the surnames of the people on Richard's list of burials which were unknown to her. The directory was not an exhaustive list of inhabitants, but only the names of householders and businesses, but it did offer some clues. She soon found several persons who might well be related to the deceased on the list. Regarding the late Bertram Veale, there was a company, Veale and Sons which owned two confectioner's shops. Hector Samprey could well be related to brothers Mortimer and Charles Samprey who were in partnership as property agents. The late Frederick Soules might have been the father of Soules Brothers, manufacturing chemists. There was no one listed, however, of the surname Porterson-White, or Mulgrew.

Mina's late father, Henry Scarletti, had been buried in the Extra Mural Cemetery and the family had been provided with a booklet about its history. This included a map showing its areas and pathways on which they had marked the place where the grave was located. Given the information on Richard's list,

Mina felt sure she would be able to locate the family plots of the named individuals.

For a brief moment Mina wondered if she was being too suspicious. If any other photographer had been involved, she might have assumed it was nothing other than a means of promoting his business. Then she pushed the doubts aside. She recalled with distaste her first meeting with Mr Beckler at Hollow House, his sickly smiles, his fawning insincere compliments, the way his thin form had hunched over her like a threat. Then there was his obvious adulation of Arthur Wallace Hope and willingness to do any despicable thing for the man who Mina knew was bent on destroying her reputation.

Even with Mr Hope abroad, his influence had long tendrils and Mina had no doubts that Mr Beckler was engaged on some project designed to please his master on his return. The enterprise probably did not directly concern her, but she feared that it might be something underhand, possibly even criminal, in which her brother was now innocently playing a part. She needed to know more, to be forearmed in case Mr Beckler's plans were exposed and Richard was left to take the blame.

Mina did not wish to write on the printed map, but she used a page in her notebook to draw a sufficiently good copy of it, on which she marked the approximate location of the eight graves. She wondered if there might be some pattern to the locations, but if there was she could not make it out. They were not especially close to each other and were in more than one section of the cemetery.

She decided to pay a visit as soon as there was time, most probably after the betrothal party. It would be an ideal opportunity to see Nellie again.

CHAPTER SEVEN

Mina had an appointment the following morning for her regular vapour bath and massage at Dr Hamid's emporium. Her mother did not usually object to these visits, but on that occasion, she protested that Mina should not even think of leaving the house at such an important time when she was so desperately needed. Mina, however, would not be dissuaded. She pointed out that she required regular treatment to ease her pinched back muscles, adding that she would look all the fresher for her photograph. Louisa gave her a sour look, and muttered dissatisfaction, but Mina held firm and departed.

The Indian vapour baths were a haven of peace and restoration to Mina. Once a week, wrapped in warm scented linen, she rested in a cloud of herbal fragrance, feeling all the tensions and worries of her life float far away, and the tightness in her strained muscles slowly disappear.

Afterwards, Dr Hamid's sister, Anna, used perfumed oils to massage her back and limbs with strong yet sensitive fingers. During Mina's weeks of recovery from her recent illness, Anna had come to her home to deliver this treatment. It was these ministrations, and Anna's guidance on gently stimulating exercises appropriate for an invalid, that had prevented the long period of inactivity from wasting Mina's already small frame, and speeded her return to health.

She had recently once again been able to take up the practice of calisthenics, which had been too strenuous for her during her illness. Under Anna Hamid's careful supervision, she undertook a quota of exercise once a week, and this was supplemented by the daily use of little dumbbells at home, which she kept hidden at the bottom of her wardrobe. She was still not as strong as she had once been but was confident that a full recovery would only take a matter of time.

Once her treatment was done, Mina called upon Dr Hamid, her medical advisor and friend. He was the only doctor she trusted, since inspired by the example of his late sister Eliza, he had made a special study of scoliosis. He knew better than anyone else what might relieve Mina's pain and discomfort, and importantly he would notice the early signs of any deterioration which another man might not see. They both knew that improvement in scoliosis was not a possibility, and the best that she might hope for was an endurable stability.

He also took note of other circumstances that might affect her state of health. Having become acquainted with her family, he was well aware of the anxieties they provoked and the demands they made on Mina's fragile physical strength. Last January he had accompanied Mina and Nellie Jordan to Hollow House, where his efforts to protect and treat the residents during a time of crisis had reached heroic levels. More recently, he had attended Mina with great care when fever and breathlessness had brought her dangerously close to death. When she was first able to go out in the fresh air, he had kindly taken her out in a bath chair to enjoy the spring weather.

When Mina called at Dr Hamid's office, he studied her outward appearance intently as he always did. He then carried out his usual examination with particular attention to the function of her lungs and pronounced himself satisfied with her progress. Nevertheless, having put away his stethoscope and noted her temperature and pulse, he sat back and observed her demeanour.

'You have something troubling you,' he said. 'I can guess what it is: the arrangements for your brother's betrothal, and the arrival of your family. This is too much for you to deal with without support, especially at present. I often feel they take too great an advantage of your willingness and your undoubted competence.'

Mina gave a resigned smile. 'Thank you. They do, I know, but Mother's demands would be even greater if I neglected to do what I can. But I have planned only a simple gathering, a luncheon for immediate family. And as far as is possible all the arrangements have been made, although to hear my mother speak of it you might imagine that nothing at all has been done and it has been left entirely to her. However, now that the grandchildren are with us, she is finding some pleasure in life. And Enid is content with her lot at last. At least she no longer complains of it, which is the main thing.'

'Your mother makes great efforts to keep you at home.'

'She does. It is my place. She makes that very clear.'

Dr Hamid looked regretful but said nothing further on the subject. 'Then what is troubling you? Is it something I can at least advise on? If not as a doctor than as a friend.'

Mina took a deep breath. 'You know better than anyone my history of conflict with Mr Hope.'

'Yes, and I was relieved when he departed for Africa.'

'Unfortunately, I have just learned that having failed to find Dr Livingstone, he has abandoned the expedition and is returning to England.'

He gave a little grunt of annoyance. 'That is bad news, but surely he would not dare come to Brighton.'

'That is his intention. He has a protégé here, after all.'

'Ah, yes. I see,' said Dr Hamid, looking perturbed at the mention of Mr Beckler. 'Well, I trust that you will be able to avoid him, and whatever happens, if there is anything I can do to keep you safe from him, you must let me know at once. If we are fortunate, the visit will be a short one.' He attempted an encouraging smile.

'Thank you. But —' she sighed. 'There is another thing.'

'Yes?'

'I suppose what troubles me most at present is Richard.'

The smile vanished. 'Oh. Is he still working in Ship Street?'

'He is.'

'I hope that Mr Beckler has not continued to annoy you.'

'Not as such. I think he wishes to be better acquainted with me, but that possibility is long past.'

'You made it very apparent at Hollow House that you did not receive his attentions with any pleasure.'

'I did not. And I told him as much.'

'I am extremely surprised, given the circumstances, that your brother agreed to work for him.'

'I am sorry to say that that is my fault.'

'It is? Do explain.'

'As you know, Richard had been working for the family business in London, but then he — he left that employment.'

Dr Hamid tilted an eyebrow, showing he could easily guess the circumstances of Richard's departure from Scarletti Publishing, but he made no comment.

'When he came to stay with us, and I discovered that he was no longer employed, I urged him to find an honest position in Brighton. Before I knew it, he had been offered a position at Mr Beckler's new business and accepted it. If I was to tell Richard how I really regarded Mr Beckler, I am not sure what he would do. And finding work in Brighton which enabled him to stay with us was something that delighted my mother and still does. So — I had no alternative — I decided to put my personal feelings aside, for my family's sake.' Despite her best efforts, Mina felt a shudder run through her.

Dr Hamid stared at her. 'You are trembling. Are you cold?'

For a moment Mina found herself unable to speak. She shook her head. He leaped out of his seat and poured a glass of her favourite aerated fruit and herb water and pressed it into her hand. 'Drink,' he ordered. 'Short regular sips. Now.'

Mina obeyed, hearing her teeth rattle against the glass.

Dr Hamid sat down and regarded her keenly. 'Now then,' he said. 'There is more. I must know it if I am to be of any assistance.'

She nodded. 'I have told no one of this,' she whispered.

He waited.

She put the glass down and composed herself. 'When Mr Beckler flattered me at Hollow House, I assumed at first that he always spoke that way to ladies, to bring custom to his business. But then I discovered that I was the only person to whom he was paying such close attention. Richard thought that he admired me and wished to court me, that he had honest intentions. I am sorry to say that my silence on the subject has allowed my brother to continue to think that. But I saw through Mr Beckler's scheme. He is the creature of Mr Hope, and Mr Hope wishes to destroy me or at least stop me from opposing him.'

'You mean it was all Hope's doing?' exclaimed Dr Hamid. 'Hope sent Mr Beckler to court you? Did he think that marriage would so occupy you that you would no longer hinder him?'

Mina bit her lips to calm herself. 'No. Mr Beckler was not ordered to marry me. That was never the intention. He was ordered to ruin me. To destroy my reputation. When I realised this, I confronted him and — he did not deny it.'

Dr Hamid could not restrain a gasp of horror. 'Please tell me he did not —?' For a moment, words eluded him.

'No, no,' she reassured him, 'it never went that far; there were only words spoken that disguised his true intent. Oh, I think Mr Beckler regrets his actions, indeed he apologised to me, although it is impossible to know how sincere he is, but no apology can ever change the fact that he was prepared to obey his master. And now Mr Hope is on his way back to Brighton. And I really don't know what will happen next.'

Dr Hamid was trying to control his emotions, but he was gripping the arms of his chair so tightly that the veins on the backs of his hands looked ready to burst from his skin. He calmed himself with a great effort. 'I agree that it was wise not to tell your brother; he is — impetuous to say the least, and who knows what he might do.' There was a pause while he collected his thoughts. 'Very well. We must try and learn all we can about Mr Hope's intentions, and how he might act against you or employ his associate in another disreputable scheme. You cannot of course engage your brother in that respect, but he might well let something slip in conversation.'

'Richard thinks I should protect myself by pretending to agree with Mr Hope's ideas,' said Mina.

Dr Hamid shook his head. 'I would not ask you to compromise your beliefs. I know you would never do that, nor should you. But it would be best not to place yourself in a position where you will feel obliged to oppose Mr Hope's wishes. In fact, it is best to stay well away from both of them.'

'I will do my best,' said Mina, 'but I am also very afraid that Mr Beckler might be engaged in some dubious business enterprise in which Richard is involved.'

'Miss Scarletti,' said Dr Hamid, impatiently, 'it is very commendable that you constantly try to protect your brother from the consequences of his own actions, but he is an adult, he is what — twenty-five, a man, and not a child. You cannot protect him forever. He will learn nothing in life if he goes through it in this way, always being rescued from his own foolhardiness either by you or your mother. And then if or rather when he falls, it will be the harder for him.'

'I know,' she sighed, 'but I don't feel I can stand by and do nothing. I really don't know what to do. If Mr Beckler is doing something underhand, then it is at the instigation of his patron, Mr Hope, or at least something that he believes will please Mr Hope. Richard told me that Mr Beckler does not own the premises in Ship Street. The purchase was made with the help of a large loan from Mr Hope. He owes him a great deal of money. He dares not offend him.'

'I can see that, although a better man might have stood up to him no matter the cost. So, what is it you believe your brother is involved in?'

Mina described the new project of photographing the grave sites in the Extra Mural Cemetery.

Dr Hamid considered this information. 'And thus far your brother has done no more than locate the graves and make some sketches at the behest of his employer?'

'Yes. Thus far.'

'Well, he cannot be blamed for that. Even if Mr Beckler has some nefarious scheme in mind, all your brother has done is carry out an apparently innocent request from his employer.'

'I was wondering —'

He raised his eyebrows.

'If I told you which gravesites they were, perhaps you could suggest a reason why those were chosen?'

Dr Hamid folded his arms and gave her a stern look. Mina knew that expression. He had been drawn into her investigations several times, often much against his will and better judgement, and he knew it was going to happen again.

Yet he also knew that if he did not advise her, it would not put an end to her efforts. It occurred to her that just as she felt bound to protect Richard from his often reckless and thoughtless behaviour, Dr Hamid felt, probably in memory of his dear late sister Eliza, an obligation to protect Mina. She felt grateful to have such a good friend and thought how much better a thing it was for a gentleman to be purely a friend and not a husband.

'Very well,' he said at last, 'I will tell you what I know, as long as it does not betray any confidences, or contravene my professional obligations.'

Mina had copied the names Richard had given her onto a sheet of paper and handed it to Dr Hamid. 'I see you came prepared for my acquiescence,' he said, with a glance of amused resignation before studying the list.

Mina observed his features as he read, the slight frowns of puzzlement, the signs of recognition or failure to recognise.

He took a deep breath. 'Mrs Eleanor Honeyacre, as we both know, was the first wife of Mr Honeyacre of Hollow House. I did not know her well, but she was brought here on occasion for relief from her symptoms during her final illness. Anna attended her. Mr Aloysius Phipps was, I assume, one of the Phipps family of solicitors?'

'He was. I believe he founded the firm.'

'I can tell you nothing about him, though. Porterson-White — the name is familiar, but I don't believe I ever met her. I have a vague memory that she was a lady of some wealth, and there was a lawsuit concerning a will. I must have read about it in the newspapers. But it was very many years ago, and I assume that it has been long settled. Frederick Soules. There is a manufacturing chemist of that name. That is as much as I can tell you.

'Now, Mr Hector Samprey I did know, as he was a patient of mine. He died about five years ago. He was a landowner who built many of the better properties in Sussex. Some years before his death, he and his wife were involved in a carriage accident in which Mrs Samprey was killed and he injured his legs and back so severely that he was unable ever to walk again. That is a matter of public knowledge. His visits here were to ease his pain with massages and herbal vapour baths.' Dr Hamid mused on the memory. 'I felt great sympathy for him. His fortune brought him no pleasure. He was a devoted family man who grieved for the loss of his wife, and there was a son, his eldest, I believe, for whom he had great hopes, but who died in very sad circumstances. A wayward boy who fell in with some dangerous and desperate criminals and came to a bad end. I sometimes wonder if Mr Samprey's death was due less to his declining health from his injuries, than his great sorrow, and his wishes to be with his poor wife.' His face clouded a little as it always did when he thought of his own late wife. 'In his last weeks he knew he was dying, but the cruel loss of his son hastened his end.'

'Do you know any of the other names?'

'They are not familiar to me.'

'I thought Mr Veale might be related to the confectioner's business which is listed in the town directory.'

'That is certainly possible.'

'And Mr Mulgrew? There is no one of that name in the directory.'

'He is a mystery. But if you are so eager to discover more, why not take a walk in the cemetery? It is a very peaceful place, and much recommended for a quiet stroll and contemplation.'

'Is that your new prescription?' asked Mina with a smile.

'It is. In fact, there is a book by a Mr Bishop which describes recommended walks for the visitor.'

'That sounds delightful. I have only ever visited the cemetery to lay flowers for my father, and Mother has always been so distressed on those occasions that we were unable to do more than that and came straight home. Perhaps after the betrothal celebration when our visitors have left, I will find a little quiet time for myself.'

Dr Hamid was expecting another appointment, and Mina thanked him for his counsel and departed. On her way home, she visited a bookshop and purchased a copy of Mr John George Bishop's *Strolls in the Brighton Extra Mural Cemetery*. But nothing could bring her as much peace as having finally unburdened herself of her horrid secret.

Her route home took her past the confectionery shop of Veale and Sons, and she decided to go in. Mina had never entered the shop before, although the window display was extremely enticing. As soon as she crossed the threshold her senses were assailed by a variety of perfumes, the aromas of sweet chocolate, boiled sugar, vanilla, rose, and violets. There were well-dressed young ladies behind the counter in crisp white aprons and starched caps, and an older lady looking on with a managerial eye. A temperance notice behind the counter assured customers of the purity of all ingredients used in their stock of comestibles which were guaranteed to be free of any intoxicating liquor. Mina was able to move about at her leisure, inspecting what was on offer. The young ladies smiled politely, although there was no denying the way their glances lingered on her tiny tilted body and awkward gait.

The countertop supported tiered cake stands with whole chocolate cakes, ready to be cut into elegant slices, iced fancies decorated with candied fruit, fresh custard tarts, and crisp wafers dipped in caramel, but the main delight of the shop was its magnificent array of sweetmeats, which provided something to suit every pocket. There were jars of glistening barley sugar twists, smooth striped peppermint humbugs, boiled sweets in a multitude of colours heaped high like a sultan's jewels, sugar coated almonds, trays of creamy fudge and slabs of dark toffee, so hard it had to be broken up with miniature hammers. Below the countertop, under glass, were displays of Veale's premium cream-filled chocolates. These were either sold by weight or in special giftboxes in white, pink or mauve, printed with the name of Veale's and depicting what treasures lay within.

Mina thought that since she was intending to meet Nellie, who often treated her in the best teashops, she would purchase something to consume on their outing, something that could easily be shared as they walked. Unsure of what flavour to buy, she eventually asked for a quarter of a pound of vanilla creams, which she took away in one of the shop's decorated paper bags.

She wrote a little note to Nellie suggesting a visit to the cemetery, and later that same evening received a reply saying that the carriage would come to collect her the next afternoon.

CHAPTER EIGHT

On the morning of the betrothal luncheon, Mina arrived early at the Grand Hotel to reassure herself that every detail was in place. The table was set with a brilliant white cloth and silver cutlery, the decorative arrangements were fresh and colourful, and at one end of the oblong room appropriate seating and music stands had been made ready for the string trio. The walls were adorned with framed displays of Miss Hooper's pressed flowers, which Mina was obliged to admit were either insipidly faded in colour, or of no colour any plant ought rightly to have. Miss Hooper had evidently not made a study of botany since each plant was not given either its common or Latin name, but had been accorded some fanciful title, presumably of her own devising; 'fairy flowers' and 'sky blossom', and 'touch me not'.

Mina had arranged for a posy of fresh flowers to be there ready for Edward to present to his bride-to-be, and she received them with a blushing smile before laying them by her plate. Every so often she inspected them, as if assessing how they might appear after their decease.

The placing of the diners gave Mina a better opportunity to observe her new family connections, and she saw little glances of understanding pass back and forth, transmitted from person to person as if by invisible telegraph. If Miss Hooper required guidance, she would look at Mrs Gostelow and only then would she convey her wishes to Edward, all unspoken but no less powerful for that.

Mina's mother assumed her preferred place at the head of the table with Miss Hooper to one side and Edward to her left, where she could bombard them with opinions and advice uninterrupted. At a more comfortable distance, Enid regaled Richard with her determination to enter the high life of London and establish herself as the fashionable hostess of glittering events. Richard's career, Mina's activities and her own children did not feature in her conversation. Her husband's occasional praise of the delights of healthy exercise on the open road met with a fond smile of acknowledgement before an immediate return to the topic in hand.

The meal consisted of poached fish, roast game, and an apple charlotte, after which a stroll on the seafront to settle the stomach would have been refreshing. However, due to the importance of the occasion and Miss Hooper's suggestion, which Edward accepted without question as a command, the company was taken to Ship Street in two cabs, like some grand procession.

Mr Beckler greeted them with a series of polite obeisances, and large friendly smiles, which were not a pretty sight, as he had strange carnivorous-looking teeth, but Mina's mother seemed not to have noticed this and greeted him warmly. They were conducted to the studio, where there were velvet draperies as a formal backdrop, and a row of chairs, the subjects being flanked on either side by pedestal plant stands topped with vases of fresh flowers.

Mr Beckler employed all his experience in photographing family groups, and circled around them, busily arranging, advising, making careful placements, and then checking through the lens of the camera until they were all situated according to his requirements. Mrs Scarletti interrupted occasionally, stating where she preferred both herself and others to be placed, but he merely smiled indulgently and ignored her. When she attempted to order people to move according to her wishes, he continued to smile and talked of lighting and shadows and angles and exposure times in such bewildering detail that he could not be contradicted, and Mrs Scarletti eventually announced that she thought that he was quite right and this was what she had been saying in the first place.

The final arrangement of persons was as near symmetrical as could be achieved with so many people of differing sizes. Unusually Mina was not placed far to one side to languish as a forgotten creature at the edge of the portrait. Edward and Miss Hooper were seated in the centre, Mina's mother sat beside Edward, and Mina beside Miss Hooper. Richard, Enid, Mr Inskip and Mrs Gostelow stood at the rear. More pictures followed, with Mr Beckler expertly inserting the dark frames into the camera, then extracting the exposed plates protected from the light. In addition to the group he also took a picture of the affianced couple, and another of them with Mrs Scarletti and Mrs Gostelow. Enid and Mr Inskip were also immortalised as a couple. The final picture was of the Scarlettis: Edward, Richard, Mina and their mother.

Mina was not sure if her dislike of the photographer was causing her to imagine things, but she thought that Mr Beckler spent more time over that last portrait than the previous ones. He made several little adjustments to the camera, using the winding handle to raise and lower it. As he did so, there was a little snigger from Enid, who seemed to think this was due to Mina's lack of height.

The photography done, Mrs Scarletti was quick to compliment Mr Beckler, who departed with the glass plates for immediate development, saying only that the prints would be available for inspection on the following day. Edward fussed a little over this as he had hoped to go home next morning, where his desk called to him, but Miss Hooper persuaded him to stay on to see the finished pictures and he agreed. Richard made an appointment for them to come and view the prints in the afternoon, while Miss Hooper amused herself by examining frames.

Richard, sensing that some family duty might be assigned to him if he remained with them, chose to return to his post in the shop. The remainder of the party drove back to Montpelier Road, Edward fretting all the way about the lost day of business.

Mrs Scarletti chattered unceasingly about how relieved she was that it was all done, since the strain on her nerves had been intense and she was sure she was about to suffer one of her headaches. Mina was not sure how she felt. Yes, it had gone as well as could be expected, and her second encounter with Mr Beckler that week had at least been in company where the discomfort had been minimised, but there was something in his manner that disturbed her, and she could not describe even to herself what it was.

For once there was no opposition to Mina's plans for that afternoon; in fact, it appeared that no thought at all had been given as to how she might like to amuse herself once the betrothal celebration and photographs were over. Miss Hooper had instructed Edward to round off her special day by conducting her and Mrs Gostelow on a tour of the sights of Brighton, before enjoying a late supper at the hotel. Enid had demanded that her husband accompany her on a visit to the premier fashion shops in town, if only to look them over and complain that they were not up to the standard of London. Mrs Wheedon was taking the children out to enjoy the sunshine and sea air, leaving Mrs Scarletti to nurse a maternal headache.

At the appointed time, Nellie's little carriage drew up in Montpelier Road and Mina, clutching her copy of Mr Bishop's *Strolls* and one of the potted table decorations she had taken from the Grand Hotel, and with the bag of Veale's vanilla creams in her reticule, left the house and climbed aboard. Even if Richard was at work that afternoon, and she was under the eye of her dragon, Nellie knew better than to arouse suspicion by entering the Scarletti home. Nellie was, as always, perfectly groomed, and dressed in the best summer style, a brightly patterned costume in light silk with a large straw hat trimmed with ribbon. In anticipation of their walk, she carried a parasol of matching fabric ornamented with lace. There was no sign on her complexion that her face had ever been touched by the Italian sun.

Mina, settling comfortably beside her friend, found herself facing Nellie's new maid, Miss Fletcher. She was about sixty years of age, with a dried, bony, withered look of an aged vine that enveloped and crushed the life out of everything it encountered. Her expression was cold, stern and intensely watchful, and Mina realised that she would be observing not only her mistress, but also herself for any sign that secret messages might pass between them.

Nellie appeared to be cheerful enough and expressed her great delight at seeing Mina again. She was making the best of her position, tied to a husband who did not command her affection, given every comfort in life apart from the feeling of being loved, admired for her face and figure but nothing else. Mina did not have the option of marriage, having been told long ago that her health precluded it, but even if it had been a possibility she felt unable to imagine inviting or enduring such a fate.

The conversation covered the usual politenesses: enquiries as to the health of the parties, and a discussion of the weather. Mina gave an account of Edward's betrothal celebration, and Nellie stated that she adored Italy in such vague terms that Mina gathered that she had hardly enjoyed herself at all.

'How is Zillah faring?' asked Mina. She almost mentioned Hollow House but stopped herself just in time. To reveal that she knew Richard's news might have excited suspicion in Miss Fletcher. 'You told me in your letter that she had been unwell while you were in Italy.'

'She is in perfect health, now,' said Nellie. 'I have sent her to Hollow House to look after Mrs Honeyacre.'

'I assume that the ghosts, such as they were, are no longer troublesome.'

Nellie smiled, since there had been, after all, no evidence of any haunting. 'Zillah is far too sensible to allow such superstitions to bother her. She is comfortably settled, and very cheerful in the company of her good friend Miss Pet.'

Miss Pet, who, like the second Mrs Honeyacre had once been in the theatrical profession had adapted her talents as a dresser and costume maker to that of a ladies' maid. A quiet, shy girl, she and Zillah had formed a touching friendship during the eventful stay in Hollow House the previous January.

'And Mrs Honeyacre — I trust she is also well? When is the happy event due?'

'A first child is always a nervous time, but she is well and strong, and hopes to become a mother in about three months. But Zillah will stay on for a while after that.'

'I had hoped to pay a visit if it is not too inconvenient. Now that the weather is fine, and I am recovered from my indisposition, it would be a good opportunity to see Hollow

House at its best. January was not its most attractive month, and the company then left something to be desired.'

'You mean Mr Beckler who you found to be such a nuisance. And now here he is in Brighton. I do hope that you have not been troubled by his attentions,' said Nellie.

'I have made it very clear to him that I find his mere presence detestable,' said Mina.

To her surprise, Nellie laughed. 'Oh, do take care, my dear; that is the very thing calculated to arouse a gentleman's interest.'

Miss Fletcher frowned but said nothing.

The little carriage arrived at the entrance to the Extra Mural Cemetery on the Lewes Road, which was distinguished by a little lodge and castellated gateway topped with a round tower, all in flint and stone. The name of the cemetery was engraved on a scroll above the entrance arch, with the humbling motto, *mors omnibus communis*, as if anyone needed to be reminded that death comes to all. The general effect was both practical and dignified, but it was also inviting to the visitor.

The carriage passed through the gateway. Stretching before them was an avenue bordered by young elms in full leaf, between which were planted young oaks, yews and well-tended flower beds. Mr Bishop's guide told Mina that the cemetery had conducted its first burial in the year it opened, 1851, and offered a pleasant retreat from the bustle of town life and an open space far superior to that of crowded churchyards.

As they descended from the carriage Mina glanced at Miss Fletcher, but her features betrayed nothing. Mina wondered if anyone she knew was interred there. If so, that person could not be recently departed or mourned with any great sense of loss.

'I promised Mother that I would place something colourful on Father's grave for her and also see that the plot was tidy,' said Mina. 'She has heard rumours about thefts of shrubs from the cemetery and it threw her into a panic. I took this decoration from the table at our luncheon today. I thought that if Father could not be at Edward's celebration, then in this way, the celebration could come to him. But I also wish to take some of the strolls recommended by Mr Bishop in his book. Dr Hamid has specially recommended that I do so for my health. He says they are very calming.'

'He is so very careful of you,' said Nellie.

'He is a good doctor and a good friend,' said Mina.

Nellie nodded agreement. She appeared to be about to say something else, but then smiled as if thinking better of it and was silent. She opened the parasol, which was a good size, and was able to ensure that Mina could enjoy some of the shade.

Unknown to her companions, Mina had already devised a route for her walk. Once she had tended to her father's grave, she could wend her way apparently at whim, but with Mr Bishop's volume in hand it would appear only that she was following one of his recommended strolls. Her intention was to follow a course that would allow her to examine the graves that Richard had been tasked with sketching. If Miss Fletcher had not been present, she would have spoken openly to Nellie of what she was seeking and also her concerns for Richard, but she did not feel it wise to confide secrets in front of Mr Jordan's appointed spy, and even the most casual mention of Richard was dangerous in the extreme.

Mina was pleased to find her father's resting place perfectly tidy and untouched by flower thieves and placed her little potted decoration in front of the headstone. Nellie was silent as Mina stood deep in thought. In those moments of contemplation, she mourned that beloved parent, remembering the mischievous twinkle in his eye as he regaled her and her siblings with stories. He lived on in her memory and she felt sure they would see each other again, but she could not help wondering if the possibility that her mother might marry the odious Mr Beckler would rouse his angry ghost.

'I bought a little treat for us,' said Mina, opening her reticule. 'I hope you like Veale's vanilla creams.'

'Why yes, how thoughtful,' said Nellie, selecting a chocolate and popping it into her mouth, while Mina ate hers in small bites.

'Perhaps, Miss Fletcher, you might care for one?'

Miss Fletcher's mouth pursed as if she had eaten a slice of lemon. She peered into the little bag with a suspicious look, and Mina realised that she was searching for hidden slips of paper. Satisfied, the dragon withdrew its head. 'No thank you,' she said.

Mina made a great play of consulting her book. 'I would like to visit the grave of the first Mrs Honeyacre,' she said. 'I know Mr Honeyacre frets about it when he is not able to visit, and I would like to write to him and reassure him that all is well.'

No one dissented, and they walked on, along well-trimmed pathways where leafy fragments fluttered prettily in the sunshine. The monument they reached was a tasteful plinth of white marble on which stood a cross carved with an angel. It was inscribed 'Sacred to the memory of Eleanor Honeyacre, a devoted wife, 1810-1865, asleep with God'.

'That is an unusually large construction up ahead,' said Mina, indicating a mausoleum the size of a small cottage. 'I should like to take a look at that.' She did not wait for agreement but moved on.

This grand affair, as Mina knew perfectly well from her research, was the vault of the Phipps family, purchased by them when the cemetery opened. 'Oh, this is the Phipps mausoleum,' she exclaimed, pausing to read the inscriptions, noting that the first burial was that of Aloysius Phipps 'esteemed by all who knew him' 1768-1856. In subsequent years he had been joined by his wife, a son, an unmarried daughter, and two brothers.

As they walked on, consuming the occasional chocolate, Mina took care to divert any suspicion of her interest by remarking on other burial sites, those not on Richard's list but which were marvels of the stonemason's art, or commemorated notable persons. At the same time, she carefully threaded her way to the grave of Charles Peasgood 1800-1862, whose headstone, carved with the caduceus, the symbol of his profession, bore abundant tributes to his qualifications and prowess as a medical man. In this case, her family's acquaintance with Mrs Peasgood was excuse enough for her interest.

The Samprey gravesite was next. This was one of the larger monuments, a small tower, square in section with a series of steps leading up to its four faces and a carved stone canopy on top with an ornamental spire. One face of the column commemorated Hector Samprey, 1804-1867, and the other his wife, Amelia, 1809-1859. One face was blank in the expectation of future Sampreys, but the other commemorated Hector Samprey junior, 1834-1867, presumably the eldest son who had come to a bad end. When Dr Hamid had mentioned this, Mina had entertained the possibility that due to his criminal associations young Hector had committed a murder and been hanged. Had that been the case, however, he would not have been buried in a public graveyard, but in the prison where he had suffered the penalty for his crime.

Mina was about make a comment, but then a gentleman walked up the path and approached the monument. Sombrely dressed, he wore round lensed spectacles that gave his eyes an unusual staring quality, probably due more to the thickness of the glass than the organs themselves. He mounted the steps and touched the inscription on the senior Hector's side, then stood for a while with bowed head. It was obviously a very personal moment, and they decided to move on.

'Oh,' exclaimed Mina, a few minutes later, 'what a strange coincidence, since we are eating Veale's chocolates; this is the grave of Mr Veale.' Mr Bertram Veale, confectioner, 'sadly missed', had a monument resembling a classical column twined about with ivy. He had died in 1868 aged only forty-three.

'I hope he did not die from eating his own chocolates,' said Nellie with a smile. Miss Fletcher gave a surly look but said nothing. Nellie glanced at her. 'Were you acquainted with the family?'

'Not as such,' said Miss Fletcher. 'But I know that the gentleman's excesses were not in the nature of confectionary. His unfortunate wife had much to tolerate.' She set her mouth in a firm line to draw a very determined end to the conversation. Mina recalled the temperance notice in the shop and drew her own conclusions.

It was fortunate that it was such a fine day, or there might have been objections to the lengthy winding walk, but Mina persevered, dipping her nose into Mr Bishop's book, and commenting brightly on the fine weather and fresh air, doing her best to conceal her own increasing weariness.

The next grave she observed was that of Frederick Soules, chemist, 1808-1866, deeply mourned by his devoted wife and loving sons. A sorrowful angel was a nicely carved tribute, but, thought Mina, nothing out of the ordinary.

The grave of Mr Robert Mulgrew (1785-1863) was an even simpler affair, a plain cross on a plinth. The inscription read: 'Humble in his perfect scholarship. Charitable and pious'. It was so unremarkable, Mina had to wonder why this one had been chosen for Mr Beckler's list.

One of the gravesites proved much harder than the others to find. Mina was obliged to wander as if at random when she actually had her little sketch map folded up in the pages of her book. She didn't like to be too obvious in consulting it. At one point Nellie even asked her if there was something she was especially hoping to find, and Mina had to assure her that this was not the case, she was just enjoying the quiet and the pretty flowers. But then she saw it and it was something of a surprise. The headstone was small, the standard rectangle with a bowed top found in abundance in older, humbler burials in Brighton churchyards. The plot was not even ringed with stones; it was a simple raised area of grass. There were neither urns, nor flowers, nor shrubs. It was tidy enough, but whether that was because it had been tended by a relative or made neat by a cemetery official, unable to bear the appearance of neglect, it was impossible to say. This was the grave of one of the wealthiest women of Brighton, Miss Edith Porterson-White, 1780-1862.

'Oh, my word,' said Mina. 'How sad that this grave of all the ones here should be so mean and little cared for. Does the lady have no one to honour her memory?'

'I don't know the name,' said Nellie.

There was a brief growl, something that might from the throat of Miss Fletcher have served as a derisive laugh, but her face was not smiling.

'Did you know her, Miss Fletcher?' asked Mina.

'I knew of her,' said the maid. 'She was said to have all the wealth a person might wish for, and yet she lived like a pauper. But she died without leaving a will.'

'Were there no living relatives?' asked Mina, hoping to learn more.

'It would have been simpler if there had not been.' Once again, Miss Fletcher's mouth clamped into a tight line.

Dr Hamid had told Mina of an old dispute over the inheritance which had taken place so long ago he felt certain it must by now have been settled, but Mina, looking at the dismal tombstone, felt sure that it was not.

As they walked back to the carriage, Mina reflected on the visit. As far as she could see, there was nothing the eight families on Mr Beckler's list had in common apart from having burial plots in the Extra Mural Cemetery, and she saw no special reason why those particular graves should have been chosen for photographs. Was she simply imagining some subtle device? Was there some obvious reason right in front of her eyes which she had missed? Or was there something hidden from her knowledge which she had yet to discover?

CHAPTER NINE

Breakfast at the Scarletti house next morning was unusually cheerful. It was Mrs Scarletti's mood that generally prevailed at the family table, and she had been keeping herself amused with the twins, who liked to chatter to each other in their own language. It was unintelligible to anyone else, although the proud grandmother pretended to understand every word.

'Do you know,' she said, attacking a plate piled with scrambled eggs and kidneys, 'I think I might invite Mr Beckler to tea. As he is Richard's employer, I really ought to. Richard, I am most surprised that you have not already done so.'

Richard said nothing but glanced at Mina. He had not made any such invitation at her express instructions, as she had informed him without a hint of ambiguity that she did not want Mr Beckler to come to the house.

Edward drummed his fingertips impatiently on the table, then consulted his pocket diary. 'I cannot remain in Brighton much longer. Our appointment to see the photographs is two p.m., I believe. If it could be managed a little earlier, then it would be all the better. Then I really must return to London. My dear Agatha and Mrs Gostelow are also departing this afternoon, and we intend to travel by the same train.'

'I shall invite him for next Sunday, as I assume that he is not able to be away from his business before then,' said Mrs Scarletti, as if Edward had not spoken.

Mina now faced a dilemma. She could not object to the idea without venturing into subjects she had no intention of discussing, neither did she see any real future in opposing her mother's wishes. Her first instinct was to accept the inevitable and devise some way of being absent for the occasion, but at the same time, she felt that someone who was both in possession of common sense and alert to the dangers ought to be with her mother. Looking around the table, she realised that with Edward back in London the only family member meeting that description was herself.

'In fact, I shall extend the invitation this afternoon,' Mrs Scarletti went on. 'We are very nearly friends, after all. Mina, you must make the arrangements with cook. Perhaps you can make some enquiries as to what he might like to eat.'

Mina did not need to enquire as to what Mr Beckler liked to eat since she had observed him at Hollow House and seen him savage anything that lay within his reach. If her mother imagined she might fatten him into a suitable husband, she would be disappointed in that endeavour.

'I will make the arrangements, of course, Mother,' she said. 'Tea for six.' She glanced at Mr Inskip and Enid, who did not object.

'Unless Mr Beckler has a sweetheart, in which case —' said Mrs Scarletti hesitantly.

'He does not,' said Richard. 'At least —' he glanced at Mina — 'if there is a lady he admires, she does not return his feelings.'

'Isn't it time you were at work, Richard? You don't want to be late,' said Mina.

'Yes, my dear, we know how much Mr Beckler relies on you,' said his mother.

Richard sighed, gulped his tea, forked hot bacon in between two slices of toast and went away, munching.

'He is such a good boy,' said Mrs Scarletti. 'Edward, you must have been so upset when he chose to make his fortune in Brighton.'

Edward said nothing.

'We would like to stay a few days longer if that is convenient,' said Mr Inskip. 'There is so much to enjoy in Brighton. I saw an advertisement in the *Gazette* for Harrison's Velocipede School in Queen's Road. They are sole agents for the new Coventry machine, and I really must pay them a visit.'

'But you already have a velocipede, my dear,' said Enid. 'Why do you need another? You cannot ride them both at once.'

Mr Inskip was momentarily speechless.

'I am only sorry that my dear Henry is not here to see how well the family thrives,' said Mrs Scarletti. She put down her knife and fork and dabbed the edge of a handkerchief to one moistening eye. She did not say it, but Mina knew that in such moments her mother's thoughts were also of her daughter Marianne, lost to consumption ten years ago, a tragedy that she could hardly bear to speak of.

'We must pay our respects at his grave while we are here,' said Mr Inskip. 'I am told it is a very fine location.'

'The cemetery is like a garden of sculpture,' said Mina. 'A place of peace and beauty. It is also an education about the notable families of Brighton. I took a walk there only yesterday. In fact, I can lend you my book of recommended strolls for the visitor. There was one grave, however, which surprised me. It lay hidden amongst all the noble statues and fine monuments. It was a low, mean sort of grave, almost like that of a pauper, a mound of grass with just a small headstone to mark the spot, and yet I understand that the lady buried there was one of the richest women in town.'

'Oh, who might that be?' exclaimed Mrs Scarletti. 'I might have known her.'

'She passed away before we lived here,' said Mina. 'A Miss Porterson-White.'

Mina's mother gave the little frown that always appeared when she did not like to admit that she did not know something. It was clear that she did not recognise the name of the prominent person. Mr Inskip, however, whose head had been bent over his breakfast plate with a loaded fork, looked up, and it was clear that Mina had his earnest attention. 'Ah,' he said, 'the Porterson-White case, a veritable Jarndyce affair.'

'Jarndyce?' queried Mrs Scarletti, who was regrettably unfamiliar with the works of Mr Dickens and was plunging rapidly out of her depth. 'Is he a Brighton man?'

'That is the name we give to a law case which is unlikely to be settled soon,' said Mr Inskip, kindly.

'This is very interesting; do tell me more,' said Mina.

He smiled. 'My firm is not involved in the case and that is a matter for which we can only be grateful, as it is more trouble than it is worth, but it is widely spoken of amongst legal men. Miss Porterson-White was a spinster, the only child of a gentleman who possessed a substantial fortune in rented properties, mainly in London. When he died, he left all his fortune to her. Many men sought her hand, but she refused them all. I think she suspected their motives.

'When she was very aged, she came to live in Brighton for her health. She passed away a good many years ago, and it was then discovered that she had left no will. The nearest heirs were two distant cousins; I forget their names. But the two gentlemen disliked each other. In fact, it would not be an exaggeration to say that they hated each other. One of them was believed to have been a favourite of the deceased and it was claimed that she had intended to leave all her fortune to him, whereas the other one she is supposed to have disliked and had threatened to cut him off with a shilling.

'But that is all rumour and supposition. There is no proof that either man can bring. Since there is no will, the fortune was destined to be divided between the two.'

'If it was so large, there ought to have been enough to satisfy both of them, surely?' said Mina.

'That is very true, but I am afraid that enmity can overcome reason. One of the cousins actually accused the other of finding and destroying the will, and they came to blows. Then they went to law.'

'And it is still not settled?'

'Not at all.'

'Why are men always so quarrelsome?' said Mrs Scarletti. 'They should have asked me. I could have told them what to do.'

'I assume the cousins are responsible for the upkeep of the grave?' said Mina.

'I expect so,' said Mr Inskip.

'They might have paid her more reverence.'

'I suppose they didn't want to spend any more than they were obliged to. Neither is especially wealthy, and both have taken out large loans in anticipation of the legacy in order to pay their legal men.'

'What a horrid family!' said Mrs Scarletti. 'I am glad not to know them, for all their fortune.'

'If there had been a will,' said Mina thoughtfully, 'then someone would have drawn it up and witnessed it. Was there no solicitor?'

'Not that anyone can discover,' said Mr Inskip. 'I believe the lady is supposed to have composed it herself. Wills may take a very simple form and still be quite legal. If it was witnessed, then it must have been done by the two aged servants who predeceased her and left no note of the event.'

Edward looked at his watch. 'We must send Rose to order the cab,' he said.

As soon as Mina had finished breakfast, she returned to her bedroom and took out her notebook, jotting down an idea for a new story. *Missing will, brothers in dispute — duel — death — haunting.* She had not devised a suitable ending but given the subject matter did not think that either of the quarrelling relatives would survive.

CHAPTER TEN

Mina did not relish the prospect of going to Mr Beckler's shop with her family in order to view the betrothal pictures, but reluctantly decided that she ought to be one of the party if only to keep an eye on her mother. She was fairly sure that the young photographer could have no romantic inclinations in that direction but feared that if he was invited to their home to take tea and saw how comfortably they lived, he might develop strong feelings for the Scarletti fortune. The contrast between the three-storey townhouse nestling in the pale elegance of Montpelier Road and his bachelor apartments above the shop was bound to engage his attention. She could already imagine him eyeing the furnishings and appraising them for value, guessing correctly that on being widowed Louisa had inherited the house and contents for her lifetime use. Therefore, Mina, having determined only a few months ago never to set eyes on the loathsome man again if she could possibly help it, found herself about to visit his shop for the third time in a week.

Edward had spent much of the morning in a state of barely concealed frustration, supervising the packing of his bags with the intention of heading to the railway station as soon as the business at the shop was completed. When the cab arrived to convey Mina, her mother, Enid and Edward to Ship Street, he almost vaulted into it and fidgeted impatiently all the way to their destination. Mr Inskip, announcing what a fine, bright day it was, elected to walk, and strode away energetically.

There was a new notice in the shop window, a large printed card with a decorative border announcing that 'Lady Brighthelm', the famous Brighton seer and mystic was available for consultation within, mornings and afternoons, by appointment only. There was a portrait of the lady, a close image showing only the upper part of her form and head. She was seated at her consulting table, leaning slightly forward in an intent yet confiding manner. The table was littered with small gewgaws and trinkets.

The new medium must have been uncertain as to which of her jewellery to wear since when dressing for her portrait she had decided to wear all of it. Multiple necklaces covered her bosom, while her hands were fat with rings, her arms heavy with bracelets. A thick veil completely covered her face, so that only the glint of her eyes could be seen. Lady Brighthelm could therefore ply her trade invisible, unrecognised, although Mina thought it would be hard for her to conceal her true identity once she opened her mouth.

When the little party arrived, Miss Hooper and Mrs Gostelow were already at the shop. They were deep in consideration of suitable frames, studying the catalogues Richard was showing them with grave attention, and pointing out the most expensive items with mutual expressions of approval. Edward had no patience for this, and on being consulted assented at once to their choosing whatever most pleased them. Enid and her mother, while not being especially interested in the display of photographs, pretended to be in order to pass the time.

'I haven't seen the pictures, yet,' said Richard. 'But I am told they are very remarkable.'

'Has the mysterious Lady Brighthelm been much in demand?' asked Mina.

'She has, and her fame is growing. Some of her clients are grateful enough to bring her little gifts. But the best news is,' he added confidentially, drawing Mina a little aside, 'she may have a suitor. At least, she thinks she has. There is a young fellow who has visited her twice already, and he has just made another appointment, which to her way of thinking means they are engaged to be married, even though he is not yet aware of it. I have seen her practising her new signature, Mrs S Clover. She makes a very great fuss of the curls and flourishes, as there are so few opportunities in H Hartop.'

'Do her clients actually leave their names?'

'Most do not, but as she has a veil, she is able to see them while they cannot see her and some of them are undoubtedly known to her. That may be why she is able to tell their fortunes so convincingly.'

'I doubt that she would dare to see me,' said Mina.

'You never can tell,' said Richard, opening the appointment book and selecting a pencil. 'Will tomorrow suit?'

'I'll let you know,' said Mina. 'After all, Mr Clover may have romanced her away by then, and she will be a one-day wonder.'

'I don't think he will,' said Richard. 'He is very young, he can't be much above twenty, and he has only seen her through a veil. And he comes here with a worried face and goes away with the same face.'

Mr Inskip arrived, rubbing his hands together and pronouncing himself much refreshed by his walk. He had only just joined Enid in contemplation of the display and wondering if he might ask to be pictured balancing on his velocipede, when Mr Beckler appeared and glanced about the shop, noting that all the party was present.

'The prints are ready for your inspection,' he said, 'and they have been mounted on card. Please come to the office and select which ones you wish to have framed. I will in any case put copies into an album for you.'

'You are so kind!' exclaimed Mrs Scarletti.

There was something about Mr Beckler's expression that put fear into Mina's heart. When she ventured to glance at him, he was looking at her in a way very similar to that in which he had stared at her when they had first met at Hollow House. Cautiously, nervously, unsure of how their meeting might progress. She turned her face away quickly. He conducted the little party through the door at the rear and into a small office. Chairs had been provided for the ladies while the gentlemen were obliged to stand. A large portfolio case rested on a desk. Mina stared at the plain black surface of the portfolio and she was suddenly visited with a grim apprehension of what it might contain. Mr Beckler took his place and rested his long fingers on the desktop.

Once they were all assembled, he opened the portfolio carefully, reverentially, as a man might who was revealing some great treasure to the nation, and lifted the card-mounted image that lay on top, tilting it upright for all to see. It was the picture of Edward and Miss Hooper. Everyone nodded and Mina's mother said how very fine it was and how the flowers in the posy looked so fresh with a careful emphasis on the word 'fresh', and then she pressed a handkerchief to her eyes and reached out to Edward, who took her hand and patted her fingers.

The photograph was lifted out of the case and laid to one side. Each picture was interleaved with a layer of thin paper tissue to protect its glossy surface. One at a time, the photographer drew the tissue aside and revealed the next portrait. The picture of the Inskips was also admired, as were those of the affianced couple flanked by Mrs Scarletti and Mrs Gostelow and the entire betrothal party.

Mina, usually so secure in her own body with the size nature had made her was rarely aware of how small she was compared to others, and it was only in the group picture in which she appeared that she could see her frail lopsided form next to persons of the usual dimensions. Seeing herself through the eyes of others, she knew why she drew such looks of surprise and pity.

There was a short pause. One photograph remained. Mina peered into the portfolio but could not see the final image clearly through its translucent covering. 'Before I show you this, I — er — I suggest you all prepare yourselves for what you will see in the last picture,' said Mr Beckler. 'It may come as something of a surprise.'

But Mina had already guessed what she was about to see. Through some craft, the nature of which she could not imagine, there would be a filmy shape, a cloudy indistinct presence on the image. Perhaps there might be more than just one, floating serenely in the air above the family group, without any great precision of feature, but only the mere suggestion of one male and one female. Mina's mother would easily be able to delude herself into imagining that these were the spirits of her deceased loved ones, her husband Henry and her daughter Marianne, coming together to celebrate with them. Mina would have done anything to stop the viewing at that very moment, but she was powerless to do so.

Mr Beckler allowed the fine paper to drift away and raised the final portrait in the set. Everyone, including Mina, gasped. The Scarlettis stood in a row, Louisa Scarletti in the centre flanked by her four children, Edward and Richard on either side of their mother, then Enid and Mina at each end of the row. Beside Mina there stood another figure, that of her deceased father.

Mina was the first to move. She reached forward and took the picture. Mr Beckler made no attempt to dissuade her; in fact, it appeared from his expression that he had hoped for precisely this reaction.

This was no delusion, no filmy wisp of vapour, but a picture of great clarity. Much as Mina wished to deny it, and she tried very hard, there could be no doubt at all that she was gazing upon the image of her late father; not as he had been when they moved to Brighton, a semi-invalid, but in the full vigour and health of his forties. It was he without a doubt, the easy way he had of standing, one hand tucked into a pocket in an almost jaunty manner, suggesting that little spark of humour that was always ready to emerge from fatherly solemnity, the light of amusement in his eyes.

Mina dropped the picture back on the desk, biting the inside of her lips to try and stop herself from crying.

'I don't understand,' said Edward. 'What is this? How has this happened?'

'Oh!' gasped his mother, pulling her hand abruptly from Edward's grasp and reaching out to touch the edge of the image with reverence.

Miss Hooper and Mrs Gostelow, neither of whom had met the late Henry Scarletti, glanced at each other and said nothing.

'I do not recognise this gentleman,' said Mr Beckler. 'I have never met him, but I now gather that he is Mr Henry Scarletti?'

Louisa Scarletti gulped and nodded. Mina said nothing.

'That is Father,' said Enid. She pulled a sulky mouth. 'Though I do not see why he comes to Edward's betrothal and did not come to my wedding.'

'He may well have done so,' said Mr Beckler, 'but you would not have been able to see him. It is the recent advances in the photographic art that have enabled this image to appear.'

Mrs Scarletti stared at the picture again, and indicated a faint pale thread hovering beside Enid. 'Marianne,' she whispered. 'Oh, Mr Beckler, I cannot thank you enough for what you have done! This picture brings such joy to my heart! How I ached to have all my dear ones around me on this day, and you have answered my prayers!' She extended her hand towards the young photographer, a gesture of gratitude as if reaching to touch the figure of a saint, then withdrew with a nervous tremble.

Mina stared at the picture again. She felt sure that what her mother believed to be the spirit of Marianne was only light reflected from a fold in the curtain but decided to say nothing. If it added to her mother's happiness, then nothing should be said. She glanced at Edward, who was staring at the picture with suspicion, but he also appeared to have decided not to comment, almost certainly for the same reason as Mina.

'Frames,' he said curtly. 'Frames for all of them. Whatever Miss Hooper decides. We'll take one of each. And an album.' He handed his card to Mr Beckler. 'Send them to this address with the invoice. Now I really must go.'

'Yes,' said Mina, glad at Edward's breaking of the mood. 'Frames and an album. Send them to me. I will settle the fee.' She dropped her card on the desk and glanced at her mother, who was gazing speechlessly at the picture, her handkerchief clasped to her lips. 'I must get Mother home at once.'

Edward nodded. 'I will order a cab,' he said and hurried from the office, the speed and determination of his stride marking his relief at leaving the premises.

'I will see to your account,' said Mr Beckler. He rose and returned to the shop. He was followed by Miss Hooper and her chaperone, saying that they intended to supervise the selection of frames.

Mina remained in the office with her mother. Enid, who despite reassurances had not got over her annoyance at being ignored by her father's ghost, was being mollified by her husband. Richard, who must have been alerted by his employer to the results of the pictures, peered in. He stared at the image of his father in silent wonder before being hugged by his weeping mother.

Before long, Edward, Miss Hooper and Mrs Gostelow were on their way to the railway station, and the rest of the family went home. Mina's only comfort in the horrible situation was that her mother had entirely forgotten to invite Mr Beckler to tea.

Mina found a letter awaiting her on her return home. Once her mother had been persuaded to take a nap assisted by a glass of warm milk with more than a touch of medicinal brandy, Mina opened her correspondence.

Phipps and Co
Solicitors
Middle Street
Brighton

Dear Miss Scarletti,

I do hope this finds you well. I hesitate to trouble you on a personal matter; however, there are areas of special study where you have demonstrated both expertise and sound common sense, and I would appreciate it if you permitted me to pay you a visit in order to seek your advice.

Sincerely,
R Phipps

Mina read this note with interest and not a little curiosity. She had often sought the professional advice of Mr Ronald Phipps, the youngest partner in the long-established firm, but for him to seek her advice was something of a novelty. She wondered what was troubling him and hoped that his recent betrothal to Miss Adeline Cherry was not the cause of any unhappiness. Miss Cherry had been a highly efficient day nurse in the Scarletti house during Mina's illness, and when Mr Phipps had visited it was clear that he had been as much impressed by her professional skills as her attractive green eyes. He had engaged her as a nurse companion to his elderly aunt Mrs Phipps, a role in which she had quickly become essential to his family happiness. Their betrothal had been announced not long afterwards.

The last time Mina had seen Mr Phipps he had seemed very contented. She had been making the final arrangements for her will, in which she had left all her personal fortune, such as it was, to create a foundation for the care of people who, like herself, suffered from scoliosis. Dr Hamid, who was an expert on this condition, had agreed to make any arrangements, although he was taken aback by the prospect of dealing with her demise, since she was younger than he by some twenty years. He had agreed only on the condition that his eldest son, who was studying for a medical degree, might in the fullness of time be appointed to take over that duty as the event was, he hoped, not due to take place for very many years hence.

Mina was eager to take a closer look at the portrait of the late Aloysius Phipps that hung in the firm's office, so when she replied to Mr Phipps to make an appointment she stated that since the house was busy with visitors, she would call and see him the following morning at his place of business. Given the events of the day, she dared not leave the house that afternoon in case she was urgently required by her mother.

Mrs Scarletti, having retired to her room, had failed to sleep, but lay on her bed, a turmoil of emotions, clutching in her hand the last portrait of Henry Scarletti, one taken long before his illness when they had celebrated their twentieth wedding anniversary. Mina's presence might be demanded at any moment.

CHAPTER ELEVEN

The following morning Mina was unsurprised to receive a letter from her older brother.

Scarletti Publishing
Regent Street
London

Dear Mina,

It was obvious to me as soon as I saw that outrageous picture that the photographer must be a great fraud. I don't know if Mr Beckler is aware of this, but as a publisher I need to keep abreast of advances in photography and while I am no scientist, I know all too well the kinds of tricks that can be played on the unwary. However, I said nothing about it when we were in the shop, and I must implore you also to stay silent. It was obvious to us both that Mother was very pleased with the picture, and I would not wish to upset her or cause any disruption or quarrels, which I know it will do if either of us attempts to expose the scoundrel's activities. I must also take into consideration that Richard is currently employed there. This may turn out to be a blessing or a curse, but either way it is sure to be of short duration.

I feel that we are of the same opinion on this matter; however, it would set my mind at rest if you would respond assuring me that you will take no action against Mr Beckler. I am sure I can rely on you to watch over Mother in case he makes any attempt to cheat her out of large sums of money. I would also ask you to try and ensure that Richard does not get into trouble, but I do not want to burden you with the impossible.

Trusting that all is otherwise well,
Affect'ly, Edward

Mina quickly penned a note to Edward reassuring him that she would make every effort to avoid upsetting their mother. She would have liked nothing better than to expose Mr Beckler as a criminal, but she understood Edward's feelings on the subject. He, of course, was quite unaware that Mr Hope had engaged Mr Beckler as the instrument of her destruction and that she feared he might do so again. Although her hands must remain tied for the time being, she felt certain that should Mr Beckler have the temerity to respond favourably to her mother's interest, Edward might feel very differently on the subject, and would have no hesitation in taking the appropriate action. There could well come a time in the near future when any information she was able to acquire about how Mr Beckler produced the spirit pictures would be extremely useful.

That morning, as Mina waited at the solicitors' office to see young Mr Phipps, she paid more than the usual attention to the oil portrait of the firm's founder. There was something warmer and more friendly about an oil painting than a photograph, she thought, and it was not just because of the use of colour. An artist in oils had more time to observe his subject, to move around him and decide on the best view without worrying about any difficulties imposed by light and shade. He could capture the personality of the sitter seen over a period of time and not just in the few moments that the camera lens was exposed.

Mr Aloysius Phipps as depicted was in his seventies, relaxed, comfortable and just a little stout. He was seated in a substantial brown leather armchair, one hand on the arm of the chair, the other on his lap, holding a book. His grey hair was an abundance of waves, his beard long and streaked with white. He was smiling with contented pride. On the wall behind him hung a number of certificates, and a row of silver trophies which suggested that he had been a devotee of croquet.

'It is a delightful portrait,' said Mr Ronald Phipps, appearing behind her.

'So it is. I have never really looked at it before. Of course, I never met your grandfather. Do you feel it captures the character of its subject well?'

'It does. The artist has reproduced very faithfully his expression of intelligence, the posture of ease and confidence, yet also his essential benevolence. He was considered by all to be accomplished, wise, and fair in his profession. In his private life he was good company, a kind man with a delightful sense of humour. I have many fond memories of him.' He turned to Mina. 'I am pleased to see that you are improved in health.'

'I am. I hope that Miss Cherry is well?'

'She is indeed. Our wedding plans continue apace. There is so much to do!'

Mr Phipps conducted Mina to his private office, which was, she thought, looking a little better furnished than she remembered it, in keeping with his new position as junior partner. He then turned to the subject of his letter.

'This is all a little strange,' said Mr Phipps, hesitantly. 'You are aware of course that I share your views on the spirit mediums who have been preying on the residents of Brighton, and like yourself I have not experienced anything that could be proven to be a visitation by a spirit, however…' Mina waited. 'It is an interesting coincidence that I found you just now paying such close attention to the portrait of my grandfather, since this does concern him. My aunt was very fond of him, as we all were. After his death, she did sometimes attend seances hoping to receive a message, and occasionally she was granted a few words of a reassuring nature. But never an actual appearance.' There was another pause. 'Just recently my aunt received a letter which she found very surprising. It came from a Mr Beckler, who not long ago opened a photographic shop in Ship Street. She asked me to look at it. Mr Beckler informed her that he had been taking photographs of some of the more notable monuments in the Extra Mural Cemetery, which naturally included the Phipps mausoleum. I don't know if you have seen it, but it is very handsome.'

'I have, yes, it is very fine,' said Mina, making every effort to conceal her growing apprehension.

'He said that when developing the picture, he saw a gentleman standing beside it. A gentleman who had not been there at all when the picture was taken. He wondered if the man could be identified. Naturally, I did not want to trouble my aunt with this, and so I visited Mr Beckler's premises and he showed me the picture.'

'Did he say when this picture had been taken?'

'Only a few days ago. I am sure he was correct, because some new shrubs had been planted very recently and they were pictured. The monument was seen from the side with the inscription relating to my grandfather, and to my astonishment he was there standing beside it, as clear as day.'

Mina was thoughtful.

'I know what you are going to say,' said Mr Phipps, hurriedly. 'I have seen the image in the window, the one supposed to be Miss Hartop's mother. All I can say is that it is the image of a lady, but the features are not at all distinct, and really it could be almost anyone. I know that persons who are grieving are eager to see in a faint image or a glowing apparition the features of a loved one, because it comforts them, but I can assure you that the image in the portrait taken by Mr Beckler was very clear indeed, and it was my grandfather without a shadow of a doubt.'

'You are quite sure of this?' said Mina. 'What I meant was, he passed away quite some years ago.'

'I know, I was a child at the time. You are suggesting that my memory may have become — I don't know — blurred over time.'

'Do you have a photograph of him to make a comparison?' asked Mina.

Mr Phipps smiled. 'That is the irony of it. I have never seen one. In fact, I don't believe he ever had a photograph taken. He sometimes spoke of photographic portraits very distrustfully; he said they were supposed to capture a truthful likeness, but he did not believe they could. Of course, the art of photography has made great strides since then. But given his beliefs, it is very curious indeed that he should appear in a photograph after his death.'

'What did you say to Mr Beckler?'

'I hardly knew what to say. I think I said that the man portrayed looked like my grandfather, but I would have to give it some thought and consult with the other members of the family. He seemed content to accept that. I felt obliged to ask him not to place the picture on public display, and he promised that he would not. It seemed prudent to buy a print to show to the other partners. I did so, and there was no doubt in anyone's mind that this was my grandfather.' Mr Phipps opened his document case and extracted a photographic print mounted on card. 'This is it. Whatever it might be, Mr Beckler certainly saw it as an opportunity to acquire more business. He said what an honour it would be for him to photograph all the partners in the firm and how impressive such a picture might look in our window. A portrait of dignified, professional gentlemen inspiring confidence. I must admit, I could see his point.'

Mina examined the picture. In the centre of the print was the Phipps mausoleum she had seen so recently, but to one side of it was the figure of a man. Mina was forced to admit that the image of the man was very clear and distinct and bore a strong resemblance to the oil portrait of the late Mr Aloysius Phipps. Mina wished she had her magnifying glass with her. She had learned the value of such an item not long ago and had purchased one for her own use. Instead, she peered very closely at the photograph, trying to judge the quality of the main image against that of Aloysius Phipps, and saw quite unmistakably the edge of the wall of the mausoleum showing through the body of the man. The figure was translucent.

'You may have noticed that he has a cast in his left eye,' said Mr Phipps, pointing out that detail. 'It was a little thing, but he could sometimes be sensitive about it. He did not like to look in mirrors too often. That was what made it quite certain to the family that there could be no mistake. Perhaps that was the real reason for his dislike of photographs; while complaining of their lack of truth, he actually found them too truthful. If you look at the oil painting, it is obvious that he has asked the artist to correct that feature.'

'And yet,' said Mina, 'one supposes that in the spirit world where all things are healed, his spirit body would not have reproduced that defect. I have often been told that in the afterlife my spine will be perfectly straight.'

'Might I ask your opinion on this portrait?'

'I will need some time to consider it. I might be able to discover more. I certainly intend to try.'

Mr Phipps looked relieved.

'Might I ask you some questions?' said Mina.

'Oh, please do. I promise I will not charge it as a consultation.'

'When I was last in the Extra Mural Cemetery visiting the grave of my father, I enjoyed a short stroll as recommended by Mr Bishop's guide and noticed some monuments which caught my attention. I was told that some interesting stories were attached to them. I wonder — could you indulge my curiosity?'

'I will do my best.'

'There was a small and rather mean headstone for a Miss Porterson-White. I was told there was a dispute about a will.'

Mr Phipps almost chuckled. 'Oh yes, a most savage dispute. And it is still not reconciled. But our firm was not involved. It was a London family.'

'If you discover any more, please let me know.'

'I will.'

'And the family of Mr Hector Samprey?'

'Ah, yes,' he said very solemnly.

'I believe the poor man succumbed to injuries in an accident, one in which his wife died?'

'So I have heard.'

'And he had a son who died in the same year?'

'Yes, I am sorry to say that he was murdered by his criminal companions.'

'Murdered! How dreadful!'

'He was one of those young men who believed he could live better on his wits than by working. He became involved with a gang of cutthroats and thieves who mainly dealt in stolen goods. I don't know the precise circumstances — maybe there was a quarrel — but he was killed by one of his erstwhile friends. The grief undoubtedly hastened the father's demise.'

'I don't suppose you know anything about Mr Frederick Soules, the manufacturing chemist?'

'As a matter of fact, I do. My uncle dealt with his affairs and often shook his head about the foolishness of it all.'

'Oh?'

'Soules had a business rival, a man named Harvey. Soules had developed new manufacturing methods which enabled him to undercut his rival. It was all perfectly legitimate, but there was bad blood and jealousy. The enmity ran far deeper than that because Soules had married the woman Harvey loved. Soules came to us because he suspected that Harvey had tried to bribe one of his employees to steal the process, but he couldn't prove it. There was nothing we could do about that.

'Then there was an outbreak of cholera and Harvey spread the rumour that it was caused by Soules' contaminated products. Not only by word of mouth, but he actually distributed printed leaflets. On that occasion, Soules was able to prove that it was Harvey who was responsible and took him to court for libel and slander. Harvey had to pay a fine and costs. He came close to ruin.'

'When did this happen?'

'About ten or twelve years ago. But the story doesn't quite end there. Soules was so afraid that Harvey was plotting still more revenges that Mrs Soules went to plead with him, for her sake, to desist.'

'And did he?'

'To my uncle's surprise, he did. Harvey had loved her for over twenty years, and that emotion won him over. He gave up the business, sold his assets to Soules and went into retirement on a small annuity. When Soules died a few years later, Harvey married the widow. The company is run and owned by Soules' two sons.'

'That is quite a romance,' said Mina, wondering how she might include it in the plot of a story. She consulted her list of names, but Mr Phipps had nothing to say about Mr Veale the confectioner, although the name of the business was known to him, and the late Mr Mulgrew continued to remain a mystery.

The framed photographs and album were delivered to Mina that afternoon, and she took the opportunity to make a detailed examination of the betrothal pictures before letting her mother know that they had arrived. Taking the ghost picture to the window and using her magnifying glass, she studied it in a good light. Much as she wished to deny it, she was sure that there was no subterfuge, at least none that she could detect. The figure who stood beside her was without a doubt that of her father, but as he had looked when Mina was a child. Unlike Mr Phipps's picture, there were other people present who Mina knew to be composed of solid flesh, and she was able to compare her father's form with that of the other individuals. His image had a noticeably different quality. Mina and her family were solid, whereas the lines of draped curtains at the rear of the studio could be seen through her father's form.

She needed expert advice, and she knew exactly where to obtain it. Mina wrapped the album of betrothal photographs carefully, placed it in a stout bag, and hired a cab to transport her to the fashionable emporium of Mr J E Mayall.

On the way to Mr Mayall's studio, Mina berated herself for acting so impulsively. She had no appointment to see the proprietor, whom she had never met, and who she felt sure must be an extremely busy man. Instead, she had foolishly given in to a sudden burst of impatience to have answers from a person of expertise. She reflected on what she knew of the eminent Mr Mayall, whose activities often featured in the Brighton newspapers. She had never heard of him taking, advertising or selling spirit photographs. He was a member of the Brighton Natural History Society and was mentioned in reports of the society's meetings where he displayed a keen interest in such diverse subjects as volcanoes and microscopes. He was without any doubt a man of science. He was also a noted philanthropist, holding exhibitions and bazaars to fund schools and hospitals. The more Mina thought about her errand, the smaller and less important she felt, but she had cast her die and she would go on.

When Mina entered the premises of Mr J E Mayall, the renowned photographer of Brighton, it was like entering a gallery of fine art. Compared to this, the entire shop of Mr Beckler in Ship Street looked like the humble antechamber to something larger and more distinguished. Where the Ship Street premises were simply neat and well kept, Mr Mayall's was also refined and luxurious, with smooth oak panelling, oil paintings in deeply carved frames, a huge gallery of photographs, and everywhere the boldness of gilding and ornament, a proclamation of pride blended with good taste. There was a special place for photographs of members of the Royal family, which as the gold-painted legends made very clear had been taken personally by Mr Mayall. There was a pronounced scent of polish and paint, with just a hint of money.

Mina approached the reception desk, where a gentleman clerk watched her limping slowly towards him. He gazed with some curiosity at the bag she was holding. 'May I assist you?' he asked.

'Yes, thank you, I wish to see Mr Mayall.'

He opened a leather-bound appointment book. 'Certainly. Do you have an appointment, or do you wish to make one?'

'I — regret I do not have an appointment. But I only wish to speak with him. I do not wish to sit for a portrait.'

He looked her up and down. He made no effort to persuade her to have a portrait taken. 'I see. Might I ask why you wish to speak to him?'

'I want to seek his expert opinion on some photographs that were taken of my family recently.'

The clerk's expression hardened, and he closed the appointment book. 'Were these photographs taken by Mr Mayall or another photographer?'

'Another.'

There was a meaningful pause and a cold little smile. 'I am not sure that Mr Mayall would wish to comment on another photographer's work. My suggestion is that you write to him, explaining what it is you would like him to review, and he will I am sure respond.'

Mina found herself warming to the challenge. Small and insignificant she might be, but she had a mission that she felt sure would interest Mr Mayall, and a rising determination in the face of the clerk's dismissive manner to see the celebrated gentleman that day. 'I am not seeking a review; it is a scientific consultation. The pictures show something which seems to me to be impossible. I require the opinion of an experienced man, a man of science.'

'Be that as it may —'

Mina had one more card to play, and it was her own. 'I am sure he will want to see me. My name is Scarletti, of the Scarletti publishing house in Regent Street.' Mina took one of her cards from her reticule and placed it on the desk as if playing a winning ace. 'Mr Mayall's late son was a friend of my brother Edward, who is betrothed to a cousin of Mr Mayall's wife, a Miss Agatha Hooper.'

The clerk picked up the card and gazed at it. 'I suggest —'

'*I* suggest that you take my card to Mr Mayall immediately and tell him that Miss Mina Scarletti is here and wishes to speak to him.'

The clerk raised his eyebrows. He stared at Mina. Mina stared back. At length he operated a bell pull and moments later another, rather more junior clerk appeared. 'Please take this card to Mr Mayall and ask him when he might next be free to speak to this lady.'

The junior clerk departed. 'I cannot of course anticipate Mr Mayall's response.'

'Thank you,' said Mina. She waited, rather expecting the junior clerk to reappear, but instead the man who entered the gallery with Mina's card in his hand was a gentleman in his late fifties, very serious-looking and rather handsome. He was fashionably dressed without being ostentatious and wore a black armband and a heavy mourning ring.

'Miss Scarletti,' he said, warmly, 'I am very pleased indeed to meet you. I have heard so much about you in recent years; in fact, I was intending to write to you suggesting that I might take your photograph as one of the notable personages of Brighton.'

'I am very flattered,' said Mina. 'I have never thought of myself as particularly notable.'

They shook hands. 'Please, come through to my office,' said Mr Mayall. It took all Mina's willpower not to glance at the desk clerk as she made her way.

Mr Mayall's office was comfortably but not ostentatiously appointed. The chair Mina was offered had a seat and back of soft leather for which she was grateful, and there was even a little cushion which enabled her to adjust her posture. Behind the desk were deep shelves with bound copies of photographic publications both English and American, going back many years.

Here, Mr Mayall was less concerned with photographs of royalty than of his own immediate family. A silver mounted portrait on his desk was draped in black crape.

'May I offer my condolences for your sad loss,' said Mina. 'I never had the pleasure of meeting your son as my brother did, but I know that he was a man of many talents.'

Mr Mayall acknowledged the politeness with dip of his chin. 'Thank you for your kind words.' He drew a deep breath. 'But tell me why you have come to see me. I am very curious, especially in view of what I know of you.'

'My younger brother Richard recently obtained a position as a clerk with a Mr Beckler, who opened a photographer's business in Ship Street earlier this year.'

'Ah yes, I know of him, but we have never met.'

'When my older brother Edward was betrothed to Miss Hooper, he therefore arranged to have some photographs taken at Mr Beckler's studio. The result, on one of them, was — unexpected. I do not feel I can entirely accept any explanation Mr Beckler might offer, which would suggest the operation of psychic forces as yet unproven. I seek an answer in science.'

From his expression, she had clearly captured Mr Mayall's interest. 'May I see?'

Mina took the album from her bag and opened it to display the picture in which her father appeared. Mr Mayall did not seem shocked, only surprised. He took a magnifier from his desk, a much larger and she guessed more powerful one than the instrument she owned, and made a close study of the image. 'Where was this taken?' he asked.

'At Mr Beckler's studio in Ship Street.'

'I assume he employed only sunlight. The light has been very good of late.'

'Yes. He has some reflectors in the studio. Are there other forms of light he might have used? I know about the magnesium ribbon. He didn't use any of that.'

'Yes, the ribbon is not suitable for portraits. It gives a brief but very intense light, but unfortunately this is followed by clouds of ash. Candles and gaslight are insufficient. Sunlight is undoubtedly superior, but of course it is not reliable. I have been looking at electrical arc lamps as a possibility. I assume Mr Beckler did not use them?'

'No, only sunlight.'

'And who are the persons in this picture?'

Mina leaned forward, pointing to the individuals. 'Apart from myself, there is my mother and my two brothers. The figure standing beside me is that of my father, Henry Scarletti. He passed away three years ago. None of us saw him or anyone else present in that location when the picture was being taken. I wanted to know if you have seen anything like this before, and if so, can you explain it?'

Mayall nodded thoughtfully. 'There was another picture Mr Beckler took recently which he claimed to be the portrait of a ghost. It was said to be that of a lady's mother. It was displayed in his window and when I learned of it, I went to see it out of curiosity. It was not at all distinct. Sometimes what the eye sees builds a picture in the mind, making a rough and undefined shape into something that looks familiar. I would not myself have accepted that image as a portrait of a ghost, but of course the lady customer had very strong opinions on the matter. A result such as that can be produced by simple carelessness in preparing the glass plate. If an old plate is used, one which has been employed for an earlier photograph, and the image has been fixed by chemical means, it must be very thoroughly cleaned before it can be used again. If it is not properly cleaned, then part of the former image will remain on the glass, and it will appear on the new picture, giving the impression of a ghost-like figure.'

'I see,' said Mina. She recalled that when Richard went to work for Mr Beckler, he had complained very vociferously of being asked to clean old glass plates, a task he had felt did not properly employ his talents. 'But this portrait of my father is very clear indeed. It is he, without a doubt.'

'Extremely clear. In my opinion, this could not have not been produced by poor cleaning of the plate.'

'Have you ever taken a picture of this nature?'

'No, never.' Mayall smiled and paused a little before he went on. 'The plain fact is, Miss Scarletti, that I believe myself to be motivated to understand our world by the means of science, and my specialities are optics and chemistry. I have never seen a ghost and cannot therefore offer any opinion as to whether they exist or are objects of the imagination. But there is much we need to learn about light and chemicals and how one acts upon the other. If there are such things as disembodied spirits, I would not rule out the idea that there is something on the coating of Mr Beckler's plates which is sensitive to the material of which spirits are composed. What it might be I could not say. If he has discovered something of importance then one day, he may tell the world, but as a man of business I suspect that that will be some time in the future, and if he is a sensible young gentleman, will involve the taking out of a patent.'

'Do you know of anyone else who has taken pictures of ghosts?'

'There is a London man who has attracted some attention very recently, a Mr Hudson, but I have grave doubts about his methods. The best known in that field is an American photographer, Mr William Mumler, who caused a great deal of excitement a few years ago and made a substantial business of it.'

'Did he ever reveal his secrets?'

'He did not. But the result was he was arrested for swindling and put on trial. Experts studied his photographs and most of them assumed that he had resorted to trickery. But while they suspected fraud, they were quite unable to prove it and he was therefore acquitted.'

'When did this occur?'

'I can show you.' Mr Mayall rose from his desk and examined his bookshelves. Selecting a volume, he leafed through the pages. '1869,' he said at last. 'It was widely reported in America and discussed at great length in the photographic journals which published some of his photographs. I am not sure it was in the general newspapers in this country. Here, you may take a look.' He carried the volume to the desk and placed it open in front of Mina.

Mina examined a picture printed in the magazine. It was not made on photographic paper but reproduced by means of the engraver's art to create a good facsimile. It showed the transparent figure of a woman whose image appeared to be blending with the more solid seated subject, a gentleman, almost if the lady was embracing him. Mina was struck immediately by the impression that it bore more resemblance in quality to the image supposed to be that of Miss Hartop's mother than the picture of her father. 'It is not as refined as the one Mr Beckler produced. The features of the woman are not distinct, and there is no detail on the clothing. I think even if one knew who it was supposed to be, one might be hard put to identify it.'

'That is so. Although there was one he took of Mrs Lincoln with the late President hovering behind her. He at least was unmistakable.'

'I wonder if Mr Beckler knows about this and was trying the emulate Mr Mumler?'

Mr Mayall smiled. 'I don't think anyone would be advised to do that.'

'But you say he was acquitted.'

'He was, but the trial was a disaster for his business, which went into a decline. He produced no more spirit pictures. If Mr Beckler had attempted to sell pictures like those of Mr Mumler, then experts in photography would be drawing a comparison, and he would be in some difficulty, as the London man is already.'

Mina thought about this. 'But if Mr Mumler was genuine, and could not be proven a fraud, why did he stop? If the spirit photographs were genuine, something that simply appeared without his causing them, how was he even able to stop? Was there some chemical he had given up using?'

'Perhaps he felt that even if genuine, if he were to continue, he would be in constant danger of a more careful examination of his process and new accusations.'

'To my way of thinking,' said Mina, 'he was an outright fraud who had turned to honesty rather than find himself in court again. The cessation of the spirit pictures is the strongest possible indication that he was a fraud. If the ghosts were real and had appeared by some means Mr Mumler did not initiate, and possibly did not even understand, then surely the suspicion that attached to him would not have prevented them from appearing again. The spirits would have been eager to appear in order to prove him genuine. If they stopped appearing then he must have created the pictures in some way, a way that was no mystery to him, and after the trial, he stopped doing whatever it was he did to avoid further prosecution.' Mina studied the Mumler pictures again. 'Did other photographers offer suggestions as to how the pictures were created?'

'Oh indeed, a number of men came forward and there were several theories about how it might have been done. Of course, it is easy enough to theorise in retrospect, but there is nothing to prove how Mumler actually did it. The practitioners of photography, while they might not have been able to explain the mystery, did not believe in ghosts. Even Mr P T Barnum, the showman, asked for copies of the pictures only to display them in his museum of humbugs.'

'What explanations did the photographers offer?'

'One man suggested that Mumler had an accomplice hidden in the room, dressed all in white, who came out, posed for the picture and then hid again.'

'I can think of a dozen reasons why that is not feasible. But there is nowhere in Mr Beckler's studio where a person might hide. I know because I looked. And even if there was, the figure would appear solid.'

'I agree. As I mentioned before, a glass plate not properly cleaned will produce the effect of a ghost. This may well be something Mr Mumler discovered through his own carelessness and used to his advantage.'

'He would have to match the old image with the new subject, though, surely?'

'That would help if he was able, but the ghost image is usually not very clear in any case. This plays very well into the hands of frauds, since their victims are eager to interpret any image as that of a departed loved one. Another trick would be to have a pre-prepared translucent image of a ghostly figure and insert it into the camera behind the lens. The light would pass through and imprint the ghost on the glass plate. Most subjects having their picture taken would not be familiar with the photographic process and would therefore not be aware that any trickery had taken place.

'Another way would be to re-expose the glass plate to a second image while the coating is still sensitive. He would have to work quickly, of course. There were some suggestions that an image might be introduced while the plate is in its silver nitrate bath; that is the chemical that provides the light-sensitive coating. I think many of these might be possible, but all would result in quite blurry images. That might have been good enough for Mr Mumler and his clients, but what you have shown me is far more advanced than anything Mr Mumler did.'

Mr Mayall thought again and picking up his magnifying glass made another examination of the betrothal picture.

'Something of this nature is more in the style of a caricature. It is a kind of novelty in which two pictures are combined to produce a new impossible one.' Mr Mayall went to his shelves again and brought out an album of caricatures, one of them being that of the figure of a man with a very large head. This resembled the way that satirical pen and ink artists liked to represent well-known personalities, but it was in the form of a photograph. 'To achieve this, one has to start with two photographs of the same man: one close portrait of the head and one of the whole body. The head of the first is cut out and pasted to the other. Any joins are concealed with ink. The new image can then be photographed. One can even create a picture of a man's body with the head of an animal, such as a rabbit.'

'Why would anyone want such a thing?'

'A question I often ask myself.'

Mina studied the caricature picture. 'It is very strange, but no part of it is translucent, as in my picture.'

'That is so. The quality of the image of your father does point to something unusual.'

'Supposing,' said Mina, 'I were to come to you and ask you to create a picture like this one? How would you go about it?'

Mr Mayall considered it. 'Well, first I would need to have the original photograph of your father. If I had the actual glass plate negative I could reuse it, cleaning away all the surrounding details very carefully. Alternatively, if I had the original print of the picture, I would take a photograph of that picture, clean away any surroundings and then use the exposed glass to take the picture of your group. How effective that would be I am not sure, but as you see from the caricatures, a little touching up with ink is always possible. If I were using the wet plate method it would all have to be done within minutes, but there is a new coating recently developed which enables plates to be prepared well in advance. I don't know if Mr Beckler uses them.'

Mina thought about that and recalled what had been said during her tour of the studio. 'Yes, he does, for when he travels outside.'

'Precisely,' said Mayall, nodding. 'Then that is how I might consider producing a convincing ghost picture. Of course, my theories are in no way proof that that is what Mr Beckler actually did.'

'You are not a spiritualist?'

'I am not. If I had ever been tempted to turn to spiritualism, I would have done so by now. My dear first wife passed away two years ago, and now I have another terrible loss to endure. Many people are understandably driven to spiritualism in such circumstances, but I believe I must remain content to live out my life with only the memory of my loved ones to console me, to be reunited with them in heaven where they surely are.'

A gentleman arrived with whom Mr Mayall had an appointment, and Mina thanked him for his advice and returned home. She had learned one very important thing: if Mr Beckler had committed a fraud, the quality of the images of both her father and Mr Aloysius Phipps required him to have a picture of the deceased person, or at the very least a fixed negative on glass which he could copy.

Richard, she recalled, had complained at great length about Mr Beckler asking him to catalogue the old photographs he had acquired from the estate of Mr H G Simpson when purchasing the business. Such a collection could well be the source of suitable portraits. Young Mr Phipps, however, had assured her that his grandfather did not like or trust photography and had never had his picture taken. Her own father, she felt sure, had not had his portrait taken after their move to Brighton. It would be useful, however, to discover if any of the other people on Mr Beckler's list had been customers of Mr Simpson.

Once home, Mina set about examining the family photograph album to see if there was a match between any earlier portrait of her father and the one in the betrothal photograph, a hearty-looking figure, bearded and standing.

'What are you doing, Mina?' her mother demanded.

'I was thinking that since Mr Beckler's shop has some attractive photograph frames, there might be some pictures of Father we could have framed,' said Mina.

For once, Louisa Scarletti had no objections; in fact, she became very engaged with the idea and on her own initiative set about finding every family picture in the house. There were few enough: a very stiffly posed tintype of Louisa and Henry on the occasion of their engagement, wedding portraits, and a family group of Edward, Mina, Richard, Enid and their younger sister Marianne as a baby, her tiny nose peeping out from a nest of frills. Mina allowed her mother to sigh and exclaim, and there were tears shed.

'Are these the only pictures we have of Father?' she asked.

'Yes, dear. I wish there had been more.'

'And you are sure that he didn't have any pictures taken in Brighton? He was never photographed by Mr Simpson?'

'No, he — he knew he did not look at all well, and — perhaps if he had lived to see Enid married, he might have consented, but — no.'

Mina studied all the pictures of her father very closely. In the tintype and wedding portraits he was beardless with a moustache and side whiskers. In the family group he was seated, holding a very small Mina on his lap. There was no resemblance between any of them and the image of her father on the betrothal picture.

CHAPTER TWELVE

The next day Mina received two more letters. One, addressed in an elegant script and with the postmark of Hurstpierpoint in Sussex could only have come from Mr Honeyacre of Hollow House. Anxious for news of the expectant Mrs Honeyacre, Mina opened this one first.

Hollow House
Ditchling Hollow
Sussex

Dear Miss Scarletti,

I do hope this finds you well. I am happy to say that my dear Kitty is blooming most beautifully, although of course it is a situation in which ladies must always be careful. I expect you know that Mrs Jordan's maid Zillah is with us. She is such a sensible girl, and she, Kitty and Miss Pet are well able to amuse each other. Since you last visited us Mr and Mrs Malling have worked almost without ceasing on the repairs and redecorations of the house and improvements to the estate. I anticipate a time when it will be possible to entertain large parties of visitors, and Hollow House will be the talk of the county for all the reasons I had hoped for when I purchased it. The gardens are already a delight to the eye and the kitchen garden has been quite restored and shows the promise of abundance. I do hope that we will be able to receive a visit from you as soon as circumstances permit.

I received an unexpected letter last week, and wished to consult you about it, as I was unsure of how to respond. Mr Beckler the photographer, whom I am sure you recall all too well, has written to me saying that he had been taking pictures of some of the tombs in the Extra Mural

Cemetery in Brighton, and in his photograph of my dear late wife, Eleanor, had achieved an unusual result which he thought might interest me. I have to say I was not impressed by this young gentleman, still less so now, as I cannot imagine why he sought to take such a picture without at the very least seeking my opinion on the matter. In view of these circumstances, and also the dreadful disturbance caused by his patron Mr Hope at my house last January, I am disinclined to do any business with him. Do you have any observations to offer?

There have been comments in the Sussex newspapers of late that Mr Beckler has taken a photograph of the spirit of a deceased person which he has placed on display in the window of his shop. You know my interest in the supernatural and I wondered if you had seen the picture. If you have, I would value your opinion.

Respectfully yours,

B Honeyacre

Mina thought long and hard before she responded.

Dear Mr Honeyacre,

Thank you for your good wishes. My health is improving, and I am permitted to make careful excursions about Brighton, which is very attractive at this time of year. The air is extremely invigorating.

I am happy to know that Mrs Honeyacre is in good health and spirits. Please convey all my best wishes in anticipation of an event which will bring great joy to you both. A visit to Hollow House in good company and pleasant weather is certainly something I look forward to.

I am not sure if you know this, but my brother Richard is now employed in Mr Beckler's business. He has told me that there is a scheme in hand whereby they are taking pictures of important monuments in the Extra Mural Cemetery. I assume that this has been done with the intention of providing an excuse to approach the prominent families in Brighton as he wishes to acquire their custom. You may make your own *conclusions from that information. You are not alone in receiving a letter from Mr Beckler.*

I have seen some ghost portraits produced by Mr Beckler, and since I have no expertise in this area, I have recently consulted the premier photographer of Brighton, Mr J E Mayall, whose portraits of the royal family are of particular note. It is not yet possible to say with any certainty whether Mr Beckler's pictures are portraits of actual spirits, artefacts produced by the camera or a deliberate trick by the photographer. My advice would be to reserve your judgement for the present time.

Yours in friendship,
M Scarletti

Mina's second letter was from her mother's friend, Mrs Peasgood. Mina, recalling that the late Charles Peasgood was one of the names on Mr Beckler's list of monuments, had a strong suspicion why the lady might be writing to her. When she opened it, her fears were realised.

Dear Miss Scarletti,
I do hope this letter finds you well.

I would be most grateful if you would consent to take tea with me at four o'clock this afternoon. I hesitate to trespass on your good will, but I do so value your good sense, and wish to consult you on a question of great personal importance and delicacy. I know that you will treat this with the confidence it requires.

Assuring you of my great good wishes,
Respectfully,
M Peasgood

Despite the lack of explicit detail, Mina had no difficulty in guessing what had provoked the letter. She was not one to place wagers but if she had been, she would have been prepared to risk a large sum that Mrs Peasgood had also received a letter from Mr Beckler and now had a photograph of her husband's spirit. Having said that, she was unsure of why Mrs Peasgood had deemed the question to be a matter of great delicacy. Her natural curiosity was aroused.

Mina looked once more at the list of individuals whose graves had been photographed by Mr Beckler. Aloysius Phipps, Eleanor Honeyacre, Charles Peasgood, Frederick Soules, Hector Samprey, Edith Porterson-White, Bertram Veale, Robert Mulgrew.

The families of the first three she now knew to have received letters from Mr Beckler and suspected that as in the case of Mr Aloysius Phipps, relatives of the other two would also find that a ghost of their deceased loved one would be standing by the family grave. Even though Mina had not met any members of the other families, she now strongly suspected that all of them would, if they enquired, receive similar spirit pictures. Why Mr Beckler had chosen these families she did not as yet know.

She did wonder briefly why her father's image had appeared on the betrothal picture rather than one taken of the grave. On reflection she guessed that had Mr Beckler decided to take a picture of the Scarletti grave Richard would have told her, and Mr Beckler had quite rightly anticipated not only objections to this but also arousing Mina's deep suspicions. The betrothal pictures, however, had been taken at the request of the family. The fact that the image of Henry Scarletti had been positioned beside Mina was to her mind a clear ploy to induce her to accept Mr Hope's views.

Following her discussion with Mr Mayall, Mina realised that if Mr Beckler was a fraud of Mr Mumler's ilk, it would be an extremely hard thing to prove, even for an expert photographer. Crucially, Mr Mayall's judgement was that such convincing fakery required an existing photograph. Mr Aloysius Phipps, however, had never had a photograph taken and the image of Henry Scarletti did not match any known photograph of him. With these mysteries on her mind, Mina wrote a note to Mrs Peasgood accepting her invitation to tea.

Mrs Peasgood, a lady approaching the age of sixty without noticeable regret, had been left in comfortable circumstances on the death of her husband. She occupied a tastefully appointed home in Marine Square, together with her sister, Mrs Mowbray, whose late husband had not treated her with similar generosity. There, in a drawing room of substantial size, they regularly hosted musical soirees and dramatic readings of plays and poetry which were attended by those who considered themselves to be the most discerning members of Brighton Society. It went without comment that an invitation to Mrs Peasgood's entertainments was a singular honour to be mentioned at every opportunity to others less fortunate.

Mina and her mother had recently received a notice of future events, which were to include evenings of recitals of the sonnets and great speeches of Shakespeare. This cheered Mina, as it revealed that her friend Mr Merridew would be returning to Brighton next month. She wondered if he would go to Mr Beckler to be photographed in his pantomime costumes.

Mina was shown to Mrs Peasgood's parlour, a less formal, and more intimate location than the drawing room where comfort rather than display was paramount. A table was set with tea things, and Mina was pleased to see little tartlets filled with sliced apricots, redcurrants, and sweetened cream as well as a tempting lemon-yellow sponge cake, and tiny savoury sandwiches.

Mrs Peasgood believed that life should be lived with calm and dignity, although these outward appearances did not conceal her essential kindness. She was not easy to get to know well but had good reason to be grateful to Mina. In the previous year she had suffered an embarrassing emotional breakdown in the Royal Pavilion, when old memories of a ghostly sighting she had hoped was long buried had risen once more to her consciousness. Mina's guidance on the subject had afforded her considerable reassurance.

Only once had Mrs Peasgood hosted a display of mediumship, which unknown to her, was one of Richard's many hopeful enterprises. He had appeared before the company as Signor Ricardo, sporting a black mask, a dreadful Italian accent and an even worse moustache, promoting the extraordinary skills of the medium, who was called Miss Foxton. The medium was actually Nellie. A former magician's assistant, she was an accomplished trickster and illusionist in her own right. It was at this event that she had appeared as a flying spirit in a form-fitting spangled costume and her exuberant charms had drawn the attention of Mr Jordan and led to their subsequent marriage.

Mrs Peasgood, shocked by the performance and the emotions it had aroused in the audience, had since declared that she would not host entertainments of that nature again. Following her fright in the Royal Pavilion, she had, as far as Mina was aware, shown no further interest in spiritualism in any form.

The maid, under Mrs Peasgood's instructions, ensured that Mina was comfortably seated, then deftly poured out the tea and supplied plates and dessert forks, then departed like a spectre without a whisper of sound. Mrs Peasgood tasted the edge of a sandwich, but her mind was not on food.

'It is very good of you to come,' she said at last. 'I feel ashamed to burden you with my troubles once again.'

'If there is anything I can do to alleviate them, it would be my pleasure to do so,' said Mina.

Mrs Peasgood laid aside the remains of her sandwich and touched her fingertips to a folded napkin. 'I — received a letter yesterday from the photographer, Mr Beckler. I understand your brother works for him. It was a most — unexpected letter.'

'I guessed as much,' said Mina.

Mrs Peasgood studied her expression. 'Have *you* received a letter from Mr Beckler?'

'No, but I am aware of others who have.'

Mrs Peasgood looked relieved. 'Then you will know to what I am referring. I went to see him. And I saw a picture he had taken of the grave of my late husband.' She allowed herself a moment of reflection. 'May I show you the picture?'

'Please do.'

Mrs Peasgood took an envelope from a side table. 'I purchased the picture,' she said, unhappily. 'I didn't know what else to do.' She drew a photograph from the envelope and handed it to Mina.

Mina recognised the Peasgood grave she had seen so recently, but this time the figure of a man, clear yet slightly translucent, stood just in front of it. He was tall, and appeared to be in his middle fifties, a little portly perhaps, but robust. He wore a broad cravat with a floral design fastened by a pearl stickpin and held what appeared to be a medical book open in one hand. 'I regret that I never met your husband. Can you assure me that there is no doubt in your mind this is he?'

'None whatsoever.'

'That is a very distinctive cravat.'

Mrs Peasgood managed a fond smile. 'A favourite of his. He was known for his colourful cravats. Ask anyone who knew him. And the pin was a gift from me on the occasion of our silver wedding. I wear it often in his memory.' Mrs Peasgood touched a hand to her collar, which, Mina noticed, was adorned with the pearl-headed pin.

'And does the image you see here match any previous photographs you have of him?' Mina was about to elaborate but decided against it. It was best to have the widow's untrammelled opinion without planting suspicion.

'I do have another picture of him.' Mrs Peasgood rose and went to the mantelpiece and brought a framed portrait. In this picture, Charles Peasgood was seated at a table, on which lay some medical texts and an old-fashioned wooden monocular stethoscope.

Mina compared the two, and there was no doubt that they were portraits of the same man, though one could not be a copy of the other. The man beside the monument stood facing the observer. The man at the table was seated and half turned towards the camera. There was something that looked like a certificate displayed on the wall. Not only did he appear to be the same age in both portraits, but he wore the same suit of clothes, cravat and stickpin. The two pictures might well have been taken within moments of each other.

'When was this taken?'

'Oh, it must have been about twelve years ago. Charles was awarded a memorial by one of the medical societies — you can see it in the frame behind him.'

'Who was the photographer?'

'I really don't know. I believe the medical society arranged it. You might think this strange, but the thing that heartens me is that he is holding one of his medical volumes. It means that

Charles's spirit is still engaged in doing good, in doing what he loved.'

Mina wasn't sure if there was a need for physicians in the afterlife but did not mention this. 'Would you be willing to let me see the back of the photograph?'

Mrs Peasgood looked surprised but said, 'You may look if you wish.'

Mina unfastened the catch at the back of the frame and eased up the back plate. The picture had been mounted on card, but it was blank. Frustratingly there was no indication of the name of the photographer.

Mina restored the picture as it had been. 'Do you wish me to offer an opinion on whether the picture taken by Mr Beckler is genuine?' she asked.

Mrs Peasgood looked startled. 'But it is Charles. It could not be anyone else. I am quite satisfied of that. No, it is something else. I have hesitated and thought about it, but I feel that maybe Charles was trying to send me a message. Do you think I should consult a medium?'

'But is this not message enough?' asked Mina, choosing to deflect the question. 'Your husband is content. Do you need to know more?'

Mrs Peasgood clasped a hand to her face. She was on the brink of displaying some deep emotion, something that haunted her memory more powerfully than any ghost could. Mina poured more tea and her hostess gratefully took a deep gulp, coughed and almost choked then dabbed at her lips with her napkin and recovered herself.

'Miss Scarletti,' she said at last. 'I must take you into my confidence once more. I know I can trust you. In fact, I am about to tell you something I could not even share with my own sister. She is a dear thing, but sometimes, she says things without thinking, and — well, you know what I mean.' She set down her cup. 'Towards the end of his life, Charles began to experience feelings of deep melancholy. What a doctor needs above all is confidence. He needs to feel confident in his treatment, his knowledge and the effectiveness and purity of the medicine he administers. But that seemed to desert him.

'I discovered that he had been suffering from a painful affliction, one that he did not think was curable, and all he could do to help himself was relieve the pain. He became very dependent on medicines to alleviate the pain, and I think they clouded his judgement, which he realised to his great distress that he could no longer depend upon. I do not believe that he made any errors due to this, only that he was afraid he might do if he continued to practise medicine. He was not an old man, but he decided to retire. He continued to read the medical journals. He took an interest in architecture and history. But sometimes the pain did overwhelm him, although most of the time be bore it stoically.

'One afternoon he told me he was going to take a rest and did not wish to be disturbed. I did not see him for some hours, and when I eventually went to see if he required anything he was quite gone from the world. He seemed to be at peace. There was an enquiry, and it concluded that he had died of a failure of the heart. But that failure was due to what was presumed to be a large injection of the drug that alleviated his pain. An injection which any doctor in full health would have known might prove fatal.

'The coroner decided that Charles was in such in severe pain from his disease that he had had a momentary lapse of judgement and might have miscalculated the dose. His death was recorded as accidental. I shall never truly know what went through his mind. He never left me a note or a message. I did,

I confess, visit a medium shortly after his death, a Mrs Ragdon, but she told me no more than she might have read in the newspapers and gave me her sincere assurance that he was at peace.

'And now — and now this. It is Charles, it is undoubtedly Charles. Not some shadow or cloud that I could delude myself is he, no, the figure is Charles, the way he stands, the way he looks. The way I remember him in full health, as he was more bowed towards the end. He looks quite his old self, confident, assured, happy. Perhaps that is the message he wants to convey. To tell me that all was well and he did not as some people suggested take his own life from despair. I don't know. Do you think I should consult a medium again? Can you recommend one?'

Mina was moved by the widow's obvious distress and took some time to consider her reply. 'Mrs Peasgood, I have no recommendations for you except to say that if you do decide to visit a medium, do not succumb to increasing demands on your purse. There are charlatans who have no desire other than to make money by cheating. Others only look for fame, or to amuse themselves. Some are honest and wish to benefit others. Whether they are genuine or not I can't say. But all of them I can tell you with some confidence will tell you only what you most wish to hear. People go to mediums for comfort when they are in distress, for certainty when they are mired in uncertainty.'

'Do you think my husband took his own life?' said Mrs Peasgood pathetically.

'I cannot answer that,' said Mina.

'But it is a sin, and I fear that we will never be reunited in heaven.'

'None of us is without sin,' said Mina, 'the Bible teaches us that. Even if your husband committed one sin in his life, that will be far outweighed by the great good he did. And see, in this picture, he holds a medical book. He is still engaged with the thing he loved. Is that not a sure sign that he is in heaven?'

Mrs Peasgood nodded. 'You are right, of course you are right. What a comfort you are, Miss Scarletti. I am sure the good Lord has a place reserved for you where one day you will sit and dispense your words of wisdom to the world.'

'Then be content, Mrs Peasgood. You know your husband to have been a good man, dedicated to the wellbeing of others. Is there really anything more you need to know?'

Mrs Peasgood gazed at the portrait of her husband and was reassured.

CHAPTER THIRTEEN

It was the final evening in Brighton for Mr Inskip, Enid, and their family. Louisa Scarletti was miserable to lose their company, protesting repeatedly that the dear grandchildren brought so much brightness into her life, adding that she hoped to receive good news as soon as possible after Edward's wedding. Almost in the same breath she went on to wonder why Richard, now that he was a successful man of business, did not marry, since when he did and became a father then she could die content. She had bought some extravagant parting gifts, and all three of her 'darling babies' were showered with toys and sweetmeats and therefore took twice as long to settle into their nursery as usual.

Care of children was at least one skill that Mina was not expected to acquire or demonstrate. It was acknowledged without comment that this was something she would never need for herself, neither was she asked to entertain her sister's offspring. Enid worried that scoliosis could be transmitted through the air, and even if it could not be, feared that the children could be unnerved by their aunt's twisted body, and their spines frightened into a sudden collapse.

While they waited for the dinner bell, Mina took the opportunity of her mother's distraction to talk to Richard. He was not lounging in the parlour, and she found him at the window of his bedroom. He was trying unsuccessfully to encourage cigar smoke to fly away out into the street, while the passing breeze clearly had other ideas.

'Don't worry, I'll get Rose to air the room,' he said, as Mina entered. She paused in the doorway and he took the unspoken hint and pinched out the little cigar. 'I'm hiding from Mother,' he said. 'All she talks about is grandchildren. Aren't three enough for her?'

Mina sank into the armchair beside the bed and adjusted a cushion for her comfort. 'Richard, I was wondering if you had seen the pictures taken at the cemetery? The ones you did the sketches for. You haven't mentioned them.'

He propped himself languidly against the wall. 'No, I've not seen them. They aren't amongst the ones ready for collection by customers. I think Beckler has been working on them.'

'Aren't they to be made into a display? I am surprised they haven't been put in the window as an advertisement. I thought you said that was the reason for taking them.'

'I think it was. But Beckler has written to the families first to see if they want the pictures, so he can offer them the choice of buying them before they get displayed. A few people have come in. Mind you, Beckler was a bit out of sorts this morning. Some fellow came in waving one of the letters at him and gave him no end of a wigging. Said he took pictures of his family's grave without asking his permission. Some people are never happy.'

'How is the mystical Lady Brighthelm doing?'

Richard controlled his enthusiasm for that subject without difficulty. 'She seems to have attracted some interest. But you know what Brighton is like. A novelty of any kind always brings the crowds. Did you know it was Miss Hartop who gave Beckler the idea of photographing the graves? She happened to mention one day that she wished she had a nice portrait of her mother to put on her grave so that everyone could see how beautiful she had been, and that was what made him think of it. So she can be useful. Somewhere in that awful run of tattle a few things do emerge.'

'And you say she brings business in, too,' said Mina. 'It only wants a few well-connected customers to add to the roster, and fashion will do the rest. I imagine she is a good source of information on the notables of the town.'

'It's hard to stop her talking,' said Richard, glumly. 'She goes on at such a rate I don't think she knows what she is saying half the time, all about the rich men her father knows, their daughters who are her bosom friends, and the handsome young men of good breeding she is convinced want to court her. And Beckler listens to her. I think he makes notes.'

'Mother and I were looking through the pictures we have of Father yesterday. I only wish there were more of them. I don't recall that Father was ever photographed by Mr Simpson, was he?'

'No, I don't think he was.' Richard gave up on the cigar, put the stub in his pocket, and went to perch on the edge of the bed.

'I am sure you are right,' said Mina. 'He was so unwell when we came here. I remembered the other day that when you first went to work for Mr Beckler, one of the tasks he set you was to make a list of the names of all persons photographed by Mr Simpson who had not collected their pictures, pictures he still has in his shop.'

'Yes, and a tedious trial that was, too. But there was no picture of Father there. I would have mentioned it if there had been.'

'There might have been pictures of people whose families we know,' said Mina, lightly, 'like the Peasgoods and the Honeyacres.' She was interested to know if any of the persons whose graves had been photographed were on the list, thus supplying Mr Beckler with material for his ghost portraits, but she thought it wise not to mention her true motives.

'I suppose so,' said Richard vaguely. 'There might have been. It was a very long list. Anyone might be on it.'

'Could you take a look at the list for me? Or better still, I could borrow it and see for myself. That will save you the trouble. Our friends might be very interested to know if there are some family photographs there that they have no copies of.'

'I haven't got it anymore, Beckler has it. He's been working on it, and the old pictures, too. But you don't need to see it. I think he's having some advertisements printed and he is making a note of people to send them to. So they will all be told about the pictures in any case.'

'Well, that is a good thing,' said Mina, carefully concealing her disappointment. She knew that she was coming close to the edge of what she might say without making Richard suspicious. The last thing she wanted was him making a careless remark to his employer and alerting him to the fact that she was making enquiries. 'Richard — has he given any kind of explanation for the ghost portrait of Father? Why and how it appeared? Or any ghost portrait for that matter? I have heard that other people can take them too.'

'Oh yes, well, he's very clever with that sort of thing,' Richard assured her. 'I was thinking about it a lot, and I couldn't help but say to him what a strange business it was, and he explained it all.'

'He did?'

'Yes. He said that the spirits are around us all the time, only we can't always see them. Except for some people, like mediums. But that makes me glad I'm not a medium. I mean, it must be a terrible bother having all those spirits floating about and giving you messages all the time. They always seem to want something. And if they do, they never say it clearly like "give five guineas to Aunt Jemima". No, it's always such a riddle that no one can make it out.' He started musing absently, then shook his head. 'No, I shouldn't like that at all.'

'But about ghost photographs?' Mina reminded him, pointedly.

'Oh, yes, those. Well, Beckler says that cameras and eyes work differently. He couldn't exactly explain how, because even the best scientists can't, although he was sure that they would one day. But that means that cameras can see things our eyes can't. Except for mediums' eyes, that is. They have a special kind of eyes. They can see the things that cameras can.' He paused with a little frown. 'I wonder if mediums can take photographs?'

'With their eyes?' queried Mina.

Richard shrugged. 'You never know. Perhaps they have all these photographs in their heads.'

'They should try staring at pieces of paper,' said Mina, teasingly. 'Maybe pictures will appear.'

'That's a good idea! Anyhow, Beckler said that the reason that spirit pictures have only just started to be seen on photographs is that cameras a few years ago weren't as good as the ones we have now, and there are better chemicals and things like that. I don't know if you know this, but once you have the picture on the glass, you have to put it in a lot of chemicals, or it just goes all dark. Ghosts especially — they go dark very quickly, so even if they are on the glass you won't see them. Beckler used to use something else — I forget the name, hypo something or other — to put on the glass, but now he uses cyanide. I know, it's quite a nasty poison, but it's so strong that it makes the ghosts stay in the picture. You can see them clear as anything. So the ghosts were always there but even if the cameras could see them, we couldn't make them stay long enough for us to see them. And now we can.' Richard thought over his argument as if searching for inconsistencies, and finding none, gave a satisfied nod.

'Well, that is very helpful for today's photographers,' said Mina. 'I wonder why Mr Mayall doesn't take spirit pictures. He is supposed to be the best photographer in Brighton. He uses cyanide just like anyone else.'

'Oh, he is all well and good for pictures of royals looking very stiff and serious,' said Richard, dismissively, 'but Beckler is the coming man, with new ideas.'

'Did he say why the picture of Father was so very clear while the one of Miss Hartop's mother was not?'

'No. I mean, I didn't ask him. But that is a good question. Shall I ask him for you?'

'No, I beg you, not on my account,' said Mina quickly.

Richard hesitated as if about to impart something of importance and leaned towards Mina confidingly. 'But here is a very interesting thing he told me. I think it might be a big secret and the world does not know it yet. He said that when someone takes a photograph of a person, someone alive, that is, the picture has some of that person in it. I didn't quite understand it, but I think it was to do with sunlight. Or maybe it's that vital force Mr Hope was talking about. Or they could be the same thing. The sunlight is reflected from the person as if the person is a mirror. I mean, we can't see it, but the camera can, and it goes into the camera, and it makes the picture on the glass plate. But it takes a part of the person with it and puts it on the glass. But the black and white on the glass is the wrong way round, so to turn it the right way about the glass and some paper are put in the sun, and then the light makes the photograph. But when it does that it isn't just making a picture, like a drawing. It's actually putting some of the person into the picture. Isn't that interesting?'

Mina was briefly at a loss for words. 'I — have never heard of or even imagined such a thing,' she said at last.

Richard gave a triumphant grin. 'Well, there you are. I know you are very clever and all that, but you don't know everything!'

Mina was full of questions, but she felt sure that she was unlikely to learn anything more from Richard.

There was a solemn farewell dinner for the family, and the following morning the Inskips and their nursemaid returned to London. Mina's mother decided that she was too ill for company. She retired despondently to her bed, tended upon by Rose, who ensured that she had enough scandalous reading matter to keep her occupied. Louisa Scarletti often denied reading the popular newspapers since the contents were too shocking, which meant that when she wished to peruse them, she was obliged to do so in private.

Having established that she was not required, Mina decided to pay a visit to the newspaper reading rooms before her mother changed her mind and demanded her presence. Since the individuals mentioned on Richard's list were all prominent Brighton people and their tombstones had supplied the years of their deaths, she hoped to find notices of their demise, and even some obituaries. The *Brighton Gazette* was a weekly publication, so it was not too arduous for her to examine the death notices for the years in question.

The issues for each year were bound into heavy books with covers like tombstones, and Mina had to ask the assistant to carry each one to the table and lift it onto a reading stand. Her diminutive size meant she was unable to sit at the table to read, as it was impossible for her to see the upper half of the pages unless she was on her feet. It would be a long day.

Mina decided to begin with the most mysterious of the names, Mr Mulgrew who had died in 1863, and found, by good fortune, Miss Porterson-White who had expired just after Christmas 1862. In the following January there was a short obituary concerning her death from the natural decay of old age, and details of her history and rumours of her great wealth. She had resided in Brighton for the last ten years of her life and had been a common sight on the sea front in a bath chair, attended by her servants.

She finally discovered Mr Mulgrew in the autumn of 1863 but was very little the wiser. All she found was a single-line announcement, no obituary, and no inquest. *The death is announced of Mr Robert Mulgrew the theological scholar, at the age of 78.*

In February 1866 Mina found, *The death is announced of Mr Frederick Soules the manufacturing chemist, aged 58, who passed away after suffering a severe attack of pneumonia. He is survived by a widow and two sons.*

The death of Mr Veale had excited considerably more attention. Mina's back was already aching, but she knew that it was about to ache very much more.

Brighton Gazette, May 1868
Coroner's Inquest

On Thursday last, D. Black Esq., the Coroner for Brighton held an inquest at the Sussex County Hospital on the body of Bertram Veale, confectioner, aged 43. From the evidence of two witnesses, William Harper and James Best, it appeared that on the evening of the 10th of this month the deceased was walking home from a tavern when he tripped and fell, resulting in a heavy blow to the head. He was removed to the hospital where he died without regaining consciousness three days later. The evidence of the surgeon Mr Preston, who attended the patient and later conducted the post-mortem examination, was that Mr Veale had been in a state of inebriation when he fell, and death was due to a swelling of the brain occasioned by the fall. The injury had been on the front of the skull, suggesting that the deceased had fallen forward and been too far under the influence of alcoholic liquor to save himself. The coroner summed up and the Jury returned a verdict of 'accidental death'. At this, the widow, Mrs Martha Veale stood up and objected very strongly. She denied that her husband had been addicted to drinking and claimed that his death was no accident but murder. She became very distressed and had to be assisted from the court.

There followed a series of letters in the *Gazette* from Mrs Veale, who from their tone had strong personal reasons for wanting to deny that her late husband was addicted to drink. This was followed by a letter from Mr Preston, who stated that his examination had been most thorough and had taken into account the general state of health of the deceased as well as the injury. He fully understood the reasons why the widow wished to preserve the good reputation of her late husband; however, the evidence was all too clear. He had discovered changes in the liver of the deceased which strongly suggested that he had been in the habit of drinking to excess for some years. This finding had been supported by friends of the deceased who had frequently observed him in a drunken state.

Mrs Veale wrote to the *Gazette* once more, stating that her husband had been the best of men, and she had never seen him take drink except in very small amounts for medicinal purposes. She had recently visited a noted clairvoyant and medium who had confirmed what she had said in court. A full account of the consultation had been handed to the police, who she was sure would soon arrest her husband's murderers.

Mina continued her search through the papers, and found that Harper and Best had later been brought before the police court charged with theft, having abstracted money from the pockets of their unconscious friend, Bertram Veale, but there was no suggestion that they might have been concerned in his death.

This was interesting enough, but she soon found that it was the Samprey family that promised far more.

Brighton Gazette, May 1867
Coroner's Inquest

The inquest was held on Monday evening at the Town Hall, before D. Black, Esq., the Borough Coroner, on the body of Hector Samprey Jnr, aged 33, whose body was discovered on the seashore near to the fish market on Saturday night. Mr William Woodruffe, boatman in the Coast Guard service stated that on Saturday evening at about ten o'clock he was on duty near the fish market when he heard the report of a firearm a short distance from him. Witness saw a man running from the scene, but it was too dark for him to make an identification. After making a search he went to the east end of the groyne and saw the body of a man lying on the edge of the water. He sent to the Town Hall for the police and the body was removed to the dead house. He made a thorough search of the seashore as soon as it was light, but no weapon was found.

Mr Taaffe, surgeon, stated that he was called to look at the body of the deceased on Saturday night. There was a large wound in the chest. The bullet had penetrated the heart, which would have proved instantly fatal. Charring of the skin showed that the weapon had been discharged close to the deceased, most probably by someone standing facing him. He believed that the weapon would have been a pistol of a kind easily concealed in a pocket.

The deceased's father, Hector Samprey senior was brought to the court to give evidence. He was conveyed by bath chair and attended by his younger sons Mortimer and Charles Samprey, who were visibly distressed and did their best to care for their frail parent. Mr Samprey, his voice painfully weak, stated that his eldest son had fallen in with some bad men whose trade was dealing in stolen valuables. There was, he insisted, no evidence to suggest that his son had been involved in their crimes. Here, the poor gentleman's composure almost failed him, as he attempted to convey the impression that his son had been no more than a convivial companion with these desperate individuals, in their enjoyment of beer. Nothing was said out of sympathy, but onlookers glanced at each other, as if to say that they knew better. One of these dubious associates was a man called Barnes who had a reputation for violence and was known to own a gun. Hector junior had recently promised his father that he would have nothing more to do with these unsavoury persons, or indeed, places where beer was sold and consumed. His father had been overjoyed by this, and agreed to take him into the family firm, in the hope that he would join his brothers in partnership. Charles Samprey confirmed that Hector junior had told him, his father and his brother Mortimer that he was going to lead a better life. On the night of his death Hector junior planned to meet Barnes and tell him that he wanted nothing more to do with him and his companions. Charles had begged his older brother to be careful, and even offered to accompany him, but Hector junior had been confident that he could manage the situation and it would be better if he did so alone. Mr Dyer, another boatman, stated that only two days previously he had seen young Hector Samprey and Barnes walking together on the seashore, and they appeared to have been arguing. Barnes had shaken his fist in a threatening manner.

Inspector Gibbs of the Brighton police stated that Barnes was a known criminal who had served several terms of imprisonment for assault, theft and handling stolen goods. The Sussex police were searching for him.

The jury after some consideration brought in a verdict of murder and named Barnes as the chief suspect.

Mina read on. As Dr Hamid had said, the loss of young Hector had been a fatal shock to his already declining father.

Brighton Gazette, June 1867
Obituary

The death occurred last Wednesday of Mr Hector Samprey, aged 63, who passed away peacefully at his home. He had been in poor health since 1859 when he suffered severe injuries in the carriage accident that claimed the life of his wife, Amelia. In his youth he had served in the army, attaining the rank of Major. For the last twenty-five years he was by profession a builder and renovator of fashionable properties in the county of Sussex, his works being widely acknowledged as being of the highest quality. In character he was a fair and good-tempered man, who bore any personal afflictions with courage and stoicism. Only two weeks ago he was struck a terrible blow by the tragic death of his eldest son, Hector Jnr, aged 33. We cannot comment on this here, but we are told only that the police are confident that an arrest will soon be made in the case. Mr Samprey is survived by two younger sons and a daughter.

Mina was now thoroughly engrossed in the story. She read on and learned that 36-year-old Barnes had been arrested a week later. It had required the efforts of three police officers to take the violently struggling prisoner into custody. Once at the police station a pistol was found on him which had been recently discharged, and there were live rounds in his pockets which he attempted unsuccessfully to throw away. It could not be determined whether the pistol was the one that had killed young Samprey, but the man was known to have been in possession of more than one weapon at various times in his criminal career. In the police court, Barnes's representative confirmed that his client had been an associate of Hector Samprey junior and admitted that the men had met two days before the murder. There had however been no quarrel. Both men had been drinking and this had resulted in what he termed a 'high spirited conversation'. This statement led to some hilarity amongst the spectators which drew sharp words from the magistrate. Barnes claimed that he had not seen Samprey since that night and denied murder.

The woman who lived with him, who gave the name of Jenny Jemson, was a forlorn creature, probably quite young but looking older than her true years, meanly dressed, with dark patches on her cheeks that might have been grime or bruises, or something of both. She made a pathetic figure in the witness box and evoked much sympathy from the onlookers, who could only speculate on the kind of life she must have led with the brutish creature in the dock. Her evidence, given in a whisper, was that Barnes had had no quarrel with Samprey, and he had been in her company at the time of the murder. The general impression was that the unhappy woman had been browbeaten into giving that account.

Barnes was charged with the murder of Hector Samprey junior and sent for trial at Lewes Crown Court. There, his female companion, deprived of his company during the previous few weeks, was still defiantly loyal, the Nancy to his Bill Sykes, as some whispered. Although still clad in poverty, she was tidier and cleaner than she had been, the bruising faded, her head held higher, her voice stronger, but she still gave the same story. It was no surprise to Mina that Barnes was found guilty of the murder of Hector Samprey junior and hanged.

Out of curiosity, Mina ordered the 1859 volume for the earlier history of the unfortunate Sampreys.

Brighton Gazette, July 1859

FATAL ACCIDENT TO MRS SAMPREY. MR HECTOR SAMPREY DESPAIRED OF.

On Wednesday afternoon last, a shocking accident resulted in the death of Mrs Amelia Samprey, aged 50, and injuries to Mr Hector Samprey so serious that it is feared he may not recover. Mr Samprey was due to drive to Ovingdean to inspect a piece of land he was interested in purchasing. The weather being fine, Mrs Samprey decided to accompany her husband as she wished to see the Grange, the historic building immortalised in the famous novel of Mr Harrison Ainsworth. Unfortunately, they had not proceeded far when something caused the carriage to make a sudden lurch. The horses took fright, and the coachman, Mr Pendry, while trying desperately to control them, was flung bodily from the vehicle. He suffered fractured ribs and bruising but is expected to recover. Mrs Samprey received a blow on the temple which was so severe that when she was brought out of the carriage it was apparent that she had expired. Mr Samprey broke both his legs and also received injuries to his spine. He was brought home, where he remains in a very serious condition under the constant care of his physicians.

Brighton Gazette, July 1859
Coroner's Inquest

The inquest on the body of Mrs Amelia Samprey was opened before D. Black Esq., Borough Coroner at the Town Hall. Evidence of identification was received, and a report was read regarding the injuries suffered by the unfortunate lady which were believed to be the immediate cause of death. Mr Pendry the coachman was too indisposed to attend, and the proceedings were adjourned for one week in anticipation that he might be able to give evidence as to the cause of the accident.

Brighton Gazette, July 1859
Coroner's Inquest

The adjourned inquest on the body of Mrs Amelia Samprey was held before D. Black Esq., Borough Coroner, at the Town Hall.

There could be no doubt from evidence given at the first hearing that the cause of Mrs Samprey's death was the striking of her head on the interior of the carriage. The only question remaining to be determined was the reason for the terrible accident. Mr Pendry the coachman, who had been too badly injured to attend last week, was now able to appear, although it was obvious from the way he took great care as he walked, that he was in severe pain. He stated that the carriage had been in perfect order before the journey commenced, as he had given it his usual thorough inspection shortly before departure. He had since ascertained that a wheel had come loose from the axle, causing the sudden lurch which had so frighted the horses. He could only imagine that the wheel must have struck some obstruction lying in the roadway and that this had caused the damage.

After a brief deliberation the coroner's jury brought in a verdict of accidental death and confirmed that no blame could be attached to Mr Pendry. Mr Hector Samprey continues very ill, although his condition appears to be more hopeful.

Her work at the reading room done, Mina called in at the bookshop next door. Having noted that Mr Robert Mulgrew was a theological scholar, she wondered if he had ever published a book or pamphlet which might furnish her with more information about the author.

She could not help but notice an abundance of volumes by Mr Hope; those with the author's signature appended commanded a higher price than those without. There were a few stories by Robert Neil on display, the little booklets tucked into a wooden stand with other similar publications. Mina, under a pretence of examining the merchandise, moved some of the storybooks about to bring her own to more prominence. The bookseller, unaware that he was speaking to the author, was a little disparaging on the subject of sensational literature, saying that it was not in his opinion suitable for ladies. Mina asked if he had anything in stock by Mr Robert Mulgrew, but the name did not sound familiar to him, and he shook his head.

Mina next tried the library, where their catalogue showed that they had some religious tracts by Robert Mulgrew, which had been privately printed in Brighton. These bore such titles as *The Message of the Gospels*, *The Power of Prayer Revealed*, *What is Faith?* and *Christ the Healer*. At some point it had been decided to publish the tracts in a collection as a single volume, and Mina asked to see this. A brief biography in the frontispiece stated only that Mulgrew, a schoolmaster by profession, was no preacher but a quiet man, who studied the scriptures with great earnestness and occasionally wrote his personal observations. There was an insert on shiny paper printed with a photograph of Robert Mulgrew. Mina had imagined him to be an ascetic-looking scholarly gentleman and was a little surprised to see a large hearty individual with a ruff of white hair above his ears and muttonchop whiskers. He was standing by a small platform piled with religious works and had an open bible in his hand.

The photograph had been taken by H G Simpson.

CHAPTER FOURTEEN

The following morning, a letter appeared in the *Brighton Gazette* which Mina read with some amusement.

To the Editor,

A number of Brighton residents have recently received letters from a certain photographer of this town, whom we take care not to name, advising them that he has taken a picture of their family monument in the Extra Mural Cemetery. These pictures, it should be emphasised, were taken not at the request of the family concerned, but at the photographer's own whim, and for reasons known only to himself. In these letters the recipients are invited to come to his place of business and view the photographs, as there is something of interest in them.

Anyone who receives such a letter is most strongly advised to place it in the wastepaper basket where it surely belongs. The photographer concerned should cease and desist from sending these tasteless communications. Should anyone be unwise enough to go to his shop and make enquiries, they will see an image of their family monument with what is supposed to be their deceased ancestor's ghost beside it. We would like to remind the general public of Brighton that there are a dozen methods employing chemical means by which such pictures can be produced, none of them involving any intervention of the supernatural. The only profiter from these pictures is the photographer himself. If anyone is in any doubt, they should consult the photographic magazines and learn of the fate of Mr William Mumler, an American gentleman who made a great deal of money from the sale of similar pictures and found himself in court on a charge of fraud. We say nothing about the Brighton gentleman, only that he is in grave danger of being tarred with the same brush as Mr Mumler and should beware.

W and T Soules, Manufacturing Chemists, Brighton

The most peaceful times in Mina's life were those when she attended the baths for her weekly vapour cure and massage, exercised alone with her dumbbells, or sat at her writing desk on her little wedge-shaped cushion creating harrowing stories. Her most recent tale concerned a man called Seckler, who had fallen victim to a terrible curse. Overnight he had turned into a giant carnivorous insect in which form he attacked the members of his family and devoured them. His neighbour, a deceptively diminutive lady called Miss Lettie, was about to put paid to the monster. Mina had been debating whether her small but formidable heroine should set fire to the creature and watch him burn or dispatch him with a few well-aimed blows of an axe, when she was disturbed by a loud noise.

It was highly unusual to hear running footsteps in her home, but that evening with half an hour still to go before dinnertime there was a frantic thumping on the stairs. The hurried steps were coming her way, and she had little doubt that she would not like whatever it was she was about to learn. Only Richard could have made such a footfall, and she wondered if the letter in the *Gazette* from the Soules brothers had caused a commotion in the shop.

She had laid her pen aside and turned from her desk in anticipation when the door to her room opened rather more abruptly than was normal. Richard stood in the doorway, breathless, as if he had run all the way from Ship Street, which he might well have done. He was clearly very frightened. 'Mina!' he gulped.

She rose to go to him, and he pushed the door shut and leaned against it. 'Richard, what is it?' She took his hands while he composed himself. 'Tell me at once,' she insisted. 'Is someone dead?'

'No, but *I* might have been!'

She quickly looked him up and down but could see nothing obviously the matter. 'Are you hurt?'

'No, no, I am well and unharmed, but Miss Hartop is not. Someone has tried to murder her! I expect all Brighton will know about it before long.'

Mina led her brother into the room, induced him to sit on the edge of the bed, and loosened his collar before it strangled him. She poured a glass of water from the carafe on her night-table, pressed the glass into his hands, and sat beside him. 'Now then,' she said, speaking calmly in an effort to convey some of that calmness to Richard, who was trying not to spill the drink down his shirt front. 'Tell me everything, from the start.'

He nodded and took some deep breaths. As he did so, she studied him more carefully in case there was some injury he was too upset at present to feel but could see no sign of anything other than a general distraction.

At length he was able to speak more evenly. 'You remember I told you that some of Miss Hartop's clients for her mediumship as Lady Brighthelm have left her gifts? She doesn't ask for money, so it's usually little things like a flower, or one of those scented sachets. Well, yesterday she received some chocolates. Veale's violet creams, all done up in some coloured paper with a ribbon. They arrived when she was with a client, so I kept them behind the counter and handed them to her as she was leaving. She opened the paper and offered me one.' He whimpered. 'Thank heaven I detest violet creams, or I might have taken one. If I had, I might not be here now.'

'She did not eat any herself?' asked Mina, with an uncomfortable feeling as to where this account was leading.

Richard blinked. 'Um, well, now you mention it she did put one in her mouth. Just as she was going out.'

There was no inhabitant of Brighton who did not recall with horror and in some detail the dreadful poisoning case of 1871. A Miss Christiana Edmunds had used poisoned chocolates in an attempt to murder the wife of a Doctor Beard, for whom she had developed a wholly inappropriate passion, an emotion which he did not return. Mrs Beard survived, and while there was no definite proof that Miss Edmunds was responsible, her erratic behaviour led to her being suspected of the crime. At this point the love-struck maiden ought to have considered herself fortunate not to be arrested, and left well alone, but instead she decided to deflect suspicion from herself by distributing poisoned chocolates around the town and sending poisoned cakes and fruit to prominent citizens. Her intention was presumably to make it appear that the doctor's wife was simply one victim of another individual's mass poisoning campaign.

These cruelly thoughtless actions had resulted in the tragic death of a small child. Miss Edmunds had purchased her chocolates from Maynards, not Veales, some of which she had adulterated with strychnine and then returned to the shop. She had even complained that she herself had been made ill by poisoned chocolates. Miss Edmunds's theatrical protestations had not, however, deceived Inspector Gibbs of the Brighton police, whose investigations had uncovered the evidence he needed to demonstrate her guilt. She was arrested and tried for murder. The notorious poisoner, having terrified the town into the belief that the days of the Borgias had returned, was currently residing in Broadmoor Insane Asylum from where it was unlikely that she would ever emerge.

'I assume from what you say that Miss Hartop has been taken ill,' said Mina, 'but is there any reason to suspect she has been poisoned?'

Richard rubbed his eyes and nodded. 'She had some appointments this afternoon, and when she didn't come to the shop Beckler asked me to go and see if she was coming. She only lives about ten minutes' walk away; they have one of those big townhouses on the seafront. So I went there and all the house was in a terrible uproar. I spoke to Mr Hartop — he really is the most agreeable fellow — and he was extremely miserable, but he was very forthcoming and told me what had happened. It seems that after today's luncheon she ate another of the chocolates and almost at once complained that it was burning her. He thinks that she only swallowed about half of it. Next minute she was taken dreadfully ill, and they called in Dr McClelland. He was there when I arrived. He has taken charge of the remaining chocolates and they are to be sent to a chemist to be tested for poison. Everyone in the house ate the same luncheon and no one else was ill, so it is thought that if anything was wrong it was the chocolates. And to think I might have had one and eaten all of it. Has that Miss Edmunds escaped from the asylum and is trying her horrid business again?'

Mina squeezed his hand comfortingly. 'I doubt it. But someone might have been inspired by her example. Do you know who gave Miss Hartop the chocolates?'

Richard shook his head. 'No, I didn't see who it was. I had gone to the storeroom to get a frame for a customer, and when I came back, I was told that a messenger boy had come in and left them on the counter saying they were for Lady Brighthelm. No one thought anything of it at the time.'

'We must hope the lady recovers,' said Mina, wondering if Richard would be ordered by his mother to leave photography as too dangerous a profession. She thought of all the poisons Mr Beckler kept in the darkroom, and that reminded her of her one visit there. This in turn suggested where she might obtain further information. 'Now then, my dear, you are looking very hot and rumpled. You must make sure to wash your face and brush your hair and put on a fresh cravat before dinner or you will never hear the end of it.'

Richard nodded gloomily, and though he was fresher of appearance at the dinner table he was unusually quiet. Louisa Scarletti had by now heard rumours of further ghost pictures in Brighton, all of them emanating from Mr Beckler's studio. She was torn between praising the skill and acumen of the young photographer, declaring what a fine thing it was for Richard's career which would undoubtedly lead him to making his fortune, and an unspoken jealousy that she had not been alone in receiving this special favour. She had not seen the other pictures in question but had decided in her own mind that hers was both the first and the finest. If she had read the letter from the Soules brothers, she had chosen to ignore it.

After dinner Louisa demanded Mina's company in the drawing room. Here, the widow spoke in lengthy monologue concerning her late husband, speaking of him with great affection, saying that she could never as long as she lived love another, a theme she repeated rather too often for Mina's comfort. It was late before Mina was able to return to her desk, where she found the card given to her by the doctor's wife, Mrs McClelland, and penned a note inviting her to tea.

'It appears,' said Mrs McClelland, as she prepared to sip her tea, gazing knowingly at Mina over the rim of her cup, 'that we have some secrets to share.'

'Ah, yes, so we do,' said Mina.

They exchanged conspiratorial smiles.

'It does not take an especially observant person to see that you are not on good terms with Mr Beckler,' added Mrs McClelland. 'Your manner towards him suggested to me that there has been some friction between you in the past — an insult, or a quarrel, perhaps —' she gave a tilt of the eyebrow — 'even a broken engagement?'

Mina felt her face grow warm, and she put her teacup down hastily in case the slight tremor of her hand resulted in a spill. Her guest noticed the gesture but made no comment. 'Oh no, nothing of that kind,' said Mina, hastily. 'He did at an earlier meeting pay some attention to me, but I soon discovered that his motives were not honourable. He knows where he stands with me now and is all politeness, but I have no wish to have any but the most distant dealings with him. I have not told any member of my family about this, as my brother is employed by him and I do not want to harm his prospects.'

Mrs McClelland nodded understandingly. 'Then that will be our secret,' she said.

Mina was grateful that her guest was too polite to pry any further. She had probably assumed that Mr Beckler had courted Mina solely for financial reasons and if so, Mina was not going to correct her.

Relieved, Mina refreshed herself with more tea and offered the plate of pastries which she had ordered from the bakery. Mrs McClelland had already eaten one and had no hesitation in helping herself to another.

'My brother told me last night about the sudden illness of Miss Hartop,' said Mina. 'In fact, he was dispatched to her house to enquire after her when she did not appear at the shop, where she had an appointment, and he spoke to Mr Hartop. I do hope she is improving.'

'Then you will know that my husband is the Hartops' doctor and was called to the house,' said Mrs McClelland. 'He applied the necessary treatments. She was extremely ill, but he is now satisfied that she is out of danger.'

'I am pleased to hear it. Richard also told me about a gift of Veale's violet creams that was delivered by a messenger boy. Does your husband believe that they are responsible? Is there another Miss Edmunds in Brighton? Should we all be very afraid?'

Mrs McClelland paused mid-pastry to consider the question. 'That is to be decided,' she said at last. 'One thing I do know: the chocolates looked very fresh, and they were in a new clean bag. They cannot have been purchased long ago.' She paused. 'I could tell you more, but it would be in strict confidence,' she added.

'Of course,' said Mina, encouragingly.

Mrs McClelland finished the last of her pastry and dabbed her lips with a napkin. 'My husband was told that Veale's violet creams are a particular favourite of Miss Hartop's. It appears that she had already consumed two of the chocolates without taking any harm, but yesterday she ate another one. She was talking and eating at the same time, which is a bad habit under the usual circumstances, but on this occasion, it may have inadvertently saved her. She had already bitten into the chocolate and it got stuck in her throat and made her choke. She began to complain that it was burning her. She managed to cough out a piece into a handkerchief and told her maid to throw it on the fire. The maid, being an intelligent girl, kept back the piece as she thought it suspicious. Miss Hartop therefore swallowed only a portion of the chocolate but soon developed alarming symptoms, which I will not describe. The maid gave her milk and water to drink, which was very sensible indeed, and sent for my husband. He was able to establish that all the family had eaten the same luncheon and suffered no ill effects and deduced that if anything she consumed had caused Miss Hartop's illness, it was the chocolate.'

'Does he believe it was poisoned? Or could it have been some fault in the manufacture?'

'He has sent the piece saved by the maid and the remaining chocolates to a chemist to conduct tests. One or two of the others have markings on them which suggest that they have been tampered with. Given this fact and the nature of the symptoms, he is privately of the opinion that poison was added to some of the chocolates, although when and by whom it is at present impossible to know. Judging by the symptoms, he suspects arsenic. Had Miss Hartop eaten the whole one, she might very well have died. If the chemist's report proves him right, it will of course be a police matter.'

More tea and pastries were consumed in a companionable but reflective silence.

Mina received her answer later that day when Richard returned home and told her that a policeman had been to the shop, questioning Mr Beckler and himself about the delivery of the chocolates and the identity of the clients for the mysterious Lady Brighthelm. 'None of them left their names,' he said, 'although I know she recognised young Mr Clover and took quite a fancy to him. And there was Mr Winstanley as well, who I knew because he had come for his photograph not long before.'

'What about the messenger boy?' asked Mina. 'Can he be found so he can describe who gave him the chocolates?'

'Well, I didn't see him. And the gentleman in the shop who did see him didn't leave his name.'

'The man who bought a photograph frame?'

'He didn't buy one. He asked to see one. I showed him a catalogue and it didn't have what he wanted; a larger one than we had at the counter. So I fetched one from the storeroom, but it didn't suit him.' Richard sighed. 'What a depressing business this is.'

'Yes, poor Miss Hartop.'

'I meant work. It's terribly dull.'

'Did the man leave without making any purchase?'

'Yes.'

'Would you know him if you saw him again?'

'That's what the police asked me,' said Richard, mournfully. 'No, I don't remember anything particular about him. Why would I? There was nothing to make him stand out from another man. I suppose he might come in again if he changes his mind.'

'And since there is no criminal charge, it will not be in the newspapers,' said Mina, 'although if he knew of the interest of the police he would surely come forward with his story. I know, why don't you put a nice display of frames in the shop window? With a sign saying there is a bigger selection inside, and customers can order anything they don't see. That might lure him in again.'

'It might. You are full of ideas, Mina.'

'Have there been many such deliveries of gifts to the shop?'

'None, as far as I know. This is the first one I can remember. I know people bring along little gifts to Lady Brighthelm when they consult her, but they hand them to her, so I never see them.'

'Have the police interviewed Veales?'

'I don't know. Did that horrid Miss Edmunds go to them?'

'No, she went to Maynards. And the chocolates when bought were not at fault; she poisoned them herself. The one thing we should be careful of doing,' she went on, 'is suggesting to the public at large that there is a second Miss Edmunds about. You know how people like to panic. But this is undoubtedly an attempt to murder a very specific person, not a general madness as it was with Miss Edmunds, who after she failed to poison Mrs Beard didn't seem to mind who she harmed. Which leaves me with the question, why did someone try to poison Miss Hartop? Did they know the medium was she? Was it Miss Hartop who was their quarry? Or did they just wish to silence Lady Brighthelm? Miss Hartop is a gossip who likes to collect rumours about society, and she may have unwittingly acquired dangerous information which she is passing on. Or, as Lady Brighthelm she has made a guess in one of her readings and hit her mark more accurately than she knows. I suppose the police will interview her when she is well enough. Do we know how she is?'

'Yes, I was sent there again today. Beckler asked me to deliver flowers and a card with our good wishes. I gave them to the maid, Tilly, who is still concerned but says her mistress is strong and will recover. But she is unable to speak at all at present, which as you can imagine, is very trying for her. It was her favourite pastime. She was asked if she had any idea who might have done this, and she just shook her head.' He paused. 'Oh, and there is one other piece of news you ought to have.'

Something in his tone and his glance told Mina she would not enjoy what she was about to hear.

'Beckler received a telegram this morning. Mr Hope arrives in town tomorrow.'

The next day, true to Richard's predictions, he informed Mina that Mr Hope had arrived in Brighton and paid a visit to the shop. The gentleman had admired the window display which featured several of his portraits and a substantial selection of his books, was given a tour of the premises, and inspected the progress made on the painting of the jungle backdrop. 'He was especially pleased with the spirit photographs, which he declared ought to be advertised everywhere,' Richard added.

'Not if the Soules brothers have any part in the debate,' said Mina.

'Oh, he has seen the letter and he laughed at it,' said Richard. 'Told Beckler to take no notice. He has already written to the *Gazette* in reply. And he is writing to all the spiritualist magazines. I have to say, though, when he first arrived, he gave me the unfriendliest look. I have hardly had worse, except from Mr Jordan on account of the fact that he is jealous that Nellie likes me very much better than him.'

'That is not an unreasonable reaction from a husband,' said Mina. 'Did Mr Hope say anything to you?'

'No, he didn't speak to me at all, but he took Beckler into the office for a private interview, and I think I was the subject. Anyhow, it seems that whatever Beckler said to him, he has smoothed it all over. When they came out, I heard Beckler telling Hope that you had been extremely impressed with the picture of Father and he was sure that you were convinced it was genuine.'

'Did he now? Well, I am not sure I am convinced, but I certainly can't explain it, and would very much like to.'

'I really do believe it, Mina,' said Richard, earnestly. 'It is Father's spirit in the picture, I know it is. How could it be anything else?'

'It is certainly his image, I don't deny it,' said Mina.

'Well, there you are! And he was very sorry to hear of Lady Brighthelm's awful illness, especially as Beckler had told him what a promising medium she is, and a veritable magnet for the spirits. There have already been rumours of poison in town, probably due to the police enquiries, which of course we could say nothing about, and the gossips are talking about a second Miss Edmunds and trying to identify the guilty party. So he is going to pay Miss Hartop a visit tomorrow morning, which I am sure will cheer her up.'

CHAPTER FIFTEEN

Mina was surprised the next morning to receive a note from Mr Hartop entreating that she receive him for a private conversation of great importance. She lost no time in responding, stating that he might call on her that afternoon. Whatever he had to say, she felt sure it resulted from the recent visit of Mr Hope to Miss Hartop's bed of sickness, and she hardly liked to imagine what it might be. She rather thought that it would not be a friendly conference. Mina asked Rose to serve tea in the parlour and bring whatever pastries in the house might prove most palatable, and then to remain in the room.

Rose, who had been present at several of Mina's less friendly conversations and was clearly from her expression expecting another such confrontation, brought a laden tea tray with a generous pile of strawberry tartlets. It was a cheerful sight. Cook's heavy hands made light pastry, and one could hardly go wrong with jam and fruit.

Mina had never met Mr Hartop, but Richard had spoken well of him. He was a small gentleman, not a great deal more than 5 feet in height, but with a well-proportioned and active figure. He was about sixty-five years of age, with grey hair thin on the crown and a short, neat beard. He greeted Mina and when she offered him a seat, took it with alacrity and regarded her with an interested stare. He declined the offer of a strawberry tart, and on being served a cup of tea, held it in his hands and stared down at it as if uncertain what to do with it next. Eventually, he placed it rather gingerly on a side table.

'Miss Scarletti,' he began, in a business-like manner, 'it is very good of you to receive me at such short notice.'

Mina offered what she hoped was a friendly smile. 'It is very good of you to come. I believe we have matters of some significance to us both to discuss.'

'We do, but I confess I hardly know where to begin.'

Mina waited a little and sipped her tea, but he appeared unable to gather his thoughts. 'Please begin by reassuring me that Miss Hartop is making a good recovery.'

He blinked and nodded. 'She is, yes, thank you. The symptoms when they struck were quite violent and distressing, but they were also short-lived, and thereafter it was a matter of rest and getting her strength back. The only concern is —' He paused, then glanced at his tea and back at Mina, who was alternately drinking her tea and eating a strawberry tartlet with as much delicacy as she could manage, since cook had been generous with the jam. 'Dr McClelland has said that she has suffered damage to her throat as a result of something corrosive in nature. She was unable to speak at all at first but is now able to converse in a whisper. We don't know how much her voice will recover, but we hope that further improvement is possible. This means that for the time being she is unable to continue her calling as a medium.'

Mina nodded. 'I am glad to know that she is out of danger. I never consulted her as a medium, although my brother Richard told me that she enjoyed some success.'

'Ah yes, your brother.' There was an awkward pause. 'Hannah speaks very highly of him. She speaks of him quite often, and I had the impression — in fact, I was quite sure — that she had developed a strong liking for him.'

'That is understandable,' said Mina. 'Richard can be very charming and is well-liked by all his friends.'

181

'He visited us on two occasions, bringing gifts and good wishes from Mr Beckler, and I must say on that on brief acquaintance I thought him a very polite and pleasant young man. I confess that I was wondering if the friendship might become something more, but I now believe, and Hannah's maid Tilly has indicated to me as much, that the — interest, for want of a better word, was all on the side of my daughter. Is that the case?'

'I am sorry to disappoint you, but I can confirm that that is the case.'

Mr Hartop did not appear disappointed, or even very surprised. 'Well, one cannot force affection. The fact is, I have to be very careful of my daughter. Most fathers are, of course, but in Hannah's case, any man seeking to marry her will undoubtedly be aware that she may expect a substantial settlement. Last year a young gentleman, apparently respectable, asked my permission to pay his addresses to her. I decided to make enquiries about him, and it was a good thing I did. I discovered that he had heavy gambling debts and little inclination to change his ways, so I sent him packing.'

Mina could say nothing about this, but simply nodded, grateful that Mr Hartop had not made similar enquiries about Richard.

'I believe,' continued Mr Hartop, 'that Hannah has been much admired recently by a young man who consulted her in her capacity as a medium. A Mr Septimus Clover. Do you know the gentleman?'

'No, we have never met.'

'I know of him,' said Mr Hartop, but without displaying any enthusiasm. 'He comes from a good family, professional gentlemen, well-known in the county, but — it is a family that has had its troubles.' He sighed. 'And he is very young, too young for Hannah, hardly more than a student. He has no special prospects given that, as you can guess from his name, he is a younger son.'

Mina drained her teacup and refilled it. Mr Hartop glanced at his but did not touch it. 'Is there something the matter with your tea, Mr Hartop? I do hope a wasp has not got into it. They can be very persistent at this time of year.'

'Er, no, it is — perfectly good, thank you.' He paused for thought. 'I understand that you are acquainted with Viscount Hope, the author and explorer, Mr Arthur Wallace Hope as he prefers to be known.'

Mina did her best to keep her voice steady. 'I am. We have met on a number of occasions.'

'He came to visit my daughter this morning. He had heard from Mr Beckler of her development as a medium, and he was both delighted for her achievements and concerned for her health. He wanted to know if the rumours of poison were true, and I was obliged to inform him that a chemist has just confirmed that a chocolate given to Hannah contained arsenic in potentially fatal amounts and it was fortunate that she had not swallowed all of it. He was extremely shocked to hear it.

'I told him how much I appreciated the support of Mr Beckler. I also chanced to mention that your brother had kindly visited my home with gifts for Hannah and that she is friends with you both. The moment I said that, I could see that Mr Hope was not pleased. He told me, with the greatest candour and sincerity, that he was very unhappy that your brother was working for his associate Mr Beckler, whom he regards as a promising young businessman and a psychic sensitive of almost limitless potential.

'He also told me that you are a great enemy to spirit mediums; that you do all that lies in your power to harm their

183

work and put a stop to their séances. I recalled then reading in the newspapers last year that you had given evidence at the trial of some mediums, but that the persons concerned were making money out of people by fraudulent means. I did not think you could be an enemy to my daughter, as she does not seek any reward.'

'I do not regard myself as an enemy to mediums,' said Mina. 'I am an enemy to those who use deception to profit from another's grief. The mediums I denounced in court had already been publicly exposed as frauds, so mine was not the only word against them — there were many witnesses — but Mr Hope continues to believe in them despite abundant proof of their crimes.'

'He told me that you are a materialist,' said Mr Hartop, accusingly, 'that you believe only in what you see or hear or touch or what science can prove. That you deny the world of the spirit.'

'I go to church, Mr Hartop. I read the Bible and I pray. I do not deny the world of the spirit. My mind is open. If I were to receive a message from my late father which I knew could only come from him, then I would welcome it.'

Mr Hartop hesitated, as if bracing himself. 'He went on to advise me in the strongest possible terms that any friendship between my daughter and your family must cease at once. He suggested that you were a danger to her. In fact —' he took a deep breath — 'he asked me if I could be quite certain that you and your brother were not behind the attempt on my daughter's life.'

Mina was momentarily speechless. Thus far, the conversation had proceeded much as she had expected, but she now quite suddenly understood her visitor's reluctance to eat or drink the refreshments he had been offered. 'I hardly know how to answer that,' she said at last. 'I can give you verbal assurances, of course, that neither I nor my brother have had any thought of causing harm to your daughter, but I understand that since we have only just met, you must weigh what I say against the pronouncements of Mr Hope. But we will cease the association if that is any comfort to you.'

Mr Hartop nodded. He gazed at Mina for some moments, then abruptly rose and paced about the room. At last he turned to face her, with fresh resolve in his expression. 'I will tell you something of myself, Miss Scarletti, so that you will better understand me. I started my working life very young, as a boot-boy in a hotel where my father was doorman. Through diligence I achieved better employment over time. As a young man, and newly married, my wife and I became housekeepers at a Brighton lodging house. But I had ambitions, and I could see where the real opportunities lay. We led a frugal life, accumulated some modest savings, and eventually I was able to purchase a small house which was in a very dilapidated state. Over many months I became builder, carpenter, decorator, whatever was required of me, to restore the house to good condition in order that I might let it. And with that income, I was eventually able to buy another property, and restore that one, and so it went on, until you see me now, a man of substance, every bit of it of my own making, much of it from my own hands' labour.

'I have met many people in my business life, honest men and flagrant cheats, rich and poor, high and low, and I have learned to judge them, not by their monetary worth or any position they might have inherited, but by their characters, the way they treat others. And one thing I will not tolerate is someone, however wealthy, however important, however noble, who sees fit to come to me at my home and give me orders as to what I may or may not do.' With that, Mr Hartop returned to his seat, picked up his tea, and drained the cup almost at a gulp.

'Thank you for your trust in me,' said Mina, although she was sure the tea drinking was just a gesture, as she had already drunk two cups.

'Mr Hope's insinuations were nothing short of malicious,' Mr Hartop continued. 'I can tell you now that I was horrified, not only by his words, but the manner in which he delivered them. I pointed out to him that the chocolates were not a gift from you but were brought to the shop by a messenger boy, who is currently being sought by the police. Mr Hope demanded a description of the boy, but I informed him that the only person who saw him was a customer in the shop who is also being sought to give evidence. When he asked who saw the customer, I was obliged to say that it was your brother.

'At that, Mr Hope laughed. He declared that it was all a trick; a story invented by you, as he does not believe your brother to be capable of devising such a clever deception. In his opinion, there was no messenger boy and no customer. He claimed that you poisoned the chocolates and gave them to your brother to leave on the counter when no one else was present, and then schooled him to tell the story of the customer and the boy. I tried to protest that this was all speculation, but Mr Hope was not to be interrupted in his denouncements. He then, on a sudden thought, told me that the last time he had encountered you he had been taken very ill, and at the time he had put it down to a bad bottle of brandy, but that now he was not so sure.'

Mina hoped that Mr Hartop would not notice any change in her expression, or if he did, he would simply view it as her natural alarm at the mere idea. In this instance, Mr Hope was correct on more than one point, since he had been dangerously ill after drinking brandy during his visit to Hollow House the previous January, and he had been poisoned. Richard had been suffering from a toothache, and Dr Hamid had given him some drops with instructions to rub a little on his gums to deaden the pain. When Mr Hope inexplicably lapsed into unconsciousness, Richard confessed that he had added the drops to that gentleman's glass of brandy. His intention was to place Mr Hope in a sound sleep, thus preventing him from pressing his unwanted attentions on Nellie. Only Dr Hamid's swift action had saved the man's life.

'When I was able to get a word in,' said Mr Hartop, 'I protested to Mr Hope that he had no evidence that you even had poison, but he said that there was a packet of white arsenic in the darkroom at Mr Beckler's shop, and he knew that you had been in there. He then announced that he would go to the police and let them know of his suspicions. And then he departed.

'When I next visited Hannah, I found that she had heard the loud conversation and she demanded to know what had been said. I had the choice of upsetting her by repeating the information or upsetting her by withholding it. I chose the former, as she was becoming very agitated. She said she was sure that neither of you would want to do such a terrible thing to anyone, least of all herself, and she begged me to go and see you so you could be warned about what Mr Hope was saying about you. I have no doubt that he will be repeating his slanders in private to his friends.'

'I am very grateful to you, Mr Hartop,' said Mina, warmly. 'You ought to know that Mr Hope has made previous attempts to discredit me without success. He cannot bear any opposition to his views, and his response is to try and crush his opponents by any means at his disposal. I expected that he might make another attempt on his return to Brighton, although I did not know how. At least now I know the nature of his actions. I assume he will not publish these accusations generally about town, and in any statement to the police he will have disguised them as merely the suspicions of a concerned citizen. Anything further and I promise you he will find himself in court.'

Mr Hartop nodded his agreement but with an expression of deep misery flooding his eyes. 'The one thing I cannot deny is that the poison was meant for my daughter, no one else. And think as I might, I cannot imagine why anyone might want to harm her. She is such a kind-hearted, well-meaning, inoffensive soul.'

'Do the police have any theories?'

'No, they have interviewed all the family and talked to her friends, but if there are no clues, no apparent motive, what can they do? Can it be the work of another Miss Edmunds, in which case no one is safe? I believe that lady went into shops and left poisoned sweets behind, caring nothing for who ate them. And she sent poisoned food to notables in the town.' He sighed. 'I rather think, when all is done, it will be proven to be the work of a maniac. A jealous person, perhaps. Or a man disappointed in love who dislikes all single ladies. Perhaps the police think that, too, in which case they must be waiting for another crime.'

'We must hope the culprit is caught soon,' said Mina, 'and before anyone else can fall victim.'

'At least I am now on my guard, and will protect my daughter at all costs,' he said, sitting up and squaring his shoulders as if for battle.

'Might I ask you about the spirit photograph, Mr Hartop?'

'Yes, of course.'

'Do you believe the spirit portrayed is that of your late wife?'

He gave this question careful thought before he answered. 'I can only say that I see no reason why it should not be she.'

'Do you have a photograph for comparison?'

'Regrettably, no. My dear wife passed away some twenty years ago. The only images we have are those that we hold in our memories of her.'

'Thank you for your openness, Mr Hartop. I will advise my brother that he ought not to visit your house again, at least while the criminal remains free. The visits were under the instructions of Mr Beckler who must be advised of the situation. And please do accept my warmest wishes for Miss Hartop's full recovery to good health. If I have anything further to impart, would you permit me to write to you?'

'Yes, please do. And I will let you know of anything I learn in the matter.'

The interview ended with expressions of goodwill from both parties.

Mina was left wondering what she might do about Mr Hope's insinuations, but there seemed to be nothing she could do but wait and see if he dared stoop to slander or worse. She reminded herself of his many ardent supporters, even in Brighton. It would be hard, if matters turned only on the spoken word, to prove a case.

When Richard returned from work, Mina was obliged to tell him what had transpired, but as he reeled from the information, she added a stern warning to take no action against Mr Hope, since anything other than ignoring him might attract more suspicion.

'If the delivery boy could only be found!' she exclaimed. 'The boys who ran errands for Miss Edmunds were discovered easily enough. Or perhaps it was not one of the usual messengers but a young relative sworn to silence or bribed. And the gentleman customer. Where is he? Can you recall anything at all about him? His age, perhaps? Old, young, middling?'

Richard shrugged. 'Middling, I suppose. I mean, not a boy but then not an old man.'

'There was nothing unusual in his appearance?'

'No. I can't recall anything of his features at all. I didn't really study him. Why would I?'

Mina tried to recall anything she knew about the customer. 'You said he asked to see a larger picture frame than the ones you had in the shop. That would be an expensive item?'

'Well, yes, but we didn't have one of the size he wanted.'

'What size was that?'

'I can't remember. I don't think he said a size. Just bigger than the ones we had.'

'He didn't bring a picture he needed framing?'

'No.'

'But he looked well able to afford the expense?'

'Oh, yes, he —' Richard pondered this. 'Now you mention it, I suppose he was well-dressed and groomed. Not short of a shilling or two. I did wonder why he had come to us and not to Mr Mayall.'

'Perhaps he had already been to Mayall's and not found what he wanted. But I am sure the police will be asking at all the photographer's shops in Brighton, so they should find him eventually, and then Mr Hope's theories will be proven false.'

'Perhaps the fellow was a ghost, and he has vanished?'

Mina gave him hard look. 'He might as well be. And in the meantime, it would be best if you did not visit Miss Hartop again. You must tell Mr Beckler that this has been agreed with her father, and when Mr Hope next comes to the shop, arrange to be somewhere out of his way. I shall not be content until he has left Brighton.'

Richard had no difficulty in agreeing to Mina's suggestions.

'I suppose it was inevitable that he would come to Brighton to visit his disciples,' she added drily. 'I can only hope that his stay will not be long, and he will not outrage decency while he is here.'

'I think he might be here for some weeks,' said Richard. 'He is planning to give a series of lectures at the Town Hall. Actually, I think Beckler is dreading his visit more than you.'

'What do you mean?' demanded Mina, surprised. 'He worships the ground the man treads on. He revels in his favour. Mr Beckler is a leading warrior in Mr Hope's army, engaged to destroy all his enemies.'

'Not all, surely,' Richard hinted, but Mina refused to be drawn. 'Well, it's mostly true, I mean the admiration, but sometimes I think Beckler is frightened of him.'

'If he isn't, he certainly ought to be,' said Mina. 'If he doesn't toady up to Mr Hope and do his bidding, he will be thrown aside, or even ruined. Well, that is his choice, and he must live with it.'

'We're expecting Hope back at the shop very soon,' said Richard. 'Beckler insists it is scoured daily, so I have become a maid of all work and a destroyer of dust. Have no fear, I will take care to hide my cuffs from Mother. But it is not all bad. Beckler wants to take a picture of his illustrious patron leading his expedition through the jungle, so he is buying a big curtain and a lot of paint, and I am to start on a backdrop as soon as we have them. And the new window display...' He paused.

'Don't tell me; I can imagine it. Heaps of books.'

'Mina, dear, I think it would be better if you didn't come to the shop while Mr Hope is in Brighton. You don't want to risk meeting with him again and having another quarrel.'

'Especially as losing to a woman makes him so angry,' said Mina. 'But rest assured I have no reason to go to the shop again, and will stay well away from it, and Mr Hope and Mr Beckler too. In fact, I would wish them both to live on the other side of the world, as far away from me as they can be. If I could send them to the moon, I would do so. But when Mr Hope found you working there, he must have objected on my account? Did he not demand that you should be dismissed?'

On considering this possibility, Mina found that she was divided within herself. While she was unhappy that Richard was working for a man she detested, the situation did have its advantages. First of all, there was the important fact that Richard actually had regular paid employment in a respectable business that did not have to be concealed from their mother, a situation that had not always been the case in the past. It also meant that he was an avenue of information as to what Mr Beckler and Mr Hope were plotting, and therefore a means of keeping herself forewarned and forearmed against her enemy.

Richard gave one of his airy, confident smiles. 'Oh no, Beckler said I was not to worry about that. Whatever you might think, he is still very sweet on you, Mina, and I think he will do what he can to advance me for your sake. In fact, I rather think one of the reasons he employed me was to get to know you better. But of course —' he gave himself a proud pat on the chest — 'I am indispensable to his business now. It's not only the backdrop painting. I thought I would try my hand at tinting photographs to colour eyes and hair and gowns, and make the ladies look generally prettier. It doesn't really work with gentlemen, of course, and babies always look hideous whatever you do. Anyhow, I undertook some and he liked what I did, and thinks that it will be a great novelty.'

'As long as he doesn't ask you to paint ghosts,' said Mina, although she did not mean it seriously.

Richard raised his eyebrows.

'He hasn't asked you to do that, has he?' she said, in sudden concern.

'No,' said Richard, thoughtfully, 'but now you mention it, I can see how that could be done.'

'As an amusement, perhaps, a novelty like those ugly caricatures of people with large heads, but not to be sold as genuine, to delude and defraud customers,' Mina warned him. 'Richard, please promise me you won't do any work of that sort. In fact, whatever happens, you must not get involved in anything to do with producing or selling or advertising ghost pictures. Especially after that letter from the Soules brothers. You don't want to end up in court like Mr Mumler. I am hoping that that letter will put paid to the whole thing, and Mr Beckler will be obliged to avoid arrest by returning to his less controversial trade.'

Richard gave her a sulky look as he always did when he felt she was spoiling his fun.

CHAPTER SIXTEEN

Mina was left with a puzzle. Mr Hartop's words still echoed in her head, and when she thought about them, she had to agree, there was no obvious reason why anyone should wish serious harm to Miss Hartop. While the crime had nothing to do with Mina or Richard, she hoped it would be solved soon, to put an end to Mr Hope's ridiculous insinuations. Was it simply the random act of a maniac, she wondered, or could there be some reason behind it? Murders — and this was undoubtedly an attempt at murder — were usually committed for the old reasons of love and money. If removing Miss Hartop would elevate another person to a rich legacy, that would be a good motive, but Mr Hartop would surely know if that was so and would have told the police. Did Miss Hartop stand in the way of another person's affections? Did the ardent Septimus Clover have an admirer jealous of his visits to the medium? That was a possibility, and a situation Mr Hartop would have known nothing about.

Mina turned to the Brighton Directory, where she found W Clover and Sons, Architects and Surveyors, Upper North Street Brighton. Mr Hartop had said that young Septimus was from a good family, but he had hinted at something else, something about them with which he was not entirely comfortable. She examined the lists of burials in the Extra Mural Cemetery and found only one under that name, a Mrs Elizabeth Clover, in 1867.

Septimus Clover was clearly not the gentleman who had asked for the picture frame and seen the messenger boy bring the chocolates. From Mr Hartop's description he was too young, and in any case, Richard would have recognised him. Mina toyed briefly with the idea of Mr Clover adopting a disguise, either as the unknown gentleman or even the messenger boy, but dismissed both ideas as the stuff of fiction, the kind of ploy that worked so much better on the pages of a novel than it did in reality. Disguise, as her friend the popular actor Marcus Merridew had told her, was an art requiring many years to perfect. An attempt by an amateur with badly fitting wigs and false beards would produce results both unconvincing and laughable.

Even before Mr Hartop's visit, Mina had expected that Mr Hope's return to Brighton would mark the end of Richard's employment at Mr Beckler's studio, and despite her brother's airy confidence she was now quite certain that before too long he would be dismissed. As he always did under such circumstances, he would do his best to conceal the news from Mina for as long as possible and from his mother altogether.

Mina therefore determined to look for the signs each day on his return home for dinner. The clearest indication would be a change in his conversation. He would become abruptly unforthcoming about the events of the day and deliberately vague when questioned. It would only be when Mina spoke to him privately and took him to task about his situation that he would be forced to admit the truth. She was therefore surprised when Richard returned home the next day in a buoyantly talkative mood.

'Well, it seems I am making some sound advances in my career!' he announced at the dinner table, helping himself to wine and piling his plate with meat and vegetables.

Louisa Scarletti glowed. 'I had no doubt that you would.'

'I have been painting a new backdrop for the studio, and Mr Beckler is very pleased indeed with the result. In fact, he has paid me a bonus for the work, and has asked me to do more of them. He said that even Mr Mayall has nothing so fine.'

Mina suspected an ulterior motive for this generosity, but said nothing. She feared that Mr Hope must be keeping Richard close the better to observe him, the better to destroy them both.

Louisa did not protest when half a roast bird was served on her plate and began attacking it energetically with knife and fork. 'I saw Mrs Peasgood today and she told me that a friend of hers went to see your new medium, Lady Brighthelm, but was told that she was unwell and has had to stop. She was very disappointed, as she had heard good things of her.'

Richard and Mina exchanged glances. Richard was about to say something, but Mina quickly silenced him with a frown and a shake of the head. She was about to make some anodyne comment on the situation when their mother continued, 'And there is a rumour going about town that Lady Brighthelm is so very wonderful that she puts all other mediums to shame, and the reason she is ill is because a rival medium tried to poison her with chocolates.'

Mina had no doubts as to where that story came from. Her determination not to alarm the public with rumours of poison was clearly not shared by Mr Hope. He would be making sure all of Brighton knew of it. 'I have heard it too,' she said, 'but I take no notice of it. In fact, I have it on the best authority that the story of the rival medium is quite untrue and has been put about by the friends of Lady Brighthelm in order to increase her fame.' Mina felt confident that her mother was more interested in the content of the rumour than the source and would not question it. All the same, she saw that her mother was as ever not happy about being contradicted. Fortunately, she was devouring roast chicken and was unable to protest. There was only one thing to do, and in the brief interlude available Mina seized her chance. 'In fact,' she continued, 'there is another rumour which I do believe, that a young gentleman who consulted Lady Brighthelm has fallen violently in love with her and the poisoner is a lady to whom he is affianced.'

Richard was so startled he dropped his fork. 'Really?' he exclaimed.

Mina ignored him. 'The persons concerned are all prominent names in Brighton society, and it will be very scandalous when it comes out.'

'Oh, my word!' said her mother.

'Apparently, when the young man thought that Lady Brighthelm would spurn him, he flew into a passion and threatened to cut his throat with a razor. But she did not spurn him, and they have been exchanging love tokens, several times a day.'

'The scoundrel, he is promised to another!' Louisa objected.

'He is, but he did not tell Lady Brighthelm of this, so she is wholly innocent in the matter and has been sadly deluded. When he tried to break his engagement, the father of the betrothed lady threatened him with a gun, but he said he would rather die than live without the woman he loves.'

'How dreadful!'

'It is said that in a fit of desperation the young lady decided to follow the example of Miss Edmunds and sent poisoned sweetmeats to Lady Brighthelm, who, thinking they were a gift from her admirer, ate one.'

'Shocking!'

Mina leaned forward earnestly. 'But this is all very, very secret. You must tell no one.'

Louisa was silent for some time, and Mina, feeling sure her mother was busy deciding which of her friends she was going to tell first, smiled.

'Mina, is any of that true?' demanded Richard after dinner.

'Of course it isn't. Most rumours are falsehoods and exaggeration. I just made it all up.'

'But — but, you know what Mother is like! She'll tell everyone she knows!'

'I am counting on it. The only way I could crush Mr Hope's story, which was a deliberate attack on me, was to oppose it with a far better one. If Mr Hope wants a storytelling war, he has one, and I am determined that he will lose it.'

Richard was not reassured. 'I hope Mr Clover will not hear your story and think it is about him. He came in today to ask about Lady Brighthelm, as he had heard the same rumour Mother heard. He was extremely agitated.'

'Agitated?' queried Mina. 'Not just concerned? Why was that?'

'I don't know.'

'What did you tell him?'

'I am on strict orders from Beckler. If anyone asks about Lady Brighthelm, I am to say only that we have been told that she is indisposed, and we know no more than that.'

'Have there been many such enquiries?'

'Yes, customers asking after her and offering good wishes for her recovery. That sort of thing. Some of them asked who the rival medium was, the rumoured poisoner. I didn't tell them it was you.'

'Thank you. Was Mr Clover the only person who was disturbed?'

'Yes. He even asked me where Lady Brighthelm lived and if she was well enough to receive clients at home.'

'I hope you didn't tell him.'

'No. I said she had given up being a medium. He said he was sorry to hear it and went away.'

Mina was thoughtful. 'Miss Hartop recognised Mr Clover through her veil, but do you think he knew who Lady Brighthelm really is? If he knew she was Miss Hartop, he could have found her father's address in the directory.'

Richard thought for a moment. 'I don't think he did know. I saw her in the veil once; you couldn't see through it from a distance. And she put on a foreign accent.'

'What sort of foreign accent?'

'It was hard to tell. And it was a different one every day.'

'Then her clients might not have been able to guess it was she?'

'Is that important?'

'It is. Because it suggests that the attempt was not made on Miss Hartop but on Lady Brighthelm, the medium. And I find it hard to believe that a rival medium would feel so threatened that he or she would plan murder.'

'Then why — who?'

'Miss Hartop is a collector of news and gossip and scandal about the notables in Brighton. She talks about it all the time. I think she made use of this as Lady Brighthelm, and it enabled her to make some good guesses even about things she didn't know. She must have appeared to know a great deal by psychic means. Supposing she guessed at something or even partly knew something which one of her clients found so threatening they decided she must be silenced?'

Richard sighed. 'We can't go and ask her, can we? We promised not to be friends anymore. But she probably doesn't even know what it was herself. I swear she never listens to a thing she says.'

'Whatever it was, it impressed someone,' said Mina. 'People hang onto every word of a medium. They see meanings that were never there and put aside what doesn't suit them. Does Mr Clover have secrets he wishes to keep concealed?' She paused for thought. 'There was something Mr Hartop said to me. He knew nothing against Mr Clover personally, but there is some shadow on his family.'

'Then we should have nothing to do with them, if they are going about poisoning mediums,' said Richard. 'I know you say you're not one, but they might think it.'

'At least if the target was Lady Brighthelm and they don't know her true identity, she is safe for now,' said Mina. She wondered if there was something she ought to do. Her new rumour should throw Mr Hope's into obscurity, and her concern about the Clover family might be unfounded. 'Have the police been to the shop recently?'

'Yes, one fellow came in, and he went into the office to talk to Beckler. And he asked to see the appointment book.'

'But the people who came to see Lady Brighthelm did not leave their names?'

'No, not to be written down, but some were customers we already knew.'

'What about Mr Clover?'

'Oh, we had a whole patch of Clovers last month. Gentlemen partners in business. Gathered round some sort of certificate they all looked very proud of.'

Respectable, honest and trustworthy, thought Mina. *A reputation to protect. But would they kill to protect it?*

Mina found two new letters waiting for her, one of which was in the printed envelope of Scarletti Publishing, while the other was engraved with the name and address of Inskip Law, her brother-in-law's firm. He had never written to her before, and she opened this first with some curiosity.

Inskip Law
Piccadilly
London

Dear Mina,

I trust this finds you well. Enid and our dear children are in the most perfect bloom of health. After my ordeals I am happy that I have been spared to take care of them. My rides on the new velocipede are the best possible exercise to preserve my strength. I hope we will be able to visit Brighton more often to enjoy the wonderful weather and fresh air.

Please do tell Mrs Scarletti she has no need to be concerned about wolves, which can be noble creatures when one gets to know them. She is, however, most unlikely to encounter one, except in zoological gardens where in my opinion, they really ought not to be confined.

On our last visit you made mention of the Porterson-White case, with which I was not personally familiar; however, in view of your interest I did mention it to a business acquaintance, and he gave me some further information. I was astonished to learn that the enmity between the two cousins is still unresolved. One of them resides in London, where he has business interests which keep him there; however, the other is in Brighton. When Miss Porterson-White went to live in Brighton for her health he also went there, in order to be near her and take care of her if need be. I believe the London cousin may have been an occasional visitor. Each of the cousins has accused the other of attempting to ingratiate himself with the lady and besmirching the reputation of his rival in order to inherit all her fortune. Each has accused the other of finding and destroying the will, although there is no proof that a will ever existed.

I have also heard it rumoured that the cousin who was her favourite was actually no better than the other, only he concealed it more skilfully and only went to live in Brighton so as to get into the lady's good books. I doubt that we will ever know the truth of it.

Following her demise, and the declaration of intestacy, both have gone to law. One of them even consulted a spirit medium, although with what result I do not know. I fear that the dispute may continue until one of the cousins dies, and as they are both under forty, we could well find that when the time comes to distribute the inheritance all the estate has been absorbed by costs.

Yours respectfully,
Peter Inskip

Mina could only shake her head at this foolish demonstration of avarice when all might have been settled with a simple handshake. She opened Edward's letter, hoping for better news.

Dear Mina,

I hope this finds you and all the family well.

I have been asking some business associates who are knowledgeable in the art of photography how the picture of Father might have been accomplished, assuming of course that it was not a genuine spirit picture. I had my doubts about it from the start because there are so many persons willing to make their fortunes by underhand means, and there is something about the photographer in this case that arouses my suspicions. There is a London man doing something very similar and attracting criticism.

My friends made a close examination of the picture and I was assured that it was not produced by the means of any paint, or any art applied after it had been printed. I was asked if some double of my father could have been concealed in the studio, behind a curtain, perhaps, and crept out to stand there while we were all instructed to look at the camera, then concealed himself again. I did note that there was a curtain in the room, but whether there was enough space behind it where a man might stand without being discovered, I do not know. They also asked me if I noticed any unusual actions on the part of the photographer as the photographs were being taken. Was the lens cap removed only the once for each picture or was there a second exposure? Was more than one article inserted in the camera? I replied that I did not see anything of that sort, but then of course I was not looking for it.

They did ask me if the image of Father resembled in any way a portrait he had had taken in the past. Had that been the case, an old picture might have been used to impose it on the new one, possibly during printing. I was obliged to say that the image did not remind me of any former portrait, although this thought did produce an old memory of seeing him dressed as he appeared in the picture. Perhaps you can recall something of the sort? Or you might have been too young.

I remain mystified but still unconvinced.

Affect'ly

Edward

CHAPTER SEVENTEEN

'There is a policeman to see you,' said Rose to Mina, a few days later, her normally impassive face showing an apprehensive cast.

'Ah,' said Mina. There was a time when she would have immediately feared that such a visit heralded the fact that Richard had disgraced himself in some way, but now she feared that due to Mr Hope scattering rumours, it was she who was under suspicion.

'An Inspector Gibbs. He seems like a very gentlemanly person.'

'Really?' said Mina. This was oddly exciting news. She had never met Inspector Gibbs, but she had read his evidence in the Christiana Edmunds trial. It was his sound instincts, insight, and imaginative and industrious investigation that had led the poisoner to the dock and eventually Broadmoor. He had employed a particularly clever ruse, writing to Miss Edmunds and, on receiving a reply, comparing her handwriting to that on the address labels of parcels of poisoned foodstuffs. 'Please, show him into the parlour. I will speak with him. Bring tea if he wishes it.'

A minute or two later Inspector Gibbs was comfortably settled in the parlour, with all the ease of a frequent visitor. He was a respectable-looking man of about forty, with dark curly hair and nicely trimmed whiskers. 'No, thank you, no refreshments,' he said with a smile. 'I have made a good many calls today, and if I was to accept any more hospitality I would not be able to enjoy my wife's good dinner when I go home.'

'How may I help you?' asked Mina. She was doing her best to be accommodating without appearing over-eager, which might, judging by Gibbs's concerns when he called on Miss Edmunds, have aroused his suspicion.

'I am sure that you are aware of the subject of my enquiries, since I have already interviewed your brother concerning the unfortunate case of Lady Brighthelm, and the chocolates delivered to Mr Beckler's shop.'

'I am, of course.'

'The chocolates were from the stock of Veale's Confectioners, and I am speaking to everyone who has purchased from them recently. I understand that you made a purchase a few days ago.'

'Yes, I did. I bought a quarter of a pound of vanilla creams. I can tell you the date I did so if you like. I can recall it exactly, since it was the same day that I met with my friend Mrs Jordan — she is the wife of Mr Jordan of Jordan and Conroy's Emporium — and we paid a visit to the Extra Mural Cemetery. I know she enjoys sweet treats and so I bought some chocolates for us to share as we walked along.' Mina had brought her diary to the parlour and provided the date of her purchase, which was two days before the poisoned violet creams were sent to the photographer's shop. 'Do Veale's keep a record of what individual customers purchase?'

'Only if the customer has an account with them. Some households make regular purchases and pay monthly. Some might send a servant with a large order to be delivered. And the assistants remember regular customers and their preferences. Other than that, they simply replenish the stocks on display and keep a record of quantities to determine when a new order is due.'

'So an individual purchase such as mine…' Mina paused. 'I suppose the assistants were able to describe me. I am aware of course, since my brother mentioned it, that the delivery to the shop consisted of violet creams. I do hope you will find the culprit.'

'As do I. Have you purchased from Veale's before?'

'No, that was my first and only visit. And our household has no account with them. If you wish to view our purchases, you may. I make a regular inspection of our household expenses and I will ask cook to show you our record book if you would like to see it.'

He smiled and made a detailed note. 'I have already seen Veale's accounts. Your name is not included. The main sales of chocolate creams are vanilla. The violet and rose are fortunately fewer. But I feel as if I have traced every single violet cream in Brighton, including a small box Mrs Veale herself gave to Lady Brighthelm only a week ago. Every single one has either been consumed without harm, or if not, has been examined and found to be untampered with.'

'And you have not discovered the delivery boy or the man who was in the shop when the delivery was made?'

'I regret not, although of course our enquiries continue. It is very possible that the customer was a visitor to Brighton who has since left.'

'I would have thought that after the case of Miss Edmunds, an anonymous delivery of chocolates would be a memorable event,' said Mina.

'It certainly would. Of course, Miss Edmunds did repeat her purchases and draw attention to herself, which is not the case here.'

'After her first attempt on Mrs Beard, Miss Edmunds did not care whom she poisoned. This person may have wanted to poison only Lady Brighthelm and having succeeded will not offend again.'

'I sincerely hope not, although I am sorry to say it would make my task easier if she, or possibly he, did. We don't want to alarm the public, but since there have already been rumours of a second Miss Edmunds it would do no harm and some good to issue a police warning notice in the newspapers.'

'You said that Mrs Veale brought a gift to Lady Brighthelm?'

'Yes, chocolates, all of which were eaten.'

'But they were in a box, not a bag?' asked Mina, recalling the pretty boxes she had seen in Veale's shop window.

'Yes, a decorative pasteboard box. We saw it amongst the trinkets and gewgaws on the medium's table. Once the chocolates were eaten, she used it for the little gifts of coins some of the customers pressed on her.'

Mina ruminated on this. 'Then is it possible that the customers who came to consult her might have noticed the box, and could have guessed that she might enjoy a gift of chocolates, and Veale's violet creams in particular?'

Inspector Gibbs paused and stared at Mina.

'I am sorry,' said Mina, 'I have no wish to offend you. It is not my place to question you, rather the other way around. I am sure this is something you have already considered.'

'Er — yes,' he said, thoughtfully. 'You have not consulted Lady Brighthelm, I believe?'

'I have not. I think it would be easy to confirm that.'

'And neither has your brother?'

'No. The lady was somewhat sweet on him, and had he done so we would never have heard the end of it.'

Inspector Gibbs smiled and closed his notebook.

Once the policeman had departed, Mina reflected that during the interview no mention had been made of Mr Hope, which was probably to the good. She was left with the feeling that she would no longer be the subject of police enquiries, and it was an extremely fortunate thing that she had purchased vanilla and not violet creams and had Nellie as a witness to the fact.

Richard had mentioned that violet creams were a particular favourite of Miss Hartop, but only a limited number of people might have known this and deduced that Miss Hartop and Lady Brighthelm were one and the same. The presence of Veale's chocolate box on the medium's table, however, opened up further possibilities.

'I had a visit from Inspector Gibbs today,' said Mina, when Richard returned home.

'Oh? What was that about?'

'I think he wanted to assess me as a suspect in the attempted murder of Miss Hartop,' said Mina. 'Fortunately, I have never purchased Veale's violet creams, and can prove it. He tells me he has not been able to locate either the delivery boy or the gentleman who saw him, so we do not even have a description to go by. Do you recall if the gentleman had ever consulted Lady Brighthelm?'

'I don't think I had ever seen him in the shop before.'

'If he was a visitor to town, he may never be found.'

Richard shrugged. 'Even if you found the man, how would he recall a delivery boy? People don't usually notice delivery boys. Especially as he had such bad eyes.'

'Bad eyes?' queried Mina.

'When I showed him the catalogue, he squinted at it.' Richard demonstrated by squeezing up his face to indicate extreme short-sightedness. 'The man needed spectacles.'

'You didn't mention that before.'

'Didn't I? Perhaps not. No one asked me about his eyesight. Everyone just asked me what he looked like.'

'Well, since you have remembered something new, I think you ought to tell the police,' said Mina.

'I suppose so. But it wouldn't help much, would it, though? If the man was half-blind, he wouldn't be of any use at all in identifying a delivery boy.'

Mina was obliged to agree. 'But you said the man was well-dressed. If he needed glasses so badly, why did he not have any?'

'Maybe he had broken them,' Richard offered.

'Whether or not he can describe the delivery boy, if we could only find him then we could refute at least one of Mr Hope's insinuations. He says the man doesn't exist at all.' Mina sighed. 'I really do fear that Mr Hope isn't going to stop. If he can't discredit me one way, he will only try another.'

Mina was surprised to receive another letter from Mr Inskip, advising her that he was due to come to Brighton on business for a day, and would like to talk to her. He would arrive next morning on the early train and refresh himself with tea at the Grand Hotel at 10 a.m. before going to his appointment and would be most obliged if she would join him for a conversation.

Mina was extremely curious to know what he was about to reveal, especially as he was deliberately choosing not to come to her house, which rather implied that he did not want her mother to be present. She responded at once, accepting the invitation.

When Mina arrived at the Grand Hotel, she found that Mr Inskip had already ordered a pot of tea for her and coffee for himself, with a selection of buns and sandwiches, the bread cut so thin it hardly seemed to be there at all.

'Mr Inskip, I do hope nothing is the matter?' asked Mina as she took her seat. 'Are Enid and the children well?'

'Oh, yes,' he reassured her, cheerfully, 'they are all very well indeed. Babies are so tiny and delicate, are they not, but they do grow and thrive!' He poured tea and coffee for them both, and moved the cut-glass cake stand so that she could more easily reach it. 'You may wonder what business has brought me to Brighton,' he said. 'Well, it is a matter of some importance. When I was in Romania, I was so enthusiastic in telling the Count about the delights of Sussex, and the healthy fresh air of Brighton that he thought he might like to come and live here when he has sold his estate. I have just received a letter from him asking if I might look out for something suitable.'

'What is his name?' asked Mina. 'I have to say your description of his person and property reminded me of the terrors of what Mr Horace Walpole called "The Gothic Novel", the kind of fiction that Mother always says she would never allow in the house and has to keep secretly under her pillow.'

Mr Inskip smiled. When he did so, his face became more animated, and his weathered features, amused eyes and bristling beard made his face not as displeasing as it had once seemed. 'Oh, Count Andrey is a gentle soul, very quiet and pious. There is nothing sinister about him, I am sure.'

Mina wondered what a novelist might make of Count Andrey. Something in the nature of the old serial story *Varney the Vampire*, which still enjoyed some popularity. A new title, *The Sussex Vampire* had something of a ring to it. She took out her little notebook and pencil and made a quick jotting. 'If he does make his new home here, my mother will insist on an introduction,' she said.

'I am sure she will,' said Mr Inskip. 'However, that is not the reason I have asked to speak to you. You may have read in the press that Mr Arthur Wallace Hope has announced a new series of lectures in connection with his forthcoming book *Africa Awaits*. I believe he is in Brighton at present and will begin his tour here before moving about the country. He seems to think that Africa is an excellent opportunity for trade and investment. I happened to mention this to my dear Enid since I know she has read some of his earlier works, and asked if she would like to accompany me to his lecture when he comes to London, and she became — well, I can hardly describe her reaction. She was extremely unhappy at the suggestion but would not say why. And then I recalled that your mother said that Mr Hope had a reputation but would not say any more on the subject. I was hoping that you would enlighten me. I would not wish to unwittingly do anything that would affect Enid's happiness.'

Mina toyed with a lacy biscuit for a while. 'Mr Hope has a strong liking for the company of attractive ladies. He appears to prefer married ladies. Last year, when he was in Brighton, he was obliged to leave town very quickly to avoid a scandal. It involved the wife of a respectable gentleman, a partner in a professional practice, and caused considerable talk. The gentleman in question gave up his business, and I believe he and his wife have both removed to Scotland. I feel sure that that was what my mother was referring to.'

Mr Inskip had raised his coffee cup to his lips but lowered it unsipped. 'Good heavens! I had only heard that he was very charming and sociable, but I had no idea of this fault in his character.'

211

'Last January I was visiting the Honeyacres in Ditchling Hollow together with a great friend of mine, Mrs Jordan, whose husband is a partner in Jordan and Conroy ladies' fashions. Mr Hope arrived at the house unexpectedly and had the audacity to send a love note to Mrs Jordan in an attempt to arrange an assignation. The implications were all too clear. She was naturally disgusted with his behaviour. Some of the gentlemen present were alerted to the situation and spoke very severely to him. He was so disappointed that he drank a great deal of brandy and was so much under its influence that he was incapable of annoying her further. Soon after he had recovered, he left.'

'How appalling!' Mr Inskip exclaimed. 'And how distressing for you that you should have been present to witness such things.' He paused and suddenly went pale. 'You say that Mr Hope has a preference for married ladies. And he caused a scandal in Brighton last year. Was that during the time when I was abroad, and Enid was staying here?'

Mina chose her words carefully. 'It was, but I can assure you that Mr Hope did not bother her with any unwanted attentions.'

Mr Inskip made a great exhalation. 'I am relieved to hear it. If he had dared to offer such an insult to my dear Enid, I would have torn him apart with my bare hands.' He made the appropriate gesture and uttered a little growl.

'You are as fierce as the wolves you admire,' said Mina.

He smiled, baring his teeth. 'I like to think so, just a little. They are strong, savage yet noble creatures. They defend their own.'

Mina wondered if she might write a story in which a man was scratched or bitten by a wolf and acquired wolflike characteristics. Mr Inskip produced a handkerchief from his pocket and pressed it to his brow, then refreshed himself with more coffee. Mina used the pause in the conversation to make another note in her little book.

'I am very grateful to you for that information,' said Mr Inskip. 'I will take care to avoid the company of Mr Hope in future, and of course I will not mention his name to Enid again.'

'That is very wise,' said Mina.

'But — didn't I see that scoundrel's picture in the window of the shop in Ship Street? The photographers?'

'Yes, he is the patron of the owner, Mr Beckler. He is interested in the ghost portraits.'

'And your brother works for him?'

'He must make his way in the world somehow, and it has not been easy for him to find employment.'

Mr Inskip shook his head. He offered Mina the last of the sandwiches and when she declined, he ate them and glanced at his watch. 'And now, I must depart. I am seeing Mr Samprey about some properties very shortly.'

'Mr Samprey?'

'Yes, Charles Samprey. Do you know him?'

'Only by name,' said Mina.

'He is a partner in one of the premium property businesses in Brighton. They have an office on West Street, not two minutes' walk from here. They are currently offering a manor house for sale, which I think might do very well for the Count. I am hoping to take a look at it.'

'Where is that?'

'In Rottingdean. I thought the Count, being used to a rural life, would prefer something quiet and genteel rather than the bustle of town. The village has a handsome windmill and a very pretty church.'

'That sounds delightful. I should like to see that,' said Mina. 'I don't suppose I could accompany you?'

Mr Inskip appeared surprised by the request. 'Well, it is good weather for a carriage ride. I am sure Mr Samprey won't mind.'

They walked to West Street, where a smart office front was painted in crisp dark green with gilded lettering, Samprey and Sons. They were greeted by a youthful gentleman at the front desk who bore the earnest look of someone who accepted his junior status without difficulty and wished to appear desperately keen to learn from his seniors. Mr Inskip announced his arrival for an appointment with Mr Charles Samprey.

'You are expected, please come this way.' The young clerk glanced quizzically at Mina.

'This is my sister-in-law, Miss Scarletti,' said Mr Inskip. It was very apparent that the youth recognised her name. Mr Inskip turned to Mina. 'Would you like to wait here for me?'

There was no reason for Mina to attend the business meeting and she agreed. A comfortable chair and some reading matter were provided, and Mr Inskip was conducted to an office further back in the building.

The young clerk returned to his desk, but he continued to observe Mina. 'It is a warm day,' he said. 'Would you like me to bring you a glass of water?'

'Thank you, yes,' said Mina.

He scurried about, fetching first a little side table then a carafe and a glass. 'Are you sufficiently comfortable?' he asked.

'Yes, thank you, I am.'

He made no move to return to his desk. 'Might I ask you a question?'

Mina sipped her water. 'Please do.'

'Are you Miss Mina Scarletti?'

'I am.'

'And Richard Scarletti is your brother?'

'He is. And you are?'

'My name is Clover. Septimus Clover.'

Mina did her best not to show she knew that name.

'The thing is,' Mr Clover went on, 'I have met your brother at Mr Beckler's shop, although I doubt that he would have mentioned me. But I wanted to ask you —'

'Please sit down,' said Mina, since he was hovering over her nervously.

'Yes, thank you, of course.' He drew up a chair. 'I was wondering if you had any news of Lady Brighthelm, the medium? I had consulted her once or twice, but when I went to the shop again, I was told that she was indisposed, but no one would tell me anything more, and there have been the most dreadful rumours in town.'

'I would strongly advise you to take no notice of gossip,' said Mina. 'It is almost always more sensational than the truth.'

'Yes, yes, I agree. But do you know if she is recovered? Will she resume her calling again?'

'My only information is that she is very much improved in health, but it seems very unlikely that she will take up mediumship again.'

He gave a disappointed sigh. 'I can't even write to her. I asked Mr Beckler if he would pass a note to her, but he said he could not.'

'Might I ask you a question, Mr Clover?'

'Yes, of course, anything!' he said eagerly.

'Is your intention towards Lady Brighthelm one of courtship?'

His expression of astonishment told Mina all she needed to know. 'No, I —'

'I am sorry to have asked such a question, but you must be aware that the usual reason that young gentlemen wish to pass notes to ladies is to further a romance.'

'Well, that is as maybe, but that thought never occurred to me. I know nothing of the lady, except judging by her voice she is of foreign extraction. I wish only to consult her as a medium, and I was hoping that even if she intends to retire, she might relent one last time for me.'

'There are other mediums in town,' Mina observed.

'I know, and I have consulted several, but she is the only one who is able to receive messages that convince me that she is in direct contact. I — I don't wish to say any more on that subject.' He looked very despondent.

Mina said nothing but waited in the hope that he might be tempted to speak further, but at that moment another client arrived, and he was obliged to return to his duties.

Mina pretended to be absorbed in her reading matter, which was a pile of leaflets describing properties for sale, but her conversation with Mr Clover had given her food for thought. If he was being truthful, then he had no romantic inclinations towards Lady Brighthelm, was not aware of her true identity and had no wish to do her harm.

Another gentleman arrived asking to see Mr Charles Samprey and sat waiting for him to be available. There was no further opportunity to speak to Mr Clover alone.

After a few minutes the office door opened, and Mr Inskip emerged, with a gentleman who Mina felt sure she had seen before. It took only a moment for her to recall the circumstances. He was the man she had seen in the Extra Mural Cemetery paying his respects at the Samprey monument.

They both approached the desk. Samprey passed over some documents.

'Clover, could you call a cab and take Mr Inskip to Rottingdean so he can take a look at the old parsonage? Do accompany him and make a note of any questions. I'll send Bentley to take charge of the desk.' He took no notice of Mina but turned to the new arrival, greeted him and conducted him to the office.

A cab was soon procured and as they left the office to board it, Mina noticed a figure lurking on the corner of the street. A man was standing there peering at them, and very quickly withdrew and turned away as if not wanting to be seen. Once settled in the cab, Mina looked out of the window. The figure had advanced a little more, and she could now recognise him. His name was Stevenson and he was the private detective who Mr Jordan had hired to spy on Nellie, sending him to watch over her at Hollow House last January with a pair of binocular glasses. His guise of being an expert in natural history writing a book about the flora and fauna of Sussex had not been especially convincing, especially as he was terrified of spiders.

As Mina stared at him, he looked up. Their eyes met, and it was clear that he had recognised her. He glanced at his watch and this was followed by much energetic scribbling in a notebook. Mina recalled that Mr Hartop had told her that he had once made enquiries about a potential suitor for his daughter, and she wondered if Mr Stevenson had been hired by Mr Hartop to spy on Mr Clover.

At their last meeting Mina had been obliged to treat the detective with some cruelty, making use of his extraordinary fear of spiders, but she had done so not out of personal malice, but desperation, in order to protect Nellie's reputation. Nellie's sojourn at Hollow House under the same roof as her former admirer Richard, and the noted philanderer Mr Hope, might have been enough to ruin her. The sequence of peculiar events at Hollow House had finally led to an uneasy understanding in which Mina and the detective had formed a mutual agreement not to reveal certain secrets. The result had been a delicate balance of trust and mistrust. Since Mr Stevenson was obviously acting in his professional capacity by lurking outside the Samprey offices and had seen her in the company of Mr Clover, Mina thought it was only a matter of time before he arranged an interview.

The genteel village of Rottingdean and its old parsonage looked like an ideal home for an antiquated Romanian Count of reclusive habits. The tour of the house did suggest to Mina that some improvements should be made to the amenities, unless the Count's interest in the preservation of historical buildings extended to the plumbing. Mr Inskip was enthusiastic about the possibilities of the property, observing that there was space in the grounds to establish a wolf sanctuary so his client would not be bereft of their company. He proposed to write to Count Andrey recommending that the property be surveyed at once to estimate what repairs and renovations were advisable. Mina had little opportunity to speak privately to Mr Clover, but was able to pass him her card, saying that if he ever needed advice, he was welcome to write to her.

CHAPTER EIGHTEEN

The next morning Mina left the house for a gentle walk, which took her down to the sea front where she stood resting her palms on the railings that bordered the promenade. The Brighton sea, which had been known to rage and even cascade onto the public walkway when the mood took it, was calm that day, its movement a soothing velvety ripple, its briny scent invigorating. She had not been there long before Mr Stevenson came to stand nearby, also leaning on the railings and staring out to sea, although he appeared to take no joy from the sight. She had received a note from him the previous evening, asking if they could speak, and she had agreed.

'I trust you are well, Miss Scarletti,' he said. 'I had heard that you were indisposed earlier this year.'

'I have recovered, thank you,' said Mina. 'And you, Mr Stevenson, I assume you are still busy with your trade in secrets?'

'Extremely. A town such as Brighton will always have them.' He took a deep breath. 'Since you have agreed to speak to me, I hope you are amenable to answering some questions?'

'I am. Of course, I have always believed that information should run in both directions.'

'I appreciate that. To begin with, I observed you yesterday in a carriage with two gentlemen. Might I ask their names and the reason for your journey?'

'Of course. The elder of the two is Mr Inskip. He is married to my sister Enid, and they live in London. He manages transactions in property and has been looking for something suitable for a client in this vicinity. That was the purpose of his meeting at the Sampreys'. The journey was to look at a property in Rottingdean. I thought that it would be a very pleasant little excursion, and I asked to accompany him to see the village. The other young gentleman is a Mr Clover, who is a clerk at Sampreys'. He was conducting us to the property.'

Mr Stevenson nodded. 'And when you went to Rottingdean, did you meet anyone else there?'

'No, we simply viewed the property and returned.'

Mr Stevenson extracted a notebook and pencil from his pocket and made an entry.

'I may be able to assist you further,' said Mina. 'I can hazard a guess at the name of your client, a gentleman whom I have met once. Since I doubt very much that you are following either myself or Mr Inskip, I can only assume it is young Mr Clover who is the object of your interest. Your client believes that Mr Clover may be intending to pay court to his daughter and wishes to reassure himself of the gentleman's character and circumstances.'

Mr Stevenson said nothing, but his eyes had turned to Mina, and he was watching and waiting.

Certain now that her supposition was correct, Mina continued. 'Mr Clover, as I am sure you know, has been consulting a medium known only as Lady Brighthelm. Unless he is not being truthful, he does not know her real name. But you and I are both aware that she is the daughter of your client. When Lady Brighthelm became indisposed and was obliged to cease her practice, Mr Clover was very concerned and tried to discover her address as he wished to resume the consultations. Again, unless he is not being truthful, his interest in her is solely due to the information she is providing or promises to provide, and he has no wish to court her. I appreciate that her father is anxious to check the credentials of any suitor, and Mr

Clover does not seem to be ideal due to his youth and the fact that he is employed as a junior clerk. My feeling is that the lady's father does not need to have any anxiety concerning Mr Clover's intentions. They are not of a romantic nature.'

Mr Stevenson smiled a little. 'Thank you for that information. Her father will also be anxious that Mr Clover must not attempt to visit the lady since he is demanding more of her than is reasonable in her current state of health. Did you only meet him yesterday?'

'Yes.'

'And you have no information to his detriment?'

'None.' There was a silence. Mina studied Mr Stevenson's features. 'But I think you do.' She recalled that Mr Hartop had expressed some doubts about the suitability of Mr Clover's family. 'Your client told me that he is concerned about the Clovers because there is some fault in their history, but I know nothing about them.'

Mr Stevenson mused for a while before he spoke. 'They are respectable people, but the profession of architect is not without the occasional drama. In the case of the Clovers, there have sometimes been allegations of flaws in buildings which have led to legal action for damages. About three years ago, there was an action brought by a Mr Bawtree, whose daughter, his only child, died after being trapped under a falling iron gate when passing by a property that was in the course of construction. He alleged that the accident was due to the architects' negligence. He took them to court, but the ruling was that it was an act of God, occasioned by stormy weather, and he went away unsatisfied. From time to time he wrote to them, threatening further action. That may be one reason why young Mr Clover did not follow his brothers into the profession but joined the Sampreys in their business.'

'But you know nothing against Mr Clover personally? I assume that being very young and without appreciable fortune, he is not paying court to another lady?'

'Paying court,' said Mr Stevenson, with a mirthless grin. 'An interesting expression. What I can say is that I have observed him making frequent visits to a lodging house, and my enquiries have revealed that while there he conducts interviews with a young person, who is the between stairs maid. I doubt very much if he is courting her in the usual sense of the word.'

'Does his family know about this?'

'Not yet.'

'Will you tell your client? If Mr Clover has no intentions towards his daughter, then it should not be necessary. As to his family —'

'I will retain that information to use as a bargaining counter should the need arise. But tell me, do you know why Mr Clover was visiting Lady Brighthelm?'

'I do not. That secret lies between him and the medium. In general, people visit mediums to find answers to their most pressing questions; questions about their own personal future; about loved ones who have passed away; or to reassure themselves about the prospect of eternal life. It is not unlike consulting a detective, except that you question the living whereas a spirit medium questions the dead. In Mr Clover's case, all he would reveal to me is that he was attempting to make contact with a deceased person. He was unwilling to say more.'

'And you say that Mr Clover was very concerned about the illness of Lady Brighthelm?'

'Yes, my brother works for Mr Beckler, and he said that Mr Clover was quite agitated. He had come for an appointment only to be told it had been cancelled, and he was very anxious to consult her. I asked him why he did not go to another medium, but he intimated that only Lady Brighthelm seemed to be able to provide him with the answers he sought.'

Mr Stevenson appeared satisfied with that reply. 'I will report back to my client. It may well be that my work in this case has been completed.'

'You are not investigating the attack on the lady?'

'That is not my remit. I leave serious crimes to the police.'

Mina and Mr Stevenson solemnly exchanged cards before they went their separate ways, but Mina was left with the feeling that despite the openness of their discussion, there was still something Mr Stevenson had chosen not to reveal.

As Mina climbed the steep road to her home, she was thoughtful. On balance she believed that Mr Clover was genuine, that he did not know the real identity of Lady Brighthelm, and his agitation at her illness was simply because he was anxious to consult her. Had Mr Clover sought to consult the spirit of the deceased Miss Bawtree to finally free his family from blame? What had Miss Hartop suggested she might know? Given her interest in local scandals, she would know all about publicly reported court cases. Perhaps she possessed some nugget of information, or at the very least by dint of a good guess that had unwittingly hit the mark, was able to suggest that she did. And if that was true of Mr Clover's enquiries, then it could be equally true of all the others who had consulted the medium, the people who had made appointments and not revealed their names. The people who might also know that the medium's favourite sweetmeat was Veale's violet creams.

Mr Beckler's exercise in photographic ghosts to drum up custom for the shop and Miss Hartop's resultant emergence as a medium had had unintended consequences. One of the consequences, Mina realised, could well have been the attempt on the life of Miss Hartop.

The next weekly edition of the *Gazette* was one which Mina studied with more than the usual care.

To the Editor:
SPIRIT PHOTOGRAPHS
Sir,

Might I suggest before the Soules brothers impugn the honesty of a businessman that they actually take the trouble to examine the product he offers? By their own admission, they have failed to do so. Really it is too bad dismissing something out of hand in such a careless manner. I would also like to remind them that Mr William Mumler, the American photographer whose example they quote, was not shown to be a fraud at all, and left court without a stain on his character.

Meanwhile, it grieves me to inform the town that a lady who is the newest shining star in the already bright firmament of spirit mediums has been the victim of a deadly assault. Only the hand of the Almighty, the most powerful, saved her so that she might continue her good works. Truly greatness will protect and nurture greatness, while the small and mean will perish.

Arthur Wallace Hope

Mina was in no doubt as to whom the 'small and mean' person might be but trusted that not everyone would see the allusion. So carefully worded was the letter that she dared not make a protest because of the risk of identifying herself as a suspect.

There was a large advertisement in the *Gazette* for a series of lectures Mr Hope was giving in Brighton at the Town Hall on the subjects of the trading opportunities in Africa, his great friend Dr Livingstone, and spiritualism, the new hope for the world. Mina hoped that he would not be detained in town for too long.

She was reading the more palatable general news when her eye was caught by an interesting headline.

DEATH OF A SEER

The death has been announced of Mrs Mary Ragdon, who once enjoyed the soubriquet of 'the Brighton Oracle', after a long illness. She was aged 74. She will be interred in the Extra Mural Cemetery at 4 p.m. on Thursday, where a small service will be performed at the chapel. She is survived by her sister, Miss Mulgrew.

Mina read this several times. The first thing that struck her was the name Mulgrew. Could Mrs Ragdon have been a relative of Mr Robert Mulgrew, the theological scholar? A sister, perhaps? And where had she heard the name Ragdon mentioned quite recently? Mina searched her memory and finally it came to her. Mrs Peasgood had described consulting a medium called Mrs Ragdon in her efforts to discover the truth about her husband's demise. That had to be the same person. If Mina was right, then she had discovered a direct connection between two of the subjects of Mr Beckler's spirit pictures. The final thing that struck her was that since the *Gazette* was a weekly paper, the death had occurred some days before and the funeral was that afternoon.

The newspaper also carried a small appreciation.

THE BRIGHTON ORACLE

Many of our readers will recall Mrs Ragdon in her heyday some ten or twenty years ago, when she received visitors who were anxious to learn their future fates, have her lay healing hands upon them, or hear messages from their deceased loved ones. Mrs Ragdon was sadly struck down in her prime by a seizure of the brain which left her unable to move or speak. Despite this and being confined to bed for the remainder of her life, Mrs Ragdon continued to act as an oracle to a devoted circle of adherents. This correspondent once visited her in her humble home and found her surrounded by flowers and objects of religious significance. She was regarded by some as a saint on earth. Although her powers of speech were gone, it was, so I was informed, only necessary to hold her hand, think deeply of the enquiry one wished to make, and the truth would be revealed. I was warned that she did not concern herself with mundane matters such as the result of horse races or the movement of the stock market, only questions of the soul. I was not asked to make a financial contribution, that would have been an indelicate request to make so blatantly, nevertheless I spied a china teapot placed in a prominent position in which there were both coins and banknotes, and I took the hint. I did sit for a while touching the lady's hand, and thought deeply of my late grandmother, but my only thoughts were of what she had previously said to me in life, so I was unable to come to any conclusion as to whether this was a message from beyond the grave.

Mina consulted the Brighton directory and found an entry for Mrs M Ragdon, *clairvoyante*. Presumably her sister resided at the same address.

Mina ordered a cab, asking the driver to take her to the cemetery. Apart from the late Mrs Ragdon, there were two names she was interested in: Miss Bawtree, whose father had accused the Clovers of negligence, and the one member of the

Clover family buried in the Extra Mural Cemetery. There was just time for her to call at the office before the funeral.

As she travelled, she gave further thought to the individuals whose gravesites had been photographed by Mr Beckler, and an emerging theme, an interest in spiritualism. Mr Mulgrew was most probably related to the medium Mrs Ragdon. Mrs Peasgood had once consulted Mrs Ragdon. Mr Honeyacre had made a study of spiritualism. According to Mr Inskip, one of the disputatious cousins of Miss Porterson-White had consulted a medium. Martha Veale had said at her husband's inquest that she had consulted a medium about his death. Young Mr Phipps's aunt had certainly attended séances, but then she went to any event where refreshments were served and had never exhibited any great interest in the proceedings. Regarding Mrs Soules and the Sampreys, she knew nothing of any interest they might have had in spiritualism but thought it would be a useful subject to pursue.

The office clerk gave her the location of the 1867 burial of Mrs Elizabeth Clover and the Bawtree grave in which there was more than one interment, and Mina made a careful note, identifying the sites she needed on her map.

With no further need of the cab, Mina walked on to the chapel. It was a delightfully neat little building; a miniature church formed in the Gothic style and clad in flint and stone. Had Mina elected to go to the chapel first, the carriage would have brought her directly underneath the tall stone canopy that protected the entrance where visitors were able to alight from their cabs and carriages unconcerned about the vagaries of the weather. Instead, as she approached on foot, she saw a small cluster of persons gathered under the canopy in earnest conversation and to her discomfort recognised one figure. He had his back to her but the height, the broad shoulders and abundant dark hair could only belong to one person, Mr Arthur Wallace Hope, the man she most wanted to avoid. Thankful that he could not see her, she diverted her intended route and rounded the chapel. Pausing by a side wall, she peered around the corner to see if he had finally vanished inside. At length she approached the entrance and was able to see into the chapel to observe how the congregation were seated and judge whether or not it would be best for her to retire without attending the service.

Unlike the usual arrangement in a church, the chapel seats were not laid out in rows facing an altar but faced each other on either side of the length of the building. The coffin had been placed on trestles in the aisle. There was an attendance of some thirty or forty persons, and Mr Hope, in the company of a lady who Mina assumed must be Miss Mulgrew, had gone to take a seat close by a lectern beside the altar. The last thing Mina wanted was for Mr Hope to see her and start denouncing her to all and sundry, which would not assist the dignity and solemnity required at a funeral.

After some hesitation, she calculated that as long as she stayed at the end of the chapel, near to the door, and exercised her special talent of hiding behind persons larger than herself, she would be able to observe the service without Mr Hope noticing that she was there.

She crept in, and took a seat beside an extra-large lady, who was in conversation with a slightly smaller lady, picked up a hymn book and bent her head over it, perusing the contents with great attention.

The service began with a brief encomium from a clergyman, regaling the mourners with the long career of Mrs Ragdon, her devotion to helping others, her goodness, her selflessness, her essentially spiritual life. There was a hymn for which the congregation was asked to stand, and even so far removed Mina could hear Mr Hope's baritone boom above every voice in the chapel.

They were seated again, and the lady to whom Mr Hope had been speaking rose and went to stand at the little lectern.

'My sister,' said the lady, 'was a saint. She was placed on earth for one purpose, and that was to help others. Countless numbers had cause to be grateful to her, countless individuals came to ask her for the answers to the questions that most troubled them, and all without exception received comfort and reassurance. Many were sick and were healed. Even when Mary was struck down by disease, exhausted from her valiant work giving her own strength to those she felt needed it more than she, even when unable to see or hear or speak, she was bathed in an atmosphere of special grace. Her fame was not diminished, her powers never left her. Those who came to pray by her bedside had their prayers answered. I do not feel now that I have lost my sister. Her soul is in heaven, where she continues her holy work. But I feel her presence is here still; she lives in my heart, and her example will guide me for the remainder of my earthly life.'

There was a murmuring of approval amongst the congregation.

There followed a reading from the Bible, and then Mr Arthur Wallace Hope stepped up to speak. Mina shrank further back into the shadow of the extra-large lady.

'I first met Mrs Ragdon some years ago, on my return from the Crimea,' said Mr Hope in his best lecturing voice. 'She was then at the height of her powers. She told me of the tragic death of her husband and how she had for a short time lost all her motivation to live. Then, as if by a miracle, his spirit came to her, and urged her to live on, as she had important work to do. God's work. Since then, she has been an example to the world. Her gifts were unparalleled, her achievements without equal. She could see both into the future and the past. She could heal the sick. She will live in fame forever. It was my honour to know her.'

Mr Hope resumed his place. As the congregation rose for a final hymn, and the parade of the coffin out of the door, the slightly smaller lady whispered to the extra-large lady, 'What did Mr Ragdon die of?' There was a guttural rumble which might have been a cough or a laugh before the answer came. 'Vice.'

Mina realised that the parade would take Mr Hope past her, but fortunately he was on the other side of the chapel from herself. He had taken the arm of Miss Mulgrew and was patting her wrist comfortingly. All his attention was therefore devoted to the sorrowing sister, and he did not notice Mina's diminutive presence.

Mina waited just inside the chapel door for the moment when she could depart unseen by Mr Hope. Instead of attending the interment, however, he turned and made his apologies to Miss Mulgrew, then bowing respectfully he boarded a waiting carriage, presumably, thought Mina, on his way to one of his speaking engagements.

She decided to join the little procession, which headed for the open grave. Once the brief service was performed and the coffin lowered, little clusters of people gathered about Miss Mulgrew, who remained in steadfast good humour. Mina was unsure of whether to approach Miss Mulgrew for a conversation or wait for another more appropriate moment, but then Miss Mulgrew chanced to notice her. Making her excuses to the sympathetic faithful, she came to speak to Mina. Her expression was not especially friendly.

'Miss Scarletti, I believe?'

'You are correct,' said Mina.

'I am somewhat surprised to see you here, unless of course you have come to pay your respects to a genuine medium?'

'I was never acquainted with your sister, but I am always respectful to those who bring peace and comfort to others. I have been told that she did a great deal of good in the world.'

'She did,' said Miss Mulgrew, proudly. 'She numbered amongst her devotees all the most renowned personages in the town. They all flocked to see her.'

'How gratifying,' said Mina. 'I wonder — did my good friend Mr Honeyacre of Hollow House ever consult your sister? He is a great student of matters spiritual. I must ask him when I next see him.'

'Oh, I can assure you, he did. I remember him well. He brought his first wife to see us when she was suffering in her last illness. She was very weak, and in great pain much of the time, but she never complained. She always said that her visits gave her great relief. She was an angel on Earth, and it was always certain that the Lord would soon take her into his Heavenly choir, but with the blessing of my sister, her passing was eased.'

Another connection, thought Mina. She decided not to push further with her questioning on that subject in case it aroused suspicion. 'You have some wonderful memories,' she said. 'Perhaps, dare I suggest it, your sister's career should be memorialised in a volume? It would be a monument to her work and a benefit to society.'

Miss Mulgrew smiled agreement. 'I am no writer, but my late brother was. He led a simple and blameless life, devoted to study. He wrote a great number of religious tracts. It was always his belief that Mary was a great mystic and holy healer. He wrote a short history of her career.'

'Was your brother Mr Robert Mulgrew? The respected scholar?' exclaimed Mina.

Miss Mulgrew looked gratified at Mina's response. 'Indeed, that is he.'

'I am familiar with his writings. Was his history of Mrs Ragdon ever published? I have not seen it for sale or in the library.'

'He had a number of copies privately printed. A dozen, perhaps. They are mainly in the hands of the family and close friends.'

'Then I suppose there are none for sale. What a shame.' Mina took a card from her reticule. 'Miss Mulgrew, you may not know this, but my brother Edward is a director of a publishing house in London. He publishes histories and works of scholarship. I would be delighted to recommend that he take a look at your brother's book with the object of bringing out a new edition.'

'Oh,' said Miss Mulgrew, taking the card. 'That is very kind of you, I will consider it.'

'I am surprised that this has not been suggested to you before.'

'Indeed. I presented Viscount Hope with a copy when he visited Brighton last year, and he is a very renowned author, yet he has not suggested that my brother's little work merited a wider edition.'

Mina was silent for a moment. 'Miss Mulgrew, if there is a copy of the book in your possession which I might purchase or borrow, I would regard it as a very great favour.'

'Certainly. I will see what I have.' Miss Mulgrew handed Mina her card. 'I wonder — would you attend our next séance tomorrow evening?'

Mina hesitated. 'Will Viscount Hope be there?' she asked, trying to make it appear that she was eager to meet him, rather than the opposite.

Miss Mulgrew smiled indulgently. 'I am very sorry, but no. I did invite him, but he is engaged to deliver lectures every evening for the next week. He may be free to visit us in future, but I cannot guarantee it.'

Mina stared at the card. 'I would very much like to attend. Forgive me, I am not used to such invitations; many mediums are fearful of me.'

'Your reputation is well known, but you will find nothing to disturb you. We have an excellent medium. She is the best in England, perhaps the world.'

'Do I know her?'

'No, it is my sister. A little matter such as death does not diminish her powers. Her work continues.'

The mourners were departing, and Miss Mulgrew took her leave expressing how eager she was to receive the renowned Miss Scarletti at the forthcoming séance. Mina remained in the cemetery and with the aid of her map was able to discover both the graves she had been looking for. The Bawtree grave recorded the burial of the young woman who had died from the falling gate, her mother who had passed away some ten years previously and also her father, the man who had blamed the Clover family for his daughter's death, and who had died only six months ago. Given that the father was no longer demanding redress from the Clovers for the death of his daughter, Mina wondered if it was likely that Septimus Clover would feel any urgency in resolving the dispute by contacting the spirit of the deceased.

The Clover grave was rather more interesting. *Sacred to the memory of Mrs Elizabeth Clover, beloved wife of Samuel, only sister of the late Hector Samprey, much mourned by her seven children, nephews and niece.* Septimus Clover, Mina now realised, was first cousin to the Samprey brothers and sister. Mr Hartop had mentioned that young Mr Clover's family had been troubled. But had he meant the Clovers or the Sampreys? This discovery opened up new possibilities.

CHAPTER NINETEEN

Mina hired a cab from the cemetery gates, and on her way home reflected on what she had discovered. She now addressed her thoughts to the possibility that Mr Clover's enquiries of Lady Brighthelm related not to the Clovers at all, but to the Samprey family, his deceased uncle and aunt, and the murdered cousin.

The Samprey monument had been one of those photographed by Mr Beckler, and even though Mina had not seen the picture she felt sure that it would show deceased Sampreys convening amicably about their tomb. As a family member, Mr Clover might have seen or at least been told about that photograph and this might well have inspired him to consult a medium. It had not inspired the Sampreys to do so, but not everyone was agreeable to consulting a medium. Mr Clover's interest in the history of his family was understandable. But why had he been so agitated? What questions had he asked the medium to answer? As far as Mina was aware, the only death in the family which was not fully explained was that of his aunt, Mrs Samprey. Was this what concerned him? Had her death been a pure accident? The result of negligence? Or something more sinister?

Mina felt sure that Miss Hartop, avid collector of gossip and scandal, was well acquainted with the turbulent history of the Sampreys. If as Lady Brighthelm she had hinted that she might be able to reveal the truth behind the death of Mrs Samprey, that could have provided a motive for someone to silence her.

Mina decided to write a letter.

Dear Mr Hartop,

I do hope that Miss Hartop is well on her way to recovering her health in full.

I hope you will not object to my asking some questions which may or may not have a bearing on these unfortunate recent incidents. Would Miss Hartop be able to recall if any of her clients as Lady Brighthelm asked her to contact deceased members of their families who had expired under particularly notable circumstances?

Assuring you of my very greatest good wishes,
M Scarletti

Mina received a reply the following day.

Dear Miss Scarletti,

Thank you for your enquiry. My daughter is gradually regaining her strength, although her voice is still very weak.

I asked her your question, and she was able to tell me the following which she thought especially interesting.

She recalls a very persistent gentleman who sought to contact the spirit of a cousin regarding a lost will which he felt sure would be greatly to his advantage. She did not know how the cousin died, and he refused to supply a name, but the behaviour of the gentleman did not recommend him to her. The spirit had few words to say, and the gentleman left in a dissatisfied state and did not return.

A lady, who wore a ribbon which proclaimed her to be a devotee of the temperance movement, hoped to discover that her late husband had not been addicted to the consumption of alcohol, as had been alleged, but had been done to death by unnamed persons. The husband's spirit told her that he was in heaven where he drank only sweet water. I think the widow was a little mollified by that thought. Hannah also recalls that she received a little box of chocolates from the lady, which she consumed without ill-effect.

Also, Mr Septimus Clover, as we know, visited a number of times. He was very anxious to contact the spirit of his late cousin, Hector Samprey junior. That was a death that upset all the family. The sister, Clarissa Samprey, actually dreamed about the murder before the family knew of it, a circumstance which she still finds highly disturbing. I believe young Mr Clover was hoping to soothe Miss Samprey's anxiety on the subject by discovering more about the events of that night. I know Hannah had promised Mr Clover a conversation with his deceased cousin in due course, and he was keenly anticipating this, but Hannah needed time to establish a path to the spirit. The attack happened before she could do so.

Hannah has informed me that as a result of her illness, her powers have quite evaporated. Whatever one might feel about the brief flowering of her abilities, I for one am relieved that her career as a medium is over, as I have felt that it drained her energies. I have asked Mr Beckler to place a sign in the shop window for the information of her clients.

Respectfully,

H Hartop

The information about Clarissa Samprey was an unexpected development, but Mina had had little time to consider it when Richard took her aside just as she was preparing to go out to Miss Mulgrew's séance and handed her a magazine. It was a recent edition of a weekly publication, *The Spiritual Banner*.

'Where did you get that?' Mina demanded.

'It was at the shop. Beckler was reading it. Mr Hope insists he should. I don't think it cheered him up much. But he thought you ought to take a look at it.'

'I'll read it when I am back,' Mina said, going to lock it in her desk with her private papers.

'Umm,' said Richard. 'There's something on the last page you really ought to see.'

There was a disturbance in his look and tone of voice that made her comply. The last page was for correspondence, on which was a letter headed *How shall we bring the disbelievers into the fold?*

It is a sad fact that there are so many scientists and materialists in the world who cannot use their intelligence to see the truth. How may we save them by showing them the truth of the world of the spirit when they are so blinkered by prejudice? Alas, after many years I am obliged to think that this is an impossibility, and I should better utilise my energies to advise those who are as yet undecided rather than try to change the minds of those with entrenched opinions. Worst of all are those who undoubtedly have the power to converse with the spirit world but reject their own abilities and do not develop them. I have learnt to ignore them, but there are some who one ignores at one's peril, those who are using their powers to oppose or even harm the great and the good in this world. I name no names. They know all too well who they are. They will stop at nothing, even murder, to work their evil. But they should beware, for I know them and will stop them. We must all be vigilant.

AWH.

Mina flung the publication into her drawer and locked it.

'What are you going to do?' asked Richard, nervously.

'I don't know yet.'

'Where are you going?'

'To a séance with a dead woman,' said Mina.

She put on her bonnet and went out.

Miss Mulgrew lived in a first-floor apartment on West Street, attended only by a maid. It was the kind of accommodation usually occupied by respectable persons who placed themselves above any hint of trade but were obliged to live frugally. There were three rooms, a small parlour, with facilities for making tea, and two others, one of which had been the sickroom of Mrs Ragdon, and was now her shrine. Washing and cooking amenities were shared with other residents.

There was a small group of persons attending, and all were silently conducted to what had been the bedroom of Mrs Ragdon. The bed was made with fresh white linen and covered with a spotless quilt. There were pillows edged in deep lace frills, and a nightgown and nightcap were laid out ready for the occupant who would never come. The nightstand still bore bottles of salves and a water jug. If other more personal items had been employed in the care of the patient, these were not on display.

Mina was well aware that the burden of caring for a stricken sister must have been both exhausting and expensive. She could not blame Miss Mulgrew for using the fame of Mrs Ragdon to continue the gatherings even when the medium had been unable to conduct a séance herself.

The mantlepiece and several small tables scattered about the room were crowded with items of religious significance, crucifixes, statuettes, bibles, and little notelets and printed cards, which Mina assumed must be gifts from the grateful. There was also within easy reach the famous china teapot. One item could not help but catch Mina's eye, a framed photograph. It was a picture of Robert Mulgrew's grave in the Extra Mural Cemetery, and standing beside it there was a familiar figure. Mina did not have available the bound copy of the author's collected tracts, which she had seen in the library, but she judged that the image beside the grave and that in the volume were not merely of the same man, but identical. She decided that it would not be a good idea to point this out.

Chairs were placed around the bed, and all present were asked to take a seat, lay a hand upon the quilt and silently pray.

Mina was no stranger to prayer, but this time she felt she needed additional guidance. The readers of *The Spiritual Banner* would probably be familiar with the authorship of the AWH letter. She wondered how many would read it and demand to know more. Had Mr Hope told Mr Beckler to show her the letter to frighten her, or was Mr Beckler, for his own reasons, trying to warn her? Was it just an empty threat, or did Mr Hope mean further harm? Was there anything in Mr Hartop's recent letter which might assist her?

The little group of communicants finally declared themselves refreshed. A number did no more than shake Miss Mulgrew by the hand and depart after placing some coins in the teapot. Mina felt she ought to make her own contribution, and as she searched her reticule, wondering what would be appropriate, she found Miss Mulgrew standing by her side, holding a slim book bound in dark leather.

'This is my brother's history of our sister,' she said. 'I do not lend copies, but if you wish to purchase it, it is five shillings. My poor brother passed away before he could record all her story, but I have added my own notes of her later achievements, so it is complete up to the year 1870. You will find much in these pages to enlighten you.'

Mina supplied the necessary funds and the book was hers.

Once home, Mina perused again the horrid letter from Mr Hope, but it only made her angry. She saw, however, that there was a lengthy debate in the *Banner* on spirit photographs, particularly describing the wonderful results of the London man, Hudson. There were hard words said about the 'hostility of professional photographers', with the comment that 'the "experts" are always the most determined opponents of any great novelty out of their accustomed track.' One gentleman who declared that he had been connected with the profession for twenty years commented 'I never knew an honest photographer except two in my life.' The overwhelming tenor of the *Banner* was understandably in favour of Mr Hudson. It had been suggested by a few cavillers that his pictures might have been produced by a method called 'double exposure', and there were even some spiritualists who were having their doubts, but this, it was asserted, did not prove that the ghost pictures had actually been produced in that way.

Mina could see that this debate might not make pleasant reading for Mr Beckler, and she wondered if he was beginning to regret going down that path.

Mina turned to Mr Mulgrew's memorial of his sister. The prose was earnest but turgid. The author was clearly intending to do no more than declare the essential saintliness of Mrs Ragdon and then provide notes of persons of significance whom she had advised.

There was only a brief mention of Mr Ragdon, who had expired after a long illness. More space was given to the eminent Viscount Hope, who had been a devoted adherent.

There were other names, many she did not recognise, but there were seven in particular who were very familiar, some of which were necessarily in Miss Mulgrew's addendum.

Mr Honeyacre, described as a noted scholar and historian, had brought his ailing wife for healing, with 'excellent results.'

A Mrs Phipps, the widow of a professional gentleman, had received messages from his spirit which had brought her great comfort.

Mrs Peasgood, the widow of a medical man, had also received messages from him and expressed her great gratitude to the medium.

Mrs Veale, whose husband, the proprietor of a Brighton business, had passed away under distressing circumstances, wished to be assured that he had found peace in the spirit world.

Mr Hector Samprey senior, the respected man of property who suffered from the effects of a tragic accident in which his wife had died, had received messages of comfort from her, and found relief from his pain.

Mrs Soules, the wife of a manufacturer, had asked Mrs Ragdon to read the future of her husband's business and predict the actions of a bitter rival determined to destroy him. She had departed with the firm belief that her difficulties could be solved.

There was no one of the name Porterson-White, but there was mention of a Mr Winstanley, who was determined to contact a deceased cousin to trace a missing will. Mina had only encountered him once, recalling him as the gentleman with the heroic moustache who was a customer of Beckler's and also, according to Richard, Lady Brighthelm.

Aloysius Phipps was the only one of the deceased who, she had been assured, had never had his photograph taken, but she now knew that all the families on Mr Beckler's list were connected by their interest in spiritualism and through this volume, were known as such to Mr Hope.

In the meantime, what was she to do about Mr Hope and his damaging insinuations? She needed to know more about the work of Lady Brighthelm, and there was one person who had consulted her who might agree to an interview. She wrote a letter to Mr Septimus Clover asking to speak to him again.

Mr Clover responded to Mina's letter agreeing to an interview but saying that he preferred that it should not take place either at his business or his home. Mina did not wish to meet him at her own home in case questions were asked, neither did she want to risk being seen with a young single gentleman in a teashop for fear of misinterpretation. She had been thinking of suggesting either the esplanade or the pier, but Mr Clover mentioned that he was going to be about all the next day inspecting empty properties in Brighton and she could meet him at one of those. This was certainly a good opportunity for a private interview, but Mina found herself becoming concerned in case Mr Clover, for all his meek manners, should turn out to be a homicidal maniac. Unfortunately, she was not sure what a homicidal maniac was supposed to look like. Newspapers and sensational literature often suggested that they could be readily identified by their staring eyes, dishevelled appearance and rambling speech, but she was not convinced. Perhaps they could just look like anyone else. She made another entry in her little notebook.

Mina agreed to the appointment but decided to ask Rose to accompany her. Rose could be relied upon to ask no questions and spill no secrets. It was also an important fact that if Mr Clover did suddenly decide to commit violence, Mina could not wrestle him to the ground, but Rose, a sturdy girl, certainly could.

CHAPTER TWENTY

On Monday afternoon, with Richard at work, and her mother out paying calls, Mina and Rose left Montpelier Road in a cab which took them to a small house on Duke's Lane, not far from the Sampreys' place of business. Mr Clover had brought with him a bundle of leaflets about properties available for purchase or letting. Mina rather thought that these were to provide an excuse for their meeting in case anyone was to enquire. He handed her the leaflets, and she took them but did not trouble herself to look at them.

At the front of the house, which was bereft of any floor coverings, was a small parlour with a blackened fireplace and a rusty grate. The only furniture was two very dusty chairs, and Mr Clover tore a scrap of material from a ragged curtain and cleaned them for the use of Mina and himself, then found a trunk full of old linen that Rose could sit on. Rose perched on the trunk and favoured Mr Clover with one of her warning looks before folding her arms with an air of determination.

'Do you have any news of Lady Brighthelm?' he asked Mina hopefully.

'I have heard that she is considerably improved, and her doctor anticipates her eventual return to full health, but it seems that her ability as a medium has quite evaporated.'

Mr Clover slumped despondently. 'There was a notice in the shop window that she no longer accepted clients, but I had hoped...' His voice trailed away.

'I am interested to know what means she employed to read fortunes or receive spirit messages? Did she use cards, or palmistry, or teacups?'

'No, no, nothing like that. She simply talked. I asked questions and she waited for a spirit to come through and answer me.'

'And you felt that she had a special insight into your enquiries?'

'Yes, I did. Most certainly I did. She knew a great deal about my family and its history. It was quite remarkable. They were things that we hardly ever talked about amongst ourselves, and she just knew.'

'Was your enquiry concerning the accident to Miss Bawtree?' asked Mina.

Mr Clover looked surprised. 'No, not at all. How do you know about that?'

Mina was hardly about to reveal her source. 'A legal gentleman chanced to mention it to me. It was not a spirit, if that was what you were thinking.'

From his expression, she had guessed his thoughts correctly. 'The Bawtree case was very unfortunate, of course, but it was settled out of court last year. No, I consulted Lady Brighthelm about my poor cousin Hector. He — he was killed. It was a dreadful thing. My uncle was a sick man and it shortened his life.'

'That happened before our family came to live in Brighton, but I have heard a little about it. I understand that a man was found guilty of the crime and hanged.'

'Yes, but —' Mr Clover paused. He had linked his fingers together and was wringing them distractedly. 'It's all so confusing. Sometimes I don't know what to make of it at all. I thought if I could contact Hector in some way… I hadn't really thought of trying it before, but when Mr Beckler took that photograph… Mortimer showed it to me, he thought it was a fraud, but I saw Hector's spirit standing there beside his grave. Smiling, just as I remember him.'

Mina waited, but Mr Clover seemed lost in his own ruminations. 'Were your questions to Lady Brighthelm concerning your cousin's murder?' she asked eventually.

Mr Clover chewed his lip and nodded. He had started to look a little afraid. 'I only heard about it later, from my cousin Clarissa,' he said. 'The things she saw that night. She can be very — imaginative — sometimes. But I have never known her tell a deliberate untruth.'

'Forgive me,' said Mina, 'but Clarissa — she is a younger sister to Hector?'

'Oh, yes, of course, I should explain. Hector was my uncle's eldest son, and then there is Mortimer, he is married and has his own establishment, then there is Charles, and Clarissa is the youngest.'

'And at the time of the murder, Hector, Charles and Clarissa were living with their father?'

'Yes.'

Mina nodded. 'Go on.'

'The night Hector was killed, Clarissa woke up quite suddenly, from a bad dream. It was something about her brother and seeing him with a gun in his hand. She knew at once that something terrible had happened. She got out of bed and started walking about and wailing, and the noise woke Charles. He found her and calmed her down; reassured her that it was just a dream. When she was able to describe it, she said she had seen Hector with one of her father's old army pistols and it had frightened her. She wanted to know if it was missing from its display case. Fortunately, Charles was able to show her that it was still there, secure and locked away, where it had always been. Eventually she went back to bed.'

'And this was before they learnt of their brother's death?' queried Mina.

'Oh yes. That night, Hector had said that he was going to see his friend Barnes. The man who was hanged. Hector —' Mr Clover gave a sorrowful shake of the head — 'he had never really settled to work the way Mortimer and Charles did. Maybe he thought as the eldest son he didn't need to trouble himself. I don't know. I never really knew him well; I was only seventeen when he died. But I had heard that his father despaired of him ever making an honest living. Barnes was a criminal of the worst type. He'd stoop to anything for money. I think Hector used some of his well-connected friends to help Barnes dispose of stolen property. But not long before he died, Hector told his father that he was going to reform, cut off all connection with Barnes. In fact, that was the purpose of his meeting with Barnes that night.'

That much Mina knew from her reading of the trial. 'When did the family discover what had happened?'

'The following morning Hector was not at breakfast, and it was obvious that he had not returned home or slept in his bed, but they weren't too alarmed as they knew he sometimes stayed with friends and came home next day. Soon afterwards, they heard a rumour that the body of a well-dressed man had been found murdered. Clarissa became very distressed and begged Charles to go to the police, and just to set her mind at rest, he went. And it was Hector.'

Mina glanced at Rose, in case she felt any concern at this tale of violence, but the maid sat squarely in place, unmoving, expressionless. 'Does Miss Samprey think that she had a premonition of her brother's death?'

'Yes. Although Charles always believed it was just her natural anxiety playing on her mind. Hector was a wayward soul. But she was fond of him. She used to worry about him.'

'And had he used a gun before?'

'No, never. That is the strange thing. Although he was going out to meet a man of bad character, and there was every chance of a dispute, and Barnes was always armed. Perhaps on that night, he felt he ought to take a weapon for his own defence.'

'Was a gun found with him?'

'No.'

'Was he seen leaving with one?'

'No.'

Mina considered this information. 'I'm not sure I understand,' she said. 'If your cousin had never used a gun before and was not seen leaving the house with one, why did his sister dream that he carried one? Also, if she had actually had a premonition of his murder, she would have seen him being threatened with a gun, not holding one. And in the end, you say that the gun in question wasn't found with him. Although I suppose the murderer could have taken it away.'

'I know. But is that not the nature of dreams? Two events occur and when we dream about them, they sometimes come together as one.'

'That is very true,' Mina admitted. 'What does Miss Samprey believe?'

Mr Clover gestured helplessly. 'It's hard to tell. When she talks about it all, the ideas seem to get mixed up. And she can get very upset. I once asked her to visit a medium to find out more, but she wouldn't hear of it. Clarissa is a very — unusual girl. She gets overwrought very easily. I know Charles is eager to have her married; he thinks she will be much better then.'

'How old is she?'

'Twenty-seven.'

'Is she betrothed?'

'No, that is the thing. She is terribly shy and has no sweetheart. Charles even held a tea party for her recently. He ordered in all sorts of cakes and fancies and invited some friends and young gentlemen from good families so she could be introduced. I was there, and I don't think it went well. She just sat in a corner eating sugared almonds all afternoon.'

'And she dwells on her brother's death? Does she talk of it often?'

'All the time,' said Mr Clover, miserably.

'I do think,' said Mina, gently, 'that if Miss Samprey finds the memory of that dreadful night so very painful, the family should find some means of alleviating her distress. There is a doctor I can recommend —'

'Oh, but you don't understand!' said Mr Clover. 'The thing is, and the whole reason I consulted Lady Brighthelm, and urgently need to see her again, is that I don't believe Barnes murdered Hector.'

Mina received this pronouncement with some astonishment. 'Really?' she exclaimed. 'Do you have any evidence on that point?'

'Yes, there is the testimony of his poor wife, Jenny Jemson,' said Clover with increased energy. 'I saw her give evidence for Barnes's defence at the police court and the trial. If you had seen her, you would have believed her, too. She had lived a hard life, a terrible life, but I could see her honesty and sincerity shine through. She declared that Barnes was at home in her company that night. In fact, she also said that there was no arrangement to meet Hector. There never had been. Hector may have said there was, I don't doubt that, but he was not I am sorry to say a truthful person. Hector always said whatever he needed to say to serve his own purpose.'

'Take care,' said Mina. 'You are claiming that British justice hanged an innocent man.'

'I am, and I know that it is an unpleasant thought, although Jenny —' he coughed — 'Miss Jemson feels sure that he had committed capital crimes in the past, and deserved to be hanged several times over, but they couldn't be proved against him and he was never charged. You might wonder why she was with such a man, but she said he was kind to her at first, all sweet talk. But when he got into drink, he struck her. She never had the courage to get away from him. She had nowhere to go except the streets, and she would never do that. He used to say that if she ran away, he would find her wherever she went and make her sorry she left him. So I think that justice has been served on Barnes, although not as intended.'

'And she still defended him?'

'Yes. She believes in telling the truth.'

Mina paused. Little of what Clover was telling her had been reported in Miss Jemson's evidence at Barnes's trial. Her statements were clearly a more recent communication. 'I assume that you have spoken to Miss Jemson since the trial. Did she reveal to you who she believes is the real murderer?'

Mr Clover's blush was confirmation of Mina's statement. 'She cannot know for certain. Her suspicions fell on one of Barnes's associates. But the motive is unclear, unless there was some kind of quarrel. With men like that, it might have been over anything at all, and of course there was probably drink involved.' He frowned. 'It's a side of life most of us never see. Talking to Miss Jemson has taught me a lot.'

'You have said that it was Hector's intention to sever his association with the criminals. Even if he didn't meet Barnes that night, it could have been another member of the gang. That intention alone might have provoked a quarrel. They might have suspected that he was about to denounce them to the police.'

Mr Clover hesitated. 'That was said in court, yes.'

'By both his father and his brother.'

'Yes, but I think my cousin was lying about that. Miss Jemson told me that she had heard Hector telling Barnes how he had fooled his father into thinking that he was about to change his ways, so as to get into his good books. He knew that if he didn't, he could end up being cut out of his father's will.'

'And his father believed him?'

'Yes, he did; after all, it was what he had wanted — prayed for.' Clover shook his head. 'My uncle was never able to see Hector for the villain he truly was. He had vain hopes of redemption right up to the moment of Hector's death. None of the family dared tell him otherwise for fear of a relapse.'

'But one of Hector's brothers lied in court as well?'

'Neither Charles nor Mortimer believed that Hector intended to reform, but they would never have said what they really thought in front of their father. It would have upset him too much.'

'I take it,' said Mina, after some thought, 'that the real reason for your concern in this matter is not to exonerate Barnes, who must be roasting in eternal flame as we speak, but with regard to Miss Jemson?'

Mr Clover's blush deepened. 'I admit I was impressed by her. I wanted to help her. I asked Mortimer and Charles if they could do something for her, but they both refused. She had defended Barnes, who they were sure was guilty, and that was enough for them. When I sought her out after the trial, she was hard to find, but eventually I found her in the Elm Grove workhouse. She had to go there or starve, since because of her association with Barnes no one would offer her work. She had nothing to her name, not even her own clothes. The workhouse uniform, the blue and white gown which was all she had to wear, announced to the world where she came from. It's a harsh place. She had been set to work picking oakum, but even in her poor condition she still had some measure of dignity. She was just nineteen, Miss Scarletti. That man had been the terror of her life for two years. She had had two children by him, both of whom had died.

'But she still said that she had told the truth and had not been mistaken. Whoever had murdered Hector, it was not Barnes. I decided to find her some respectable work. I knew of a rented house looking for a general maid, and I bought her new garments — her old rags had been burnt — and had her looking presentable. She knows how to clean and is not afraid of hard work and long hours. She calls herself Jenny Jones now. But she lives in terror that her old life will find her out. She has been branded as a disreputable woman who lied in court. If I could prove that she told the truth, she would have a happier future.'

'That is very charitable of you,' said Mina.

Mr Clover gave a faint smile, then abruptly rose from his seat and walked about the room. Rose stared at him suspiciously as he turned impulsively to face Mina. 'I have learned something even more shocking. I have told no one else of this, but I will tell you as I see you need to be convinced. Hector once told Barnes that he was responsible for the accident in which his father was injured, and his mother killed. He had loosened one of the carriage wheels.'

'Why ever did he do that?'

'He intended to kill his father. He hadn't known that his mother would join his father on the journey. It was decided on an impulse. He didn't have a chance to dissuade her.'

'Did the coachman not check over the carriage before setting out?'

'So he claimed. But who could prove otherwise? He would hardly admit to negligence. After that happened, Hector was so afraid of being found out and arrested that he went away for a time. He only came back when he thought he was out of danger. His father killed the proverbial fatted calf, of course.'

'And do you believe that if you were able to interview the shade of your cousin, he would reveal the true identity of his murderer, and exonerate Miss Jemson?'

'I do,' said Mr Clover.

'What of his brothers, Mortimer and Charles — do they not share your views?'

'No. They were sure that the spirit picture was a fraud. I went to the shop to make enquiries about it, and that was when I learned of Lady Brighthelm. She knew all about the murder of my cousin, even though I didn't give her my name. She told me that the spirit of my dead cousin had secrets to reveal. I told Mortimer and Charles about Miss Brighthelm, but they treated her with derision. They both believed that justice had been done, but I wasn't about to give up. I was going back to see her again when that awful thing happened. So now I fear I shall never know the truth,' he finished miserably.

'Mr Clover, when you consulted Lady Brighthelm, you didn't happen to notice what sweetmeats she preferred?'

He was evidently surprised by this question. 'Well — she — er — liked chocolates.'

'Did you notice which kind?'

'Yes. Now I think about it, she had a box of them. Violet creams. Veale's does them. Why?'

'Did you ever give or send her any?'

'No.'

'Did you mention her preference to anyone?'

'I — don't know. I might have mentioned it when I was talking to my cousins. They thought she was a figure of fun. Mortimer said she must be a secret drinker, or something worse. I said that as far as I knew, her worst vice was chocolate. I might have said Veales, I can't remember now. Charles said that all mediums are liars who make up stories for money. Is that what you think?'

'I know many mediums who are sincere about what they do and accept no reward. I know others who are criminals.'

'Lady Brighthelm never asked for a reward. Do you think her genuine?'

'I cannot judge.'

'There are many in Brighton who say that you are a medium.'

'I am not and have never claimed to be. Anyone who suggests that I am is mistaken.'

'I was hoping…'

'Yes?'

'I suppose I was hoping that you might be able to help Clarissa.'

'I'm not sure what you mean. How might I help Miss Samprey?'

'I think she may be a sensitive and would benefit from development.'

'If she is, it could prove to be a burden she would rather she did not have. My advice to you, Mr Clover, is to leave well alone.'

'But I can't!' he cried. 'I must know the truth!'

Mina, too, would have liked to know the truth. And the thought did occur to her that if Jenny Jemson had given honest and accurate testimony, then the killer of Hector Samprey might still be free.

When Mina returned home, a letter from young Mr Phipps was waiting for her, which, combined with what she had recently discovered was very informative.

Dear Miss Scarletti,

Further to our recent conversation, I have some news which you may find interesting.

I recall informing you that my grandfather, Aloysius Phipps, who founded this firm, had never had a photograph taken, since he was distrustful of the process and also wished to avoid any record of his appearance due to the cast in his eye about which he was extremely sensitive. This led to him commissioning the portrait in oils which you have seen.

I mentioned this recently to my great aunt Flora. She is the younger sister of my grandmother, the late Mrs Charlotte Phipps. She had a slightly different recollection of the matter. According to Aunt Flora, my grandfather had once been persuaded to have a photographic portrait made. It was about two years before his death in 1856, when glass plate photography, which is the thing nowadays was just starting to become popular. She couldn't recall the name of the photographer but felt sure that it was a Brighton man. She does remember, however, that when my grandfather came back from seeing the pictures, he was very annoyed and said that they were not at all good. He never showed them to her, or indeed anyone else as far as she is aware. He had paid for the work but ordered the photographer to destroy all trace of it. I assume that means both the glass negatives and the prints.

I showed my aunt the picture of the grave with what appears to be my grandfather's spirit standing beside it, and she agreed that it was him to the life. Not only that, but she was heartily amused by it. When I asked for an explanation, she said that he had always been very sceptical of the claims of spiritualists. He did not believe that the dead paid visits to the living but maintained that after death they slept until the day of judgement to be raised, as the Bible has said. This had greatly upset my grandmother, who was a passionate devotee of the medium Daniel Dunglas Home, who first came to England in 1855. Apparently, they used to have quite heated debates on the subject. My grandfather would denounce Home as a conjuror and charlatan, and my grandmother did all she could to change his mind but without effect.

After his death, my grandmother attended a number of séances to contact him, as she wanted to reassure herself that not only was he happy in the spirit world but that he now acknowledged that she had been correct all along. It appears that there were mediums who were able to provide her with messages that satisfied her that they came from my grandfather and that he accepted the reality of the spirit world. I asked my aunt what she thought of the photograph; did she think it was a message from my grandfather? She could not say; she only hoped that he and her sister were now together in harmony.

Sincerely,

R Phipps

There was no means of knowing whether Mr Simpson had been the photographer in question and if he had been, whether he had, as promised, destroyed all evidence that Mr Aloysius Phipps had ever been photographed. The records of past customers and the list that Richard had once made of images and plates acquired from the estate of the late Mr Simpson were materials which Mr Beckler was holding very close to his chest.

CHAPTER TWENTY-ONE

Mina was not especially interested in mingling with fashionable crowds of visitors on the West Pier, but their noisy chatter and colourful jostling helped to conceal her real intention, which was another conversation with private detective Mr Stevenson. What her mother might have made of a second meeting with a gentleman who was a stranger to her, she did not know. Mina thought that for safety such occasions should be made to appear as chance encounters and not planned assignations. She realised that she did not know if Mr Stevenson was married or single and had no intention of asking him.

Mina did not venture far along the walking deck. The sun was high, and she decided to find a seat at one of the ornamental shelters. She had brought her little wedge-shaped cushion and made herself comfortable, opened her notebook and waited. A few minutes later she heard the approach of a gentleman, who sat down within speaking distance.

'It is a fine morning,' said Mr Stevenson.

'So it is,' said Mina. She glanced about, but no one was near enough to overhear them. The shelters were octagonal, so the seating under the canopy formed separate sections, which was very convenient. 'I have had a recent conversation with Mr Septimus Clover, in which he imparted some very interesting information,' she went on.

Mr Stevenson listened intently to her account. 'Do I have the impression that Mr Clover has an attachment to Miss Jemson which goes further than a mere friendly concern for her wellbeing?' he asked.

'That could well be the case. He was clearly impressed by her. But what the future may hold, I cannot say. However, what occupies my mind is the suggestion that it was one of Barnes's criminal associates who murdered Hector Samprey and not Barnes himself. Barnes's conviction has never really been questioned, and Miss Jemson's testimony was not believed. She was thought to have been coerced. But Mr Clover's determination to rehabilitate her is stirring up suspicion. If Lady Brighthelm was offering him an opportunity to converse with Hector's spirit, whether or not she knew the truth of the matter, that could be a reason for the attack on her.'

'You mean it was not another medium who wished to dispose of a rival?' said Mr Stevenson, but he was smiling. 'Yes, I know of Mr Hope's insinuations, and I can see why you would like this matter resolved. But if you wish me to investigate on your behalf, I am afraid I cannot do so.'

'Why not?'

'There is a limit to the types of cases I undertake. I watch the actions of erring husbands and wives. I observe those thought to be cheating in business. I find evidence of blackmail, fraud and theft. What I do not do is confront dangerous criminals who are armed with guns which they are unafraid to use.'

'I can understand that,' said Mina, regretfully. 'And I doubt very much that it would assist me to inform the police, especially in a case which they must regard as resolved. Miss Jemson has no more to offer beyond her original testimony. I cannot point to another culprit. I assume the members of Barnes's gang were all known to the police?'

'Not all. A few were merely violent cutthroats. Some are in prison. Others, like Hector Samprey, made a show of respectability and may still walk free and unsuspected amongst us.'

'That is what I had feared.'

'If we hope to resolve the question, we will need either a confession or an informant, and there should be verifiable facts, not mere suspicion. Either way, the source should be living. The courts will not countenance the evidence of a ghost.'

'I understand.'

'Mr Hope may be making insinuations against you, but he has no evidence, and he cannot be explicit for fear of prosecution. He may tire of the theme in time and turn to other matters.'

'If you could be alert to any further action he might take against me, I would be grateful,' said Mina.

'I think we are agreed to a free exchange of information,' said Mr Stevenson. 'Oh, and one other thing, for what it is worth. There are conflicting accounts of Hector Samprey's intentions, but I am convinced that Mr Clover told you the truth. The Samprey brothers believed that Hector had lied to his father, but they dared not say anything to him about it in view of the old man's health. They came to me and asked if I would follow their brother and secretly witness any meetings he might have with his criminal associates. Naturally, I declined.'

'Perhaps they went to another detective.'

'If they had done, he would have witnessed the murder, but no one has come forward. In fact, now I think about it, their appeal to me took place only the day before the murder, so if they had found another man willing to undertake such a risky commission, it would have been too late.'

Mina received another letter from Edward.

Dear Mina,

I hope you and the family are well. London is very hot, and my dear Agatha has been spending much of her time at Mrs Gostelow's cottage where the air is so much better. She is cultivating a herb garden, which I am told is quite enchanting. I am to be invited to view it very shortly, although I am not sure why it is believed that such an activity could possibly occupy an entire afternoon. She has made some flavoured waters which she is very anxious for me to try.

Now, as you know, I do not wish Mother to be advised that we in any way consider the supposed spirit photograph of Father to be a fraud, as it brings her so much happiness to look upon it. However, the matter has continued to weigh upon my mind, as I am convinced it has also done on yours. I mentioned in my last letter that I had spoken to some knowledgeable acquaintances, and they asked me very pointedly about other pictures of Father, which might have somehow — possibly by accident — managed to be superimposed on the recent one. There is a London gentleman called Hudson who has been doing something similar very recently and has created a great deal of excitement, although I believe it is mainly amongst those who are already devotees of spiritualism and needed no further convincing. I was shown one of Hudson's supposed spirit photographs, and I have to say if ghosts really do look like persons wrapped in linen shrouds with their faces concealed, then he has made a very fine job of it.

I chanced to mention the matter to Greville as he was Father's oldest friend, as well as his business partner, and he asked to see our picture. When I showed it to him, he stared at it for quite a while then said that it was slightly familiar to him and he would make some enquiries. This morning he brought me a family album of his. There are a number of pictures of a picnic which took place many years ago, possibly in the summer of 1855 or 1856. They show a family group in which the members were either sitting or standing in a London park. I at once recognised Greville and his wife, and there were his brother and sister and their spouses. And Father was in the picture, standing to one side. As soon as I saw it, I recalled the event. You were there too, and Richard and Enid. But we children were not pictured. I think we had been taken aside to be amused with ball games or some such, and there was little chance of us standing still long enough for a photograph, as things were then. Mother wasn't there; either she had a cold or was looking after Marianne who had a cold, I can't quite recall.

When I compared the picture of Father in Greville's picture with the one at the betrothal, they were similar but not identical. The clothing was the same, and his hair and beard were the same, and he was standing, but not in the same pose, and he was facing the other way. I looked through the whole album, as you can imagine. There were no pictures of Father at other events, although I did find several others of the picnic. I think the photographer must have been experimenting with different views of the scene and maybe also the light. Some pictures had not come out well, as they were too dark, or someone had moved, and the face was a blur, or a hat was in the way, so the only one properly mounted was the one I have mentioned. But Father was in several of them, usually sitting. Greville said that he had never had copies made of the pictures, neither has he lent them to anyone.

I would have suggested having a copy made for Mother, but there would always be the risk that she might draw the same conclusion as we have, that there is something underhand being done if we could only discover what it is.

Affect'ly
Edward

Mina gave considerable thought to Edward's letter. She had no doubt of the accuracy of his observations. Neither was there any doubt in her mind of the honesty of Mr Greville's reply. There had been occasional summer picnics when she was a child, but she had never seen any photographs of them. Nevertheless, this was evidence that photographs of her father had been taken at a time when his hair, beard and clothing were the same as those in the betrothal picture. Supposing there had been others? Supposing he had liked the results and arranged for another more formal sitting? The family had occasionally visited Brighton before coming to live there. Had her father been photographed by Mr Simpson during such a visit?

Mr Greville had recently written to Mina to send her payment for one of her stories, and she had every excuse to write to him.

Dear Mr Greville,

Thank you for your cheque on the publication of Horrid Tales from a Haunted House, *and your very complimentary remarks on the work. You may indeed wonder where my ideas come from, and I sometimes wonder that myself, but in this particular case it is no mystery. A recent visit furnished me with ideas for a score of stories, and I only hope I shall have time to write them all.*

I was interested to learn that Edward has shown you the picture recently taken at his betrothal in which the image of our father appeared. He tells me that you were kind enough to show him some pictures in your family album showing my father at a picnic, which bear some resemblance to this new portrait. Please could you let me know the name and address of the photographer, as I would find it very interesting to speak to him. I am wondering if he might have some other pictures of my father, which would be greatly appreciated. Sincerely, M Scarletti

Mina was pleased to receive a letter from her friend, the actor Mr Merridew, who informed her that he would be returning to Brighton in a week's time and hoped to meet with her to be apprised of all the most important news of the town. Mina, who was interested to know his views on the matter, responded that the town was all a-chatter about Mr Beckler's claim to produce spirit photographs, one of which was displayed in his shop window. She knew as she wrote the words that one of Mr Merridew's first actions on his return to Brighton would be to pay a visit to Ship Street to examine the great novelty of the hour.

She received a reply from Mr Greville in the next post.

Dear Miss Scarletti,

Thank you for your letter. If your ideas for Horrid Tales *from a* Haunted House *came from personal experience, I can only be amazed. It is not a house I would ever care to visit.*

The photographs of the family picnic were taken by my wife's cousin, Thomas Gooding. He had a small photographic business in London. The picnic photographs were done as a favour, as he was trying out different lenses and settings at the time, which does explain the varied results. Sadly, he passed away some eight years ago, and his business was sold to Mr J E Mayall of Regent Street. I made some enquiries there on your behalf, but it seems that only the equipment and materials were purchased, and Mr Mayall took over any existing accounts. They have no record of any pictures taken of your father.

Sincerely,

G Greville

It had been a promising trail to follow, but there it had ended. Mina did not even know if there had been any further pictures taken, but if there had it was unlikely, under the circumstances, that they had survived. It was like finding two ends of a chain. She could not help feeling that the ends were part of the same chain, but there was a gap she could not bridge.

CHAPTER TWENTY-TWO

At Mr Beckler's shop, a new sign had been put on display which stated, 'The Management regrets to advise that Lady Brighthelm has retired from her practice as a medium.' Few customers had stopped to read it, and so Richard had been asked to paint a decorative border on the notice and move it to a more prominent position. This had made very little difference. Nothing, it seemed, would stop customers from coming in and requesting a consultation, even those who it appeared had troubled to read the sign. There were always those who hoped that despite the advice given to everyone, they might be regarded as an exception to the rule.

Mr Beckler had ordered Richard to polish the picture frames on display, and was examining the appointment book when young Mr Clover arrived, bringing with him a lady he had not met before.

'What may I do for you, Mr Clover?' he asked. 'I am occupied this morning, but I have time for a sitting this afternoon.'

'Oh, it is not for a sitting,' said Mr Clover. 'Allow me to introduce my cousin, Miss Samprey.'

Mr Beckler glanced at the lady. 'I am delighted to make your acquaintance, Miss Samprey.'

She lowered her eyes suspiciously and shrank back from him.

'Might I ask a few minutes of your time for a discussion?' asked Mr Clover.

Mr Beckler felt little inclined to give either of the visitors any of his time but consulted his watch and bowed. 'Of course, I do have a few moments to spare before my next appointment.'

Mr Clover raised no objection to Richard's presence, and Richard made sure to remain as the conversation commenced.

'As you know, I was extremely upset to hear of Lady Brighthelm's indisposition,' said Mr Clover. 'I don't suppose there is any possibility…?' he ventured.

'None, I am afraid. Her powers have quite vanished,' said Mr Beckler, firmly.

Mr Clover accepted the situation without further comment. 'The fact is,' he said brightly, 'I was thinking that if you wished to employ another medium, I might have the answer.'

Mr Beckler risked a look at Miss Samprey, who was staring at the floor. 'Please go on.'

'I do not pretend to have any gifts in that line myself, but it is my belief that the Samprey family all have some measure of psychic abilities. My cousins Mortimer and Charles, who are Clarissa's brothers, have both told me that following the death of their older brother Hector some years ago, they have had vivid dreams in which he has appeared to them.'

'That must be very distressing,' said Mr Beckler. 'Of course, many people dream of loved ones, family members they have lost, but that is not in itself evidence of psychic powers, unless of course the spirit provided them with some information they did not have before.'

'He was murdered,' said Clarissa, looking up so suddenly that Mr Beckler flinched. 'Shot to death. They found his body by the sea. The bullet went through his heart.'

'Yes,' said Mr Clover, 'and that fact was not known until the day after his death, when his body was found, but the important point is that Clarissa dreamed about Hector's death at about the same time it happened, but before the family learned of it.'

'He had a gun,' said Clarissa, 'and his eyes were wild and staring. I knew something was wrong. But no one would believe me.'

'I believe you,' said Mr Clover, patting her hands, which she had bunched convulsively into lace-mittened fists.

She pouted with annoyance. 'Charles said it was all a dream, but I know what I saw!'

'And it *was* a dream, my dear, it was,' said Mr Clover, soothingly, 'but a dream in which you saw what others could not see.'

Mr Beckler looked at his watch again. 'Mr Clover,' he said politely, 'what is the purpose of this conversation? Are you offering Miss Samprey's services as a medium?'

'Oh, I know her powers are as yet unformed, undirected,' said Mr Clover. 'I would not suggest that she comes here straightaway and sets up her booth as a replacement for Lady Brighthelm. Not yet. But I think if she could be developed by a suitable individual, she could in time achieve greatness in that line. Might I ask you — would you be willing to develop her?'

Mr Beckler stared at Clarissa Samprey. 'I have no talent in that direction. Lady Brighthelm's talents may have blossomed here, but they did so entirely without my assistance.'

'Then might I ask if you could arrange for her to be introduced to Viscount Hope?'

'Of course,' Mr Beckler said, 'I will arrange an introduction as soon as Mr Hope is available. He is at present engaged in giving lectures with which he is planning to tour England, and writing a new book, so I cannot anticipate when that might be.'

'I am so very grateful,' said Mr Clover, presenting a business card.

'It wasn't a dream,' said Clarissa Samprey through gritted teeth.

'And now I have an appointment for a sitting and must bid you good day,' said Mr Beckler, a little sharply.

Soon after the visitors had gone, two policemen arrived. There was something about their manner that suggested they had not come to arrange a sitting. The more senior of the two consulted a notebook. 'Mr Anthony Beckler?'

'Yes.'

'Might we have a word with you? In private?'

It was not a request.

When Mina made her next weekly visit to the Oriental steam baths, she told Dr Hamid about her attendance at the funeral of Mrs Ragdon and the subsequent séance. Both of these accounts interested and surprised him, although he was anxious that she might be overtaxing herself before she was fully recovered. His examination, and review of the list of exercises she was undertaking under his sister's supervision were able to satisfy that concern.

'I don't suppose you can enlighten me on the demise of Mr Ragdon and the illness of his wife?' asked Mina.

'I did not treat either of them, but I understand that Mr Ragdon ended his days in an asylum. He suffered from a disease of the brain. It is possible that Mrs Ragdon suffered in the same way but escaped that fate due to the care of her sister.'

'Would she have been able to conduct séances?'

'Towards the end of her life that would have been very doubtful.'

Mina found the idea of being alive and conscious but not able to express herself very frightening. 'Would she have been aware of her surroundings?'

'I feel certain that she would have known nothing.'

'We prayed by her bedside. I was hoping for answers, but I am not sure I found them.'

'It is not good to dwell excessively on our troubles. We must prepare for the future, of course, that is always wise, but sometimes we use all our energies in worry when we would be better advised to use the greater part to consider the present.'

'That is what I tell other people,' said Mina, ruefully, 'and likewise what they tell me.'

'You should listen to them,' he said. 'Is Mr Hope causing you any concern? I saw his letter in the *Gazette*. My advice is to ignore it.'

'He is being very careful not to make a direct attack in print. But he is giving a series of lectures in Brighton, and who knows what he is saying?'

'If there is anything I can do to assist you, you must let me know,' said Dr Hamid.

'I will be sure to do so,' Mina replied.

When she returned home, she found Richard there earlier than expected. He was avoiding a conversation with their mother, and the sunshine had gone out of his manner. Something was obviously the matter.

'I need to go out for a smoke,' he said, when Mina asked him how he was.

'Do you want to be alone, or would you like me to come with you?' she asked.

He managed the ghost of a smile. 'It's always better when I can talk to you,' he said.

Mina didn't press him to say more. He would talk when he felt ready. They walked down to the sea front together, arm in arm, and leaned on the railings, looking out to sea. Richard lit a small cigar and looked thoughtful. The air was delicious. Mina could never understand why anyone would taint it with cigar smoke.

'It was a very peculiar sort of day,' said Richard, at last. He recounted what he had heard during the visit of Mr Clover and Miss Samprey to Mr Beckler's shop. 'Beckler was quite shaken up by it. All that talk of ghostly dreams and murder and guns. He said he thought they were both mad. Clover wanted him to introduce Miss Samprey to Mr Hope, but I could see he didn't want to as he had no idea how that would end. For all he knew, the woman would go wild and be more trouble than she is worth. I know you don't feel sorry for him, but I have to admit I rather did.'

'There is nothing too strange in this world for Mr Hope,' said Mina. 'If someone came to him saying they had seen goblins and pixies and fairies dancing in their garden, he would claim it as the most wonderful discovery.'

'Anyhow, that wasn't the oddest thing. Two policemen came to the shop this afternoon asking to speak to Beckler. I overheard enough to know that they were from the Middlesex force. They all went into the office to talk, and when they came out Beckler was very shocked indeed. He'd obviously had some bad news. He wouldn't tell me what it was, only that he had to go away and he didn't know when he would be back, but he would send a telegram to let me know.'

'Middlesex?' said Mina, thoughtfully. 'I know he has another business in Twickenham. That's where he lived before coming to Brighton. Perhaps he has family there. If the police have come to see him, it must be serious.'

'From the faces of the policemen, it was very serious,' said Richard, gloomily. 'Perhaps he'll be arrested. And then what am I to do?'

'Is the shop to be closed while he is away, or are you to manage it?'

'Closed. I hope I'll be paid. I mean, it wouldn't be fair if I wasn't. I had to stay on for a bit this afternoon because Mr Nye Chart from the theatre was sending a messenger to collect some pictures which he absolutely had to have today for some reason, but Beckler said that once that bit of business was done I was to lock up and go home.' Richard frowned suddenly. 'Now where did I put those keys?' He patted his pockets, then dipping his hand in one, pulled out a bunch of keys. 'Ah, yes, here they are.' He pushed them back into his pocket.

'I think you should take good care of those,' said Mina. 'Best put them in a drawer at home rather than walk about with them.'

He nodded and flicked the stub of his cigar over the rail, then rested his chin on his hands and sighed.

'You did remember to lock up the shop, didn't you?'

'Mm? Oh yes. Well, I think so. I'm almost sure I did.'

Mina seized his arm and gave him a little shake. 'Richard! Almost sure isn't enough. A business like that has hundreds of pounds worth of equipment, not to mention a stock of poisonous chemicals. Arsenic, cyanide. There must be enough poison there to kill hundreds — thousands of people.'

'That's true. I could go along tomorrow morning, I suppose.'

'No, Richard,' Mina insisted, 'we will get a cab and go there now. I know you'll sleep soundly without making sure all is safe, but I certainly will not.'

Richard knew better than to make other than the most token protest. He summoned a cab and before long they had alighted at the end of Ship Street to walk up to the shop. To Mina's dismay, the 'Open' notice was still showing and when she pushed the door, it swung inwards and the bell tinkled.

'I'll just lock up now, then,' said Richard, groping for the keys.

'No, you won't. You will go in and check that nothing has been taken.'

Mina entered the shop and changed the notice on the door to 'Closed'. Richard gave a sigh of resignation and followed her in. A quick examination showed that the doors of the darkroom, studio, storeroom and office were all locked. Richard cast an eye over the items on display, but nothing appeared to have been stolen.

As Mina looked about her, she realised that as they were the only persons present it was possible to undertake a useful exercise.

'Shall we go now?' Richard asked plaintively.

'Not yet. There is something you can help me with.'

'Oh?'

'I am thinking about the day the poisoned chocolates were left here. And the gentleman customer.'

'But I've already told all I know to the police.'

Mina ignored his protest. 'Let us pretend it is that day again. Where were you when the customer came in? The gentleman who wanted to buy a frame?'

'I was standing behind the counter.'

'Good. Just go there now.'

Richard shrugged. 'All right.' He moved to stand behind the counter.

'Now, imagine that I am that gentleman. I have just walked in.' Mina went and stood by the door. 'Where do I go from here?'

'Well, you would walk up to the counter and stand there looking at the frames.' He indicated the tiered wooden display stand on the counter stocked with a selection of frames.

Mina moved to the counter to view the frames. 'Is this where he stood?'

'Yes, just about. I mean, he was taller than you.'

'If you didn't move, then this display is in between us. Were you able to see much of his face as he stood there? You didn't move to look at him?'

'No, why would I? I just let him look at the frames.'

'So, here I am looking at them, but I don't see what I want. What next?'

'I must have said to him, "we have more in our catalogue", or something of the sort, and put it on the counter for him to look at.'

'And he looked at it?'

'Yes, but not for very long. He said something like "do you have anything larger?"'

'What was his voice like?'

'Nothing in particular. Quiet. Mina, it's very hard to remember all this.'

'But there was nothing unusual? An accent?'

'No.'

'I see. What happened next?'

'He said something about my going to have a look for him, so I went into the storeroom.'

'Then you went at his suggestion, not on your own initiative?'

'Yes.'

'How long were you there looking?'

'Not long. About a minute. I mean, I didn't really bother to look because I knew we didn't have anything else. Then the bell rang.'

'The shop bell?'

'Yes, so I came back because I thought another customer had come in.'

'Go to the storeroom now.'

'It's locked.'

'Then unlock it.'

Richard obeyed, shaking his head, and after a minute, Mina crossed to the door and opened and closed it as if someone had entered. It was less than half a minute before Richard reappeared.

'Who was in the shop when you came back?'

'Just the man.'

'And where was he standing? Was he still by the counter?'

'No — he — I think he was on the other side of the shop. He was looking at the pictures on the wall.'

Mina crossed over to the wall display. 'Here?'

'Yes.'

'With his back to you?'

'Yes.'

'What conversation did you have?'

'Not much. He just said that a boy had come in and delivered something. That was when I saw the little bag of chocolates on the counter.'

'Whereabouts on the counter?'

'I don't know. In the middle somewhere.'

'So — you can hear the shop bell when the door opens quite clearly from the storeroom?'

'Oh yes.'

'Which means that someone had come in. When you came back into the shop, you were expecting to see another person there?'

'Yes, well, that would be usual.'

Mina went to the door and opened it, causing the bell to ring. It was on a spring, so when she released the door it began to swing shut again and closed under its own momentum in just a few seconds.

'But you didn't hear the door open again after that?' Richard scratched his head. 'The thing is, if the delivery boy had come in and put the chocolates in the middle of the counter, then the door would have swung shut behind him. Then he would have had to open it again to leave the shop. The bell would have rung twice.'

'I suppose so,' said Richard.

'Unless,' Mina continued, 'the boy held the door open, handed the bag to the customer who was standing looking at the pictures, and left, so the door only opened and closed once.'

'Mina, I really don't know. I found the bag lying on the counter and I guessed that the boy had just put it there.'

'It would be very unusual for the delivery boy to hand something to a customer, I agree,' said Mina. She crossed over to the counter and put her reticule in the middle of it. 'Is that about the right place?'

'I think so.'

'Now you have to pretend to be the delivery boy, because I can't walk smartly enough.'

Richard had given up arguing with Mina and came out from behind the counter. She handed him the reticule. 'Go to the door, open it as if you have just come in, walk to where the bag was placed then go back to the door.'

Richard obeyed. As he opened the door, the bell sounded. On reaching the counter he put the reticule on it, then he turned and walked back to the door. By the time he had reached it, it had swung shut again.

'So,' said Mina, 'unless the boy was actually running — a possibility we can't altogether dismiss — he would have had to open the door a second time to leave the shop. But you only heard it open once.' She thought further. 'How did you know the chocolates were for Lady Brighthelm? Was there a label or marking of some kind?'

'No.'

'Then how did you know they were for her?'

'The customer told me; he said a boy had delivered something for Lady Brighthelm.'

'But how did he know?'

'He didn't say. The boy must have said something.'

'Did you hear a voice?'

'No.' Richard searched his pockets for his cigar case. 'Can we go home now?'

'Not yet. I want to try something else,' said Mina.

'If we must.'

'I am the customer, and you are going to the storeroom to look for a frame.'

Mina stood looking at the display stand, and Richard reluctantly but obediently returned to the storeroom. Mina placed her reticule on the counter. She then walked to the shop door, opened it and closed it, and walked over to view the pictures on the wall opposite the counter. At this point, Richard returned to the shop. 'A boy just delivered something,' said Mina, pointing to her reticule.

'I don't understand,' said Richard.

'I think I may do,' said Mina. 'There was no delivery boy. The man came to the shop with the bag of chocolates in his pocket. He sent you away to look for something then dropped the bag on the counter and walked away. Then he opened and closed the door as if someone had come in. When you came back, he told you that a boy had delivered chocolates for Lady Brighthelm. There was no label or marking on the gift because he feared that his handwriting would give him away.'

'Why would he do that?'

'Because he knew they were poisoned.'

'How?'

'Because he poisoned them.'

'Oh!' exclaimed Richard, suddenly wide-eyed as he understood.

'How long did he stay after that?'

'He — left almost at once. He said he would come by another day. But he didn't.'

'I would hardly have expected him to do so.'

'Oh. Oh, I see. He didn't really mean it.' Richard grimaced. 'Do we have to tell someone?'

'I will write to Inspector Gibbs with my observations. But he is very clever and must have already come to the same conclusion. He caught Miss Edmunds, after all. If he cannot catch this villain, no one can.'

'All right,' said Richard, looking relieved. 'Now can we go home?' he added, hopefully.

'Not yet,' said Mina. 'I have one more thing to do. Let me have the keys.'

Richard delved into his pockets again and handed her the bunch. 'What do you want them for?'

'I want to look in the office.'

'What for?'

'The list you made. Remember I wanted to see it?'

'Yes, but —'

'I won't be long.'

Richard leaned his elbows on the counter with a groan.

'And no smoking,' said Mina.

He groaned again.

It didn't take long for Mina to identify the various keys. She first made sure to relock the storeroom, then opened up Mr Beckler's office, and began by examining the contents of the shelves. She recognised the same photographic magazines Mr Mayall had in his office, but there were also some old leather-bound ledger volumes which she realised were account books from the time of Mr Simpson. One, neatly kept in alphabetical form, listed all the individual customers and their accounts with brief descriptions of what work had been done. She turned the pages and found names she knew. Samprey, a family group portrait, Bertram Veale standing outside his shop, Miss Porterson-White walking in her garden, Frederick Soules with his chemical apparatus, Aloysius Phipps with croquet mallet, Charles Peasgood with ancestral portraits, Eleanor Honeyacre with puppy, Robert Mulgrew with collected books, and the Scarletti/Inskip wedding. Her father's name did not appear, and neither did that of any member of the Hartop family.

There was a small key on the bunch that unlocked the desk. It helped that Mr Beckler kept everything very tidy, and Mina soon located a folder which contained the list that Richard had made of the unclaimed pictures. Every one of the individuals whose graves in the Extra Mural Cemetery had been photographed was recorded there. Again, there was no record of any unclaimed photographs featuring either the Scarlettis or the Hartops.

A thicker folder caught her attention and when she opened it, she knew she had found what she had most hoped for: copies of all the cemetery pictures. She had to admit, Mr Beckler was a master of his craft. As she examined them, she noticed another significant thing they all had in common: all the subjects were portrayed standing. It was a clever twist, but she saw that a picture of someone seated in an armchair by their own grave would have been far less convincing. Her discovery inevitably raised the question of how the pictures had been achieved, and she thought it was most probably by the method Mr Mayall had described. Mina realised, however, that the portraits themselves and her suspicions, even the expert opinion of Mr Mayall, did not constitute actual proof of how the results had been achieved. There was nothing she could take to a court of law.

At the bottom of the pile was a stiff envelope. It was unsealed, and Mina peered inside and saw a single photograph. When she eased it out, she gasped aloud. It was a portrait of her father, one that she had never seen before. Or at least, not in that form. It was the very image that had appeared beside her in the betrothal picture taken by Mr Beckler.

Her father was standing at his ease, healthy, smiling. He was outdoors and behind him was a pleasant sweep of grassland, with a cluster of trees in the distance. And all of a sudden, Mina remembered it, the precise event. It had been a sunny day, she didn't know where or when, but she could feel the warm air on her face, and how hot her clothes felt. There was a fresh smell of new cut grass, and she heard the clatter of teacups from a small table about which the adults were gathered. She had eaten cake and drunk lemonade; she could taste them. Other children were there, larger than she, and there was a brightly coloured ball to chase. She had tripped and bumped her knee, but jumped up again, and kept running and running until she was allowed to catch the ball. She stood up, clasping the ball in both hands triumphantly. A boyish Edward was smiling. Her spine was straight.

But where, she wondered, had Mr Beckler obtained such a picture? There was nothing on it to say who the photographer was. Then Mina remembered the images Edward had described to her, those in Mr Greville's family album, ones he said had never been copied; and the horrible truth dawned.

At that moment, Richard peered through the office door. 'Have you finished? Can we go now?' He paused. 'Mina dear, why are you looking like that? What's the matter? What have you found?' He stared at the open drawers, and the papers on the desk. 'I do think you ought to put all those things back, or he'll think I've been rummaging through his desk.'

Mina held up the picture to his view. 'Richard. Please explain this.'

He was visibly taken aback. 'I — er — well, it's a picture of —'

'I know what it is. It's a picture of Father. One we never had taken. Please tell me how it got here. And also let me know why you allowed it to be used by Mr Beckler to falsify a ghost portrait.'

'How do you know it was me?' he said, sulkily.

'Richard, it's always you.'

He shuffled his feet.

'Don't stand there like that; come in and sit down. And I want the truth. All of it.'

'I don't want Mother to know,' he pleaded, as he sat down.

'Mother is the very last person I would tell. Can you imagine?'

'I don't want to imagine. But Mina, it isn't a fraud, not really. Beckler explained it all. I told you all about it.'

'You told me some nonsense about photographs absorbing part of the subject.'

'It's not nonsense! It's science!'

'The science that suits Mr Beckler's schemes. Just tell me first of all how did you get the picture?'

'It was when I was working in London. I had dinner at Mr Greville's. Did you know he has three daughters? Quite pretty, too. All married, not that I ever thought of —'

'Richard!'

'Yes, well, they are nice enough ladies. One of them showed me the album, and I saw that there were pictures of Father in there. She said that I could take one and have it copied. She fetched an envelope for me, and I put it in my pocket. I suppose I must have forgotten about it.'

'That does not explain how it came into Mr Beckler's possession.'

'No — well —'

'The truth, Richard. Now.'

'Don't be so cross, Mina,' he protested.

'I will be even more cross in a minute if you don't tell me what I want to know.'

'All right.'

Mina allowed a few moments for him to collect his thoughts, and for her furious breathing to settle.

'The thing is, I was thinking about the picture with Miss Hartop's mother, and I said to Beckler how happy our mother would have been if Father's ghost had been in the portrait that she sat for. When I asked him to take the pictures of Edward's betrothal, I did wonder if Father might appear there. You remember how Mother was when she thought about it; I knew she would have liked him to be there.'

'I do remember, yes. And when you say you wondered if Father might appear, did you actually mention it to Mr Beckler?'

'Umm — yes — I suppose I must have done. I asked how he thought ghosts happened in pictures. He said that for a ghost to appear there had to be an essence of a person's spirit in the room. When his first ghost picture appeared, that was at his other business in Twickenham. He was at the beside of a dead man, and he thought that being so recently deceased, some of the essence of the gentleman must have remained in the room. I suppose it must float about in the air — I don't really know. But for others it can be a part of something that belongs to them. Miss Hartop wears a locket, and he thought it must once have been her mother's. So I said I could ask Mother to wear some memento of Father when she came for the betrothal pictures.'

'Mother always wears some little memento of Father,' said Mina.

'Yes, I thought that too. But then Beckler told me about the way that photographs can have some of the essence of the person in them. He thought that it would work even better than something like a locket. He asked me if I had a picture of Father he could borrow. He said all that was needed was to leave it in the studio for a short while, maybe just for a morning, and then I could return it. During that time, some of the essence from the photograph would pass into the air of the room. And then when he took the pictures, Father might appear. But he said I mustn't tell anyone I had borrowed a picture. He said if I told Mother and nothing happened, then she would be disappointed and upset. And he also said I especially mustn't tell you, because Mr Hope thinks your influence frightens away ghosts, and if you were to know of it the ghost might not want to appear.

'I thought about the pictures Mother already has of Father. There is the one by her bedside, but she would probably notice if I took it away, as she looks at it so often, and there are some others in her escritoire but that is always locked, and then I remembered the one from Mr Greville's album. So I said he could borrow that one. When I told him no one else had seen it yet, Beckler said in that case he would keep it for a while and have a copy made and put in a special frame for Mother as a gift. But it would be a while before he could do it, as it takes time for the essence to rebuild.' Richard gazed at Mina hopefully.

She remained unmoved. 'I imagine Mr Beckler was delighted when he learned it was a picture we had never seen. And I have no doubts as to why he has chosen to retain it. I don't know if Mother would have had suspicions, I am sure she could have found some way of convincing herself of a reason why the images were identical, but Edward and I would have seen at once that it was a copy, and Mr Beckler knows it.'

'You think it wasn't really Father?' asked Richard, plaintively.

'What I think doesn't matter. The betrothal picture brought so much peace and pleasure to Mother, I have no intention of suggesting to her that it is a fraud. The cost to us was not exorbitant, and it was a small price to pay for Mother's happiness. For myself, I need no photograph in order to live in the hope that Father is watching over us and that he is with Marianne in heaven.'

Mina tidied away everything, taking great care that the contents of the drawer were placed exactly as she had found them.

'What are you going to do?' asked Richard, apprehensively. 'I don't want to be dismissed. I've just started doing the colour tints of ladies.'

'I am not going to do anything, Richard. And you must promise me not to tell Mr Beckler I have seen these pictures. I do think he is a fraud, but I can't prove it. In a way, I suppose he is like the mediums who entertain people for a shilling. I have no quarrel with them if they make their customers happy.

I am hoping that the letter in the *Gazette* from the Soules brothers will prove to be warning enough. Not everyone will be taken in, and the example of Mr Mumler in America and his false ghosts is not unknown over here. But I shall keep my eye on your employer, as I do not know what he may do in future to stay in Mr Hope's good books.'

Mina did not say so, but she could see that Richard, while bored by some of his work, did enjoy painting backdrops and tinting photographs and was more settled there than he had been anywhere in the past. She was satisfied that for now, there was no great danger of Mr Beckler's arrest for swindling. Better than that, based on what Mr Mayall had said, the techniques used to produce the spirit images were far beyond Richard's capabilities, so even if his employer did come under suspicion, it was unlikely that he would be implicated.

CHAPTER TWENTY-THREE

The following morning, Richard received a telegram to say that Mr Beckler would be back in Brighton the next day and the shop could then reopen. When Mina eventually learned the reasons for his absence, it was not good news.

The man who Beckler had left in charge of his Twickenham business had neglected it disastrously, and his reports on takings had been false. He had finally absconded with all the funds and the valuable equipment, leaving the rent of the premises unpaid. There was no alternative but to close the business and sell what small stock remained to a dealer to pay off the debts.

'I am almost inclined to feel sorry for him,' said Mina. 'But he has the Brighton business, which seems to be doing well.'

'Oh yes, and Mr Hope called in again,' said Richard. 'He is writing another letter to the *Gazette* to say that the Soules brothers are materialists and he knows the truth, and he is also composing a special article for the *Spiritual Banner* so that believers will flock to Brighton for Mr Beckler's pictures. He is taking out advertisements in all the newspapers, and he is going to deliver a talk on the subject to the Brighton Photographic Society. There will be a card in the shop window with all the details. He's taking a room at the Town Hall. Everyone welcome. He says Mr Beckler will make his fortune.'

'I expect he was very pleased about that,' said Mina.

'Do you know, it was rather strange, but he didn't look pleased at all.'

Mina's first thought was that this new endeavour would keep Mr Hope in Brighton for still longer. She wished he would go away. She wished she knew if he was planning some new scheme to discredit her. Now that Mr Beckler had lost his other business and was completely beholden to his patron, what dreadful demands would he be obliged to undertake?

Mina's great comfort was that she was not alone; she was not without friends: good, kind, sensible friends. Dr Hamid was always her most reliable support, and he knew more of her concerns than most people. And there was Mr Merridew, who would be in Brighton again very soon. She would tell him everything, and she knew she would have his sympathy.

One thing she knew she must never do. Whatever the temptation, however burning her curiosity, she must not under any circumstances attend the talk Mr Hope was planning to give to the Brighton Photographic Society. Having very firmly and irrevocably made up her mind on that point, Mina opened a letter from Mr Merridew.

Dear Miss Scarletti,

What a joy it is after such a long time spent going about the Sussex coast to be back home in Brighton, which must be the prettiest and freshest town in the world. I have stories to tell of the thrills of the stage, our wonderful audiences and the great acclaim that was heaped upon us, which would take almost as long as my absence to describe.

But we must leave that for another day. At your instigation I hastened to Ship Street, where I saw in the window the astonishing portrait of the buxom young lady and the figure in profile of the female she owns as the very image of her mother. My amazement at this sight may only be imagined.

I entered the shop and had the most fascinating discussion with Mr Beckler concerning the provenance of the wonderful spirit picture. He has assured me, and I believe him, that it was something which occurred without any intention or artifice on his part.

There was a large card in the window and another inside, saying that Mr Arthur Wallace Hope will be delivering a talk at the Town Hall tomorrow at 6 p.m., under the auspices of the Brighton Photographic Society. All are welcome to attend. I shall certainly be there. It would be my very great pleasure to escort you to this event, which I am convinced will be one of the highlights of the Brighton summer season.

Yours respectfully,
Marcus Merridew

A year ago, Mr Arthur Wallace Hope had been the lion of Brighton. He had arrived to give a series of lectures on his travels in Africa, although all his talks whatever the subject always tended to veer into his great crusade on behalf of spiritualism. Mina was perfectly content for him to have his own opinions but found it distasteful when he insulted his critics. She could understand a natural eagerness to convert others to his views, and a certain vigorous exhortation was usual in such things, but she could not approve of his trying to bully or bribe or threaten.

He liked to deliver his Brighton talks in the Town Hall, a solid and serviceable building which, while not having the beauty of the Royal Pavilion or the Dome, nevertheless played more than one vital role in the life of the town. On the ground floor and basement, it housed the police offices, magistrates' courts, and cells, while on the first floor in rather more decorative surroundings, there were meeting rooms for societies and public lectures. Mr Hope had, as he had done previously, engaged the largest room available in anticipation of a large attendance.

Last year, the room had been packed with impressionable young men who fancied themselves adventurers in the making, and impressionable ladies who liked the look of Mr Hope. As

Mina entered in the company of Mr Merridew, she could see that there were fewer seats taken than before, and fewer and smaller clusters of persons about the room gathered in conversation. Mr Hope was less of a novelty, and worse than that, his reputation was such that many gentlemen were averse to their wives so much as being seen in the same room as he. It had been said that he was a hunter by nature and that young married ladies were his preferred sport. There were, Mina observed, no married ladies present under the age of fifty.

There was a platform at one end of the hall, with a long table and two chairs. An official of the Town Hall was busily overseeing the arrangements to ensure that everything was in order. Mr Beckler appeared, bringing with him something that looked like a large picture frame wrapped in a cloth, and a wooden display easel. He placed the easel carefully on the table facing the audience, and positioned the cloth-wrapped item on it, but did not reveal it to view. The official had brought in an album and some books and documents, which he laid on the table, and Mr Beckler arranged them to his liking and then stepped back to check the display. Quite suddenly, he lifted his eyes to glance at Mina and Mr Merridew, then he puffed a little exhalation, compressed his lips and looked away.

'What a curious fellow he is, to be sure,' said Mr Merridew.

Mina said nothing. She was glad to see Dr Hamid arrive. She had written to him asking if he would attend the talk as she had decided to go, and he had immediately agreed. He came to greet them at once. Mina had previously been unsure as to whether the two gentlemen had ever met. She had learned, however, that Mr Merridew on her recommendation had been visiting the baths to refresh himself in exotic vapours and restore his energies with invigorating massage, and they had struck up an acquaintance.

'Do you think this is wise?' asked Dr Hamid, but he was smiling.

'Most unwise,' said Mina.

Richard arrived, burdened with a box of glass plates, the camera in its case, and its tripod, which he helped Mr Beckler place on display. He had not been assigned any further part in the event and took a seat on the front row. Mina was pleased to notice the arrival of Miss Hartop, who looked well, if a little paler and thinner than before, in the company of her father. Mr Hartop made a polite little bow in Mina's direction, and also to Richard, but as had been promised, the two families made no move to speak with each other. Mr Clover was also there, accompanied by a young woman who stared about her in a very unsettled manner. 'That is his cousin, Miss Samprey,' said Richard. 'I expect Clover has brought her here for the opportunity of introducing her to Mr Hope.'

As he spoke, Charles Samprey arrived in a hurry, looking very annoyed. He glanced quickly about him, and seeing Mr Clover and his sister he strode up to them in a very determined manner. Mina edged closer to hear what was being said.

'What do you think you are you doing, Septimus? What madness is this?' Charles hissed. 'I am only glad Clarissa told me about your foolish plan.'

'Who is that angry fellow?' asked Richard.

'Charles Samprey, Miss Samprey's brother,' said Mina.

'I see nothing wrong in advancing Clarissa's abilities,' Mr Clover protested.

'No? You want to place my innocent sister under the influence of Viscount Hope? The man has a reputation! She should be respectably married, not disgraced! Just showing her in this room could ruin her!'

'I want Mortimer!' announced Miss Samprey. 'Where is Mortimer?'

'One of us has to mind the office!' snapped Charles. 'Come, Clarissa, I'm taking you home!' He made an attempt to remove his sister from the hall, but she struggled against him and squealed, her arms flailing. One hand caught his spectacles and knocked them from his face. They bounced on the ground, and Richard quickly darted forward and rescued them, or they might have been trampled underfoot. He handed them back to Samprey, who was looking about him in confusion, then as he grasped the spectacles, he thanked Richard gruffly and put them on.

Meanwhile, Mr Clover had conducted his cousin to a seat and placed himself beside her. Charles Samprey, faced with the very firmly seated Clarissa, was obliged to give up the attempt to remove her, which might have caused an even bigger disturbance than had already taken place. Finally, he sat down on the other side of her in a thoroughly aggrieved manner.

Mina was interested to see Mr Mayall arrive. She didn't know if Mr Hope recognised the premier photographer of Brighton, but saw that other people did, as he was greeted very warmly by a number of gentlemen. 'I think you might take this opportunity to be introduced to Mr Mayall,' Mina told Richard, but his attention appeared to be elsewhere. For once her brother was not glancing about the assembly to see if there were any fine ladies to gaze upon, but merely looked puzzled and thoughtful.

Mina was about to ask what the matter was, when the supervising official mounted the stage and requested everyone to be seated as the lecture was about to begin. He retired to the side of the room, and Mr Hope entered and stepped up onto the stage to be greeted with polite applause. Mr Beckler simply sat down. He looked nervous and unhappy. Mina guessed that addressing a large audience, some of whom would be more expert than himself, was something new to him. He was doubtless anxious not to disappoint his wealthy patron on whom all his fortunes now depended.

'Ladies and gentlemen,' began Mr Hope, 'believers and unbelievers. I am about to tell you about the most important discovery in the history of the science of photography. A discovery that will change forever our understanding of the world we live in. Yes, there are sceptics, but it is my opinion that the evidence I will show you today' is so strong that scepticism will soon fade away to be replaced universally by the great joy of unreserved belief.

'I am talking of course of the new art of photographing the spirits of our departed loved ones, who still walk amongst us and watch over us. I have never doubted this, but the cavillers, the wilfully ignorant cannot, will not understand the great truth.

'I am sure that many of you will have heard of the great American pioneer William Mumler, a man hounded and derided by fools, accused of crimes not one of which could be proven against him. There is a man called Hudson doing good work in London. He, like Mr Mumler, has attracted critics who accuse him of this and that without a single shred of proof. The fact remains that wherever in the world we see these spirit pictures appear, no one, even the most determined sceptic, even those who are experienced photographers, even the greatest scientists of our day, can convince anyone, much less a court of law, that their accusations have any foundation in fact. I am entirely confident,' he added, staring hard at Mina, 'that on seeing the evidence which I am about to place before you today, even the most determined of all sceptics will finally be convinced.

'Here in Brighton, we are seeing the emergence of a new age, the coming to prominence of a new pioneer. I refer of course to my associate, Mr Beckler. Last year, he succeeded in taking his first ever spirit photograph. I pressed him to come to Brighton, where there is a strong focus of psychic power and where I knew his talent would grow. Only a few weeks ago he was engaged to take a portrait of Miss Hartop, a lady I see sitting here before you. And thus was brought to the attention of the world the first spirit photograph taken in this town. Mr Beckler has kindly made a larger copy of the picture, which will be displayed to you now, and he will answer any questions as to how it came about. Since then, Mr Beckler has refined his methods and has produced the most detailed, the most beautiful spirit pictures ever seen. There are copies in these albums which everyone here will be able to view very shortly.'

Mr Hope gestured to Mr Beckler and withdrew to take a seat and give the stage to his associate. Mr Beckler appeared to take a short interval to steady his nerves, then he stood, bowed, and walked forward to the easel. He drew aside the cloth covering to show a larger size print of the Hartop spirit picture, which could clearly be seen by at the least the front two rows of the assembled audience.

'This is the portrait I took of Miss Hartop,' he said. 'If anyone wishes to see it more closely, then once the talk is completed you may all feel free to examine it. The camera I used is the one you see before you. I also have here on display samples of the glass plates used, and the formulas I employ for collodion, the silver nitrate coating, the fixative, and all the other chemicals employed in my photographic practice.'

He laid his fingertips on the top of the frame. His fingers were trembling a little, and he withdrew his hand and clenched it tightly before continuing. 'When I took this picture in my studio, it was in full sunlight. Only Miss Hartop, her maid and I were present. The maid was seated at some distance from the subject, and it would have been quite impossible for her image to appear on the glass. She was in any case wearing a straw bonnet and not a large hat as you see here. I had not expected to see anything of a spirit nature on the image and was quite astonished by what I saw.

'When Miss Hartop first saw the picture, she was struck by a powerful emotion and as you know, declared that the spirit was none other than that of her late mother. I have, however, since established without any doubt that the image was not that of Mrs Hartop at all.' There were little vocalisations of surprise from the assembly, and Mr Hope's jaw dropped in surprise. Mr Beckler drew himself to his full height, standing far straighter than was usual for him, and looked around the room. 'In fact,' he went on, speaking strongly and more clearly than before, 'I am now of the firm belief that its appearance in the photograph was all due to a terrible mistake.'

Mr Beckler stopped speaking. For several moments there was a profound silence in the room, which was followed by an explosion of startled chatter. Mina glanced at Mr Hartop and his daughter, but it was apparent from their expressions that this news was no surprise to them. If anything, it appeared that Mr Beckler's announcement was affording them some amusement.

Mr Hope was not amused. He gave a gasp of horrified astonishment then leapt from his chair, surged forward, took Mr Beckler roughly by the arm and pulled him around until they were face to face. 'What is this, man? What do you mean? Whose is the picture?'

'The lady in the picture is —' Mr Beckler hesitated, then glanced at the audience. 'I would like to ask Mr Marcus Merridew, to whom I am very greatly indebted, to explain.'

Mr Merridew rose and came forward, then turned with his customary elegance and aplomb to address the company. 'The lady in the photograph,' he announced, 'is none other than Dame Freda Fay, who has long been an ornament of the popular stage, and who I count as a very dear friend. I am so sorry that no one in Brighton recalls her. Fame can be so fleeting. Of course, she mainly played London, and the north of England, but she did do a season in Brighton some years ago. An artist of great refinement. Music and light comedy.'

'Miss Hartop's identification of the picture was an honest error,' added Mr Beckler, who had managed to extricate himself from Mr Hope's angry grasp, 'and quite understandable, as the image is not very distinct and Dame Freda Fay and her mother had a very similar taste in hats. I wish to make it clear that I attach no blame whatsoever to Miss Hartop. It was a mistake born of a loving daughter's great attachment to her late mother.'

The audience made sympathetic noises.

'Then this figure must be the ghost of Dame Freda Fay,' said Mr Hope. He glanced at Mr Hartop. 'Is she a relative of yours?'

'I am afraid not,' said Mr Hartop, without a trace of regret.

'A friend?'

'We have never met.'

'Then for reasons which I cannot as yet explain, this lady, who I am sure was excellent in every way, has appointed herself as Miss Hartop's guardian angel and spirit guide.'

'With respect, sir, I do not think that can be the case,' interposed Mr Merridew. 'You see, she is very much alive and is even now delighting audiences in Manchester. I had a telegram from her only this morning.'

This drew a burst of laughter from the audience, bringing a flush of scarlet to Mr Hope's already darkening face. Mina was well aware that for Mr Hope, who adored adulation and thrived on opposition, there was one thing he could not bear, and that was being an object of derision.

'Then I would suggest,' said Mr Hope, glaring at Mr Merridew with growing annoyance, 'that it is you who are mistaken. After all, we have only your word that this is Dame Freda Fay. Where is your proof? You have none, sir, none!'

Mr Merridew put his hand in his pocket. 'I have it here,' he said, calmly withdrawing a *carte de visite*.

Mr Hope strode to the edge of the platform and reached out. But before he could snatch the item away, Mr Merridew made a graceful turn on the spot and offered it to Mr Mayall. 'I think an independent witness would be in order, and Mr Mayall I am sure would meet with the approval of the assembly?'

The assembly expressed its very strong approval.

Mr Mayall rose from his seat and drew a magnifying glass from his pocket. Mina wondered if he always carried such an item with him or if he had been forewarned of this eventuality. He made a close examination of the portrait of Dame Freda Fay and then of the spirit picture, then addressed the assembly. 'There is no doubt in my mind,' he said at last. 'The images are not merely of the same person; they are actually identical. One is a copy of the other. Perhaps Mr Beckler can make a suggestion as to how this occurred?'

'I believe I can,' said Mr Beckler. 'The record books of my business show that Dame Freda Fay was a customer of my predecessor, Mr Simpson. On her last visit to Brighton some years ago, she sat for a number of portraits. Not all of the negatives were printed, and Mr Simpson kept the glass plates which could be cleaned and reused. It appears —' he glanced briefly at Richard — 'that they were not cleaned thoroughly, and some of the original image remained on the surface. When the plate was used to photograph Miss Hartop, the image appeared.'

'I agree that that is the most likely explanation,' said Mr Mayall.

'Well, we will not waste any more time on this!' exclaimed Mr Hope brusquely. 'I will see to it that the best men in England will examine these pictures, and then I think we will have another story. But now I invite the company to see the pictures which Mr Beckler took in the Extra Mural Cemetery, which are altogether of a different order. The results are extraordinary, without precedent, and there can be no doubts in anyone's mind as to the identity of the spirits portrayed.' He went to open the album, but to his surprise Mr Beckler interposed himself and placed his hand flat on the cover to prevent it.

'I am sorry to be a disappointment,' he said. 'The pictures I took in the cemetery were all taken on the same day in good light; however, the images of the persons that appear, while they are very clear, are also in fact copies of pictures formerly taken by Mr Simpson of living subjects. I have abundant evidence to prove this, which I am willing to show to anyone. I know that many people did purchase copies under the impression that these portrayed the spirits of their departed relatives, but now that I have established the truth of the matter, I will be happy to refund any purchase money without quibble on application.'

There was an immediate public sensation. All the assembly broke out in excited chatter and several gentlemen jumped to their feet and made loud vocal demands.

Mr Hope's eyes blazed with rage, and he seized Mr Beckler by the lapels and shook him, letting go only to wave a large fist in his former protégé's face. 'You snake! You reptile! This is nothing short of slander! You won't get away with this! I will ruin you! I can do it in a day! You will be bankrupt by tomorrow! I will see you locked away as a madman!'

Despite the fact that it appeared that Mr Hope was on the verge of punching him on the nose, Mr Beckler seemed remarkably calm. 'You may do your worst,' he said.

Mr Hope, on a sudden thought, turned to where Mina was sitting and pointed a finger. 'It's you! You are the bad influence! You have used your horrible wiles, mesmerised and corrupted an honest psychic, destroyed his abilities.' He leaped down from the platform and advanced on Mina, but was unexpectedly confronted by Dr Hamid, who had risen to his feet and faced him with stonily determined calm.

'Have a care, sir,' said Dr Hamid, 'have a care.'

The two men stood there for a moment, one red-faced and quivering with rage, one set and immovable.

'Excuse me, sirs, but is anything the matter?' said a voice close by, and Mina saw that the official had summoned a police constable from the offices below. Mr Hope growled but was wise enough, even in his fury, to say no more, then he abruptly turned and stormed away.

'Thank you, constable,' said Dr Hamid. 'I believe the danger is past.'

'Very well, sir,' said the constable politely, but after a brief word with the official, he did not withdraw but remained to keep an eye on the room.

No one complained about the early termination of the lecture; rather, the audience began to leave their seats and mingle to discuss the remarkable conclusion. Many people, including Mr Mayall, were eager to speak to Mr Beckler and examine the photographs he had brought.

Mina noticed Mr Hartop approach Mr Beckler and shake him warmly by the hand. In the general hum of conversation surrounding the young photographer, it was hard to make out what was being said, but both men were all smiles. If Mr Beckler was concerned about the prospect of Mr Hope demanding immediate repayment of his loan, or repossession of the business, he was concealing it well.

Charles Samprey rose to his feet and turned angrily on his cousin. 'Now you can see the shameful influence to which you have almost exposed Clarissa!' he exclaimed. 'I will take her home at once. And we will have no more of this nonsense!'

'But you can't deny the power of her dreams,' pleaded Mr Clover.

'A dream is only a dream, a thing of fancy and imagination,' said Samprey. 'If Clarissa is allowed to forget all about her dreams as I have constantly advised, they will trouble her no more.'

'It wasn't a dream,' said Clarissa, sulkily. 'Everyone keeps telling me it was a dream, but it wasn't, it was real.'

'Well, I still mean to see if I can find someone to help you,' said Mr Clover. 'Not Mr Hope, I have to agree with Charles on that. But we will find the right person, I promise.'

'And I think I know what is best for my sister!' said Charles. 'You have no control over her. I do!' He went to take her by the arm, but she shrank back.

'It was real, Septimus, it was real!' squealed Clarissa. 'I saw him with the gun. I smelt it! It was like burning!'

'But Clarissa, you can't have seen Hector with a gun,' said Mr Clover, soothingly. 'Unless — did you follow him?'

'Come home now!' insisted Charles. 'You foolish girl!'

'It wasn't Hector,' said Clarissa. 'It was Charles with the gun! Father's gun. He went after Hector that night. And when he came back, he was holding the gun and I smelt the smoke. He told me I must have dreamed it, and I got it all mixed up in my head.'

'You see, Septimus, she is insane! I have done my best to manage her and find her a husband, but all you do is stir her up, and she will never be free of these delusions!' Charles Samprey pulled his sister to her feet and despite her protests and Mr Clover's objections, hustled her roughly from the hall.

Nearby, the police constable was writing busily in his notebook.

Mr Clover slumped despondently in his seat. Mina went to talk to him. 'What can I do now?' he moaned. 'Miss Scarletti, you must help me!'

'Might I ask you something first?'

'Yes, of course, anything!'

'This may appear to be a trivial matter, but I believe it is important. When your cousin held the tea party for Miss Samprey, where did he order the cakes from?'

This was clearly the last question Mr Clover had expected. 'I — I'm not sure.'

'You mentioned her eating sugared almonds. Were there any other sweets?'

'Um — yes, there were. Bon-bons and chocolates. That's right, I do recall now. Veale's creams. I forget the flavour. But they were in little bags. But why do you ask? How is that important? And can you help me?'

The police constable completed his notes, put his notebook in his pocket and left the room with a very determined expression.

'I suggest,' said Mina, 'that you go home and think very hard and try to remember all you can very clearly and prepare yourself for a more thorough questioning in the near future.'

He looked very surprised at this reply but agreed.

Richard had been deputed by Mr Beckler to compress the camera into its carrying case, and fold and fasten the tripod in preparation for removing them back to the shop. Mr Beckler was also assembling his materials for transport and had closed the album. Despite what he had said, he had received several offers for purchase but had declined them all.

Mina took the opportunity to thank Dr Hamid for his courageous defence of her in the face of her enemy. 'I hardly dared imagine what might have transpired if that policeman had not been summoned,' she said. 'I do not think Mr Hope would have held himself back from violence.'

'Mr Hope is a much larger man than I, but I sensed that his is the method of brute force without control,' said Dr Hamid, with a smile. 'I took up the art of boxing in my youth, and I still exercise when I can.'

'Then you might have surprised him,' said Mina. 'That would have been a very interesting sight to see.'

'It is better to avoid violence,' said Dr Hamid. 'But if it is unavoidable, one must engage fully.' He glanced at her. 'Are you well, Miss Scarletti? You look a little flushed. Here, sit down and rest for a while.' He conducted her back to her seat. 'I am greatly relieved,' he commented to Mr Merridew, 'that no one suggested that Dame Freda Fay was the real mother of Miss Hartop. That would have been most insulting to Mr Hartop, whose respectability has never been in question.'

'I can only imagine,' said Mr Merridew, 'that there were persons present who did recall Dame Freda Fay but decided not to speak out.'

'Oh?'

'Dame Freda could not have been anyone's mother. That was only her professional name. When not on the stage, she was Freddie Finklestein.'

'Freddie — oh, I see. Well, it was the musical stage, which does so delight in a novelty.'

'Not as novel as one might suppose in the world of the theatre.'

Richard was heading for the exit door, burdened with equipment, but he stopped on seeing Mina. 'Mina, I know my memory is wretched, sometimes, but — I had a thought, an impression — about the man who came into the shop with the chocolates. The man with bad eyes who squinted at everything.'

'I think I know what you are about to say,' said Mina. 'We will talk about it later.'

Mr Merridew kindly went to help Richard with his burdens, and they proceeded back to the shop.

Mr Beckler was walking past, carrying all his papers and pictures. He didn't look at Mina, but on an impulse, she called out to him, 'Mr Beckler.' He stopped and turned to stare at her in surprise. She rose and approached him. 'I don't know why you did what you did, and what it might have cost you to do it, but I just wanted you to know that I am grateful for it.'

There was a little hint of a smile, and he made a slight bow. 'Thank you, Miss Scarletti.' He walked on.

But Mina had already begun to suspect what it had cost him.

CHAPTER TWENTY-FOUR

On the afternoon following Mr Hope's abandoned lecture, Mina was entertaining her new friend Mrs McClelland. Her doctor husband had been amongst the audience at the Town Hall, since as Miss Hartop's medical man, he had thought it advisable to keep an eye on her during what was her first public engagement since her illness.

'She is doing very well, and he has hopes that her voice will recover a great deal of its strength in time, although he believes that it will not be as shrill as it once was.'

'I hesitate to say so, but that could well be an improvement.'

'I do not hesitate. It will be. And much appreciated by her new husband.'

'Husband?' queried Mina, although she felt sure she knew what the answer would be.

'Yes, it has not yet been officially announced, but I have heard that she and Mr Beckler are betrothed. It was quite a sudden romance and will take the town by surprise, as there had never been any suspicion of an attachment before. In fact, I must confess that I had always been under the impression that he did not care for her at all. Her father, however, is very pleased and I am sure that Mr Beckler will find the marriage settlement of great benefit to his business interests.'

'But he will not be making any more spirit pictures,' said Mina, refreshing the teacups. 'My brother tells me that a large placard was placed in the window last night advising customers that whatever they may hear to the contrary, that part of the business has ceased.'

'And is it true that in the cemetery images the ghosts were all falsified by Mr Beckler? That is what the town is saying.'

'He admitted only to making an error, not to outright fraud. The quick retraction of his claims will probably save him from any police investigation. My belief is that he made them to please his patron. Former patron, I should say. Mr Hope showed him a list of prominent Brighton families who were interested in spiritualism. Mr Beckler studied the list and found suitable pictures in Mr Simpson's collection which he could use. It was actually Miss Hartop who gave him the idea of photographing the graves. If he ever does so again, I doubt very much that the occupants will make an appearance. But the enterprise has had a good result, in that he has learned fresh skills, which will enable him to introduce a new line in novelties.'

Mrs McClelland finished her slice of marble cake with evident satisfaction. 'Oh? What kind of novelties?'

'I understand that it is possible, if one knows the art, to produce a photograph of a man with the head of a rabbit.'

'Indeed? Is there much call for such things?'

'I'm really not sure.'

Mina cut some slices of fruit tart and they helped themselves.

'I have been told,' said Mrs McClelland, 'that the posters outside the Town Hall advertising Mr Hope's lectures have all been altered to say that they are cancelled. It is rumoured that he left town last night. He is a boorish creature, despite all his connections. My husband believes that he has lost many friends due to his outrageous behaviour and may not be seen here again.'

'As he has severed his association with Ship Street, there will be little to tempt him back.'

'I assume that Mr Beckler is no longer employing a spirit medium on the premises?'

'No, the booth where Lady Brighthelm once conducted her consultations has been removed. That is a line of business which I think he will not stray into again.'

Mrs McClelland sipped her tea very thoughtfully. 'And — forgive me if you think I am prying, but — is there still a coldness between you?'

Mina hesitated. 'Mr Beckler has long made it plain that he was very sorry for his earlier behaviour towards me, and I admit that until yesterday I was still very angry with him and not inclined to accept any apology or attempt to make amends. But he has shown concern for my welfare, warning me to be on my guard against Mr Hope, and his actions last night meant a great deal to me. We will never be friends, but I believe we have made our peace.'

Their conversation was interrupted by a vigorous knocking at the front door.

'Dear me, I hope there is no dreadful emergency,' said Mrs McClelland, who as a doctor's wife must have been used to such things.

'If there is, it will almost certainly be for my attention,' said Mina. 'If you would be so kind as to remain?'

'Of course,' said Mrs McClelland, eyeing the marble cake and taking another slice.

Rose came in with a card. 'I'm sorry to trouble you, but it's a Mr Clover from Samprey Brothers house agents. He wants to speak to you if he can. He's very agitated.'

'Please show him in,' said Mina, pouring a cup of tea for the visitor, 'and refresh the teapot.'

'Ah, yes,' said Mrs McClelland, 'my husband mentioned that last night the young gentleman had some altercation with his cousin of a rather peculiar nature.' She opened her reticule and took out the smelling bottle just in case.

Mr Clover arrived out of breath. He was a little surprised to see Mrs McClelland, but on being told that she was Mina's trusted friend and the wife of Doctor McClelland, he was mollified and sat down.

'It's the most dreadful thing!' he said. 'And you were quite right in what you told me yesterday, that I should prepare myself to be questioned. How did you know? I think you must be a psychic after all, despite what you say.'

'Please calm down and be sensible, Mr Clover. You may have a cup of tea, but the only spirits I will produce are a few drops of medicinal brandy if required. What has happened?'

'The police came to see me. I told them all about what Miss Jemson told me, and they have gone to see her.' He turned to Mrs McClelland. 'Miss Jemson was the wife of Barnes, the man who was hanged for my cousin Hector's murder.'

Mrs McClelland's nod of understanding showed that she was familiar with the case.

'Jenny — Miss Jemson — she always said that Barnes was at home that night, but she was never believed. She had heard Hector speak cruelly of his father as an old fool who would die soon, and then he would inherit the eldest son's portion. He had promised to be a model son, but he never meant it. He even tried to kill his father once by damaging the axle of his carriage so the wheel would come loose and cause an accident. It killed his poor mother instead.'

Mrs McClelland said nothing. One rarely insulted a man's relative to his face, but her eyes said it all, that whoever had shot Hector Samprey had done the world a service.

Mina handed Mr Clover his tea and he drank it in a single gulp. 'I told the police everything I knew,' he continued, 'and they wanted to look at the business appointment books which I keep. Both Charles and Mortimer see clients at the office. There was one day they were especially interested in. I was in the office all day, and so was Mortimer. And Charles claimed that he was there all day, but in fact he wasn't. He went out on an errand. I remembered it because a customer called to see if he was available for an urgent consultation, and he had gone out. I gave the police the name of the customer, and they said they would talk to him. And then I realised that that was the day when someone delivered the poisoned chocolates to Lady Brighthelm. Miss Scarletti — the police have just come back to the office and taken Charles away to question him. They think he poisoned Lady Brighthelm. They even think he shot Hector!'

Rose came in with a fresh pot of tea, and Mina asked her to bring the medicinal brandy. When the maid returned, she handed Mina a letter.

Dear Mina,

Hoping this finds you and the family in good health.

I thought you would be interested to know that the Porterson-White case has, quite unexpectedly, been resolved. It appears that the lady did make a will, but it was many years before her death, and before she left London. It was lodged with an elderly solicitor who, it seems, was not aware that she had passed away. He departed this life only recently at the enviable age of 97, and it was found amongst his papers. She left the sum of £1,000 to each of the two cousins, a Mr Porterson who lives in London and Mr Winstanley who resides in Brighton, which will go some way towards settling their debts, and the remainder will go to a foundation for the establishment of a home for the relief and education of orphan children.

Respectfully,
Peter Inskip

EPILOGUE

The trial of Charles Samprey for the murder of his brother Hector was a sorry affair, the prisoner standing in the dock quietly weeping as the evidence was presented for the defence.

Expert counsel first invited the court to consider that Hector Samprey had been a disreputable individual whose associates were the lowest and most vicious of criminals. He had on his own admission attempted to kill his father and caused the death of his mother. Both his brothers had begged their father to cut him out of his will, as they believed he would dissipate the family fortune by leading an immoral life. His unfortunate father, who could not help but love his son, never lost hope that he would turn to the path of honesty. Hector had played upon his father's affection, warming the old man's heart with a promise that he would reform, but it was a cruel lie. The brothers had asked a detective to follow Hector to see who he met as proof that he had not shaken off his previous associates, but the detective, concerned for his own safety, had declined the commission.

On the night of his death, Hector had gone out to meet one of his criminal associates, and it was the prisoner in the dock who had followed him. Charles Samprey had taken their father's army revolver but had had no intention of using it on his brother. He did not for a moment wish harm to his own flesh and blood. He knew that Hector's associates were desperate men likely to be armed, and he carried the gun solely for his own defence.

That night, the prisoner was able to overhear the conversation between his brother and the man he met on the seashore. He was left in no doubt that a robbery was being planned. As Hector left his companion to walk home, the prisoner, who now had the proof he needed, accosted him. He said that he had overheard the conversation and was going to conduct his brother to the police station and hand him into custody. Although he was pointing the gun at his brother, it was not meant to injure him, but only to frighten him into complying with his demands. Unfortunately, Hector Samprey refused to comply. There was a struggle which was initiated by the deceased, and the gun was fired. Whether by chance, or deliberately when in fear of his life, the prisoner could not recall. Realising that his brother could not be saved, he rushed home in a state of distress. He was seen by his sister holding a gun. His first impulse was to protect his sister from all knowledge of the terrible events. He therefore persuaded her she had had a dream.

When his brother's body was found, the prisoner determined to spare his father all knowledge of his eldest son's lies. He told the police that his brother was going to meet his friend Barnes that night to tell him that he was going to have nothing more to do with him. Barnes was the leader of that gang of cutthroats and had been long suspected of the murder of a young policeman and other heinous crimes. It was understandably believed that it was Barnes who had killed Hector Samprey. The prisoner repeated this tale in court at Barnes's trial. He did not know that Jenny Jemson would provide Barnes with an alibi.

Jenny Jemson, whatever one might think of her former associates, had always spoken the truth. She had since thrown off the mantle that was once forced upon her to become an example of honest toil and purity. The prisoner in the dock had always been a law-abiding and respectable gentleman, but circumstances and a wish to protect his father and sister led him to make the mistakes that placed him in the dock.

The defence asked the court to acquit Charles Samprey of the wilful murder of his brother, which they duly did. They went on to find him guilty of manslaughter and perjury. He was sentenced to a total of ten years in prison.

There was another trial in store for Charles Samprey, this time for the attempted murder by poison of the spirit medium Lady Brighthelm, whose true identity was not to be published for her own safety.

The case was hotly debated by Brighton society, and the subject of cautious speculation in the newspapers. It was generally held that Samprey was guilty of the crime, which he had committed in order to hide his involvement in the death of his brother. Whether his guilt could be proved in court was quite another question. It was a case riddled with wholly reasonable doubt, and wide open for exploitation by the defence.

It was rumoured that ever since the death of his brother, Charles Samprey had suffered from recurring nightmares in which Hector had accused him of murder. When his cousin Mr Clover told him about Lady Brighthelm being able to discover the truth, the nightmares had become more frequent and terrifying than ever.

It was expected that the prosecution would advise the court that Samprey had learned all he needed to know about Lady Brighthelm from his cousin and employee Septimus Clover. He knew that she took no money but received little gifts such as chocolates and was especially partial to Veale's violet creams.

The accused had learned what mistakes to avoid by reading the trial of Christiana Edmunds. He did not buy the chocolates from the shop but had suggested to his sister Clarissa that she host a tea party for her friends and ordered some treats from Veale's, including cakes and chocolates. It was thought that his housekeeper would testify that she had believed that the shop had not delivered the right quantity of chocolates, and when she commented on this her employer had told her he had taken some for his sister. And there was arsenic kept in the house for the control of vermin. Naturally there was. But that was hardly a crime.

The prosecution would then suggest that Charles Samprey had gone to Mr Beckler's shop, removing his distinctive glasses before he went in to hinder recognition. He had then sent the assistant to look for something in the storeroom, dropped the chocolates on the counter and claimed that a messenger boy had left them.

All of these things were possible, and some of them could even be proved, but when one added it up it was a flimsy case. As the trial approached, it was generally believed that Charles Samprey would plead not guilty and an intelligent defence would heap scorn on the prosecution case and tear it into unrecognisable shreds. Richard Scarletti, who had said that he almost thought Charles Samprey was the man who had come into the shop, would be an especially unconvincing witness, and even if he was correct no one had actually seen who had left the chocolates on the counter. Charles Samprey would be acquitted. This might have been the correct result under English law, but Mina knew that if the crime stayed unsolved and unpunished, then it would remain open to Mr Hope to continue insinuating that she and Richard had been responsible.

The trial, however, opened with a surprise. Charles Samprey pleaded guilty, not to attempted murder but to the lesser offence of assault by administration of a toxic substance. His counsel maintained that the prisoner had intended merely to make the medium unwell enough to stop her consultations but had not wished to kill her. The motives for this change were unclear, but it was possible that the visits of Charles's brother Mortimer to his prison cell and their lengthy conversations had convinced him that the Sampreys had suffered enough, and for the sake of his sister's prospects it would be best not to expose the family to another scandalous criminal trial. The new charge and plea were accepted, and the judge directed the jury to find the prisoner guilty. Charles Samprey was sentenced to seven years in prison to run concurrently with his existing sentence. Shortly afterwards, Clarissa Samprey was betrothed to the son of a Brighton publican, who considered that both her notoriety and her marriage portion would be good for business.

Peace, or what passed for peace, was restored to the Scarletti household. Mr Hope was gone from Brighton, hopefully for good, there was no danger of Mr Beckler courting Mina's mother, and Richard was happily working on the art for novelty photographs. A leading London spiritualist had just exposed Mr Hudson as a fraud, and his business was collapsing. There would, Mina reflected, always be people who took spirit photographs and there would always be some who believed in them, but the fashion was fading. What the next fashion would be, she must wait to see. But for the time being, she had laid all her ghosts.

HISTORICAL NOTES

BRIGHTON AND SUSSEX

In 1872, the recently built West Pier was a fashionable promenade deck: the pavilion and covered band area had not yet been built. The bandstand was a low raised wooden platform and was gas lit. **http://regencysociety-jamesgray.com/volume2/source/jg_02_021.html**

The Grand Hotel was opened in 1864. The houses to the west of the Grand Hotel were demolished for the construction of the Hotel Metropole in 1890.

The Extra Mural Cemetery was the first private cemetery to be opened in Brighton when it was no longer advisable to continue burials in overcrowded churchyards. It was consecrated in 1851. The cemetery gatehouse described in this book was demolished in 1956.

Mr John George Bishop's *Strolls in the Brighton Extra Mural Cemetery* was published in 1864 with a second edition in 1867. The Cemetery Chapel is a Grade II listed building and is still in use for services.

Elm Grove Workhouse in Brighton was opened in 1867. It ceased to be used as a workhouse in 1930.

In 1872, Harrison's Velocipede School was open daily at 14 Queen's Road.

In 1872, Ovingdean was an agricultural village to the east of Brighton. It is now part of the city of Brighton and Hove. Ovingdean Grange is a Grade II listed manor house. It featured in the 1857 novel *Ovingdean Grange: A Tale of the South Downs*, by W Harrison Ainsworth.

Rottingdean is a picturesque village on the East Sussex coast. It is now part of the city of Brighton and Hove.

The Brighton Photographic Society is fictitious.

PEOPLE AND PUBLICATIONS

The Sussex Vampire. Mina did not in the end write a story with this title, which had to wait until 1924 under the authorship of Sir Arthur Conan Doyle.

Dr David Livingstone, the lost explorer, was located by Henry Morton Stanley in November 1871; however, news of the discovery did not reach England until May 1872.

Horace Walpole (1717-1794) wrote the first Gothic novel *The Castle of Otranto*, which was published in 1764.

The Spiritual Banner is fictional, but the quotations included here are from *The Spiritual Magazine*, July 1872.

Frederick Augustus Hudson (1818-1900), not to be confused with the respected Isle of Wight photographer Frederick Hudson (1822-1889), was a London photographer who was active in the early 1870s in the field of spirit photography. He was believed to have employed 'double exposure', although he was never arrested for fraud.

William Mumler (1832-1884) was an American spirit photographer who was tried for fraud in 1869. Although he was acquitted, the accusation destroyed his career. I am indebted to *The Apparitionists* by Peter Manseau (Houghton Mifflin Harcourt, 2017) and *The Illustrated Photographer: Scientific and Art Journal* (London, Edmund Dring, vol II 1869, May-July).

John Jabez Edwin Mayall (1813-1901), usually referred to as J E Mayall, was a prominent society photographer. He opened his Brighton portrait studio in 1864, leaving his eldest son Edwin to run his London business at 224 Regent Street. He later used electrical arc lamps for indoor photography.

Mayall was a member of the Brighton Natural History Society. He became an Alderman and later Mayor of Brighton. (See the *Brighton Guardian*, 21 November 1877 for a biography.) In November 1871, the London business dismissed an employee, Henry Newman, who took revenge by entering the premises and destroying valuable equipment. A jar containing four or five pounds of potassium cyanide was found uncorked. Newman had taken some home and used it to commit suicide. (*London Evening Standard*, 9 November 1871 p. 3). Edwin Mayall died after a long illness in February 1872, aged 37.

William Gibbs (1831-1904), Inspector of police, who brought the Brighton poisoner Christiana Edmunds to justice, was later promoted to Superintendent.

The Mayall/Hooper connection in this novel was pure serendipity. Miss Hooper's name was first mentioned in *Mr Scarletti's Ghost*, and when I researched Mr Mayall for this book, I discovered that his second wife was a former Mrs Hooper.

PHOTOGRAPHY

Cartes de visite were a popular photographic form of the period from the mid-1850s to the early 1870s. They served as small visiting cards, and those of celebrities were widely collected.

Memento mori photography was the art of photographing the deceased. It was often the only means by which a family might have an image of a loved one to remember.

A NOTE TO THE READER

Dear Reader,

Thank you for reading *The Cyanide Ghost*.

Reviews are so important to authors, and if you enjoyed the novel I would be grateful if you could spare a few minutes to post a review on **Amazon** and **Goodreads**. I love hearing from readers, and you can connect with me online, **on Facebook**, **Twitter**, and **Instagram**.

You can also stay up to date with all my news via **my website** and by signing up to **my newsletter**.

Linda Stratmann

Sapere Books is an exciting new publisher of brilliant fiction and popular history.

To find out more about our latest releases and our monthly bargain books visit our website:
saperebooks.com

Printed in Great Britain
by Amazon